Green Card

Elizabeth Adams

ISBN: 1505382696
ISBN-13: 978-1505382693

DEDICATION

For my grandmother, who told me life is what you make it.
Well, here goes.

ACKNOWLEDGMENTS

There are so many people I would like to thank. This book has been in the works for years, callously being set aside for silly things like childbirth and degree completion, and yet, through all of that, there were people who consistently told me to keep at it and supported my efforts.

I have to thank Rose, for reading every word and commenting diligently on what worked and what didn't. She truly is a gem. I am so thankful to Rachel, my intrepid sister-in-love, for cold reading and giving feedback and talking me down when I freaked out. She's positively lovely. Big love for my dear friend Lori who always believed I could be, and in fact already was, a successful writer, and of course for calmly reminding me that this was a worthy pursuit when I thought about setting it aside.

Huge props to Caitlin Daschner at Chromantic Studio, my fabulous graphic designer, who managed to take my garbled descriptions of feelings and colors and create a cover that I (and hopefully the readers) adore. She also gave me the Nutella line in chapter eighteen, one of my favorites.

I have to thank my friends Andrea, Debra, and Sarah, who have helped me in big and small ways, by listening, helping me choose names, catching errors, cold reading, and being patient soundboards. My sweet husband has put up with a lot throughout this process and made it possible for me to take this project on. He was an all out rock star at the end. And, of course, getting his green card was the inspiration for this book, though he didn't pay me to marry him.

Lastly, I want to thank my children, who, small as they are, cheered me on and clapped when I wrote my last line, and thoughtfully gave opinions on cover options, and put up with a slightly crazy mother for entirely too long. Thank you, darlings.

1
THE PLAN

Mid-April

"Hello, Jamison. Where do we stand?"

"Well, we've got a bit of a problem," he answered as he sat in front of his friend's desk.

"How so?"

"You know how it's about time to renew your visa?"

"Yeah, we do it every few years. It's never been a problem before."

"Well, now there's a problem."

"What kind of problem?" Harper sat forward and placed his elbows on the desk.

"Do you remember Alicia Winters?"

He grimaced.

"I'll take that as a yes. As it turns out, she wasn't too happy about the way your relationship ended last January."

"Relationship?" he cried. "We went on three dates!"

"Either way, she's pissed. Apparently, she thought she was going to be the next Mrs. Harper and is not too happy about the breakup."

Harper rolled his eyes.

"She has some friends in important places. A few well-placed phone calls and you've been red-flagged."

"What do you mean red-flagged?"

"I mean you are now under investigation by immigration."

"Investigation for what?"

"It looks like Miss Winters has accused you of illegal activities and something to do with off-shore accounts and tax havens."

Harper's face turned an unhealthy shade of purple. "She what?"

Jamison continued, "What this means for you is that your visa cannot be renewed until the investigation is complete"

"When will that be?"

"No one knows, but now that the FBI is involved-"

"FBI?" Harper interrupted, his voice rising slightly in pitch.

"It's just a formality. I'm sure once they do a little looking around, they'll pull back. But immigration will be on you for a while, and they're not known for expediency." Harper looked at him with raised brows. "We're not even supposed to know about this yet, nothing has officially been declared – I know someone at immigration. Best case scenario, it'll be over in two to three months. Worst case, you're looking at eighteen months to two years."

"Two years!"

"Sorry. They take this a lot more seriously now than they used to. I'm doing everything I can, but you are an important figure. It would be quite a feather in some inspector's cap to nail you."

"Yeah, but doesn't it occur to them not to fool around with powerful people?"

"You would think, but a powerful target is also a big target and you know what that means -"

"Easier to hit," they said in unison.

"So what do I do now? Doesn't my visa expire soon?"

"Four months to be exact. I'm looking at ways around it to try and keep you in the country, but there aren't many."

"How many is not many?" asked Harper.

"Well, really, there's only one."

"And what is that?"

"You're not going to like it."

"Jamison!"

"Alright, I do have one idea. It's a loop-hole and pretty risky, but if it works, your problems could be solved for the next twelve years at least."

"Well out with it, man!"

"You could get married."

Silence.

"To an American, of course."

More silence.

"It's the only way to stay in New York."

"Isn't there some sort of investment visa?"

"There is, but investment visas require a lot of financial documentation and we don't want to draw attention to your assets right now. If you marry an American, all the focus is on *her* money. With any luck, you'll slide under the radar – the different visa types aren't even handled by the same department. Of course, if you don't want to get married, you can always go back to England, wait for the investigation to be over, then we can re-apply. There's a decent chance they'll give you another one."

"And what are the chances they won't?"

"It's really fifty-fifty. A lot of it just depends on the mood of the consulate. You have some friends in useful places, that should help, but there are no guarantees."

"If my visa is suspended or denied, can I still visit here, as long as I don't do business?"

"In short, no. You wouldn't be allowed into the country again until the investigation cleared. And since you still maintain controlling interest in Taggston, they'll be keeping a close watch on your company, too. Especially since Taggston has been sponsoring your work visa all this time. You may run into some difficulty with the larger deals – like the Helgsen merger."

Harper ran his hands through his hair. "We've been working on that deal for eighteen months!"

"I know."

"We're talking *millions* of dollars here! Not to mention hundreds of jobs."

"I know."

Harper growled and hung his head back, exhaling angrily toward the ceiling.

"I know." Jamison sounded sympathetic.

"You think I should get married. To an American. Soon," Harper said.

"I'm sorry, Harper, I know this is unexpected and, well, damned inconvenient."

"Inconvenient?"

"Okay, awful. But I think it's your best option."

Harper exhaled loudly. "Give me a while to think about it, Jamison."

"Alright. Let's talk tomorrow."

Jamison quietly left the room and Harper turned his chair around and stared out the window at his view of the Manhattan skyline. Could he leave this place and the life he'd built here? Could he go back to London full time? Did he want to? What would that do to his business, to his life?

He stood and paced the room with one hand on the back of his neck.

"Bloody immigration, bloody rules, bloody Alicia Winters."

He passed his assistant on his way out. "Goodnight, Evelyn."

"Goodnight, Mr. Harper."

He paused in the hall and looked back at his always-efficient assistant and considered her for a moment. Would she marry him to keep him in the country? *She's loyal…* He quickly shook off the thought and moved to the elevator. *I can't marry my assistant. That would be damn awkward. There's got to be another way.*

**

Andrew Jamison looked up when he heard the knock on his door. "Come in."

"Morning, Jamison."

"Damn, Harper, you look like hell! You were up all night worrying, weren't you?"

"Worrying and researching. And I was only up half the night."

"And what did you decide?" Jamison asked as William Harper fell into the chair in front of his desk.

Harper sighed and looked around the room before focusing on his friend.

"I guess there's really only one option."

Andrew beamed. "I'm glad you came around, Will. Any preferences for the lucky lady?"

"I don't want one of the usuals. No high society women. For one thing, they'd want a big fancy wedding and we don't have that kind of time. I assume I need to sew this up soon?" He shot Jamison a questioning look.

"That would be wise."

"Okay. So we need a woman we can trust. Someone who won't say anything about the whole thing being a sham and who will sign an ironclad pre-nup. No one with a record or a gambling problem. And no drinkers! I don't need a repeat of that Clare fiasco from last summer."

Andrew shuddered. "No. You'll need to pay her, of course. You may be a catch, but if you are planning on divorcing her in two years, she's going to want to be compensated in some way."

Harper nodded, then looked up. "Why do you say two years?"

"When you sponsor a spouse for immigration, or a green card as it's called, if you've been married less than two years at the time of application, you're granted a temporary twenty-four month visa instead of the usual ten year green card. After two years, you re-file to prove you weren't screwing the system – it's pretty basic really – and get your ten year card."

"I see. Would we have to do all those tests like they show in the cinema? Like knowing each other's favorite films and all that?"

"Hopefully not. That only happens if they are particularly suspicious of you. Which may happen in your case, but it's never really like that anyway. Generally, you turn in a lot of legal documents, show some proof of relationship –

photographs, phone records, that sort of thing – and your friends will have to swear that you're a real couple."

"Really? Why?"

"There's the theory that you might be able to get someone to marry you and lie, but it would be harder to find several people to go along with it."

"Hmm."

"Or it could just be more bureaucratic BS." Andrew shrugged. "So it would probably be best to act like a real couple in front of your friends. Especially with you being in the public eye so much. Every time you get photographed at an event, it proves that your marriage is legit."

"I see. So who will we find to do this? An actress? You already said I'd have to pay her."

"I don't think an actress is the best way to go. Ultimately, they are out to forward their careers and if exposing you helps them with that..."

"Right. So how do we find a woman who will act like a wife without being a wife, who's trustworthy and believable and has nothing better to do for the next two years of her life?"

"Funny you should ask that. You remember Jenny, the girl I've been seeing?"

"The one from that charity organization?"

"Yes. Well, she has a sister."

"Oh, come on, Andrew!"

"Now, hear me out! Jenny and I have been together almost five months now and I've seen a lot of Katie. She's a great girl and I really think you two would get on well if you actually gave her a chance."

Will rolled his eyes. "What kind of name is Katie? And what do you mean 'if I actually gave her a chance'?"

"Katie is short for Katherine, Will, as everyone knows. AND I mean that you tend to go on one or two dates with a girl then send her packing because she didn't meet some imaginary picture in your mind of the perfect woman. Hardly a recipe for success, you must admit."

Will ignored his comments and moved to his next objection. "What makes you so sure she'd do it? No boyfriend?"

"She broke it off with her old boyfriend a couple months ago. She's in grad school now, at Columbia – literature I think. Anyway, she's got a year left on her masters and is working like a dog to pay her tuition and cover her living expenses. She'd probably be thrilled not to have to pay rent anymore – after all, she'd move in with you."

Andrew laughed at Harper's expression.

"Don't worry. It's a big place, I'm sure you can find a way to cohabit without sacrificing your peace of mind. And if you gave her a good enough allowance, she could quit her job and focus completely on grad school. Who'd turn that chance down?"

Harper took a deep breath and rubbed his forehead. "You think she's trustworthy?"

"She's the vault. I told her about a surprise I was planning for Jenny and she never caved. Even after Jenny practically begged her. If she won't tell her favorite sister, she won't talk to the press."

"Not telling about a necklace you bought for your girlfriend isn't quite the same thing, Andrew."

"I know that, Will. I was just giving an example. Trust me, I'm a good judge of character. Katie's the girl."

Will sighed and sat back. "Alright. When do I meet her?"

"Tonight. I'm meeting the girls for dinner."

**

"Man, I wish I'd had time to change," Kate said as she pulled at her loose red T-shirt. "I had to take Mrs. Patterson's dog to the vet."

"You look fine, red's your color," Jennifer replied. She walked briskly next to her sister, her skirt swishing across her knees and her blonde hair twisted over one shoulder.

"I noticed you used 'fine', not 'great'," Kate retorted.

Jennifer laughed lightly. "Well, those jeans are great."

Kate laughed and playfully swatted her sister's arm while rubbing at a splotch of dirt on the leg of her jeans.

"Who is this guy again, Jenny?" Kate asked as she took Jennifer's proffered lip gloss and applied it liberally. *I would choose today not to wear make-up. I HATE blind dates!*

"He's Andy's best friend. They've known each other since third grade, or something like that. Anyway, he's in a spot of trouble and needs some help."

"Immigration trouble. What do you want me to do again?" She pulled her long, dark hair out of its ponytail and finger-combed it before twisting it into a neat bun on top of her head.

"It depends on what the guys have come up with. He may be looking for a temporary wife."

"That's what I thought you meant when we talked earlier. What's wrong with him? Why doesn't he have a girlfriend?"

"Not sure. I've only met him once. He's some kind of business big-whig. Old money. I don't think the debutantes are up for this particular task." She gave her sister a significant look.

"So what does he want from me? Besides marrying him, of course?"

"I don't know for sure, but I'm sure he's willing to pay you something. And you know you could use the money," Jennifer said.

"Yeah, since skanky Arlene moved out on the fly, I don't know how I'm going to make rent next month."

Jenny squeezed her hand and they continued down the sidewalk, turning into a small restaurant on the corner. Kate was considering the idea. She'd seen that movie with Andie McDowell and the chubby French guy. They got married, she moved into a great apartment, and she didn't see him again for a year. What could be easier?

**

"Hi, Andy!" Kate kissed his cheek. "And you must be William. I'm Katherine, everyone calls me Kate." She extended her hand towards him. *He's tall, that's good. Blue eyes. Kind of serious looking. Geez, who died?*

"William Harper, it's nice to meet you." *Not bad. Not great, but not bad.* She turned around and he got a look at her posterior. *Maybe a little bit great.*

"Good to see you again, William." Jenny kissed his cheek.

"You too, Jennifer."

The four of them sat at the table, women on one side, men on the other, and perused the menus.

"What's everyone else getting?" Kate asked.

"I think I'll have the veal," Andrew said.

"I'm having the salmon," Jenny replied.

"Hmm. Andy, remind me again if the lamb is any good here?" Kate asked.

"It's good, but you didn't like it last time." Will looked at Andrew questioningly, but his friend was focused on his menu.

"Oh, that's right. What are you getting, William?" Kate asked.

"I thought I'd have the steak."

"Ooh, New York strip or filet mignon?"

"The filet."

"Mm. Sounds good." She screwed her lips to one side and tapped her foot under the table.

"Why don't you get the risotto, Katie? You liked it last time," Jenny suggested.

"I'm not in the mood. Maybe the beef medallions? But that's too close to Will's."

Will cocked his eyebrow at Andrew.

"Kate doesn't like to order the same thing as anyone else at the table. That way she can taste everyone's food without a repeat." Will made a disgusted face. "Don't freak out. Just say no if you don't want to share," Andrew explained quietly.

"Jen, this guy is so uptight!" Kate whispered to her sister behind the menu.

"He'll warm up once you get to know him. Andrew says he's great and they've been friends for ages. Just give him a little time." Jenny looked at her younger sister. "And maybe order your own steak tonight."

"So William, how have you been?" Jenny asked, trying to make the situation less awkward.

"Busy." Andrew kicked him under the table. "Um, good mostly. Work's been a little crazy with the new merger."

"What do you do, William?" asked Kate.

He looked at her with squinted eyes, then answered haltingly. "I manage a conglomerate of businesses."

"What does that mean?"

"I guess you could say I make sure everyone is where they are supposed to be when they are supposed to be there and has what they need to do their job."

"Hmmm. Where do you do this 'managing' at?"

"At the Taggston building in downtown. I work at Taggston Corp."

"Cool. So is your company worldwide?" He raised his brows. "I ask because you're clearly English and I was just wondering if you started with the London branch or something like that."

He opened his mouth and said nothing for a few seconds, then Andrew stepped in. "Taggston does have offices around the world, but the biggest office has been here in New York since the late nineties. Will moved here about eight years ago." He nudged Harper under the table again.

"Yes. I moved here full time after Cambridge, but I still spend time at my family's place in London." Another nudge. "I guess you could say we've always lived in both cities."

"How fun! I've always wanted to have more than one house. Our family has a beach house in South Carolina, but all the aunts and uncles share ownership, so it gets used a lot and isn't always available. So how do you know Andy? Jen says you two were in third grade together or something like that?"

"I'll take that one," Andrew answered. "Will and I met at Eton when we were twelve. He was the seasoned twelfth gener and I was the new kid quickly getting labeled as a new-money upstart. Will here stood up for me and made the other kids leave me alone. Of course, being a head taller than everyone else at the time probably didn't hurt!"

They all laughed lightly and Kate asked, "What's a twelfth gener?"

"Twelfth generation Eton boy. The men, or I should say boys, from Will's family have been going to Eton since the 1600's. There's even a library named after one of them."

"Whoa! Twelve generations! I can barely trace my family past my great grandparents. It must be amazing to be part of something so old and solid."

"Yes, it is... amazing," William said softly.

"And you two work together now?" Kate asked.

"Andy is William's lawyer, Katie. I told you that, remember?" Jenny said.

"Oh, yeah. Sorry. You do tell me a lot about Andrew. It gets hard to keep it all straight," she teased her sister as Jen blushed. Andrew took Jenny's hand across the table and they stared at each other with dreamy eyes.

Looking away, Harper asked, "So Kate, what do you do?"

"For money or in real life?"

"Uh, how about both?"

"Well, for money I do several things. I tutor high school students and freshman undergrads in English. One of my professors is writing a book and I help him out a bit – as a cold reader, research assistant, typist, and general sounding board – and I walk dogs every morning and evening in the park." Harper's eyebrows were dangerously close to his hairline. "In real life I'm studying Literature and if I ever finish," she held up her hand with crossed fingers, "I'll become a lit professor myself, or an editor, or maybe write my own book. Who knows?"

"Wow. Andrew said you were working like a dog, not with dogs." She raised her brows. "Sorry, bad joke." He straightened his fork on the table and took a sip of water. "I didn't realize you had three jobs. Are you a full time student as well or just taking one or two classes?"

"I'm full time, usually five classes per semester. Trying to get it over with as soon as possible. Not that I don't love it, but college is to prepare you for life, not to *be* your life. I'm ready to get on with it."

He nodded his head and furrowed his brow, something he did when he was thinking. "Are your parents not helping you out with tuition?"

"They covered what my scholarship didn't for my bachelor's, but after that I was on my own. And of course I had to pay my own living expenses. I could have lived at home and gone to a local school, but I was ready to get out from under the apple tree, you know?"

"Where's home?"

"Virginia."

"Do you go back often?"

"Not really. A couple times a year. What about you? Do you go back to England often?"

"Every couple of months. Most of my extended family still lives there, although some of them have homes here. My little sister moved away, so I don't go as often anymore."

"Do you live near Andrew? He was telling me that his sister still lives there; I think he said she recently married a Brit. And isn't his mom over there, too?"

"Yes, his sister Jessica married an Englishman and they live in London, in Maida Vale I believe. His mother goes back and forth. She's an American after all, but his father's family is English and they all live there still, near the family home in Dorset."

"Are you two talking about me?" Andrew cut in, momentarily ceasing his mooning over Jennifer.

"Yes, as a matter of fact we were. William here was just telling me what a mutt you are. I didn't know your mother was American!"

"Oh, yes. Mom's from Oregon originally. Dad's the Brit in the family. They moved the family over the pond when I was eight. That's why I have the quasi-accent. Not really American, but not pure English either."

"That's alright, Andy. You know, growing up, my favorite dog was a mutt, and I loved him just as much as a pure bred," Kate said with mock sweetness.

"Thank you very much, Katie. Your acceptance really means a lot to me," Andrew answered with feigned sincerity, a hand over his heart.

Jenny just smiled and shook her head. "Ignore them, William. These two are like squabbling siblings when they spend too much time together."

Before a response could be made, the food arrived and everyone tucked in. The table was filled with nothing but the sounds of flatware scraping on plates and ice clinking in glasses. Will watched surreptitiously as Kate silently stabbed a piece of salmon off her sister's plate and popped it in her mouth. Jenny simply turned her plate in her sister's direction and made no comment on her food pilfering. Before he knew it she had taken a bite off Andrew's plate as well without saying a word to anyone.

"Mmm. Remind me that I like the veal next time, Jenny. This is sooo good!" She closed her eyes and leaned her head back, taking a deep breath, before she returned to her own plate. "Here." She held her fork out to Jenny with a small bite of steak on it. Jenny turned towards her sister and opened her mouth, quickly biting the meat off the end of the fork.

"Mmm. Good choice, Katie! Andrew, you have to try this." Jenny then fed him a bite of salmon off her fork, then reached to Katie's plate to cut him a piece of her sister's steak.

Will watched it all in silent fascination, feeling a little like he was viewing a National Geographic special on tribal eating patterns. Everyone went back to eating their own food, the sisters occasionally snitching bites off one another's plates. *Fascinating,* he thought. *Strange, but fascinating.*

Once the plates were cleared and dessert and coffee was ordered, they got down to business. Jenny started, thinking it would be the least awkward coming from her.

"So, William, Andrew tells me you're having some trouble with immigration."

"Yes, I've always lived and worked here under a company-sponsored visa, and mine is about to expire. Usually I just renew it without any problems, like most people who work in more than one country do, but it looks like that's not going to work this time. Andrew thinks I should consider getting a green card instead."

"And what do you think?"

"I trust Andrew's judgment. After all, isn't that what lawyers are for?"

Jenny smiled and Andrew chuckled lightly before saying, "Basically, Harper here will have to leave in four months with no guarantee of return unless he gets a green card. The best way to do that is to marry an American."

"Well, they just legalized gay marriage here, why don't you two get hitched?" Kate asked.

Both men sat up straighter in their chairs and shifted uncomfortably, subconsciously leaning away from each other. "Um, well for one thing, we both have well-documented lives as straight men. No one would believe we just woke up gay one day."

"They might think you've been in the closet this whole time. You know, dating women as a cover up. After all, you're both in your thirties and unmarried. People might believe it," Kate deadpanned.

"I suppose we could, but then where would that leave your sister?" Will answered.

"Touché, Mr. Harper." Kate smiled and tipped her head.

Andrew sputtered and continued on. "Gay marriage is only legal at the state level right now. Immigration is a federal affair. It wouldn't work for our purposes."

Deciding it was time to get serious, Kate asked, "Okay, so what exactly are we talking about doing here?"

"Will needs an American wife. You need money and a place to stay till you finish grad school. Quid pro quo," Andrew answered.

"Okay, give me details. What happens if they find out it's fake?"

"Will gets deported and you get fined and possible jail time."

"Wow. It sounds like I've got a little more to lose here, doesn't it?"

"Not necessarily. Once you've been deported, it's very hard to get back in the country. That could be devastating for Will's business. Not to mention a publicity nightmare."

"That doesn't sound as bad as jail to me."

"True, but jail is rare. Especially if you pay the fine. Generally, the higher the fine, the shorter the jail time. And of course Will would pay the fine."

"I'm going to need that in an account beforehand."

"Does that mean you'll do it?"

"Slow down, Andy! What *exactly* will be expected of me?"

Andrew lowered his voice and leaned across the table, suddenly serious. "Here's the deal: William will cover your remaining tuition and all your living expenses for the next two and a half years. You'll live in his apartment and attend major events with him, be photographed at society functions, and generally act the part of his wife. We can hammer out more exact details when we sign the papers. After two years, you can get a quiet divorce and go about your life with a generous settlement, no strings attached. So, what do you say, Kate? Are you in?"

She pursed her lips and tilted her head to the side. She was mentally counting up the amount of money she was spending on tuition, books, food, rent and everything else she had to pay. She was working three jobs and taking out student loans to cover the rest. It added up to a pretty big number. Trading that in for a few nights out with a cute guy seemed like a pretty good deal. But, they would be *married.*

She wrinkled her brow as she thought about that part of it, then she looked at William. He was shifting nervously in his seat and looking deeply into his cappuccino. She saw he was fidgeting with his spoon and was struck with how odd this all was. She stretched out her leg under the table and tapped his foot with hers. He looked up and she smiled. He stared at her for a moment, then smiled back.

"Okay, Andy. I'm in."

2
THE DEAL

Mid-April, Wednesday
9 Days to Marriage

"Alright, Andy. Dazzle me with legal speak." Kate sat in Andrew's office in a small chair in front of his desk. He was perched on the corner, his expression a mixture of open friendliness and no-nonsense business.

"Like we talked about last night, this contract says that you'll provide all the documents necessary for Will's application – birth certificate, tax returns, etc. – and that you'll stay married for at least twenty-eight months, or until the papers go through. When the time comes to dissolve the marriage, you will each leave the union with the material possessions and finances you came into it with."

"So, basically broke?"

He chuckled lightly. "Not completely. You'll receive a settlement. These are the terms suggested." Andrew gestured to the stack of papers on his desk. "You may wish to counter them if the terms are not satisfactory to you."

Katherine looked at her childhood friend and lawyer seated next to her. "Well, Laura, what do you think?"

"In layman's terms, here's what they are offering: You have the right to live in the apartment in Manhattan until the divorce is finalized, and are required to spend at least seventy percent of your time in the same residence as Mr. Harper to maintain the appearance of a true marriage. You also have unfettered access to two of his additional homes – a beach house in the Hamptons and a townhouse in London."

"Two of his additional homes? As in he has more than that?"

Andrew answered slowly, "Yes. Harper has an ancestral home in England that is currently undergoing renovations, another apartment in the city that he co-owns, and an additional vacation home he goes to to be alone. He never takes anyone there – I've never even seen it and I'm his best friend. Not many know of its existence so you not visiting it shouldn't be viewed as a problem."

"I see."

Laura continued matter-of-factly. "You'll receive three credit cards to cover your monthly expenses. The cards themselves have no limit and can be used on whatever you like, but if you need to spend more than fifty thousand Mr. Harper asks that you check with him first."

"Fifty thousand per...?"

"Month."

"Whoa." Kate sank back in her chair.

"You'll need to clothe yourself as befits Mr. Harper's wife, so much of your allowance will go toward your wardrobe. Immediately after the wedding, you will be given a clothing fund to get you started, separate from your regular funds. You will also receive a signing bonus of ten thousand dollars to spend as you wish. There is a part-time housekeeper employed at the apartment; you turn in your grocery list to her and she'll take care of it. Your allowance is for personal items, not groceries. All utility bills are covered by Mr. Harper. In addition, when you go out together, he picks up the bill and it is not considered your personal expense. You will be provided with petty cash each month in the amount of five thousand dollars. This money is kept in the safe at the apartment and Mr. Harper will make sure it is stocked at the first of each month."

Laura turned the page and continued, ignoring the look of incredulity on Katherine's face. "As far as public appearances go, you are required to attend at least half of the public functions Mr. Harper attends, not to exceed eight functions in a month. In addition, you'll need to have a public meal or date together at least once a week. Lunch or dinner – breakfast doesn't count – to keep up the appearance of a real marriage."

"You'd think after a few months we'd just sit at home in our sweats watching *Everybody Loves Raymond* reruns – isn't that what real married people do?" Laura glared at her. "Sorry, Lar. Continue."

"You are to maintain the appearance of a happily married couple. That means no arguing in public, no flirting with other men or women," Kate's eyes got wide, "and no pulling away when Mr. Harper touches you."

"That's in there? Really?"

"I was trying to be as thorough as possible. Habit. Sorry, Kate." Andrew smiled sheepishly at her.

Laura continued, "You're required to wear the wedding ring on the third finger of your left hand at all times and, of course, you cannot have an extramarital affair. If you are caught cheating or if you tell anyone about the true conditions of this arrangement, you forfeit your claim to the settlement, and Mr. Harper has the right to sue you for any and all expenses incurred during the marriage, including rent on the apartment you'll be residing in."

"Okay, I get it, don't cheat," she said defensively. "So what about children?"

"What do you mean children?" Andrew asked.

"You know, tiny people that are born after nine months in the womb? What happens if we have children?"

"I'm sorry, Kate, there seems to be some misunderstanding. This is a business relationship *only*. You and Harper will have separate bedrooms and you're not expected to ... you know."

Kate rolled her eyes. "I'm aware of that, Andrew. I'm not pimping myself out, I'm just saying that we'll be living in close quarters for at least two years, possibly longer depending on the paperwork, and neither of us will be seeing anyone else, and we'll be cozy-ing up all lovey-dovey in public – something might happen. I want it covered just in case – as a precaution. Can you add that in, Laura?"

"No problem. I'll add a clause that says you're entitled to nothing less than fifty percent custody of any children born from the union and regular child support. I'm sure they will want to add a clause that you maintain some method of contraception. Mr. Jamison?"

"Yes, we'll need some sort of guarantee that you won't become pregnant on purpose in order to receive child support payments. Not that I think you would, Kate, but I need to cover my client."

"I understand, Andrew. Don't worry, I'm not offended. Let's put in that I will not purposely get pregnant and he will not coerce me into it either. Does that work?"

"Certainly. Now about your settlement: You'll retain everything you purchased personally during the marriage, including, but not limited to, clothes, jewelry, and household items, as well as any gifts given to you by Mr. Harper. Once he receives his ten-year green card, you'll be provided a place to live for the next year – specifics to be decided by you – and five hundred thousand dollars cash." Laura scanned further down, then added, "Mr. Jamison, rather than provide her with a place to live for a year in Manhattan, we'd like a home purchased outright and access to Mr. Harper's apartment for a year while she chooses said home."

Kate looked at Laura, but her lawyer placed her hand on Kate's arm and looked calmly at Andrew.

"I don't see a problem with that. I'll add it in." He nodded with a smile that looked surprisingly respectful.

Kate's eyes widened and she nodded at Laura's questioning glance. "When do we sign the final papers?"

"I'll make the necessary changes and have this ready for you first thing in the morning. So if you have any changes you want made or any questions, ask me today. We need to hurry so Harper's paperwork can go through before his current visa expires," Andrew explained.

"So when do we get hitched?" asked Kate.

Andrew answered, "Will has four months before he has to leave the country. Since Jenny and I have been seeing each other for a while now, we can put out that we introduced the two of you a couple of months ago. I was thinking that you could go ahead and get married next weekend. That gives you a little over a week to get seen and hopefully photographed to legitimize the relationship. Then we'll all go to Vegas and you two can tie the knot. We'll tell the press that Jenny and I had been planning on going and you decided to join us. Spur of the moment you decide to go ahead and get married. Maybe we'll tell them you were drunk – we can figure out the particulars later as long as we have you two married by the end of the month."

"I think I've got it. Walk out with me, Laura?"

At the elevator, Laura leaned in to whisper to Kate. "Katie, do you want to ask for more? I'm pretty sure he'd go to a million."

"Laura!"

"Hey, it's my job to get you the best possible outcome and he's desperate. Despite popular belief, there aren't many women who are willing to do this and keep their mouths shut. He needs you. Capitalize on that!"

"I don't know, Laura. I don't think I'd feel right asking for more. He's being really generous as it is. Half a million dollars and a house!?! I don't want to take advantage of someone in a desperate situation. That can't be good karma. Besides, I have to live with this guy for the next two years. I don't want to piss him off before I even move in!"

"Whatever you say, Kate. But think about it."

"I will. I'll see you tomorrow, Laura."

"Aren't you going down with me?"

"Nope. I'm going up to have lunch with my fiancé," she said with a sly smile as she pointed upward. Laura just laughed and rolled her eyes as the elevator doors closed.

***

"Katherine Bishop to see Mr. Harper," Kate told the receptionist outside the elevator on the thirtieth floor.

"Down the hall and to your right," she said, pointing out the way.

Kate walked down the hall reading the names and titles on the plates outside the doors. So far she'd passed three vice presidents of various departments and at the end of the hall was a double door with the label CFO outside it. Wow. If William's office was up here, he must be important.

She turned right like the receptionist told her to do and came to a set of carved wooden doors. There was no label outside the door, so she hoped she wasn't about to walk into the wrong place. Tentatively, she opened one and peeked inside. After seeing it was a sort of anteroom, she stepped in and walked toward the assistant-looking person behind the desk.

"Hi. I'm Katherine Bishop, here to see Mr. Harper."

"Please have a seat over there. Mr. Harper is just finishing up a call and will be with you momentarily."

Katherine sat down on a leather club chair and thought over the contract, wondering if there was anything she'd missed and if she should add anything.

After about five minutes, the assistant told her she could go on in.

Katherine walked into an office that was easily bigger than her entire apartment. Two walls were covered floor to ceiling in windows and the view of the city was spectacular, even from the door. There was a small bar near a round table with four chairs and a seating area that included two armchairs and a leather sofa. On the opposite side of the room was an enormous desk, and sitting behind it, in an enormous chair, was William Harper. He was facing the window, his back to her, on the phone.

"That's fine. Go ahead and make the reservations and we'll have dinner afterward at Bernard's. Yes, alright. Sounds good. Thank you, Evelyn."

He spun around and hung up the phone. Katherine stood in the middle of the room, not really knowing how to greet the man you've just agreed to marry but have no actual relationship with. She smiled, waiting for him to say something.

"Hello, Kate." *She looks better today. Maybe it's the lighting? Or her dress?*

"Hi, William."

"I spoke to Andrew. He said we should have the contract signed in the morning," he said as he gestured for her to sit in the chair in front of his desk.

"Yes, I don't see why we wouldn't."

He shifted his eyes around the room uncomfortably. "Kate, this is a rather awkward situation for both of us. I know the lawyers are going over our... relationship with each of us individually, but I thought it might make things a little easier if we covered a few of the more *intimate* details face to face."

She nodded, gesturing for him to proceed.

"We'll need to appear as a real couple in public. I've been giving this some thought, and I am not an overly demonstrative man." She bit back her sarcastic comment. "It would appear incongruous with my past behavior if I were to suddenly become publicly affectionate. However, the thought has also crossed my mind that in the past, I never would have run off to marry a woman no one had ever seen me with before – especially to Vegas. In order to make our quick elopement appear legitimate, I may need to modify my behavior to seem more..."

"Spontaneous?"

"Yes, thank you. I don't want to appear foolish or make you uncomfortable in any way, but I think we should try to seem..."

"Smitten? Besotted? Head over heels?" She may have been enjoying this a little *too* much.

"Yes, something like that."

"Don't worry, William. I minored in theatre," she said proudly.

He looked slightly terrified at that and she smiled guiltily.

"Seriously, it'll be fine. I've had a boyfriend before. I will look at you adoringly and laugh at all your jokes. Everyone will think I've bewitched you and that's why you're acting so strangely. We'll be fine. Don't worry." He gave her a relieved look.

Just then Evelyn knocked on the door, Harper bade her

enter, and she came in with two large white bags which she quickly began emptying at the table.

"I've ordered in lunch. Shall we?"

Kate nodded and followed him to the table.

After finishing her salad, she smiled and said, "May I ask you a question?"

"Of course."

"Why do you and Andrew call each other by your last names?"

"We met at Eton, and everyone there goes by their family name. It tends to stick. When we moved to the States we tried to use our given names, but it was hard to change after so many years. I suppose we use a mix of both now. Sorry if it's confusing."

"No, it's not, I just wondered."

He nodded and put the straw into his drink.

"Why does everyone keep mentioning the press? Jenny said you were some business bigwig and old money, so are we talking page six, high society stuff?"

"Uh -"

"Oh, no! You're not famous are you? Are you some big famous guy and I don't have a clue who you are?"

He flushed slightly and shifted in his seat. "No, not really, although I am in the public eye at times." She looked at him questioningly. "Well, I think Jennifer mostly had it right. The Harpers could be described as 'old money'. I am mostly known for my position with the company."

"What position is that? You must be high up to be way up here in this enormous office."

"I'm on the board of the Taggston Corporation, but most of my time is spent with HarperCo," he said plainly. "I'm the CEO."

Her eyes widened. "You're the CEO? Of the entire company? But you're so young!"

"Yes, well, my age and position combined have made me something of an oddity, hence the press. But don't worry, I'm not hounded by paparazzi or anything. Mostly just photographed at events, nothing invasive."

"So you're no Paris Hilton?" she teased.

He chuckled lightly and shook his head. "Afraid not. Sorry."

She moved on to her entree and they ate silently for a few more minutes.

"So where do you live, William?"

"Central Park West. It's a bit of a trek to work, but the security's great. I think you'll like it."

"Good. Closer to Columbia." She took a few more bites and waited for him to say something, but he ate his fish in silence. "So, Andy thinks we should get hitched next weekend in Vegas. He and Jenny could be our witnesses."

"Yes, we spoke about it. I was thinking of modifying his plans just a bit."

"How so?" she asked with interest.

"I think we should see each other as much as possible in the next week to let the press get used to the idea, then have a public engagement and subsequent announcement before going to Vegas. I think it would be more believable if we went there to celebrate the engagement, then got caught up in the excitement of it all and eloped, than if we were just dating and all of a sudden got married."

"What do you mean by public engagement?"

"I'd propose, somewhere we were likely to be seen, and some lucky person can sell the story to the Post. Of course we'll probably use a plant."

"Start a rumor that you're about to pop the question?"

"Exactly. Having someone see you at the jeweler's looking at engagement rings is usually the easiest way."

"How devious of you! I wouldn't have pegged you for the sneaky type."

"What type would you have thought me?"

"Jury's still out," she replied coyly.

He grinned and after a few minutes of eating in silence, Kate spoke.

"So let's talk about sex."

Harper spluttered and nearly choked on his fish. After taking a drink of water and a moment to calm himself, he said,

"What do you mean?"

"You know, sex. When a man and a woman-"

"I know what sex is! I'm wondering why you want to talk about it," he said with eyebrows raised.

"Oh, come on, William! We're both adults here. We're going to be in this for at least two years, possibly closer to three, and I've got a no-cheating clause in my contract. That's a long time to go without!" She made a mental note to have them put in a no-cheating clause for William as well. It was only fair.

He looked at her skeptically. "What exactly are you suggesting?"

"That we have sex with each other." His eyebrows went higher. "If I sleep with someone else, I'm in trouble. If you do, you're in even bigger trouble and will probably get deported and I'll go to jail. We'll be living together and spending time with each other and acting like crazy newlyweds. What's the harm in sleeping together? After all, we *will* be married."

He looked at her silently for a long moment. At first his expression was shocked, but then it transformed to amused and intrigued.

"I'm not suggesting we jump each other's' bones out of the blue. But if the mood strikes and we're in the moment, why not?"

He smiled broadly. "You know, Kate, I think we're going to get along just fine."

She kicked his leg under the table. "Typical man!" she muttered under her breath.

He couldn't help but laugh and reached across the table for her hand. "No, but seriously, Kate, I appreciate your forthrightness. It's a topic that needs to be covered and you're right; we're both adults and two years is a long time. Rather than put ourselves in the way of dangerous temptation, we should take care of things at home."

"Are you always this proper?"

"What do you mean?"

"Never mind. So we're agreed. Sex with each other is okay?"

"Yes, sex with each other is okay."

3
THE DATE

Mid- April, Thursday
8 Days to Marriage

"Jenny!"

Jennifer held the phone away from her ear and answered her sister. "*Yes, Katie?*"

"Guess what?!"

"What?"

"I signed the papers! And before I left, Andy gave me a big envelope filled with cash! He said I should buy clothes for the next week of 'dating' since I won't have my cards until after the wedding. Can you believe that?" Her voice calmed for a moment. "I mean, officially, I'm offended, my clothes are great, but now we get to go shopping!" Kate stomped her feet and squirmed in her seat with excitement.

Jennifer laughed at her sister's enthusiasm. "*How much did he give you?*"

"I don't know. I quit counting when I got to ten grand. Can you believe it? And guess where I am now?"

"Barneys?"

"No, not yet. I'm in the back of a limo with a privacy screen and everything. They insisted I take the car and told the driver to take me wherever I wanted to go. I won't have to carry my bags on the subway!" Katherine squealed a little and sighed, leaning back into the plush leather. "Come shopping with me? I need to get a cocktail dress for tonight. William's taking me to a show and dinner after at Bernard's."

"I'll meet you at Barneys in an hour."

Four hours later, two exhausted women stumbled into Kate's Lower East Side apartment.

"That was amazing," said Jennifer as she collapsed on the couch.

"Completely."

"Fantastic."

"Unbelievable."

"Orgasmic."

Kate held her sides as she dissolved in a fit of laughter. "Oh, Jenny! I can't believe all this is happening to me!"

"I know. Just think – last week, you didn't know how you were going to pay rent and today you spent a small fortune at Barneys."

"This is so surreal! And this time next week, I'll be in Vegas getting married. Mom is going to *freak*."

"Speaking of Mom, what do you plan to tell her?"

"Nothing now. After we get married, I guess I'll have to tell her something. Definitely not the truth, though. She couldn't keep a secret if it was glued to her."

Jennifer rolled her eyes. "What about Dad? He'll be upset he didn't get to give you away."

"It's not a real wedding, Jenny. And you can't give away something you don't have. I'm a grown woman, not a fifteen year old girl. I can get married if I want and I don't need my parents' permission."

"Okay, Gloria Steinem! Easy! I was just saying that you and Dad have always been close and he'll be sad he missed it, that's all."

"I guess I'll call them after I get settled in over at William's. We'll probably have to go down there. I certainly don't want them coming here – mom would have a field day with that. They don't read the New York papers there anyway, so hopefully they won't know about William's millions and I can just pass him off as well-off or something like that."

"It'll be hard to fool Dad. He knows you too well."

"I know. That's why we should make it a short trip."

"Good luck with that," Jennifer said sarcastically.

"Maybe you'll get engaged to Andy and take the attention off of me," she sniggered.

"I don't know, Katie," Jennifer said, suddenly serious. "We've only been dating a few months – I don't know how serious it is."

"You're exclusive though, right?"

"Yeah."

"Has he said the L-word yet?"

"No," Jennifer sighed sadly.

"Have you?" Kate asked suspiciously.

"Of course not! You know I'd never break a cardinal rule!"

"Good. Because telling the guy you love him first is just asking for heartbreak. I think he loves you, though. Or at least he's well on his way."

"You think?"

"Oh, yeah. He can't stop looking at you and brings your name into every conversation. It's getting annoying! Kind of like someone else I know..."

Jennifer hit Kate with a pillow. "Not funny, Katie! I don't bring Andrew into every conversation!"

"Alright, sorry, Jen. But tell me, do you love him?"

She let out a frustrated sigh. "I don't know. Sometimes I think I do. I swear, when he looks at me with those big brown eyes and tells me he can't wait to see me again, I nearly swoon. It's pathetic! Is five months long enough to know if it's love and not just some infatuation? I don't know if it is."

"And?" Kate asked with one raised brow.

"And what?"

"You know what!"

"Katie!"

"What? You used to give me all the details, even the ones I'd rather not know, but since you've been with Andrew you've become surprisingly close-lipped."

"Well," Jennifer answered evasively, "you've been really busy and we haven't been spending as much time together as we used to... and -"

"And you've been spending all your spare time doing the nasty with Andrew!"

"Katherine Mae Bishop! I can't believe you just said that to me!"

"Well, it's true isn't it?"

"That doesn't mean you should say it!"

"I'm sorry, Jenny! Did I offend you maiden sensibilities?" Kate said mockingly.

"Oh, alright! Yes! I spend all my time doing the nasty with Andrew. There! Are you happy now?"

Kate laughed so hard she nearly fell off the couch.

"Katie! Stop laughing at me! Stop it!"

"I'm sorry! I couldn't help it." Wiping the tears from her eyes, she looked at her sister slyly. "Soooo, how is it?"

Jennifer turned red and looked down, fidgeting with the hem of her shirt. "It's great. Really great."

"Oh no, you're not getting off so easy! Spill! And I want details."

"Well," Jennifer began, sitting up on her knees, "he's really good with his hands. And he does this thing with his tongue." She blushed and hid her face in a pillow.

Kate giggled and covered her mouth. "So, is he the best you've ever had?"

"Definitely! He's so attentive and gentle, and yet he can be so strong and forceful sometimes. When he kisses me, I can't think straight. I swear, Katie, sometimes I forget to breathe!"

"Wow. You've got it bad. This is worse than I thought."

"I know! What am I going to do? I'm turning into a puddle of mush!"

"I think it's cute. My little Jennifer's in love!"

"Stop teasing me, Katie!"

"Alright, I'll leave you alone. I like Andy. He's good for you, and not an idiot, which is a big step up from some of your other boyfriends."

"Thanks a lot, Kate!" Jennifer threw a pillow at her sister. "Enough about me. Let's get you ready for your big date with William."

"Oh!" Kate jumped up and ran to the bathroom and turned on the tub. "Jenny! Look at the time!"

Jennifer laughed at her sister and began unpacking the clothes they'd purchased, getting Kate's cocktail dress ready for the night.

**

Kate was in the backseat of a sleek black sedan when her phone rang. "Hi, Andy!"

"Hey, Katie. All set for the big night out?"

"Yeah, I should be at the theatre in about ten minutes."

"Great. Listen, I want to cover a few things with you before you meet Will."

"Like what?"

"This is your first public appearance together. Since it's opening night, there will be a lot of press and a big society turn out. Harper will likely be asked to pose for pictures. Even if they don't ask you, get in the shot. We need people to see you together. Stick to him like glue. Hold hands, take his arm, that sort of thing."

"Got it. PDA in front of the cameras. Anything else?"

"There will be a lot of society players there. They may ask you some personal questions. Try not to talk to anyone long enough for it to get that far, but if you find yourself in a conversation, be as vague as possible about yourself and your relationship with Will. Hint that you've been dating for a little while, but don't say anything outright. They'll assume more on their own than we could ever tell them directly."

"Okay. Anyone in particular I should look out for?"

"Yes. Alicia Winters is a woman Will went out with a few of months ago. It was never serious, but she's mad it didn't go anywhere, and she's the one who made accusations about Will to immigration."

"She sounds lovely," Kate said sardonically.

"And the other is Nicole Jamison."

"Any relation?"

"Unfortunately, yes. She's my cousin and has her sights

set on Will. Just between you and me, I don't think she even likes him that much, she just wants to be the one to nab him. Will's been a commodity for a while now."

"I see. Don't worry, Andy, I know how to stake my claim."

"I knew you were the right girl for the job, Katie. Good luck and feel free to call if you need anything."

"Thanks, Andy. Will do."

Harper stood in front of the theatre waiting for Katherine. As soon as he'd gotten out of his car the crowd of cameramen and reporters had turned their gaze to him, anxious to see who had arrived. He stayed on the sidewalk, close to the street, just far enough away to not be questioned by the velvet-rope-enclosed crowd. Still, that didn't stop a few reporters from calling his name and trying to get him to turn toward them for a shot. Thankfully, about two minutes later Katherine's car pulled up.

It stopped directly in front of the red-carpeted entrance. Harper stepped forward himself to take Kate's hand. The first thing he saw was a pair of dark purple heels reaching out, followed by two shapely legs. Before he knew it, Kate was standing in front of him in a short cobalt blue cocktail dress and smiling straight at him. He couldn't help but smile back. Behind them, cameras were flashing like crazy as a cacophony of voices called out Harper's name, asking him who his date was and if she was his girlfriend.

He placed her hand on his arm and led her inside, nodding to the press as he went, but saying nothing. They made it through the crowd at the entrance and into the lobby. Harper leaned down and whispered in her ear, "You look wonderful tonight."

"Thank you, and thanks for the dress."

"Anytime."

"Harper!"

Harper turned around and looked at a man in his early sixties with a mustache and gray hair. He had a bit of a round belly and Katherine expected to see a monocle in his pocket, but was disappointed.

"Hello, Stevens. Allow me to introduce my date, Katherine Bishop. Katherine, this is Reginald Stevens."

"Hello," she said simply with a small smile.

"Well hello, dear! How did you get dear old Harper out of the house? He hardly ever comes to these things if he doesn't have to. What's your secret?"

"Surely you know a woman has her ways," she said flirtatiously.

He let out a great laugh. "Aye, that they do, that they do! Well, it's good to see you out, Harper. I'll see you at the next meeting."

The men nodded at each other and parted ways. "Meeting? Are you two in AA together or something?"

Harper chuckled slightly. "No, board meeting. Stevens is on the board at Taggston. Has been since the early nineties."

"Ah." She looked around the room and said quietly, "May I make a suggestion?"

"Of course."

"You might want to introduce me as your girlfriend." He looked dubious. "It'll move things along a little faster. I mean, you're supposed to be proposing within a week. It's *kind of* a big jump from *date* to *fiancée*."

"I see your point. Alright. You know, it's strange – I've never introduced a woman as my girlfriend before."

"Never?"

"No, never. Well, maybe once in school to my parents. And there was one girl in college, but it was never very serious."

"How is that possible?"

"What do you mean?"

"Have you *seen* you?" She said with a sweeping glance up his tall, lean body and stopping on his head of thick, dark brown hair.

He chuckled self-consciously. "I didn't say I haven't had dates, just not women I introduced as my girlfriend."

"Oooh, I see. You're a player," she said, drawing out the words.

"Not at all. I just haven't been in any serious

relationships in a while."

"Well, this is definitely a topic we're going to need to talk more about, but I think it's time to find our seats."

They watched the first half of the play without interruption. When it came time for intermission, Katherine headed straight for the ladies room. It was one of those old fashioned lounges with red velvet couches and gilt-edged mirrors. It was filled to the brim with women in evening and cocktail gowns. *It looks like Barneys threw up in here,* she thought.

After finding a place in the mirror and touching up her lipstick, Katherine was approached by a tall blond in stiletto heels and a sparkly black mini dress.

"So you're William Harper's date," the Amazon said plainly.

"Girlfriend actually." Kate continued checking her hair unfazed.

The Amazon's eyes opened widely. "Girlfriend? Does he know you call yourself that?"

"Of course – it was his idea. If you'll excuse me." Katherine smiled a little too sweetly and left the room.

As she approached her seat, she saw William in conversation with a woman slightly taller than herself, with long, straight black hair and cat-like eyes. As she got closer, she could tell the woman's eyes were an unnatural violet color and her lashes looked like spiders sitting on her eyelids. Looking at William, she thought he looked tense. His shoulders were rigid and his face was expressionless. But behind his eyes was a slightly angry look, almost hostile.

"Hi, sweetie! Sorry I took so long – I got to chatting with the others." She took his arm and pulled him down slightly, kissing him on the cheek. Katherine smiled at the other woman expectantly. Spider lashes just glared at her while trying to maintain a flirtatious pout toward William. It was rather comical and Katherine would have laughed if it hadn't been completely inappropriate.

Will recovered his shock and put his arm around Kate. "Let me introduce you, honey. This is Alicia Winters. Alicia, this is my girlfriend, Katherine Bishop." Alicia nodded warily, eying Kate up and down while trying to look like she wasn't doing just that.

"It's so nice to meet you. How do you know my William?" Kate asked in a friendly voice as she leaned into his side and ran one hand over the front of his jacket.

Spider lashes looked flustered. "Our families go way back," she said slowly. "And how do you know William?"

"Through a mutual friend." Before she could say more the lights flashed indicating it was time to get back to their seats.

"We should go," Harper said, taking her elbow and beginning to turn her away. "It was nice to see you again." He nodded to Alicia and started to move.

"It was nice meeting you, Katherine," Alicia said uncomfortably.

"You too, Alina."

"It's Alicia."

"Sorry, my mistake. Enjoy the rest of the show." And just like that Kate walked away on Harper's arm, leaving a fuming Miss Winters behind them.

"Very well played, Miss Bishop," he whispered in her ear once they were seated.

"Why thank you, Mr. Harper."

The remainder of the show passed uneventfully and before they knew it, they were standing outside, waiting for their car to pull around. The cameras were flashing all around them and questions were being asked of the various critics and society elite standing nearby.

"Do you trust me?"

"What?" he asked.

"Do you trust me?" Kate repeated.

"Yes," he said slowly, dragging out the word. "Why?"

"Come on."

Kate took his hand and dragged him away from the crowd to the edge of the roped barrier. They were close enough to the road for a quick escape, but also close enough to the press to be seen, photographed, and questioned.

"What are you doing?" Harper asked.

"Andy told me to get photographed and be seen. We need to start making you look bewitched," she said close to his ear. He leaned toward her to hear better as she wrapped the hand he still held behind her to rest on her lower back.

"And how do you propose we do that?"

"Stay close like this. Now, put your hand on my neck."

"What?"

"Just do it," she said with a sultry smile toward the cameramen.

He raised his right hand and placed it on the side of her neck. "Now whisper in my ear."

"What should I say?" he whispered.

Kate laughed lightly and looked down, then looked up at him through her lashes. "Say whatever you want."

For a moment Harper wanted to kiss her. Not because the cameras were watching and he needed to put on a show, but because she looked so damn enticing looking at him like that, her skin so soft and creamy, her lips plump and inviting. Without realizing it, he had gotten about a centimeter away from her lips. She raised her chin slightly and without thinking, he closed the distance between them.

Cameras began flashing all around them and reporters were calling out, "Mr. Harper! Mr. Harper! Who is she? Is she your girlfriend?"

After a moment, Harper pulled away and stroked Kate's cheek. She smiled sweetly and placed her hand on his chest. "I think our car is here." Harper nodded to a car behind her and they slowly pulled apart. He opened the car door and followed her in, shutting it quickly behind him.

4
THE AFTERMATH

Late April, Friday
7 Days to Marriage

Kate woke to the sound of rustling in the apartment. She groggily rolled over in her bed, determined to block out whatever noises had made their way to her room. She vaguely registered the sound of the refrigerator door closing and heard the gurgling of Skanky Arlene's forgotten coffee maker.

"If you're here to rob me, there's nothing worth more than fifty dollars! But there is a futon in the first bedroom that you're welcome to take."

"Katie! It's me!"

"Jen? I want my key back!"

"Have you seen the paper?"

"Ugh. What time is it?" Kate looked at the clock next to her bed. "Jenny! It's six in the morning! I'm going back to bed."

Jenny flopped onto Katherine's bed and waved a cinnamon roll near her sister's face. "It's six fifty-five. Did Skanky Arlene really leave a futon?"

"Yup." Kate swiped the cinnamon roll from her sister and took a big bite. "And it comes with a lovely Aztec-inspired cover. Feel free to take it with you. What are you doing here so early?"

"I come bearing news. You, little sister, are in the paper." Jenny took the cinnamon roll back and sauntered out of the room.

Kate stood up and stumbled into the hall that passed for a kitchen. She noisily grabbed a plate and dropped a cinnamon roll onto it, then followed Jenny into the tiny living room and sat on the opposite end of the couch, curling up under the throw blanket. "Why are you here again?"

Jenny kicked off her running shoes and waved a paper in front of her sister. "This is why." She dropped it onto the coffee table.

Kate slowly picked up the paper and looked at the picture with sleepy eyes. After staring for a moment, it finally came into focus. There, in a picture that took up a quarter of the page, was a man kissing a woman in a short blue cocktail dress. Their bodies were pressed together and his hand was on her neck, pulling her closer. Below was a caption that read: *Business mogul William Harper kisses unknown woman at opening night of In the Garden.* She looked at the accompanying article and saw the headline: *Whoa, Harper!*

"Jenny, it's too early to see straight. Read this to me?" Kate passed the paper to her sister.

"'*Just when you think you know a guy, he goes and turns into a curb-side kisser. If you don't believe me, just look at the picture. Unfortunately, Lady Luck's identity is currently unknown. Since the kiss heard round the world only happened last night, we haven't heard anything from Harper's rep. So far, all we know is that she has legs that will have women everywhere digging their thigh-masters out from under their beds. Sources inside the theatre say the two remained close throughout the performance and Harper is rumored to have referred to her as his girlfriend. Yes, you read that right. I said GIRLFRIEND! Our man of mystery is proving even more mysterious with this latest stunt. We'll be keeping our eyes peeled for more news about Harper and his new lady love.*'"

Kate sipped her tea silently.

"Wow. This columnist really needs to get a life," Jenny said.

"And a thigh master. Who wrote it?"

"Let's see – Priscilla Jennings. I've never read her before but this says she's the regular columnist for this section."

"She certainly has a way with words. I'd like to say I won't become a regular, but I have a feeling Andy will want me to keep up with what they are saying about me and William."

"Probably."

"I'm glad I had the idea at the theatre, though. Poor William is so used to avoiding the cameras, I think it's really unnatural for him to seek attention."

"So you kissed him?"

"No. I just moved us into a better spot for being seen and got close to him and told him to whisper in my ear. He kissed me. I was really surprised – he didn't strike me as the type to kiss in public, at least not in front of a camera."

"Interesting. Is he a good kisser?"

"Not bad. I'd give him a solid seven out of ten."

"Really? He looks like he'd be at least an eight."

"Maybe next time his score will improve. We're just getting to know each other now."

"Well you're about to know him a lot better. Andy says we're all going out tonight to some posh new French restaurant. He wants to make sure we're all established as friends in the press. Apparently, this is a place you go to be seen. Reservation's for eight o'clock."

"Ugh. I'm too tired to think about that right now. What are you going to wear?"

"Probably that purple dress I bought with you yesterday. You?"

"I don't know. You pick. We'll be together in the pictures – we have to represent the Bishop women," Kate said sarcastically.

"Don't be a spoilsport, Katie. Does William know how grouchy you are in the morning?"

"I'm not grouchy in the morning!"

"Oh, really? Do you call this pleasant?"

"I call this a normal reaction to being rudely awakened at six a.m. after going to bed at two in the morning!"

"Whatever. I've got to get back and get dressed for work. Wear the pink dress – it'll flow with the French atmosphere."

Kate threw a pillow at her sister as Jenny slipped her running shoes back on. "Yeah, yeah. Bye, Jen."

"Bye, Katie." Jenny kissed her sister on the forehead where she lay curled up in the corner of the sofa and skipped out the door.

**

"Hey, Kate. Sorry to bother you."

"It's no problem, Andy. What's up?" Kate balanced the phone on her shoulder while she stuffed a notebook into her backpack.

"I just wanted to let you know that Harper will pick you up at seven-thirty tonight, then swing by Jenny's to pick the two of us up."

"Do you always confirm his plans or do you just like talking to me?" She zipped her bag and slung it over her shoulder.

"I know it seems weird, but Will's a very busy man and I offered to call for him. His assistant doesn't know about the two of you yet. He usually keeps her out of his personal life. He's private like that."

"I see. Can you give me his number?" She hung up with Andrew and dialed Harper.

*

"Harper." William answered his phone brusquely.

"Hi, William. It's Kate."

Pause. "Hello, Kate. How are you?"

"I'm fine, thanks. Andrew said you'd be here around seven-thirty to pick me up?"

"That's the plan. Does that not work for you?"

"No, it's fine. I just wondered what the plan was for tonight other than eating with Jenny and Andrew. I mean, what is supposed to be happening between us?"

"How do you mean?"

"*Well, we need to look like a couple who's been seeing each other for a few months and is in love. We'd probably be more convincing if we got to know each other a little better, you know?*"

Will let out an exasperated sigh. "What do you want to know?"

"*That's not exactly what I meant.*"

Will pinched the bridge of his nose and exhaled heavily. "Listen, Kate – I'm not very good at this sort of thing."

"*What sort of thing?*"

"This." He gestured with his hands until he remembered she couldn't see him through the phone. "Women, dating, relationships."

"*Is that why you haven't had a girlfriend since college?*"

He chuckled slightly. "Probably. Can I just be honest with you?"

"*Please do.*"

"I'm not a very gregarious man. Sure, I've asked out plenty of women, but we never went on more than four or five dates, and I never was so infatuated that I would disregard my own nature and start snogging in public." Kate held back a snort on the other end of the line. "I don't like being in front of crowds and am not naturally deceptive. Basically, I am a terrible liar. It would be really great if you could just take the lead. Andrew has told me to look smitten in public, so whatever you want to do, I'll go along. But honestly, I don't think I'm very good at making things up on the spot. I doubt I could pull it off."

"*So you're saying you think I'm a good liar?*"

"See, this is what I was talking about!" He let out a frustrated sigh. "I didn't mean-"

Kate cut him off. "*Calm down, William. I was just messing with you. I've noticed you seem more comfortable one on one, so I see what you're saying. But really, I'm not much better at this than you are. I'm just making it up as I go along.*"

"But you are acknowledging that you're better at it than I am."

She could hear the smirk in his voice. "*Well, you said you liked honesty*," she said happily.

"I know, I brought it on myself. But seriously, you did really well last night. It was all over the papers this morning."

"*Yeah, the kiss was – and that was your idea.*"

"Well, I'm not completely clueless." Was that pride she heard in his voice?

"*Okay lover-boy, you've got it. I'll take the lead. Just don't jump if I grab your leg or something, okay?*"

"Deal. See you tonight, Kate."

"*See ya. Oh, and William?*"

"Yeah?"

"*Call me Katie.*"

**

"So, how is it going so far?" Andrew asked in the car.

"I suppose it's going fine. It's only day two, so I can't really say," Kate answered.

"Fair enough. We have to make this count because Will is in Boston for the day tomorrow. You'll be back late Saturday night, right Will?" Harper nodded as he changed lanes. Andrew kept talking, "I put in a call to the Post, anonymously of course. I expect to see a photographer at some point this evening."

"I read the article this morning," Jenny commented. "The picture was great. I was a little surprised it was such a big piece, though."

"Harper usually poses for pictures at society charity functions, and up until now, that's all he has really attended. They were probably surprised to see him last night. And he'd usually go stag or have a different date for each one, so him dating someone steadily is kind of a big deal. Don't worry – you won't have anyone stalking your apartment or anything – he's not *that* popular."

"Gee, thanks, Jamison," Harper said. "You know, I did sometimes take the same woman to more than one event. I'm not completely socially dysfunctional."

"Sorry, Will," Andrew retorted insincerely. "There is a New York gossip blog that Will is not normally featured in, mostly because he doesn't really do anything worth gossiping about," he shot Harper a look, "but after today's article in the paper, they did a post about him. Since everyone seems to have a camera phone these days, you can expect pictures of you to be sent in, so even if there isn't legit press around, you'll need to be on your game."

"Got it. Any news on when this whole proposal scene is going down?" Kate asked.

"I'm thinking next Wednesday or Thursday. We leave Friday for Vegas, so it has to be done before then," Andrew answered.

"Do I get a say in any of this?" Will asked.

"Time to stop the shop talk, we're here," Jenny said.

Harper handed the keys to the valet and they went inside where they were immediately seated. Katherine slid into the booth next to Harper and sat just a little closer than she should. She immediately put a hand on his thigh and felt him jerk his leg instinctively.

"This is why I think we should get to know each other better," she whispered in his ear. He relaxed and leaned down to her ear.

"Point taken."

She smiled and he put his arm around her shoulders. At least that was a move he was comfortable with.

The four of them drank two bottles of wine between them, though Harper only had one glass since he was driving, and filled themselves on rich French food. Kate fed Harper a few bites off her spoon and rested her head on his shoulder as they were eating dessert. He smiled down at her and played with her hair, feeling more confident as the evening went on. There was something about Kate that set him at ease and made him forget to be self-conscious.

As they were standing outside on the pavement, Katherine caught sight of a man with a large camera partially hidden around the corner.

"William," she called to him quietly as she left her conversation with Jenny, "we've got company."

He looked in the direction she had tilted her head and saw the man looking around the corner surreptitiously. "Why do I feel like I'm in some sort of action film, being spied on from around corners?" he asked in a low voice that only she could hear. He smiled lightly at Kate as she reached out and grabbed his tie.

Slowly she pulled him toward her, her chin tilted up in invitation. "Is he looking?" she asked while smiling flirtatiously.

"Definitely."

"Good." She pulled on the tie more until Harper had to bend down to move with it. Finally, he was close enough to kiss and Kate lifted her heels slightly to meet his lips with hers. She heard clicking coming from nearby and could see several flashes behind her closed eyelids. After counting to thirty in her head, she pulled away. "Mission accomplished, Mr. Harper," she smirked.

"Katie?"

"Hmm?"

"Call me Will."

***

"Is he free?"

"Go on in, Ms. Bishop. Mr. Harper is expecting you," Evelyn smiled professionally at Katherine and nodded towards the door.

"Thank you, Evelyn." She stepped into Will's office.

"Hi, Katie. Come take a look at this." Will waved her over excitedly.

"What is it?"

"It's that blog Andrew was telling us about last night."

Kate looked at the computer screen. "Whoa! Did you even notice all those pictures being taken at the restaurant?"

"I saw one woman with a camera phone, but clearly this is the work of multiple paparazzi. Look at all the different angles they captured."

Kate looked at him askance when he called average restaurant-goers paparazzi, but saw his point immediately. There were over a dozen photographs: her feeding Will a bite of crème brulee, her head on his shoulder, his arm around her, them nuzzling noses and whispering to each other. "Wow. They certainly are thorough. Did they write anything?"

"Just some mess about this being my first foray into PDA and not doing anything by halves. It looks like they're buying it hook, line, and sinker."

"You must be relieved," she said.

"I am. I really can't get deported right now. I'm in the middle of a major merger that involves both Taggston and Covington Enterprises. There's a lot riding on this."

"A lot of money, huh?"

"Not just money, but we'd lose millions if we couldn't pull it through. We're talking hundreds of jobs, influence in our industry, power over our competition that will strengthen the company down the road – it's a VERY big deal."

"I see. What's Covington Enterprises?" she asked, sitting on the edge of his desk as he leaned back in his chair, resting his hands on his middle.

"It's a European company that designs guidance and surveillance equipment. They're one of the leaders in the market. They're also family." Katherine's brows shot up. "My mother was a Covington. Her older brother, Alistair Covington, runs the company now along with his children, my cousins."

"So wouldn't they still do the merger with you even if you were deported? Isn't that what family's for?"

"Yes and no. I'm handling the details of the merger for both of us, mostly because Taggston is the bigger company and has more to lose, but also because I'm more familiar with Helgsen, the other part of the merger." At Kate's questioning look, he explained. "Helgsen is a large Dutch software firm. HarperCo has done a lot of work with them in the past, hence my familiarity with them. For this particular merger, it's a marriage of Covington's designs, Helgsen's little blue chips, and Taggston's manufacturing capabilities. Various sectors of each organization will be coming together as one to create a stronger force in the market."

"I thought you were CEO of HarperCo, not Taggston as a whole."

"That's correct, but I still have an important position at Taggston. After all, I do own sixty percent of the company. I'm on the board, and because of my familiarity with the players and information involved, I'm handling this merger."

"So will there be a whole new company?"

"Sort of. The bulk of it will be under Taggston's umbrella with both Helgsen and Covington maintaining shares and a say in the direction of the company."

"Wow. I must say, Will, I'm impressed. I had no idea you had your hand in so many cookie jars." She smiled as she leaned back on her hands, still perched on his desk with her legs crossed.

He smiled appreciatively at the feminine picture she presented and asked, "And what do you know about cookie jars? Two days ago you told me you had no idea who I was. Have you been Googling, Miss Bishop?"

"You make it sound so naughty! As a matter of fact, I have not Googled you OR your company. I haven't had the time. Finals are just around the corner, remember? Besides, it was Andy who told me."

"Ah, I should have guessed. And what did good old Andrew have to say?"

"Not much. He just gave me a rundown of the company. He said you have a gajillion departments and sub companies covering everything from hotels to ship building."

"Well, not quite a gajillion, but several, yes," he said with a grin.

"If I didn't know better, I'd say you were flirting with me, Mr. Harper." He looked surprised. "Let's take some of that charm to lunch, shall we?"

He followed her out of the office, her hand in his, not saying a word until they were alone in the elevator when Kate broke the silence.

"There's something I don't understand."

"Yes?"

"If immigration has you under investigation, and the FBI is involved, won't they stop your visa from going through, no matter which kind you're applying for?"

"I thought the same thing and asked Andrew about it. Technically, I'm not under investigation – yet. Andrew just got a tip that I was being looked at, but nothing has been made official. That means that not all departments know about me, and any red flags on my file are only visible to the higher ups at this point. Hopefully, I can sneak under the radar before the red flag goes system-wide. That's one of the reasons we're wanting to apply so quickly. We want at least the first few steps pushed through by June."

"Wow. That only leaves a month. Won't all the red tape slow everything down?"

"Yes, but all the paperwork is already put together. As soon as we're married, it will be filed. As long as the initial petition gets approved, we're good. They usually do it the same day – it just means you have permission to apply. We have almost everything ready for the application, so we can file within twenty-four hours of our petition being accepted. They would look really foolish if they approved it, then turned around and pulled it three days later."

"And I'm imagining that you would make sure that was very public?"

"Of course. I have to look after my interests, Katherine, it's the only way to survive in business," he said seriously.

She was saved a reply by the elevator doors opening.

5
PHOTO SHOOT

Late April, Sunday
5 Days to Marriage

"I can't believe I'm up this early on a Sunday."

"Stop whining! The boys will be here soon." Jen handed Kate a cup of tea and walked into her sister's bedroom. "Have you decided what you want to wear?"

"Well, we decided we need several outfits, right? So I am going with mostly old stuff. I don't want to be caught wearing something I just bought in a picture that was supposed to be taken months ago."

"Got it. Why don't we do the casual shots first, since they don't require make up, then we can get dolled up for the party shoot?"

"I like that idea. I'll wear my little black dress that I wore to your real birthday dinner. If any pictures show up later, there will be continuity."

"Good thinking. I brought the pink dress I wore that night as well."

Jennifer pulled Yahtzee out of the closet while Kate changed into jeans and a warm sweater. She pulled her hair back in a simple braid and slipped on some wooly socks.

"Do I look like January?"

"Definitely. Is this believable?" Jenny gestured to the card table set up in Kate's tiny living room.

"Yes, but I don't know that Will would play Yahtzee.

He seems more like a Trivial Pursuit kind of guy, doesn't he?"

"I don't know, maybe. Want to change it?"

"Yeah, I'll take care of it while you change."

Kate swapped Yahtzee for the Trivial Pursuit board and doled out pie pieces. Then she got the tray of cheese and crackers Jennifer had brought and placed it on the corner of the table, making sure it looked half-eaten. She drew the curtains and turned on lamps to make it look like evening.

"That looks great, Katie!" said Jen when she emerged in a red knit sweater and jeans, her blonde hair pulled back in a loose ponytail.

"You think it's believable?"

"Definitely. All we need are the men and mock game night can commence!"

There was a knock on the door and Jennifer ran to let in William and Andrew. They each had a leather bag filled with various pieces of clothing and props.

"Hi, Will." Kate greeted him with a peck on the cheek, trying to get into the habit, and he reciprocated. "We thought we'd start with January game night. You guys can change in there," she said, pointing to the empty front room.

"Sounds good. What are we playing?" Will asked.

"Trivial Pursuit. Jen originally thought Yahtzee, but I thought this might be more you."

He smiled slightly. "You thought right. I like this game."

"Whoa! Whose futon?" Andrew called from the front room.

"Skanky Arlene's. Don't ask."

Andrew shook his head and the guys closed the door to change into their winter clothes.

Twenty minutes later they had several photos of Jenny and Andrew cuddling on the sofa, Kate and Jenny lording their win over the boys, Andrew looking stumped and Will looking smug. Andrew snapped a few of Kate and Will side by side arguing over a blue pie piece, and another of the reluctant truce handshake at the end of the game.

Looking over the pictures on the digital camera, they

decided their "meeting" looked believable and moved on. Andrew had come up with a time-line that the four of them were committing to memory in case of immigration questions and he quizzed them mercilessly.

"When did Jenny and I meet?"

"Early December at a charity event. You introduced her to me at a New Year's Eve party," William answered.

"Good. When did I meet Kate?"

"January fifth," Jenny answered. Andrew looked impressed. "What? I remember because I had a big meeting that day and you two met me for drinks after work."

Andrew squeezed her hand and couldn't keep the admiration from shining in his expression. Kate rolled her eyes and Andrew moved on. Time for the *creative* portion of their history.

"Kate, when did you meet Will?"

"Jen suggested the four of us have a game night to get to know each other. I offered to host since Jeremy was out of town and so was my roommate. It was the last weekend in January, a Saturday night."

"Good. What did we play?"

"Trivial Pursuit and I won," said Will.

"Only the second round. Jenny and I won the first," threw in Kate.

"Will, what was your first impression of Kate?"

"Talks a lot, nice ass."

She looked at him indignantly, mouth open and eyes blazing.

He smirked. "And feisty."

Kate covered her smile while Andrew moved on. "How often did you see each other after that?"

"A few times here or there – nothing memorable, a dinner at your house the first week of February, and Jenny and I ran into Will at the market one Saturday morning. Not much because I was still with Jeremy," Kate answered.

"And when did you and Jeremy break up?"

"February sixteenth," Will answered.

"Good, Will. When did you see Kate again?"

"At Jennifer's birthday party three weeks later."

"March ninth," Kate said.

"Kate was sad, I was there and had been interested in her for a few weeks, but she hadn't been available. I was a good listener and she told me her troubles over drinks," Will said.

"He was kind and understanding and when I had a little too much champagne toasting Jenny, he kept me together and listened to me ramble on about the idiosyncrasies of men in general and Jeremy in particular," said Kate. "You and Jenny left early and Will offered to see me home."

"But your keys were in my purse and I forgot to give them back to you before I left with Andy," added Jenny.

"So when I tried to drop Kate off, we couldn't get in and neither Jennifer nor her roommate were answering their phones," added Will.

"Hey, it was my birthday!" cried Jenny.

"So I took Kate home to my place and we stayed up talking till four in the morning when we fell asleep on the couch."

"My feet were in his lap," added Kate.

"And I had a horrible crick in my neck the next day from sleeping sitting up," said Will.

"Who asked whom out?" asked Andrew.

"I asked her the next morning. I thought it might be too soon, but I didn't want to waste the opportunity."

"It just felt right, so I said yes and we had our first date that Friday night," Kate added.

"Great. Where did you go?" quizzed Andrew.

"Will ordered take out from Jasmine's and we watched a movie at his place. I thought it was too soon to be out with a date in case I ran into one of Jeremy's friends or someone I knew."

"And I was trying to keep a low profile. I really liked Kate and I wanted to keep her to myself as long as possible," added Will.

The questions and answers continued on until they had worked up to their current activities. Andrew, the great orchestrator, ordered a pizza for lunch and when they had finished, he started talking again.

"I did some digging around about the kind of things to put in your *Proof of Relationship* file. Can you two write each other some emails back and forth? Will, you can change the time stamp on them, can't you?"

"Sure, that wouldn't be difficult. We're printing them off, right?"

"Yes. What is most convincing are long distance phone bills - which you obviously don't have, large items purchased together like cars and houses, which again, you don't have and it wouldn't make sense to do, a child together -"

"Uh uh, no way, definitely not happening," Kate interrupted.

Andrew reached out and squeezed her knee. "I know. I'd never think of suggesting it. I'm just telling you what they look for. They are looking for proof of intimacy, of a shared life."

"Don't these pictures accomplish that?" Will asked.

"Yes, but I think we can take it a step further."

Will's eyebrows shot up, recognizing the look on his friend's face. "Andrew, what are you thinking?"

"I think you should do some bedroom shots."

Kate's eyes widened and Harper's jaw clenched.

"Like the two of us, in the bed, together? And take pictures? And show them to people? To immigration?" she asked, stunned.

"No, not anything distasteful or even revealing. Just something that you might snap if you were getting up to go in the morning and you look back at her in the bed and take a picture with your phone. Simple."

"You sound practiced, Andrew," Will said quietly. Jennifer just blushed and sank a little lower in the sofa.

"I think I understand. I have a few pictures of Jeremy with his shirt off that I took for fun. Something like that?" asked Kate, her cheeks a light pink.

"Yes, that's it exactly. And since Kate will be leaving this apartment soon, it would be best to go ahead and get them done before there are boxes everywhere. You could take some more at Will's place once you move in." He looked between the two of them and stood, pulling Jenny up behind him. "We're going to go to the kitchen. I'll let you two work this out."

Will glared at him as he left, then turned to Katherine.

"Are you up for this?" he asked.

"I'm not exactly thrilled, but I suppose it's okay. I can put on pajamas and we can wrap up in sheets. That won't be so bad, will it?"

He sighed and ran his hand through his hair. "Argh. Come on, let's do this." He rose and headed toward the short hall that lead to Kate's bedroom. She pointed to the door that was hers and put a hand on his chest before he could follow her in.

"Give me a minute to change," she said as she closed the door.

Three minutes later she opened it, wearing polka dot pajama pants and a thin tank top with no bra. Will looked at her chest for a moment too long until she said, "I want to look authentic. If we're going to all this trouble, I don't want anything to be questioned. Nobody sleeps in a bra."

"Of course, you're absolutely right."

He stepped into the small room and edged around the bed to stand in front of her tall dresser. "Who's posing first?"

"I'm already in my pajamas, so I guess it can be me." As she said it, she realized that if they were alone in the pictures, she could just as easily have had Jenny take hers, but she didn't want to sound like a prude or be the whiny one. They were both adults. They could do this with no – or very little – awkwardness. She pulled her hair over her shoulders in an attempt to reclaim some modesty and stood awkwardly by the dresser.

Will picked up the camera and pointed to the bed, silently telling Kate to hop on. She sat down gingerly on the fluffy duvet, looking around in confusion.

"What do you want me to do?"

"Um, I don't really know." He laughed uncomfortably and ran his hand through his hair.

"Do you do that when you're nervous?"

"Do what?"

"Run your hand through your hair."

"Oh. I don't know. I guess I do. Nervous and stressed."

She smiled kindly in sympathy. She was feeling a little vulnerable on her bed in a room alone with a man she barely knew and not even wearing a bra. Fake dating was fun in dresses and heels, but she was not in the habit of sharing intimate moments with relative strangers.

Finally, she took a deep breath and looked at Harper. He squared his shoulders and said, "Okay, we can do this. We'll just try to relax."

She nodded. "Channel your inner photographer."

He made a face and held up the camera.

"Why don't you grab that pillow there," she did as he said, "and smile up at me. Perfect." Click. "Now drop the pillow and reach for me, like you want me to come toward you." She did and then got on all fours and crawled toward him slowly, his confidence behind the camera putting her at ease. "Yes, exactly. Lie on your belly, chin in your hand." He squatted down in front of her and snapped a close shot, "Now roll onto your back and let your head fall back a bit. Smile. Bigger. Perfect." He stood high above her and snapped away as she let her head dangle slightly off the end of the bed, her wavy hair almost reaching the floor.

"Let's get a few of us together."

"Okay. But shouldn't you be wearing something else?"

"I didn't bring pajamas."

"Boxers and a T-shirt?"

He looked uncomfortable.

"Uh-oh. Are you a whitey-tighties guy?"

"No! I am a boxer brief guy, though."

"That's okay. Here, get under the covers. I won't look."

She pulled back the blankets and turned her head to look at the wall. She heard a zipper and the sound of a belt falling to the floor, then she felt the bed shift under his weight.

"Alright. Let's do this." His voice was so grimly serious that Kate had to laugh. It started as a small chortle she tried to hold in, but when he looked at her with a mixture of confusion and sternness, it developed into an all-out giggle, then a hearty belly laugh. Her laughter eventually affected Harper and it wasn't long before he joined her.

He had the presence of mind to grab the camera and extend his arm, snapping a picture of Kate leaning on his shoulder, laughing uncontrollably.

"I know what would make this more convincing," she said between giggles.

"What?"

"Hands up."

He mechanically did as she said and raised his hands. Kate quickly grabbed the hem of his white T-shirt and pulled it over his head.

"There. Much more believable."

Before he could say anything, she snuggled into his side, wrapped an arm around his waist and smiled.

"Go on. Snap the picture."

He took a moment, but reached out and snapped a few shots, the camera angle going wide when Kate reached over and tickled Will in the ribs.

"Hey!"

She laughed again and Will kept snapping until Kate grabbed the camera and took a few of him, mussing his hair and making silly faces to make him laugh.

Finally, Andrew knocked on the door and popped his head in. "Everything alright in here?"

"Yeah, we're good, Andrew. Be out in a sec," Harper answered.

He closed the door and Kate got out of bed, suddenly remembering they were virtual strangers taking pictures in their underwear. She gathered up her clothes and moved to the door.

"You can change here, I'll go to the bathroom."

"Okay," he said.

Will sighed and pulled his jeans back on and found his shirt at the foot of the bed. With an amused look on his face, he walked out of her room.

6
SECOND THOUGHTS

Late April, Monday
4 Days to Marriage

"Have you thought about how you're going to propose?"

"Not really. I haven't had time to think of much."

Will sat across from Andrew at the small table in his office, eating Chinese takeout with a set of chopsticks.

"Well whatever you do, it needs to be public. And over the top. You're supposed to have fallen madly in love with this girl."

"Yes." Will chewed thoughtfully. "Hot air balloon? Too cliché?"

"Probably. Jumbotron at the Garden?"

Will made a face. "Bleh. Those are so annoying."

"And so public," Andrew said as he pointed a chopstick at him.

"I might as well rent a billboard in Times Square if that's all we're concerned about."

Andrew's eyes lit up.

"Oh, no you don't, Jamison! I know that look. I am not spending an obscene amount of money to rent a tacky billboard in some smelly square to propose fake marriage to a girl I met a week ago. NOT doing it!"

"Fine." Andrew held up his hands in defeat. "What about an old fashioned proposal in a restaurant? Stock it with the right people, of course. You buy her a rose, there's a violin or a piano or something, you get on one knee and she squeals and says yes, the whole restaurant applauds."

"Maybe. It just doesn't seem worthy of the whirlwind courtship, though. It should be really romantic," argued Harper.

"And public. Can't forget public."

"What if we went somewhere public afterwards? Like there is that benefit for the children's hospital this week. We're already committed to going. She could just show up with a ring on her finger."

"True, but that's not nearly as good PR as an actual proposal. Besides, who goes to a charity event right after they propose? You should go back to your apartment to shag."

"You seem to be forgetting one little detail, Andrew."

Andrew rolled his eyes. "I know that, Will. But nobody else does. We have to think of something spectacular." He tapped the table nervously with his fingers while his foot bounced on the floor. He turned his head, looking around the room for inspiration.

"That's it!"

"What's it?"

"The Empire State Building!"

"What about it?"

"For the proposal, you idiot!"

"How is that public? It'll just be filled with a bunch of tourists."

"We fill it with the right people. We leak to the press that someone overheard you making plans to go there and saw you looking at a ring in your pocket or something. We'll tell everyone *'An Affair to Remember'* is Kate's favorite movie. It'll be great! Romantic, iconic, easy to remember. All the makings of a great story. You'll be an overnight sensation!"

Andrew was so excited he was walking quickly in circles, making wide motions with his hands as he talked.

Will sighed in defeat and leaned his head back against the chair. "Alright, Andrew, you win. The Empire State Building it is. We fly out Friday, so when should I do it? I have the fundraiser Tuesday night. Wednesday? Is Thursday too late?"

"Thursday is good. It'll give you more time to pick a ring. What are your plans for tonight?"

"I'm picking up takeaway at Giorgio's while on the phone to Katherine. The maître d there has a mouth as big as the Thames, he might pass on what he hears. Then I'm meeting her at my building and introducing her to the doorman, making sure she has 24-hour access. We'll go out for ice cream at the patisserie on the corner before I take her home."

"Good. It's very Monday, nothing too flashy. But why isn't she staying the night?"

Harper raised his brows. "Because."

Andrew gave him a look.

Harper exhaled roughly. "She hasn't been seen staying the night this entire time. I can just say she's been parking under the building with me and going up in the private elevator and that's why the doorman hasn't met her before. I've always been a private man, that won't surprise anyone. We can leave the same way tonight and no one will be the wiser."

"But you said you were going back out for ice cream. If you're just walking to the corner, it will look weird if you don't walk back in."

"So we walk back in then leave in the car to drop her off."

"Will." Andrew looked at his friend who was moodily staring out the window. "Hey. Are you alright?"

"Yes. Maybe. I don't know. I know I need to do this and that it's my best option and all of that, but I never thought this was how I would get married. It's not like I sat around and dreamed about it like a little girl, but I did think that if I ever did it, I would at least have some affection for her, maybe even be in love. Hell, I don't know that I thought I would even *get* married, let alone do it so soon. Now the next two and a half years of my life are mapped out for me. Marry *this* girl, be seen in *these* places, get divorced at *this* time." He bent his neck to the side uncomfortably, as if he was trying to dislodge a collar.

"It chafes, doesn't it?"

"Yeah."

Andrew patted his shoulder. "I'm sorry, mate. If you don't want to go through with it, we can call it off. Katie's a good sport. She'll let you out of the contract if that's what you want."

Will sighed for what he felt like was the fortieth time that day. "No, that won't be necessary. I was just having a mood, but I'm past it. I can do this. I'll call Kate and ask her to pack an overnight bag for tonight."

"You sure?"

"Yes, I'm sure. Thanks, Andrew. You're a good friend."

"Anytime."

**

"Hello."

"Kate, it's William."

"Hi, Will. How are you?"

"Well, thanks. Listen, do you think you could pack an overnight bag tonight? I thought you could sleep at my place."

There was silence for a moment.

"Umm, sure. I have an early class tomorrow. Do you want to walk me to campus? It'll take half an hour, but the weather should be nice."

"Actually, an early morning walk sounds nice. I'll plan on it."

"Great. So I'll meet you in front of your building at seven?"

"I'll be there. Do you know what you want for dinner?" he asked.

"Italian, right?"

"Yes."

"Some sort of ravioli sounds good. I'll let you pick."

"Alright. See you tonight."

"See ya."

Katherine hung up the phone and turned the corner onto her street. *The First Night in William's apartment.* Reaching her building, she dashed up the stairs and ran to her room, hoping her pajamas were clean. Sleeping in an old t-shirt on their first night together was not how she wanted to start off.

7
WILLIAM'S PLACE

Late April, Monday
4 Days to Marriage

Kate looked around the room, her eyes falling on the dark leather sofa and the modern glass topped cocktail table in front of it. The windows were basic and uncovered, just simple blinds that looked as if they were always open. The whole room seemed to be focused on a massive flat screen television that took up half the wall across from the sofa.

"Well, this is it," said Will as he walked in behind her. "This is the sitting room, obviously. Kitchen is through here." He gestured to a doorway but they didn't go in. "Bedrooms are down here."

She followed him down a white painted hallway.

"Here's the bath. It's for guests mostly." She peeked into the bare bathroom as he flipped the light switch. It was well done and the tile was pretty, but the only soft thing in the room was a tiny hand towel folded neatly next to the sink. Otherwise, it was nothing but cold marble and modern steel fixtures. Will continued walking and she hurried along behind him.

"This is my study." He opened the door and she looked in cautiously. One wall was covered with a bookcase that was bursting with books, another was floor to ceiling bare windows, the third wall held a large desk with an odd looking ergonomic chair in front of it and the fourth was bare except for the door.

She nodded and he kept walking. “My room is at the end of the hall.” He pointed, then opened a door on his left. “This is your room.”

She took a few slow steps into the room, turning around slowly and taking it all in. He continued talking while she looked around. “There's a closet over there, and the bathroom's through here.” He opened a door and turned on the light switch. “I'm afraid there's no tub in here, but the shower is big.”

She nodded again and peered into the empty closet. The floor was bare dark wood and gave the room an echo-y feeling that was compounded by the austere uncovered windows and the plain white walls. Thinking back, she realized there wasn't a single picture hanging in the entire apartment, just vast white walls everywhere she looked. This room had nothing but a queen sized bed on a simple metal frame, no headboard, no dresser, just a small square nightstand with two tiny drawers on one side of the bed.

The bathroom was a little bit better, but only because the white subway tiles reaching halfway up the wall had a blue accent tile running through them. There was nothing soft in sight. Looking next to the commode, she noticed there wasn't even any toilet paper.

“Well, what do you think?” He hadn't been concerned at all about showing her his place, but now that she was there, and hadn't said a single word since they walked in, he was beginning to wonder if he should have given this more thought.

“It's very... white. And empty.” Her voice sounded louder in the square space.

“Yes, I've never done anything with it. I just bought this bed last year when my cousin came to visit. It's not old, but if it isn't comfortable to you, go ahead and change it.”

“How long have you lived here?”

“Two years. My parents had a place on the upper west side, but it was too big for me on my own, and my sister owns half of it. Making changes can be tricky, so I just bought this.”

She nodded, wandering back into the hall and looking around silently.

He continued, "I never hired a decorator – I don't really entertain and it has what I need." *Why do I feel like I need to defend myself? My home is perfectly fine. And a lot bigger than the cracker box she lives in.*

"Would you mind if I painted my room?" she finally asked.

"No, of course not. It's your room, you can do whatever you want in there. Just don't knock down any walls or anything."

She smiled and gestured toward a door across the hall. "What's in there?"

"That's another guest room. It's empty though."

He opened the door and she saw he was right. It was a white square with a small window and absolutely nothing in it.

"Can I see your room?"

"My room?"

"Yeah, the place where you sleep?"

"Umm, sure. It's down here." He led her back down the hall and opened the door at the end.

The room was spacious with an entire wall of windows, a feature that seemed to be prevalent on that side of the apartment. There was an enormous California king platform bed on one wall, flanked by two shiny black night stands. The bed was covered in a fluffy charcoal gray duvet. There was a long, low dresser across from the bed and a cozy armchair in the corner with a floor lamp next to it. Otherwise, it was as empty as the rest of the house.

"Is that your bathroom?" she asked, pointing to a door on the right.

"Yes," he answered, trying to remember if he had left any underwear on the floor.

She walked in and stopped short. "Oh, Holy face of Moses!"

"What?" he asked, coming up behind her. "What's wrong?"

"This bathroom is bigger than my bedroom." She walked in slowly, looking around in awe at the warm colors on the floor tile and the endless double vanity. "How many people can fit in this shower?" She opened the door and stepped in, shoes and all, and stretched out her arms. "I can't even reach both sides! How many heads are there?" She began counting the spigots on the wall behind her as Harper shifted from surprise to diversion at her behavior.

She looked back at his amused expression, slightly chagrined at her own excitement. "Sorry. I don't usually ooh and ah over other people's bathrooms. Guess I'm getting more comfortable with you," she said uneasily.

He looked at her for a moment, then replied, "Good. That's what we want."

She smiled in response.

"Did you see the tub?" he asked.

She looked at him with excitement and turned around. "Oh. My. G-d. That might be the most glorious thing I've ever seen."

He chuckled. "Thought you might like that. It's great to soak in on cold winter nights."

"You'd probably drain your water heater before you filled it up!"

"It's tank-less."

She gasped and faced him, her hand on her chest. "Be still my heart."

He laughed. "Feel free to use it. I guess it isn't really fair that you don't have a tub in your bathroom."

"Be sure you mean that. I just might take you up on it."

He laughed again, oddly proud of himself that he had something that made her so obviously happy.

"Come on, let's eat. Food's getting cold."

**

The next morning, Will walked Kate to her eight o'clock class. He left her outside the English building with a quick kiss and a squeeze of the hand he'd been holding. Kate said goodbye, then turned to walk up the steps and go inside.

"Damn, girl! That is a prime piece of real estate! You gonna get you some land?"

Kate laughed when she heard the familiar voice. "Thanks, Angie. William will be thrilled to know he's on your hot list."

"So it's true? You're dating William Harper?"

"Not you, too! I never pictured you as the page 6 type."

"Why? Because I'm not a skinny white girl?" she asked.

"Nice try. Because you're not vapid and shallow."

"Well, not vapid, but shallow can be fun sometimes." Kate laughed and they continued up to the third floor. "Besides, Sheila told me. So, tell me everything! Is he as hot out of that suit as he is in it? Hairy or smooth? Come on, woman! I need details!"

"You know a lady never kisses and tells."

Angie looked around. "Do you see any ladies here? Now spill!"

"Oh, alright. Yes, he's just as hot out of the suit."

Angie raised a brow. "And?"

"Hairy."

"Ha! I knew it! Has he bought you tons of diamonds yet? What's his place like? Did he take you shopping? Is he good? He looks like he'd be good. Is he good?"

"Whoa, slow down! No, he hasn't taken me shopping or bought me tons of diamonds, or any diamonds for that matter. And his place is very nice. And that is ALL I'm telling you!"

"Party pooper!" She pouted as they took their seats.

Just then, Sheila plopped down on Kate's other side. "Did I miss it? Has she spilled?"

"No, you didn't miss anything," Kate said as Angie motioned to Sheila behind her back. "William is my boyfriend, he's very nice, I really like him a lot, and that's all I'm telling you," Kate said firmly.

Angie leaned across her and spoke to Sheila. "No diamonds yet, but I think it's only a matter of time." Kate gave her a look. "What? I saw how he dropped you off. That boy is a smitten kitten." Kate rolled her eyes.

"Ten says she's sporting bling before the semester's out," Sheila said.

"Twenty says she's got it by Saturday," replied Angie. "That man comes money."

Kate let her head fall to the desk. "I need new friends," she murmured.

***

"Hey, Jenny. Ready to go?" Kate popped her head into Jen's office a little before one o'clock.

"Yeah, I'm starving! Where do you want to eat?"

"Your turn to pick."

"Let's go to that deli on the corner." She followed Kate out of the building, and as soon as they were outside, turned to her sister. "So how did last night go?"

"I got something shiny." Kate held up the key to Harper's apartment that now dangled from her key chain as Jen smiled in approval.

"What was his place like? Trust fund chic or dirty bachelor pad?"

"Neither. It was mostly empty. And white. There wasn't a single thing hung on the walls – anywhere! Except mirrors in the bathrooms, but I don't think those count."

"Are you going to redecorate?"

"I'll do my room. I have to. It's completely depressing. All stark and echo-y. The mattress was so hard, I lay awake half the night thinking I was in some sort of asylum."

Jenny laughed. "Oh, no! That's awful! What are you going to do?"

"Feel like painting with me?"

"Always. When?"

"Well, I am busy dating this week and studying, and next week is exams, but my last one is Thursday morning. We could start Thursday afternoon. What do you think?"

"Works for me. I can't get there till after five, though."

"That's fine. That'll give me time to tape it off and get everything ready. I think I'll move my stuff into the guest room first. I'm thinking of doing that room as well. It's completely empty right now, so I don't think he'd mind. If someone comes to visit, we'll have somewhere to put them."

"Do you think you'll have houseguests?"

"I don't know, but we'll be there a while, so we might. Maybe it could double as a guest room/den for me. I don't know if William will take to me sharing his living room. It's got a major man-cave vibe going on right now."

"Ugh. I hate those places. Nothing but leather and big screen TV's," Jenny agreed.

"Exactly. I'd love to take a can of paint to the whole place, but I don't want to insult him or take over his home."

"But it's your home now, too. You'll be living there just as much as him." Kate shrugged. "I know you. You say you want to be nice now, but after living in a *hospital* for a month, you'll be going crazy. Just talk to him about it. Maybe you can do it together. Be all domestic and choose paint colors and fabric swatches."

"Haha, Jenny. I can't see me getting domestic with Will. Actually, I can't really see Will getting domestic at all. He's so... contained."

Jen just raised a brow and looked at her sister. "Uh huh. Come on, let's eat. I'm starving and I've been craving this all week."

After they slid into a deserted corner booth and placed their orders, Kate passed an envelope to Jen.

"What's this?"

"Look."

Jen opened it and slid out the contents. "Oh! The pictures! Do you like them? What does William think?"

"I like them fine, Will didn't really say anything. He smiled once, but otherwise I got no feedback. He did say he thought they would suffice, though."

"Wow. He's kind of close-lipped, huh?"

"Yeah. I'm hoping he'll loosen up when he knows me better. When he has something to talk about, like something he knows and understands well, like work, he talks plenty. But if you want information out of him that he wasn't prepared to give, forget about it."

Jen made a sympathetic face and flipped through the pictures. “Oh, this one's funny!” She held up a picture of William with Kate's foot on his chest. “Love the red nail polish.”

“Thanks. I thought it was a nice touch.”

“So it looks like you were pretty relaxed together.”

“Yeah, it was awkward at first, of course, but we warmed up to each other pretty quickly. You know, it was funny,” she said thoughtfully. “When he got behind the camera, he seemed less nervous, almost determined. He actually put me at ease. You should have heard the way he was directing me. 'Look over here, arms up, smile, turn to the side'. I felt like Heidi Klum, but shorter and less blond.”

“Maybe he felt more comfortable behind the lens than in front of it. Is photography a hobby of his?”

“I don't know. I'll have to ask him. If it's not, it should be. He was really good at it.”

“How's the studying going?”

“Good. I have a final project due tomorrow and then four exams next week. I feel like all I'm doing is studying and going to dinner.”

“You're almost there, you'll make it.”

“I know. It' just that end of semester exhaustion. I am really looking forward to a free summer.”

“I thought you were thinking about taking a class or two so your load would be lighter in the fall?”

“I was, I am.” She sighed tiredly. “I know I should, but right now, I am just so tired that spending three months relaxing sounds great. But then I know the fall will be crazy hectic with everything I'll be doing with Will and classes and my work with Mark.”

“I didn't know you were still working with The Passionate Professor,” Jen said with a look.

“Yeah.” She sighed. “I quit tutoring in a few days – I have my last lesson Monday – and I’ll stop with the dogs some time after the wedding. But when I talked to Mark about not being his assistant anymore, he flipped. He offered me more money and told me he'd do anything to get me to stay.”

"Really?"

"Yeah. He said he was counting on me and that it would throw the whole schedule off for him to have to find a new assistant."

"So what did you say? Did you take the money?"

"Of course! I'm not stupid! I work my butt off for him and he knows it. So I'll keep working with him a few hours a week and just try to juggle everything. If it gets to be too much, I can always quit. He's supposed to publish in February, so it's not that long, anyway."

"Well, good luck, little sister."

"Thanks. I'm going to need it."

**

That night, Kate was attending a fundraiser with William. He came by her apartment a few minutes early to pick her up. Before she could grab her purse to leave, he handed her a long narrow box in a telling blue color.

"What's this?"

"It's a gift. Open it."

She gingerly took the top off the box to reveal a long, slender black velvet case. She opened it slowly and there sat a large diamond pendant on a dainty chain.

"I thought you could wear it tonight… if it matches your gown, that is," he said, almost shyly. The truth was he had never given a woman jewelry before (except for family and he didn't think that counted), and he was more than a little nervous about his selection. Evelyn, his assistant, had told him you couldn't go wrong with simple diamonds, so that's what he got. Now, looking at her face as she stared at the glimmering stone, he wondered if he'd made the right choice.

"If you don't like it, we can exchange it for something else. It's no problem. I didn't really know your tastes-"

Suddenly, he was cut off by Kate's lips against his and her hand on the back of his neck holding him closer. After a long moment, he responded and kissed her back, putting his hand on the small of her back and pulling her to him.

"I like it. A lot," she said when they pulled apart a moment later. "Thank you. I don't think I've ever been given anything so beautiful." She smiled warmly and he smiled back, all his nervousness gone for the moment. "Do you mind?"

She held out the opened necklace and turned her back to him, holding her hair out of the way. After he secured the clasp, he kissed the back of her neck softly.

"There. Are we all set now?" he asked.

"Yes. I just need my wrap." She grabbed a silk shawl off the back of the chair and followed him out the door.

On the way, she couldn't resist sending a text message to Angie. *Sheila owes you $20.* A minute later her phone buzzed with a reply. *Yes! I knew it! Send me a pic later!*

8
THE PROPOSAL

Late April, Thursday
1 Day to Marriage

"I can't believe that after tonight you'll be engaged!" Jennifer exclaimed.

"I know. It's all a little surreal," Kate answered.

"And we're going to Vegas tomorrow." Jennifer clasped her hands together. "If this were real, it would be so romantic!"

"Since when is Vegas romantic?"

"Not that part, but getting proposed to on top of the Empire State Building-"

"In front of a bunch of reporters," Kate interrupted.

"And being whisked away to celebrate-"

"To *Vegas.*"

"In a private plane." Jen sighed and fell back onto the pillows of Kate's bed.

"Are you sure *you* don't want to marry him?"

"Oh, Katie! Where's your sense of romance? This might be the only time you get proposed to. You should enjoy it."

"Hey! Who says I won't get married after this?"

"That's not what I meant. Nowadays people just discuss it and start planning. There's not even always a real proposal – and definitely not one this romantic. Who knows, you might propose the second time."

"Seriously? I would never propose. If he can't man-up enough to ask, what kind of marriage would that be? I don't think so. I'll start out as I mean to continue, thank you very much."

"You sounded just like mom for a minute there."

"Not funny, Jenny!"

Jenny laughed and rolled off the bed to begin shuffling through Kate's closet. "So have you decided what you're going to wear tonight?"

Kate scrunched up her nose as she looked in the tiny closet. "So far, it's between the vintage floral dress I bought last summer and the new red dress. What do you think?"

"I love the vintage, but I think it's a little more daytime. The red dress screams glamour and night on the town."

They both stood back and looked at the two dresses hanging side by side, identical expressions of concentration on their faces.

"Alright, the red dress it is."

"Good choice. Jewelry?"

"The diamond studs dad gave me for graduation and my new necklace."

Jen's eyebrows shot up. "What new necklace?"

"I can't believe I forgot to tell you! Will gave it to me Tuesday night for the benefit we went to." She handed Jen a delicate chain with a diamond pendant hanging in the center. "Here. What do you think?"

"It's beautiful! How many carats is this thing?"

"I don't know – I didn't ask. It's pretty big though, right?"

"Uh, yeah! You'll have to have it insured."

"You think?"

"Definitely." Jen nodded sagely.

Kate placed it carefully on the dresser and laid the dress on the bed. "Help me with my hair?"

"Of course."

For the next hour and a half, Jen helped Kate with her hair and make-up, gave opinions on shoes, and took Kate's final 'single' pictures.

"Okay, you're ready. When is William picking you up?"

"He said seven thirty. Reservation's at eight."

Just then, the bell sounded and Jen ran to let Will in. Kate stood in front of the mirror in her room, gazing at her reflection, hardly recognizing herself all done up. She'd been dressing up and going out for what felt like ages, but for some reason tonight felt different. She thought it might be her hair; they had spent longer on it than usual. Or maybe it was her dress; it was different than anything she'd ever worn. It was that perfect mix of modern and classic, sexy and elegant. The color was just right for her and the full skirt made her look voluptuous and feminine.

She ran her fingers along the silky fabric and looked herself in the eye. “You can do this, Katie. You know exactly what to do. Smile, act surprised, say yes. That's all. Just smile, act surprised, say yes. There will be other proposals. This is not the only one you'll ever get. You've got this. Smile. Act surprised. Say yes.”

She nodded at her reflection and left the room to meet William.

*

“Everything okay?” Kate asked.

“What? Oh, yes. Why?” Harper answered as he looked out the window at the passing traffic.

“You were staring at me with a funny look on your face.”

“Was I?”

“Yeah. You alright?”

“Yes. Perfect. Everything's fine.” He smoothly pulled into traffic and headed towards midtown.

Kate let it go and looked out the window. “It's weird, you know?”

“What's weird?”

“I've been living on this street for three years, and next week, I'll be gone.”

Her voice was surprisingly serious and Harper didn't know what to say, but thought he should say something.

"If you want longer, to move out I mean, you can. I don't mind if you want to keep this apartment for a while. This has all happened so suddenly; it's perfectly understandable if you need some time to adjust to all the changes."

She kept her head turned to the outside and didn't say anything for a few minutes. "Thank you. That's kind of you. I think a week is enough time to get my stuff out. It's time to move forward. It's just a little odd, that's all."

"Yes, I know what you mean," he said quietly.

Dinner was over before they knew it and by ten fifteen, they were in an elevator headed to the top of the Empire State Building. Somehow, their hands found their way to each other as they stood against the back wall. Will gave her hand a squeeze, and she intertwined her fingers with his.

"You ready?" he whispered in her ear.

"As ready as I'll ever be."

Just then the elevator arrived and they followed the small crowd onto the observation deck.

"You know, I've lived here five years and I've never been up here," she said.

"Really?"

"Yeah. I guess you don't do the touristy things when you live somewhere."

"Yes, I suppose. My parents brought me here when I was a kid."

"That sounds like fun."

"It was a great trip. Dad was revamping the New York offices and mother and I came along. It was the last trip we took just the three of us. Not that we took so many, but my sister was born the next year."

"How far apart are you?" she asked as she looked out at the view. Will stood behind her and wrapped his arms around her middle. She easily clasped his forearms in her hands and leaned back against him.

"She's seven years younger than me. Are you cold?"

"Hm? Oh, a little, but I'm alright."

He pulled her closer and brought the sides of his jacket around her so she was cocooned in his warmth, holding everything in place with his arms wrapped firmly around her. "Better?"

"Yes, thank you. Do you see her often?"

"Who?"

"Your little sister."

"Not really. We email regularly, though. Living on separate continents makes more contact a bit difficult."

She nodded and snuggled closer as a breeze brushed across her face.

"Come here," he said softly as he turned her around and pulled her against him. "You should have brought a jacket."

"Sorry, mom. I didn't want to ruin the look of my dress." He chuckled and she wrapped her arms around his middle under his jacket and laid her head on his chest. "You're very warm."

"The better to heat you with, my dear." She smiled and sighed. He held her quietly a moment, then said, "It really is beautiful up here. We should do this again."

"Yeah, we should. Can we bring a blanket next time?" she asked.

He laughed lightly and leaned back to see her face. "Did I tell you you look amazing tonight?"

"No. I was beginning to wonder if you liked my new dress," she answered impishly.

"Oh, I like it. I like it very much." She smiled as he stroked her cheek. She could see the reporter looking people she had noticed earlier looking their way, though no cameras had come out yet.

"Thank you. You don't look so bad yourself," she said.

"Thank you."

"Katie," he breathed.

"Yes?"

He took a deep breath and she looked at him encouragingly. "The first time I saw you, I was intrigued. The second time I saw you, I was drawn in by your charm. The third time, I knew I had to be with you. And by the end of our first date, I knew I never wanted to let you go."

He reached into his pocket and knelt down in front of her. Everyone around them realized what was happening and stopped talking, all eyes on them, plus a few camera phones.

"Katherine Bishop, will you marry me?" He opened the tiny velvet box he was holding and revealed an enormous diamond ring that he held out in front of her. Katherine smiled gently as he spoke, gasped and brought her hands to her mouth when she saw the ring, and with a voice that trembled just a little, she answered.

"Yes, William Harper, I'll marry you."

He immediately broke into an enormous smile, rose off his knee, and wrapped his arms around her. She giggled as he twirled her around, her feet off the ground. He finally set her down and placed the ring on her outstretched hand. Her eyes were wide as she stared at the giant rock and then up to his smiling face.

"It's beautiful."

His answer was to take her face in his hands and kiss her softly as cameras clicked and flashes went off all around them.

*

"Well, I'd say that was a success. Beer?" Will asked as he reached into the fridge.

"Thanks." She took a bottle from his outstretched hand and kicked off her shoes. "I don't know about you, but I'm beat."

"Me too. Do you want to go straight to bed or would you like to watch something first?"

"What do you usually do?"

"I usually relax in front of the telly before bed, but I don't want the noise to keep you up."

"That sounds good. What do you want to watch?"

He looked at his watch. "*The Daily Show* just ended, but I have it on DVR."

"Sounds good." She walked into the living room and curled up in the corner of the sofa, spreading her dress out over her curled up knees.

"Are you cold?" he asked.

"A little."

He left the room and a moment later was back with a folded blanket in his arms. "Here you go."

"Thanks." She spread it over her and watched the show, laughing and getting used to Harper's presence.

When it was over and he was about to turn the television off, she said, "You know what this means, don't you?"

"What?"

"We have to change our Facebook statuses now."

He groaned. "I had forgotten about that little program. Luckily for me, I don't have a Facebook account."

"Really? Why not?"

"No need."

"How do you keep up with people you don't see anymore?"

"If I don't see them anymore, why would I want to keep up with them?"

She thought for a moment, then said, "Well, I have an account, and it will look weird if I get publicly engaged but say nothing about it."

"Are you one of those people who are constantly updating and boring everyone with a dozen posts a day?"

"How do you know about that if you don't have an account? And for the record, no, I am not one of those people. I update every couple of days, usually."

He looked relieved. "Just because I don't have an account doesn't mean I don't know anything about it. Andrew has an account and he seems to feel the need to alert the world to all of his actions every moment of the day. Do people have no sense of privacy anymore?"

"Apparently not. But I've never seen him doing that. He seems to post a normal amount."

"Well, being with your sister seems to have relieved him of some of his more compulsive tendencies, I'll grant you that."

She laughed. "I can change my status now if you'll pass me my purse." She fished her phone out of the bag and typed quietly for a minute, then looked up and said, "Done!"

"That was quick."

"Nothing to it, really. I just went from single to engaged. Now we just have to wait for the comments to start rolling in."

He rolled his eyes and decided to change the subject. "Are you and Jennifer ready to leave tomorrow?"

"Yes. Oh, and speaking of Jenny, she's going to come over Thursday and help me paint my room. There isn't anything scheduled is there?"

"You're painting your room?"

"Yeah."

"Why?"

"Because I like color. I asked you Monday, you said it would be fine," she said a little defensively.

"No, that's not what I meant. Of course you can paint it any color you want. I just wondered why you wouldn't hire someone to do it."

She looked surprised. "Oh. Honestly, I hadn't thought about it. I suppose I could. I've just always done it myself."

"My assistant should have the name of a reputable contractor. We had my office redone last year – they did a good job."

"That would be great. Thanks, Will."

He nodded. "You know," he said slowly, looking around him uncomfortably, "if you wanted to paint some more, that would be alright. I know it isn't very homey, and I've never really done much with it. I don't spend much time here except to sleep, just a few hours in the evenings sometimes. I think it could use a woman's touch."

"Really?" she answered, trying to hold back her enthusiasm.

"Yes, just don't do anything crazy like paint the walls black and hang skulls from the ceiling."

She burst into laughter. "What on earth makes you think I would ever do that?"

"I'm just being cautious."

"How about we make a deal. I'll make this place a little cozier, but I'll run all the big decisions like paint colors by you first."

"Deal." He held his hand out and she shook it vigorously. "Oh no, you're getting excited, aren't you?"

"Just a little," she said with a barely contained smile.

He let his head roll onto the back of the couch. "This is exactly why I don't let my sister come over when she visits. She always wants to redo everything and take me shopping for light fixtures."

"I promise not to make you shop. And if you don't like anything, just tell me. I won't get upset – I promise."

He sighed. "Alright. You've got a deal, Miss Bishop."

"Thank you, Mr. Harper."

9
VEGAS

Late April, Friday
0 Days to Marriage

Kate looked around the small private plane, once again thankful that she didn't have any Friday classes. Will was across the aisle from her, looking over some documents, and Jen had fallen asleep two rows up, her head on Andrew's shoulder. Like Will, Andrew was scrolling through documents on his laptop.

She looked out the window, thinking about how this was her last day as a single girl. Well, for two years at least. And it would probably be closer to two and a half. The clock didn't start until he had his green card, and that would take a couple of months at least. Then they would have to reapply for the permanent card, and that would take another month or two. If he wanted to get citizenship, it was three years. *Whoa, don't get ahead of yourself, Kate. You're not even married yet. He might not even ask you to stay longer, and he probably doesn't want to become a citizen. He's too British for that.* She gave herself a shake and went back to studying the landscape outside the window.

Bored with the scenery, she picked up the newspaper Andrew had brought along. She knew there would be a story about them in it, but she hadn't read it yet. The day had been full and she was enjoying the last moments of her anonymity before she became the wife of (as she was only beginning to understand) a very important man.

Kate opened the paper and flipped to page 6, looking for Priscilla Jennings's article. She was unsurprised to see a photo of Will twirling her around, her skirt flaring out and her Liboutins up in the air.

Were you at the Empire State Building last night? No? Then you missed quite a show! One of Manhattan's most eligible bachelors and English man of mystery, William Harper, was seen ON HIS KNEE proclaiming love and everlasting devotion to none other than leggy Kate Bishop, the woman he's been canoodling all over town with. This whirlwind romance has taken the city by storm. Who knew Mr. Buttoned-up could be so romantic? And Kate, if you're reading, help a girl out and tell me where you found that amazing dress!

There was a photo of Will sliding a ring onto her finger and the caption read *'Check out the size of that rock!'*

Kate laughed and immediately began sending an email to Evelyn, Will's assistant and general lifesaver, asking for more details about Priscilla Jennings. This woman would be a big part of her life for the next few years, whether she liked it or not. She needed to decide how close to keep her and whether or not she wanted to play along. Andrew had told her that it might help to cultivate friendships with certain members of the press in case there was any trouble with Will's documents later. "Good publicity never hurts," he'd said. *Well*, thought Kate, *here we go, Andrew. I hope you're right!*

**

"Wow. This room is huge." Kate dropped her bag and walked over to the window to look out over the city. "What a great view. Come see this, Will."

He came up behind her and looked over her shoulder at the city below. "What do you want to do tonight?"

"I don't know. Remind me, are we supposed to be getting drunk and then married, or just caught up in the excitement of it all and then married?" she asked.

"I think the latter. If we were drunk, there could be questions about getting an annulment, not to mention that it would be completely out of character for both of us. And I don't fancy pretending to be drunk in front of people."

"Well, in that case, I think I'd like to see a show. Something exotic and strange."

"Jungle animals exotic or drag queen exotic?"

She laughed. "Animal exotic. I've seen drag before."

"How about Cirque de Soleil? I've never seen it but my assistant said it was a good show."

"Sounds good. Can you get us tickets so last minute, Mr. High-Powered CEO?"

"I think I could manage it." He smirked. "Give me a minute."

He walked to the other side of the room and spoke lowly into his phone. Katherine wandered through the suite. It was a large open space with a seating area in front of the windows consisting of two love seats and four chairs. There was a fireplace on the other side of the room with a flat screen television next to it, and two chaise lounges strategically placed for viewing. There was a sweeping staircase with a modern floating rail to her left, and she walked up the steps to explore.

The top of the staircase led directly into a bedroom. The floor to ceiling windows from below extended into the space and in front of them was the biggest bed she had ever seen. There was another fireplace across from it, a television, and a bureau. There was a frosty glass panel in the wall with some sort of round metal sculpture surrounding it. Curious, she stepped through the door next to it and into a very chic, very modern bathroom. The frosted glass panel was the back wall to the shower, so whoever was bathing was also giving a private show to whomever was in the bedroom. She raised her eyebrows looking at it, and turned around to see a sunken tub with steps leading down into it and a large, wall sized mirror behind it.

"A little overdone, isn't it?"

She jumped with her hand over her heart. "Will! You scared the crap out of me!"

"Sorry. I thought you heard me come up. So what do you think of the suite?"

She took a deep breath to regain her equilibrium and answered, "It's nice. A little modern and sleek for me, but nice."

"I know what you mean. Evelyn specifically requested something romantic when she made the reservation. Do you suppose that is what they were trying to achieve?" he asked as he looked around slowly.

She snickered. "I'd say raw sex appeal was more what they were going for, but maybe that's romantic to some people."

He nodded and continued looking around. "Does this shower look into the bedroom?" he asked in disbelief.

"Sexy, isn't it?" she teased.

"In a movie maybe, but real people don't look that sexy when they shower. Just a lot of bending and awkward poses."

She laughed out loud. "Wow. You will definitely be staying downstairs while I'm showering then."

He smiled a bit sheepishly. "Well, I got the reservation. The show starts at eight, we've got VIP seats."

She rolled her eyes. "Of course we do. What time is it now?"

"Quarter past six."

"I'd better get ready." She pushed him out of the bathroom. "You can wait downstairs while I take a shower."

He let her propel him toward the stairs, then turned when he reached the top. "Do you want me to bring your bag up for you?"

"That would be nice, thank you."

"I'll call Andrew and let him know the plan, then I'll bring it."

"Thank you, honey!" she called as she walked into the bathroom.

"Yes, dear," he answered drolly.

Harper quickly called Andrew and told him of their plans, double checked the information he had looked up earlier about all night wedding chapels that weren't *too* seedy, and fixed himself a quick drink at the bar. He checked the location of the performance venue and realized it was close enough to walk, then arranged for the car he'd hired for the weekend to pick them up after the show and take them to dinner. Another quick call to Evelyn and dinner reservations after the show were secured. They may have been there to get married, but that was no reason they couldn't have a little fun while they were at it.

Not realizing how expedient he had been with his calls, he grabbed the two suitcases and bounded up the stairs in a surprisingly good mood. Things were finally rolling and with any luck, his immigration problems would be over soon. And though he'd never admit it to anyone, he was really looking forward to the Cirque de Soleil show.

He stepped into the bedroom and set Kate's bag across the low dresser and his own on the luggage rack he found in the closet. Cocking his ears, he realized the sound he was hearing was steadily running water and a low voice singing. Was that *Hot Blooded*?

Telling himself he would not turn around and look, he began to back toward the stairs. Kate would be understandably angry if he watched her taking a shower without her knowledge. And he was not a common Peeping Tom. He paused. Of course, she would be his wife in a matter of hours. Would it really hurt to look? Just for a second? The glass was frosted, and with the steam, he probably wouldn't be able to see more than a shadow anyway. Was it really so wrong to just take a tiny little peek?

Annoyed with himself for his lack of control over his own curiosity, he slowly turned around and looked toward the glass panel.

"Holy mother of-" his whispered words died on his lips as he looked open-mouthed at Kate. As she turned her back to him, he couldn't help the slight groan that escaped as he took in her silhouette. He stared at her waist, the way it drew in above her hips before flaring out again over her ribs. He had the sudden urge to grab her there and pull her to him, run his hands over those round hips and feel her perfect ass against his -.

"Get a hold of yourself, man!" he said harshly. He berated himself mentally for not having dated anyone since the whole Alicia fiasco – and he hadn't even slept with her. *Come on, Harper! It's only been a few months – okay, six months. You can handle this!* He lectured himself internally as he went down the first few steps until he heard she had turned off the water. He waited for her to leave the shower, then banged back up the last few steps and called to her.

"Your luggage is on the bureau, Kate."

"Thanks," she called back, her voice muffled.

Probably buried in a fluffy white towel, he thought. He went back downstairs on shaky legs and flipped through the channels until she called down that the shower was available if he needed it. He needed a shower, alright. A very cold shower.

**

The show was amazing. Their seats were perfect and the foursome ooh-ed and ah-ed in all the right places. Afterward, they went to a very exclusive, very expensive restaurant for a late supper. Harper ordered champagne and toasted his fiancé and the four drank, ate, and laughed more than any of them could remember doing in a long time. Finally, dinner was over and it was time to go to the chapel.

Harper gave the address to the driver, and twenty minutes later they were pulling up to a small white building designed to look like a country church. The four piled out, raucous but sober, and headed inside. Within minutes, they had a license and were third in line to be married.

"I don't want the word 'obey' in the vows," Kate said suddenly.

"What?"

"No obey. I don't want to promise that."

Will came close and whispered in her ear, "It's kind of a moot point, isn't it? Why does it matter what the vows say?"

"Because they're vows!" she whispered back. "I may not keep all of them, like the 'as long as you both shall live' part, but

I can keep others, like no cheating and not ditching you because you're sick."

He looked at her incredulously. "Uh-"

"I know, it's kind of late to be bringing this up."

He made a face that showed he clearly agreed with that assessment. "You think?"

Suddenly she brightened. "I know! Let's say our own!"

"Our own?"

"Yeah, our own vows! It's way more romantic that regular vows, and it will make a great story," she said quietly.

"I'm sure it would, but I don't have any vows prepared and we're supposed to be reciting them in fifteen minutes!" It was clear he was not happy and beginning to get distressed.

"Andy can help you. He's great with words!" She looked at him hopefully while he just stared back at her with an I-can't-believe-this-is-happening-to-me expression. "Andy, come here."

"What's up, guys?" Andrew asked quietly.

"What do you think of me and Will reciting our own vows?"

Andrew immediately lit up and ignored Will's aggravated expression and frantic 'no' signals. "I think it's a great idea. It'll make a great story. Come on, Harper, I'll help." Andrew pulled Harper into the corner as Will shot an angry look over his shoulder at Kate.

"What's going on?" Jen asked.

"We're writing our own vows. Here, help me." She handed Jen a scrap of paper and a pen from her bag. "I would just like to lie as little as possible," she whispered to her sister.

Jennifer looked a little perplexed, but after thinking it over for a second, understood her sister's feelings and began writing.

Exactly thirteen and a half minutes later, they stood in front of the officiant, who was dressed like a country minister, and the ceremony began. The first part was relatively quick and before she knew it, it was Kate's turn to say her vows.

"I, Katherine, take you, William Harper, to be my husband. I promise to always be by your side when you need me, to listen when you need an ear to hear you, to hold you when you need comfort, and to be your companion when you are lonely. I promise to be there for as long as you want me."

Harper looked at her with wide eyes, surprised by her candor and her ability to promise things she could actually deliver without telling a single lie or saying that she loved him. No one seemed to notice that omission. He took the paper with Andrew's flowery words and put it in his pocket, deciding on the spur of the moment that if she could be honest, so could he.

"I, William, take you, Katherine Bishop, to be my wife. I promise to support you, encourage you, and protect you. I will be there when you need me and give you space when you don't. I promise to be there for as long as you want me."

They shared a private smile and the minister instructed them to exchange rings. The next thing they knew, he was announcing them husband and wife and telling William to kiss the bride.

He smiled and gave her a gentle kiss, then led her down the aisle to a bad organ recording of *The Wedding March.* They quickly got into the limo with Jennifer and Andrew and sped back to the hotel.

"Well, that was lovely," said Jennifer.

"Yes, well done, Will. You scared me for a minute when you put away your notes, but you pulled it off. I'm impressed," Andrew added.

"Thanks, Andrew. Coming from you, that's saying something." Andrew nodded silently and Will looked down at the hand he was still holding. "Well, Kate, how does it feel to be a married woman?"

"I don't know just yet. How does it feel to be a married man?"

"Ask him in the morning!" Andrew exclaimed. Will looked down, embarrassed, but before he had time to reply, they pulled up in front of the hotel.

"What are your plans?" Kate asked her sister as they were climbing out.

"Well, since you two will be heading up, we thought we'd play for a little while. Andy has offered to teach me how to play roulette."

"Sounds fun. Just don't lose all your money!"

"No worries. I only brought enough cash to play with and left all my credit cards in my room."

"Good thinking." Kate and Jen kissed each other's cheeks as they parted in the lobby. "Good luck, Jenny!"

"You, too!" Jenny called as she was pulled away by an excited Andrew. Kate laughed and took Will's arm as they waited in front of the elevator.

"Well, my husband, can you believe we're married? How do you think you'll like the ball and chain?"

He chuckled softly. "I think I'll like it just fine." He leaned down to kiss the top of her head where it rested on his shoulder.

"Oh, did you two just get married?" asked an older lady in pearls and a red Chanel suit.

"Yes, tonight," Kate answered with a smile.

"Congratulations! You know, I was a Vegas bride," she said with a knowing look to Kate.

"Really?"

"Oh, yes. It was different back then, of course. Oh, my father was so angry with me! I thought he'd never forgive me! But he did, and Henry and I have been together forty-three years now."

"Wow! That is quite an accomplishment! What's your secret?" Kate asked as the woman was joined by her husband, a dapper-looking man in a gray suit.

"Oh, I don't know. I'd have to say it's living every day like you said your vows that morning." She leaned in toward Kate and whispered, "And good sex helps!"

Kate let out a startled laugh and the woman's husband took her arm. "Come, Sophia, I see our car has arrived."

"Alright, Henry. I'm coming. Congratulations again, you two. You make a lovely couple."

"Thank you," said Katie sincerely.

"Thank you," added Will.

Just then the elevator doors opened and Kate followed Will in. "Our first congratulations. And from a happy couple. That's got to be a good sign, right?"

"Of what?" he asked.

"That we're doing the right thing."

He didn't answer but wrapped his arm around her shoulders, pulling her into his side.

10
WEDDING NIGHT

Late April, Friday
Married 2 hours

"Wow. You look..." Harper trailed off, his voice soft and his eyes wide as he took in the image of Katherine in a long white nightgown and robe.

Kate smiled mischievously. "What can I say? I'm a traditionalist." He raised his brows in disbelief. "Well, in some things. This is my wedding night after all." She sashayed toward William, her hips swaying beneath the white silk. "Who knows when I'll have another wedding night? Besides, second weddings are always much more subdued than firsts, so I thought I should milk this one while I had the chance." She stopped and looked serious for a minute. "I had to be seen buying something in the shop downstairs, and I thought, since I have it," she trailed off and shrugged. *And since I might not actually ever have another wedding night…*

He smiled at her jest, then looked at her seriously, his eyes soft and gentle. "It's alright, you look nice." He touched the hair over her shoulder for a second. "Katherine. Thank you," he took her hands in his and kissed each one, "sincerely. I don't know any other woman who would have done half so much for me."

Katherine met his eyes for a moment, then smiled slyly. "Well, you are paying me, so I'm not a *complete* saint."

Harper smiled and chuckled slightly, accepting her shift away from the serious. “Champagne? It's a shame to let it go to waste.”

She nodded and he poured her a glass. “To two happily married years.” She echoed the toast and touched her glass to his.

After taking a sip, he looked at her uncomfortably. “I had planned to kip on the sofa, but as you can see, there isn't one here. It would raise suspicions to ask for an extra bed. If you don't want to share, I can sleep on the chaise.”

“Don't be silly, Will. You're way too big for that thing.” She gestured to the chaise by the fire. “We're adults. And we are *married*. I think we can share a bed without too much trouble.” He just smiled in response. “Now, I am exhausted. What do you say we veg out upstairs?”

“Lead the way.”

After nibbling on strawberries and drinking almost the entire bottle of champagne, Harper leaned back against the headboard and looked at Katie as she lounged on the other side of the bed. She really was a beautiful woman. Her long white nightgown hugged in all the right places, one perfectly toned leg peeking through the thigh-high slit. Her robe had fallen off her shoulders and now hung round her elbows, baring her creamy shoulders and delicate collarbone to his eyes. How was it that no one had claimed her yet? It struck him that she must trust him; here they were, all alone in a hotel room, late at night, half drunk on champagne and she was barely dressed. Yet she seemed completely comfortable.

“Kate, can I ask you something?”

“Of course.”

“Why did you marry me?” She looked at him incredulously. “Seriously. In one evening, you agreed to spend more than two years of your life with a man you'd only known for an hour and lie to all your family and friends about it. Why did you do it?”

Kate looked at him, unsure of how to answer. “I don't really know. Jenny told me about the situation and it sounded intriguing. Then I met you and you didn't seem so bad.” He raised his brows. She sighed. "Honestly?"

He nodded his head. "Please."

"I don't know why I did it."

"Really?"

"Really. All I can say is that it seemed like the thing to do." He gave her a look. "And now you think I'm crazy."

"I don't think you're crazy. It just seems like an odd reason to me. Are you always so spontaneous?"

"Not always. I just go with my gut. It's rarely wrong."

"Your gut?"

"Yeah. Don't look so skeptical. It's true. Once, I applied for this college that I really wanted to go to. They had the perfect program for me and everything seemed just right, but every time I tried to fill out the paper work I got this terrible feeling in the pit of my stomach. Once I got so nauseous I actually ran to the bathroom thinking I was going to lose my lunch. So I applied to NYU and got a scholarship to boot."

"I see. And does this amazing gut instinct apply to other life decisions or just your choice of educational institutions?"

"Actually, oh doubtful one, it does. Three years ago, there was a really cute guy in one of my classes. He was constantly trying to get me to go out with him, but even though he was charming, I always thought there was something not quite right about him. My friends thought I was crazy not to say yes but *my gut* told me not to. Six months later he was arrested for slipping mickeys to freshmen at a frat party. So you see, I was right about the charming sleaze ball."

He raised his hands in surrender. "Alright, I give in. The gut knows all and shall not be questioned."

She laughed and ate another strawberry before asking him, "What about you? Was there really no other option than getting married? And why me? Didn't you have an ex or a friend who would've done it?"

"Well, as far as options went, this really was the safest one. Even if immigration never looks my way, having a green card is a much better set up for me. As far as your involvement goes, we were in a hurry, Andrew suggested you, and I agreed to meet you. You didn't seem so bad, so I-" Katie interrupted by throwing a pillow at his head. “Hey! What was that for?”

“Not so bad?” she cried.

He laughed out loud. “Well, I did think you had a great ass.”

“Thanks,” she said sarcastically.

“And I don't really have any exes. The only one I would have considered is married to someone else with a couple of kids, so that wasn't an option.”

“You weren't afraid I was a psycho killer or anything?”

“Psycho killers must be a relatively small portion of the population.” She shot him a playful glare. “And Andrew trusted you and I trust Andrew. That's what really did it.”

“You two are really close, huh?”

“Yes. He's my oldest friend. Like a brother, really.”

“How many siblings do you have?”

“One. Just my sister I was telling you about that's seven years younger than me. She got married last summer and moved to Cyprus with her husband. He has a place there where he likes to go to 'write',” he said with air quotes.

“What's so wrong with that?”

“Nothing, if you're really writing. But he sits on the beach, swims, and takes walks. He never actually writes anything. He says he's gathering inspiration and ideas, but I think he's just lazy.”

“How do they live? Does your sister work?”

“Jacqueline bought a little run down inn and is fixing it up. She's always been interested in restoration. I don't know whether she'll sell it or run it when she's finished. Possibly neither. She has her trust fund which they could easily live on comfortably, plus he has his own, though I don't know if he ever uses it.”

“Wow.”

“What?”

“It's just a little odd. I've never known people who don't need to work. Besides retired people. And they definitely aren't buying hotels in Cyprus to renovate.”

He smiled. “It's a different world. You'll get used to it. Besides, it's not all fun and spending. It's not unusual for me to work sixty plus hours a week and I know some who do more than that."

"True, but obviously there are some who are just lolly-gagging about."

"True. Enough about my sister and her lazy husband. Tell me about you. We've been so busy for the last week that I feel like I don't know much about you."

"What would you like to know?" she asked as she stretched out onto her back and stared at the ceiling.

"You're getting a masters in literature?"

"Uh-huh."

"What do you think you'll do when you're done?"

"Well, I had considered writing, but now that I know your opinion on writers, I might change my mind." She smiled at him slyly.

He hung his head in mock penitence. "I'm sorry. I'm sure you'd make a wonderful writer. Just don't put me in any of your work."

"You don't want to be immortalized in fiction?"

"No, thank you!"

"Alright, I won't then. I also thought about teaching. I could teach high school with this degree, or I could go on and get my PhD and try to teach at a university. But I've always thought teachers are better when they've lived a little bit away from the academic world. You know what I mean. Like they need to actually see the world before they regurgitate the same ideas as every teacher before them."

"So how do you think you'll go about 'living in the world', as you put it?"

"Well, currently I'm sitting in a fancy hotel room with a rich handsome man. I'd say I was living pretty decently already." She smiled as she teased him and he was surprised to find himself blushing slightly.

"You think I'm handsome?"

"Of course. Don't you?"

He looked bewildered and she laughed out loud. "I'm teasing you, Will. And yes, you are very handsome, even though you have a tendency to fish for compliments."

She had climbed up to his side while she laughed and playfully kissed his nose.

"What was that for?" he asked.

"For being so cute." She kissed him full on the mouth then, warmly, but not deeply, then pulled away. "And that is for being so handsome." She climbed under the covers while he stared at her with an odd expression. "I'm exhausted. Goodnight, my husband."

He leaned over and kissed her smooth cheek. "Goodnight, my wife," he whispered, utterly confused but with an odd feeling of contentment, like everything would be alright in the end. If he'd believed in that sort of thing, he might have said he had a gut feeling.

11
WEEK ONE

Early May, Monday
Married 3 Days

Harper Married!!!

By Priscilla Jennings

Kate, I bow at your feet. Please, teach me your ways! Ms. Bishop has done what no woman before her has managed to do. Not only did she win the heart of the elusive Mr. Harper AND get him to propose in record time (and with Harry Winston), but he then whisked her away to Vegas to celebrate and the little bitch (and I mean that in the nicest of ways) actually MARRIED HIM there! Yes, your eyes are not playing tricks on you. William Harper is MARRIED. Off the market. Gone. Finito. Done. Signed, sealed, delivered.

I'd love to hate her for stealing such a good catch (and for having thighs you can crack ice on), but I can't because she's just so damn nice! Do you know what I found on my desk this morning? It would seem that Legs read my column last Friday and took it upon herself to send me that fabulous dress she was wearing in sapphire blue. Now that's classy.

Katherine Bishop Harper, you have the Page 6 seal of approval.

Harper set the paper down on his nightstand and took off his reading glasses. He ran his hand through his hair and yawned tiredly. Well, it certainly looked like Kate had been the right choice. The media loved her and she was making all the right moves. *Hell, she's better at this than I am and I've been doing it my entire life.*

He heard a clanking sound and got up to investigate. Harper pulled a robe on over his pajama pants and padded down the hall. He followed the light spilling out of the kitchen and entered to find Kate digging through a cupboard.

"Looking for something?"

Kate jumped. "Don't you make any noise when you walk?"

"Sorry."

"I'm looking for a pan." She reached into two more cabinets and finally found what she was looking for.

"Are you going to make something?"

"Grilled cheese. You want one?"

He looked at the clock. "Isn't it a little late? It's after midnight."

"I know, but I'm starving."

He watched her set the pan on the stove and turn up the fire. She pulled a loaf of bread and a package of cheese out of a sack that was sitting on the counter.

"Did you go to the store? You don't have to do that. You can leave a list for the housekeeper."

"I know, but she doesn't come until tomorrow and I'm hungry tonight." She smiled as she buttered a slice of bread and put it in the pan, carefully placing three slices of cheese over it and covering it with another slice of bread. "You in or out?"

"In. Beer?"

"Sure."

He took two beers from the fridge and popped them open while Kate expertly flipped the sandwich in the pan and got to work buttering more bread.

"How was your day?" she asked distractedly as she threw the wax paper from the cheese into the trash and searched the upper cabinets for plates.

"Fine. I changed the time stamps on those emails you sent me. Very creative, by the way."

"I was pretty bored on the plane."

"You made a good move with that column writer. She wrote about it today."

"Did she? I haven't had a chance to look."

"Yes, she seems to like you."

"I hope it doesn't bite me in the ass by making us more interesting to the press."

"Nah, the story will die down soon enough, especially now that the wedding is over. Some salacious gossip will usurp us and no one will even remember our names. And a little good will never hurts."

"I hope so. Here you go." She passed him a plate with a steaming sandwich on it and sat herself on a barstool at the island in the middle of the kitchen. "Be careful, it's hot in the middle."

"This is really good," Harper said after a bite that he washed down with beer.

"Thanks. The trick is the different kinds of cheese you use. The more variety the better."

"Hmm. So how was your day? Do anything interesting?"

"It was good, not particularly interesting. I spent the morning polishing up my paper that I have to turn in tomorrow. Thankfully that's done. Then I had a study group for the exam tomorrow. We quizzed each other and drank too much coffee, the usual. I feel pretty ready."

"Is this the last one?"

"No, I have this one tomorrow, I have to turn in my paper to my professor, and I have one last exam Thursday. I've done really well in that class, though, so I think I'll be alright. I already turned in a big project last week."

"What was your project on?"

"Using literature to teach young learners."

"Are you studying education?"

"No, this class was one elective of several. I thought it would be useful if I ever decided to pursue teaching. And it sounded interesting."

"Hmm." He nodded and kept eating.

"I'm really glad we don't have any evening plans this

week. With all the last minute finals stuff, I don't know how I would have handled it."

"Yes, thankfully people will expect us to take a little time for ourselves. It will give us time to get sorted. When do you finish work?"

"I finished tutoring last week. I don't usually do it the week of finals and the students all have finals, too, so I'm done for the summer. I'll just need to send everyone an email telling them I won't be picking back up in the fall." He nodded. "I took the dogs this afternoon and have to take them twice more before Friday, and I'm done."

"Don't dogs need to be walked every day?"

"Yes, but I work for an agency. There are several of us designated for each family and we walk on rotation. I had already requested a light week because of finals, which is why I'm only walking three times this week. Normally I would do three mornings and three afternoon/early evenings. I also took a lot of weekends."

He nodded his head thoughtfully. "Are they requiring a long notice?"

"Not really. I told them I could give them two weeks, but she said Friday was fine. A couple of the other walkers want to up their hours during the summer, so this worked out perfectly."

"Right. Well, thank you for the sandwich," he said as he stood.

"You're welcome. Goodnight, Will."

He left the room and she looked at the plate he'd left on the counter next to the empty beer bottle.

She sighed and put the plates in the dishwasher, rinsed the empty beer bottles and put them in the recycling bin, and washed the pan by hand before drying it and placing it in the cabinet.

She filled herself a glass of water, turned off the lights and headed to bed.

***

Will walked in to the kitchen Tuesday evening to find Kate sitting at the counter and reading a textbook.

"How did the exam go?"

"Well, I think. I turned in my paper on time. Just one more to go!" She looked excited but weary. There were circles under her eyes and she clearly hadn't spent any time on her appearance. Her face was bare of makeup and her hair was in a simple braid down her back.

"I'm starving. I was thinking of ordering Indian food. I know you need to study and I don't want to go out by myself. It would look odd."

"Yeah, no, I understand. I'm sorry to mess up your evening. Indian food sounds great. I need to take a break anyway. I think my brain has officially turned to mush."

"Great. Do you want to order in or pop out for a bite?"

"Honestly, I'm really tired and don't feel like getting dressed to go anywhere. Would you mind if we ordered takeout?"

"Takeaway is fine." He pulled a menu from a drawer and placed their orders and soon they were piling plates with saffron rice and curry and settling in to the island.

"I am so looking forward to the semester being over!" she said dramatically.

"I can imagine. I'm glad my university days are behind me. How much more do you have?"

"Well, I technically have two full semesters, but my advisor has suggested an internship for the last semester, and I'd have to take one class in addition to that. But if I do that, I'll have an extra large load this fall. I won't really be working, which makes it easier, but I'm getting the feeling that we'll stay pretty busy. How full is the fall usually for you?"

"It depends. September is generally pretty quiet, though August usually has a lot of social obligations: weddings, parties, that sort of thing, but I guess it makes up for July being so slow. Most everyone spends the weekends in the Hamptons, and it's too hot to do anything in the city. October has the usual charity galas. Then holiday season comes and December is always crazy."

"So September is light, October and November are… moderate?" she asked.

"Yes, I'd say so."

"Okay, so maybe I should take some summer classes. There are two that I'm interested in. They're six weeks long, two hours every morning. Each."

"Ouch. Five days a week?"

"Four. I guess that's something. But you know, if summer is light on social obligations and I'm not working, I could handle it. Then my fall courses could be lighter. Eighteen hours is a lot to carry – six professors to please, six books and assignments and schedules to keep up with. If I do two now, I'll only have four classes. I could even do five and not take one with my internship. That seems a lot more reasonable."

"How many classes do you generally take each semester?"

"Five is the norm, though I did take six for two very memorable semesters. Four would feel like a vacation!"

"When do the summer classes start?"

"The end of May. They end the tenth of July or something like that."

"That sounds like a good plan. It would give you three weeks off now to relax and get settled in. You could take the classes, and then you'd have over a month before the next semester begins. Since you have three day weekends, we could go to the beach house to get out of the heat."

She was nodding and chewing absently while she thought it all through.

He continued, "I wanted to ask you, what do you think about going to the shore for a few days? I imagine you could use a break, I know I could. We could say we're taking a bit of a honeymoon and get out of the city… Maybe next week, after you're finished with work and exams?"

She turned to face him, suddenly giving him her full attention. *Why does he look so nervous?*

"It's been a really busy time at work and with this immigration debacle-"

"Will," Kate interrupted, "I understand. You've been

under a lot of strain. We both have. A vacation is definitely due. I'd love to go to the beach."

He looked relieved. He wasn't used to checking his plans with anyone. He certainly wasn't in the habit of admitting his exhaustion and need for escape. In the past, he would have simply told the office he would be out for a few days and gone wherever he wanted. Now, he had to take her with him, especially this close to their wedding. It would look ridiculous if he left her in the city alone while he went to the Hamptons by himself. Still, even though he knew all of this and could admit that his reticence was slightly ridiculous, he was made very uncomfortable by the entire conversation.

"Do you want to just make the plans and let me know when? I'm totally free after Friday," she asked.

"Yes, I'll do that."

"Okay, back to studying for me!" Kate said cheerfully. She put her plate in the dishwasher and placed the leftovers in the fridge and the empty containers into the trash.

"I'll leave you to it." Will nodded and went into the living room. She heard the sound of the television a few minutes later. Looking over to where he was sitting, she saw his plate was still there, along with a soiled napkin, a fork, a large spoon and several crumbs and spots of orange curry on the countertop.

Is this a rich thing or a man thing? she wondered. She put his plate in the sink but didn't wash it and wiped the countertop down so she'd have her study spot back, and then sat down to continue reading.

***

"Hi, Will! How was your day?" Kate asked cheerfully when Will came home Wednesday evening.

"You're in a good mood. I expected to find you hunched over a book." He walked into the kitchen and set the bag he was carrying on the counter.

"I was. I've been studying almost all day and it's time to quit cramming. If I don't know it by now, I'm not going to."

"I picked up Chinese. I wasn't sure what you liked, so I got a little bit of everything."

"Mmm! Smells great!" She quickly grabbed two plates and a couple of forks. "What do you want to drink?"

"I'll just have a beer."

They settled onto the sofa in the living room, food spread over the cocktail table, and happily started eating.

"I know you've been studying all week, but do you think you're up for a little more?" Harper asked.

She looked at him warily. "What do you mean?"

"We should start working on these." He held up the questionnaires Andrew had printed off for them. They had questions like "Which side of the bed do you sleep on?" and "Does your partner snore?"

"Sure, I think I can handle that."

They started simply, answering basic questions about childhood and education. Kate was doing most of the asking and scribbling furiously in her notebook.

"Okay, let me get this straight. You were born in London, but grew up between there and your country home in Somerset and traveled a lot with your parents."

"That's right."

"Your parents were James and Cynthia, both died when you were in your twenties," she grimaced and looked at him but his face was blank, "and your little sister is Jacqueline, and she's six years younger than you."

"Seven years younger, but yes to everything else."

Kate scratched something down in her notebook. "You went to boarding school when you were eight and Eton when you were thirteen years old and Andrew Jamison was your best childhood friend."

"Yes, but I didn't meet him until I got to Eton."

"Right," she said as she made a quick note on her paper.

"You know, these are the sort of questions anyone can find an answer to on Google. I think we should focus on the more personal details. At least that's what Andrew suggested."

"What kind of personal details?"

"Things like what shampoo we use and what our

favorite foods are."

"Okay," she replied, dragging out the word. "You want to start?"

"Sure. What shampoo do you use?"

"Nexxus usually, Herbal Essence when I want it to smell good."

He gave her a confused look. "Um, what's your favorite food?"

"It depends on the type. Italian, Thai, Indian..."

He made a face. "Okay, if you were on a desert island for a month and could only eat three different foods, what would they be?"

She screwed her face up in thought, then answered, "Lemon salad, pad Thai, and tiramisu."

He raised his eyebrows and looked at her incredulously. "That's quite a selection. And what is lemon salad?"

"It's a salad I make with a lemon dressing. I'll make it for you sometime. You'll like it."

"You cook?"

"Of course. I'm southern and my mother is VERY southern, which means I definitely cook. So does Jenny. It's the most useful thing our mother ever taught us."

He nodded. "Tea or coffee?"

"Usually tea in the morning, I don't really like the caffeine rush. But I do coffee during finals and when I'm with my dad. He drinks a pot a day."

"Interesting. Early Grey? English Breakfast? Herbal?"

"Usually herbal or something fruity. I love orange spice. Oh, this will be good to know! Laura, you met her as my lawyer but she's really an old childhood friend, turned me on to it. She's horribly allergic to caffeine or something like that, so she drinks herbal tea when everyone else is slogging down pots of black coffee. She's convinced that's why her skin looks so good, but that's not the point. When we were little she was our babysitter. She's seven years older than me and five older than Jen and she lived on the next farm over. Her dad raises quarter horses. Anyway, when it was the busy season and dad was watching the farm and mom had to mind the store, Laura would come spend the weekend with us. She'd sleep in the guest room and cook all the meals and everything. But she wasn't so much older that she was like a mom. She was more like a knowledgeable older sister. Anyhow, she would always have a cup of tea in the morning and got me and Jen drinking it with her. I've been hooked ever since. But I do love the smell of coffee; it always reminds me of my dad."

Will was writing furiously on his paper, his brow furrowed in concentration. He eventually stopped writing and looked up.

"Favorite color?"

"To wear or to look at?"

"Are you always this particular?"

"What do you mean?"

"You qualify every question."

"I do?"

"Yes. Now: favorite color?"

"I'm kind of in a blue phase right now, but I also love red and my childhood room was painted yellow and I loved that."

"Okay, good information." He jotted something down. "What about music?"

"I don't really have a favorite. I like everything except hardcore rap. It's a little violent and too hard to sing along with for me."

"Favorite film?"

"Hmm. *Roman Holiday* for classic, *The English Patient* for drama, for comedy, uhh, don't laugh."

"What? Why would I laugh? Is it really bad?"

"Well, it's a little bit bad. But if you want to have a legitimate answer that shows how well you know me, I think I should be honest."

"What could be worse than *The English Patient*?"

"You don't like *The English Patient*? What's wrong with you?"

"Me? It's a total sap-fest! How can you possibly take that film seriously?"

"It's wonderful and beautiful and romantic! And Ralph

Fiennes's voice gives me chills."

"Oh, I see. You like it for the eye candy."

"Did you just say eye candy? And you think Ralph Fiennes is eye candy?"

Harper blustered, "I'm not saying that I think he is, but that is clearly what you liked most about the film."

"Well, I did enjoy him in it, but if it wasn't a good story I wouldn't have liked it at all. What about you? What's your favorite movie?"

"I don't know, really. I liked Citizen Kane."

"Really? And you're making fun of my choice?"

"It's classic!"

"Yeah, and the boring choice of every man who wants to sound like he likes classy movies when he really loves *American Pie*."

"American what?"

"Never mind."

"Let's move on. How about perfume. What do you wear?"

"Allure and Gucci. You?"

"I had one I liked by Davidoff, but it's been discontinued. Jackie bought me something by Armani and it's alright, but not my favorite."

"Do you prefer showers or baths?" she asked.

"Baths. You?"

"Depends on my mood, but I usually take showers. I know, it's very American of me."

He smiled and looked at the list of questions in his lap. "What was your first job?"

"I worked for my dad on the farm, selling trees during the season and running the cash register in the gift shop with my mom. But my first real job outside the family would have been babysitting for the Beckers. Those kids were terrible! It was enough to make me never want to procreate!"

"Really? So you don't want children?"

"Oh, I don't know. Probably someday. Definitely not any time soon. I want to get certain things in my life squared away before I do."

"Like what?"

"Well, for one thing I want to finish my masters. Then I'd like to work for a little while and get at least semi-established before jumping on the mommy track."

"So do you think you would quit your job to take care of your children – if you had them?"

"I don't know. Maybe in the beginning. Everybody I know who has them says it's great to be home with them early on. But then you get restless, or that's what my friends with kids say, and I don't know if I could just walk away from work, so I'd have to see. Sometimes I think I'd be perfectly happy just being the fun aunt and never having any. What about you? Do you want kids?"

"Yes, I mean, I suppose I do. Doesn't everyone? Obviously, it's less of an issue for me since I wouldn't be the one carrying them, but I've always thought I would have them; at some point anyway."

"How old are you again?"

"Thirty-two. And you're twenty-three right?"

"Yeah. So I've got plenty of time before I become a baby factory."

He laughed. "Do you like ice cream?"

"Yes, I love it, but don't ask me my favorite flavor because it changes weekly!"

"Actually, I wasn't asking for the notes. I was going to get some and thought you might like some."

"Oh! Sorry. Yeah, I'd love some. What flavor?"

"Mint chocolate chip."

"Ooh, that's my favorite!"

"This week?" he asked as he walked toward the kitchen.

"Haha. Point taken, Mr. Harper. Now bring me some ice cream!" she called playfully.

"As you wish, Your Highness," he called from the kitchen.

She laughed and followed him to the kitchen.

***

"So what are you up to today?" Laura asked as Kate slid into the chair across from her in the corner of a small coffee shop Thursday afternoon.

"I'm packing up my old apartment. And I aced my last exam!"

"That's great!"

"And I've been setting up my back up plan."

"Sounds intriguing. Tell me more." Laura leaned across the table.

"I opened a new savings account this morning – in my name only. As you know, William and I will have a joint account now – which I still find bizarre – but I wanted my own savings account. So now I have somewhere to put all that money he's giving me."

Laura raised her brows. "I'm impressed. I thought I was going to have to coach you on financial independence."

"Really?"

"Rule number one: Trust no one - especially your spouse."

"Who better to get marital advice from than a divorce lawyer?" She grinned at her friend, then said quietly, "But really, you know the situation, so of course I am looking out for myself. I mostly trust Andy, but he is Will's lawyer, not mine. And I barely know Will. So while I'd like to think they would never screw me over, most people who get screwed never see it coming."

"So what's your plan?"

Kate leaned forward and slightly over the small round table. "Well, so far I've opened some interest-earning savings account. I can't remember what it's called." Laura rolled her eyes. "Anyway, I had enough for the minimum balance required and I plan to use my money from the professor for spending and save all my petty cash from Will. If I need to supplement, I can see if some of the stores won't give me cash for returned items. I have no bills – no rent, utilities, groceries, nothing – and I get five grand a month for spending. On what? Taxis? I have cards for everything I need and I'm sure I won't go over the limit."

"You might be surprised. You'll be going to a lot of events and those dresses can be expensive. It can add up quickly."

"Well, he gave me a big advance for clothes, and of course I have my signing bonus." Now it was Kate's turn to roll her eyes. "I swear, these people spend money like water. I've never seen so much cash in my life."

"Have you learned any more about him yet?" Laura asked with raised brows. Laura knew all about him, of course, but Kate wanted to find out on her own.

"Like I told you before, I was waiting to give him twenty questions until after the wedding."

"Hello! You're married!" Laura said as she raised Kate's left hand and looked pointedly at the ring.

"I know. We were too busy last week with all the dating and then the wedding stuff. And of course I've had exams this week. I've spent all my time cramming for tests and polishing final papers. The petition got approved Tuesday, so that's good. Andrew filed the official application yesterday. Now we're just waiting for an interview date."

"That's good news. Andrew moves fast."

"Yeah, he seems really good at his job."

The waitress brought the check and Kate quickly slid a shiny plastic card onto the tray.

"Ooh, is that your new hardware?"

"Yup! And I just got this to go with it."

Katherine held out her new driver's license which read 'Katherine B. Harper', just like the credit card she'd lain down.

"Wow. I always thought you'd hyphenate," she said thoughtfully.

"Turns out it's kind of a pain in the butt, not to mention really long when you're signing your name. Besides, it looks more legit that I change it. Isn't that what most women do? Especially those madly in love in whirlwind romances?"

"I suppose, though some never do."

"Yeah, well I'm not some famous actress that doesn't want to lose name recognition. It won't hurt anything to change it. I can just change it back when I'm done."

"You make it sound like you're changing clothes."

Kate just smiled as the waitress returned the check and she signed her new name.

"Got your new signature all squared away?"

"I think so. What do you think?" She held out the newly signed slip of paper.

"Nice. So how was the wedding? Everything you dreamed it would be?"

"Yeah, it was great. You know, we actually had a lot of fun. I played a slot machine for the first time and won fifty dollars!" Kate beamed with pride and Laura just laughed.

"Only you would be excited about winning fifty bucks six days after you married a millionaire."

"But I won! That doesn't happen every day!" Laura shook her head and Kate continued, "We had a lot of fun. Jenny and Andy were good to have along and the four of us had a great time."

"Did you do any shopping?"

"Yeah, Saturday Will took me shopping. Of course he was traumatized after the first hour and left me alone with Jenny. I think I have a whole new wardrobe."

"Well, you look great."

"Thanks!"

"So when will you be all moved in?"

"Soon. I don't have to be out until Sunday, so I'll get the rest of my things before then. Will suggested we get a moving company to pack everything, but I was just going to bring over a few boxes. I'll get rid of most of my furniture. It was all cheap hand me down pieces anyway."

"Well, you know I'll want to hear all the dirty details next weekend. Right now I've got to run. I'm meeting a client in forty-five minutes."

She kissed Kate's cheek and Kate walked out with her, hugging her tightly before she left. "Thanks a lot, Laura. For everything."

"Don't thank me. That's what friends are for."

*

Kate wandered slowly through the lower east side neighborhood where she'd lived for three years, remembering the things she thought she would miss and saying a happy goodbye to the things she was glad to leave behind. She walked the five floors up to her old apartment and packed up a few things, mostly old photo albums and pictures and random knick-knacks. Will had someone with a truck coming Friday afternoon to collect whatever she was taking with her. She'd arranged for the Salvation Army to pick up the furniture she no longer wanted earlier in the day.

Three hours later, she looked around her almost bare apartment. She had packed nearly everything and only a few tidbits remained.

"You'd think after three years I would've accumulated more stuff," she said to herself. With a shrug and a sigh, she grabbed her bag and got ready to go to Will's place. "I should probably start thinking of it as home. And I should definitely stop talking to myself. We don't want Will to think we're crazy now, do we?"

She locked the door and headed uptown.

*

Thursday night, Kate and Will sat in the living room eating salads from the neighborhood deli and watching television. She was quiet, thinking about the conversation she'd had earlier that morning. Angie and Sheila were in her morning exam and they couldn't wait to pounce on her. She even got there a little early to give them time to ask their questions before the test started. They'd been relentless, of course, like she'd expected, and she'd given them the details she thought old Kate would, before she started living a secret life, and tried to act as normal as possible.

She thought she'd pulled it off pretty well, but one thing was niggling her. Laura had referred to "knowing" about William earlier, and Sheila and Angie had both intimated that they knew all sorts of things about him, especially about his money. She played along like she knew what they were talking about, but really she had no clue. She still hadn't had time to Google him and she didn't really want to. She thought half the things on there were likely to be rumors anyway, and why read about someone when you've got the real thing right in front of you?

But still, she didn't like others knowing something about the man she'd married that she didn't. And it wouldn't do to be caught off guard.

"Can I ask you something?"

"Of course," he answered. "What's your question?"

"How rich are you?"

"Um, well, I'm… very."

"Very?"

"Yes. Very," he said succinctly.

"That's it? That's all you're going to tell me?"

"What more do you want to know?"

"How much are you worth?" He made a face and shifted in his seat. "Okay, how about I'll guess, and you can tell me when I'm getting warmer."

"Okay," he said eventually. Will was comfortable with his wealth, and money had never been an issue for him or for any of his friends. He knew very few people who weren't wealthy, or at least he didn't know them well, and he knew Kate was one of those few people. But as he had recently been informed, not everyone was as comfortable as he was. Andrew had warned him not to act like a snob, which he had taken offense to at first, but then had thought better of. He didn't want Kate to feel uncomfortable, so up to now, he had simply avoided the money topic. She must know he had plenty by the sheer fact of her presence and his ability to pay for her. *See, that's just the sort of thing you should not say out loud!* he thought.

"Ten million," she said.

"Are we talking about me personally, or my company? And HarperCo or Taggston as a whole? Because those are very different numbers."

"How about just you for now," she said with a frown. This was more complicated than she'd thought.

"Including the family trust?"

"The what?"

"Some things are in my care, but are not my actual property, or mine alone. Like the apartment I share with my sister, for example."

"Oh. How about just what you personally have and could sell without anyone else's permission, and cash that is yours alone."

"Okay. I'll have to think for a minute." He closed his eyes and leaned his head back as if he was adding numbers in his head.

Just for fun, Kate did the same. She counted her personal property, which included a nice bicycle back home, the new smart phone her mother had given her for Christmas, an iPod, and a decent sized collection of books, plus her wardrobe which was now quite nice thanks to Harper. Then she had her bank account which had had about $1200 in it from before she married (and before she paid rent) and the savings account she'd just opened with her signing bonus that had $10,000 in it. Altogether, she figured she was worth around $30,000. She was surprised by this and a little bit proud. Granted, most of that money had come from the man sitting across from her in the last few weeks, but still, she was better off than she'd been before.

"Okay, I think I've got it," he said when he opened his eyes.

"Okay, so ten million?"

"Cold."

"Five million?"

"Colder."

"Okay, so more than ten. Twenty million?"

"Cold."

"Fifty?"

"Less cold."

"But not warm?" He gave her a look. "Seventy-five?"

"Less cold."

"Eighty-five?"

"Still cold."

"Ninety-five?" she squeaked.

"Warmer."

She looked at him warily. "You're worth over a hundred million dollars? Just you? Not your company, just you and your, what, holdings?"

"Yes, much more. Some of it I inherited through various family members, mostly my father, and some I earned through investments."

"Must've been a hell of an investment."

He chuckled. "My father was great with money. He ran Taggston flawlessly. When I turned sixteen, he gave me a thousand dollars to invest. He taught me how to follow the markets, who to trust and who not to, what made a sound investment. And more than just stocks – companies, people, real estate. It was a very good lesson. That thousand dollars is now worth twenty times that – well, depending on the market."

She looked at him incredulously. "Can you teach me to do that?" The question was out before she knew what she was saying, but she didn't wish it unsaid.

He looked surprised but answered quickly, "Sure. Of course. I'd be happy to." He smiled and leaned forward, his elbows on his knees. "Do you have any more questions? It's probably a good idea for you to know about the various properties and things. That way in case they ever come up in conversation with others, you won't be blindsided."

"Various properties?"

"Yes. For starters, the Taggston Building is owned by Taggston, not by me, but I own controlling shares of Taggston. I own this apartment, half my parents' across town which I've told you about, and a couple of buildings downtown. They're all rented out right now and turn a good profit. I bought them when the market was slow a few years ago and they were in pretty rough shape, so I got an entire block for a song."

"And you own all of this outright? No payments to the bank?"

"No, I try not to deal with banks when I can avoid it. My father always said the key to a successful business was to keep the debt level down and the cash flow up."

"Makes sense."

"Yes, it does. Too many get in too deep and then when things slow down, they can't keep their heads above water. You have to grow slowly. If you go too fast, growing pains are bound to follow."

She nodded her head slowly, taking it all in. "Anything else you own here in the city?"

"I've invested in a few business start-ups, mostly small technology firms that I thought showed promise. I have an apartment building in Brooklyn that I bought as a favor for a friend, but that's it – here, anyway."

"You bought it as a favor for a friend?"

"Yes, an old family friend owned the building. He hit some tough financial times and needed cash, but he didn't have time to sell it on the open market, nor did he really want to sell it – it's a great investment. Fully occupied, long-term renters. Anyway, he offered me a deal to sell it to me privately, without the broker's fees, and I agreed to sell it back to him in five years if he could afford it."

"Wow. That's a big act of friendship."

He shrugged. "Yes and no. I wouldn't have done it for just anyone, no, but it was also a sound investment. It's made me plenty of money since I bought it, so I can't complain."

"How many years ago was it?"

"Four. So next year I'll find out if I get to keep it," he said.

She nodded, absorbing all this new information. "Wow. And I thought letting Laura borrow my lucky dress was an act of friendship."

He laughed. "If it's really lucky…" He trailed off and stifled a yawn.

She shook her head and stood. "Well, now that I know you're richer than Croesus, I'll stop feeling bad about how much money you're giving me. In fact, maybe I need a raise." She walked towards the doorway.

He smiled and followed her down the hall, stopping outside her door to kiss her head in what was becoming a nightly habit. "Night, Katie."

"Night, Will."

12
GROWING PAINS

Early May
8 Days Married

Kate and William spent the long weekend at his beach house in the Hamptons. They weren't on the road an hour before they both realized that they barely knew each other and four days in the other's sole company could potentially be incredibly boring or even contentious. Kate mentioned how much Jenny loved the beach and Will quickly suggested they invite Andrew and Jennifer to join them.

Their guests arrived Saturday morning bright and early, as only two people as energetic and cheerful as Jennifer and Andrew could do. The newlyweds were clearly relieved and the couples quickly separated by gender.

Andrew and William spent Saturday swimming in the frigid water and kicking around a soccer ball while Kate and Jen lay on the beach reading and chatting, then shopping at the local antique stores where Kate bought a dining table that had once belonged in a Long Island farmhouse and a new wooden bed frame for her room. They returned to the beach house tired but triumphant with bags full of burgers, fries, and Cobb salad. The four spent a relaxing evening eating, drinking, and in Andrew's case, telling funny stories of life at an English boarding school.

Sunday morning, everyone slept in and by the time Kate emerged from her room, Andrew and William were swimming in the ocean and Jennifer was reading on a blanket on the sand. Kate plopped down beside her.

"Morning."

"Morning, little sister. Sleep well?"

"Yes, I did. You?"

"Yes, thank you. Andrew is thinking of buying a place up here." She looked around. "It could be nice, but..."

"What's the point if your best friend has a place right down the shore?"

"Exactly." Jen smiled.

They sat in silence for a few minutes before Kate spoke. "Have you noticed anything weird about the house?"

"This house? No, why?"

"It seems really feminine, doesn't it? It's decorated so softly. I've seen how Will decorates, or I should say doesn't decorate. He definitely didn't do this."

"Maybe his sister did it or he hired a decorator."

"Maybe. But did you notice the pictures?"

"I haven't really looked. What about them?"

"Will is hardly in any of them. There are several of his sister, she's plastered all over the place, and a lot of his mom, too. There's even a painting of the two of them sitting on the beach together. But Will isn't in it. Isn't that odd?"

"I don't know. Maybe. Could he have been away when it was painted? He went to school in England, after all."

"I don't know. It's all very confusing."

"Oh, no. I know that look. You think you've just stumbled on some interesting mystery and you won't rest until you find out what's going on." She looked hard at her sister. "Listen to me, Katie. This is William we're talking about here. William Harper, heir of Taggston Incorporated and riches untold, fiercely private, and newly, your husband. This is not a game. It would not be wise to piss him off. Do you hear me, Katherine Mae Bishop?"

"Yes, but-"

"No buts!" Jennifer interrupted. "There is probably a very logical explanation for everything."

"Like what?" Kate asked skeptically.

"Like maybe his sister did the decorating. That would explain why it feels so feminine and why there are so many pictures of her and her mother."

"So Will's sister is a narcissist who loves lavender?"

"Katie!" Jenny tried no to laugh. "You haven't even met her. Maybe she was going through a phase. She might want to change it when she comes back."

"She can't. It's Will's. She only owns half the apartment on the Upper West Side, not this place."

"So you repaint it if you don't like it. Ask William. He probably won't mind. Blue would look nice."

"Yes, it would." Kate agreed with her sister while she planned to ask Will about the house tomorrow when Jen and Andrew were back in the city.

After a rousing game of volleyball, a freezing dip in the ocean, and Scrabble played in front of the fire on the patio, everyone was ready for an early night. Jennifer and Andrew were getting up before dawn to drive back into the city for work, but William and Kate had another day before they were due back.

They were eating strawberries and yogurt on the patio late Monday morning when Kate decided to ask Will some questions.

"So, who decorated the house?" she asked.

"My mother and sister. They redid it just before she died."

"I'm sorry, I didn't meant to bring up a painful topic."

"It's alright, it's been twelve years now. Jackie had just turned thirteen and the two of them made it a sort of birthday project. Mother let Jackie choose most of the colors and furnishings, only stepping in if necessary. Even then, Jacqueline loved decorating." He smiled and shook his head.

"Did your family spend a lot time up here?"

"Mother and Jacqueline did. They would spend the entire summer here, usually. Mother loved the beach and taught Jackie to love it, too. I suppose that's why living in the Mediterranean suits her so well now."

Kate nodded. "Would your dad stay in the city to work?

Maybe come up here on weekends?"

"Sometimes he came up, maybe once or twice a month. He was always busy with Taggston and one venture or another."

"Has your family always had this house or did your parents buy it?"

"My grandfather built it in forty-nine. My father inherited it when he died and I inherited it from my father."

Kate nodded, unsure of what to say. She had so many questions, but didn't know how to ask them.

"Jackie still comes up here when she comes to New York," Will continued. "She spent a weekend here just before her wedding last summer."

"She's twenty-five now?"

"Yes. Twenty-six in July."

Just then, Will's phone rang and Kate thought it was just as well. The only questions she had left were intrusive and really none of her business, but she couldn't help herself. This way, she was forced to hold her tongue.

But she couldn't keep her mind from wandering. Why did his mother and sister spend summers here but not William? Sure, he was in boarding school then in university, but he had summer breaks, didn't he? Was he working with his father? Doing internships at Taggston? What about before he was old enough for that? Where were pictures of a gangly teenaged William playing on the beach with his little sister? Surely they did that. Everybody did that, didn't they? Even rich people?

Kate tried to quiet the thoughts circling her mind while Will paced the patio, nodding and agreeing intermittently, occasionally speaking in whole sentences to whoever had called. Maybe Jacqueline didn't like William? Was that why there so few pictures of him displayed in the house she decorated and he didn't spend summers with his mother and sister? Was Jacqueline a spoiled brat?

"Sorry about that," Will said as he set down the phone on the table and sat back down. "Care for a swim?"

"This water's too cold for me. I don't know how you do it."

"A walk down the beach then?"

"Sounds great. Let me just put these in the sink." Kate collected the dirty plates and glasses, deposited them in the sink, and walked barefoot to meet Will on the boardwalk.

"The pool should be open next time we come," Will said.

"There's a pool?"

"Yes, right over there." He pointed to a group of trees broken by a small path with a gate at the end of it. "It's scheduled to be opened next week. It was too short notice for this weekend."

"What? The mighty CEO couldn't get the pool opened with the force of his will alone?" she teased with a smile and a nudge to his arm.

Will laughed lightly. "Believe it or not, there are people more powerful than me." He shrugged. "And the pool company can only handle so many at once."

She laughed a little and stooped to pick up a smooth stone and throw it into the water. "It's very peaceful here."

"Yes."

They walked on in silence for another half hour, then turned back. When they reached the house, William said he wanted to swim and Kate lay on a blanket on the sand and read. The day passed quietly, William ordered pizza for dinner and they watched a movie in the living room. Kate fell asleep forty minutes in, only to wake up when William turned off the television. She mumbled goodnight and stumbled down the hall to bed. After a simple breakfast Tuesday morning, they drove back to the city. All in all, it was a peaceful weekend.

***

Thursday, Andrew and Harper had lunch together in Andrew's office.

"So how's it going with Kate?" Andrew asked.

"She talks a lot. It's almost like she's-"

"Trying to get to know you?" Jamison interrupted. Will glared. "Is it really so bad?"

Will gave a frustrated sigh. "I don't know, Jamison. She's so, she's just so... so-"

"Charming? Nice? Funny?"

"Happy!" Andrew chuckled. "And she's always singing. Did you know the other day she sang the same two lines to a song for over an hour? She just hummed the parts in between. She's ALWAYS singing!" Andrew gave in to a full blown laugh now. "Every morning it's, 'Bye Will, have a good day.'" He did a high pitch imitation of her voice. Will shook his head and let out a groan.

"So let me get this straight. She says hello and goodbye to you and hopes you have a good day, and she's cheerful and likes to sing in the house. And this bothers you because...?" Andrew asked.

"She's just so THERE!" Will let out in one loud breath. "Studying at the kitchen counter or watching TV on the sofa. It's like I've been invaded by a perky pink smurf."

"Smurfs are blue."

"Whatever. I'm just not used to sharing my personal space with anyone. I want to come home, watch the telly in my boxers, and have a little peace and quiet. I didn't think she'd be there so much. She sounded so busy when we first talked."

"Well, she was busy. She was working three jobs. She's not working now. Maybe she needs a hobby. Or you could try talking to her about it. It's only been a week."

"Almost two weeks."

Andrew leveled a look at his friend. "Talk to her, Harper. Kate is a reasonable person. She'll understand."

"Yeah. I'll think of something."

That evening when Will walked into the apartment, it was surprisingly quiet. There was no music coming from the kitchen, no humming in the living room. He went down the hall and saw no light under Kate's door. *Hmmmm. Guess she's not home.* He let out a sigh of relief and went to the refrigerator for a beer. He looked at the stocked contents and thought that was one good thing about having Kate around. Now there was always food in the fridge. Yogurt for breakfast, fruit for snacking on, and lots of fresh salad.

Three hours later, Will was sitting on the couch in his boxers watching *The Daily Show* when he looked at his watch. It was after eleven. Where was Kate? He knew she wasn't working, and she didn't usually stay out this late. Was she with friends?

Thirty minutes later, he heard a key in the door. *Thank God!* Will was surprised at his own relief. As he was wondering about the strange turn of his own thoughts, he realized he was sitting in just his white tee shirt and underwear. It was too late to make it to his room now. *Oh, well.* He walked toward the door and saw Kate entering with a heavy-looking messenger bag over one shoulder and a notebook clasped in her arm.

"Out studying?" he asked as he took the bag from her shoulder.

"Thanks. No, working actually." *He doesn't remember the semester is over?*

"Working? I thought you quit tutoring."

"I did. This is the assisting thing I told you about. My professor that's writing a book?"

"Oh, yeah. I didn't realize you'd kept that one," he said, silently wondering why she was still doing it.

"Yeah, well, we have a good relationship and I enjoy the work. It's great experience for me and it's not easy to find the right writing assistant. It wouldn't really be fair to Mark to have to find someone else at this stage of the process. It could throw off the whole publishing schedule." *And Mark practically begged me to stay.*

"Oh. I see. Are you always out this late when you're working?"

"Why? Worried?" She smiled playfully and walked into the kitchen, obviously not expecting an answer. "No, not usually. He was out of town this last week, and when he got back he had a ton of notes to go over and straighten out before he lost the muse. Normally, I'm only there once or twice a week and am done by nine or so."

He nodded silently, gratified that she told him her schedule without having to be asked and wondering why he cared. "Well, goodnight." He backed away uncomfortably toward the living room.

"Night, Will."

Kate grabbed a glass of water and headed to her room. Her new furniture had been delivered that morning and she had gleefully unpacked all of her boxes, happy to be settled and for her room to be comfortable. Her biggest splurge was the new mattress. Harper had told her that any redecorating she did would come out of the household budget, which was basically their joint account. He put money in it every month and they both had access to the funds, but it was understood that they were to be used for the home and not for personal items.

After a week, she realized it had been necessary. She was spending a lot of time in her room. She usually studied in the kitchen and the only television was in the living room, but when Will was home she tried to give him space and control of the remote. Now that the semester was over, she would focus on cozying-up the rest of the apartment. She had plans to shop with Jen the next afternoon for some drapes to cover the huge windows in the living room; she'd already had it painted and put a few new pieces in there. She also had her eye on some red bedding for the guest room where the hard mattress that used to be in her room was. She was still thinking about turning it into a study for herself. Maybe a Murphy bed would work?

Stepping into the bathroom to brush her teeth, she noticed it was time to clean it again. She sighed. *I hate cleaning.*

Not that anyone loved to clean bathrooms, but Kate supposed she hated it more than most. But what else could she do? On the way home from Vegas, she had realized there was a glitch in their perfect plan that no one had seemed to notice: the housekeeper.

Maria came twice a week and gave the place a thorough going-over and usually baked a loaf of bread and made a casserole or roast for Will to munch on until she came again. She was a very sweet lady and everyone liked her, but with a secret as big as this one, they couldn't afford any slip ups, and if there was anyone who would notice that two people weren't really living together, it was the housekeeper.

So they'd come up with a plan. Or rather Kate had and

the men had agreed with it. They got a heavy lock for Kate's room and told Maria that it was being used to store Kate's things and not to worry about cleaning it. Kate just had to make sure it was locked up on the days Maria was due to come. She felt all the irony of having someone regularly clean the house, a longtime dream of hers, but not clean her bathroom.

They put most of Kate's old clothes into Will's closet and placed a picture of her on his bedside table. Of course, it was on the side he never slept on, but that was a technicality. She put a few personal products in his bathroom and told herself that every once in a while she would spritz his sheets with her perfume. Rather than Kate having to remember to take her dirty laundry into his bathroom on cleaning days, he agreed to take his to the laundry room the night before. Hopefully Maria would think his new wife was simply whipping him into shape and not suspect anything.

Of course, all of this meant that Kate had to clean her own bathroom, a task she was not looking forward to. *Oh well*, she thought, *it'll keep all of this from going to my head.*

***

"Bye, Will. Have a good day," Kate called as Harper headed toward the door. He stopped and turned around slowly, trying to decide if he should say anything.

"What are your plans today, Kate?"

She stopped in the kitchen doorway and looked up in surprise. "Well, the dining table is being delivered, so I have to be here for that, and I'm going shopping with Jen for some curtains in the living room. I also plan on hitting the market and cooking dinner." He looked surprised and a little interested. "You're welcome to it if you want. There hasn't really been time to cook, but now that I'm settled in and I have a couple of weeks before my summer classes start, I thought I might make something other than grilled cheese. Oh, that reminds me, I wanted to ask you if you want to have Jenny and Andrew over for dinner Saturday night."

"Umm," he answered slowly. "Don't we have a thing this weekend?"

"Friday night we have the donors' dinner for the supporters of the new homeless shelter."

"Oh, right. Well, Saturday night sounds fine. Are we going out afterward?"

"I thought we could play games if it was cool with you. Jen will probably come early and cook with me. It's kind of our thing."

"Oh, sure, whatever you want to do is fine. I'll see you tonight then. I should be back around seven."

"See ya." She went through to the kitchen and he turned back around and went out the door, kicking himself for not talking to her about the chipper goodbyes.

Is it really such a big deal? He asked himself. *Have I become such a grouch that I can't stand for anyone to even wish me a good day?*

He shook if off and went to work, forgetting all about it a few minutes later.

*

Just after seven that evening, Will pulled his tired body out of the elevator and unlocked the front door. He was immediately met with a wave of warm, homey smells. He set down his briefcase and looked around. The previously empty area to the right of the entry was now filled with a large, rustic style dining table surrounded by six chairs, but they were so far apart that it looked like it could almost accommodate twice that. The chandelier above the table was dimmed and there were two wine glasses and a bottle alongside two simple place settings.

"Kate?" he called.

She bustled into the dining room wearing an apron and carrying two bowls, one steaming and covered in a cloth, the other a wooden salad bowl filled with lush greens.

"Hi, Will! How was your day?"

He took a deep breath. "Fine. How was your day?"

"Great."

Just then a timer went off in the kitchen. "Be right back."

Will walked forward and looked into the living room, wondering what had happened to his apartment. Kate had painted the living room a warm chocolate brown. At first, he thought it would make it feel dark and small, but the giant wall of windows prevented that from happening. She had added two soft colored arm chairs and a chenille throw over his leather sofa. His glass topped coffee table had been replaced by a warm painted wood one that looked like it had at one point or another been at least ten different colors. It was distressed and peeling and incredibly homey. There was a table behind the couch with lamps and an Mp3 speaker on it, and a warm, patterned rug on the dark floor. Was this his apartment? He had to admit, the whole effect was very warm and inviting. He'd never felt so drawn to his own home before.

"You hungry?" Kate's voice interrupted his reverie.

"Uh, yes, very actually. I had to work through lunch today."

"Oh, sorry. But it kind of works out for me. I got a little carried away. I thought we could christen the new table!"

He looked at the table and saw she had brought out three more dishes. "Wow! This looks great." He quickly washed his hands and sat down. "So what is all this?" he asked, clearly delighted by what was in front of him.

"This is chicken tetrazzini," she pointed to a creamy pasta dish in the middle, "this is tomatoes and buffalo mozzarella with fresh basil, homemade garlic bread, sautéed peppers and zucchini, and lemon salad."

"Ah, the famed lemon salad. I'll have to try that first." He eagerly filled his plate with vibrant green lettuce and quickly took a bite. His eyes brightened for a moment. "You weren't kidding. This is really good." He took a swig of wine and continued to eat, suddenly in a much better mood.

Kate watched him with a small smile and a bit of amusement. She had always liked cooking and there was something about someone enjoying what she had made with genuine appreciation; it always made her glad.

"Do you cook like this often?" he asked.

"Sometimes. Usually I make less food because I have less time, but this is my usual style, yes."

"This is amazing. Really, Katie, you're very talented."

She blushed a little despite herself. "Not really. All of this is actually pretty easy to make. I just hadn't cooked in a while and I missed it, that's all."

Will was eating ravenously and had already piled his plate full of seconds when Kate was only halfway through her firsts.

"Oh, I should tell you: I saw Jamison today. He thinks we should register."

"Register? Like for gifts? But we didn't have a wedding. Isn't that a little... rude?"

"Well, according to Evelyn, she's gotten several calls from people who'd like to send a gift and want to know where we're registered to do so. Jamison heard about it and he thinks we should have a reception. We can invite everyone that we would to a wedding, but it will just be a big party."

"That could be fun. When should we have it?"

"Andrew thinks sooner rather than later and I agree. Let's get the wedding itself behind us and out of the public eye. I want people to start thinking of me as married, not as in-the-process."

"That makes sense. We could probably do it in about three weeks if Evelyn would help with the invitations."

"I'm glad you said that. I took the liberty of speaking to her about it already and if you are available, she can meet with you tomorrow to discuss details. Will there be enough time for your family to come up?"

"It's enough time, but I doubt if they'll come. Summer is tourist season and my mom's shop is usually busy – I doubt she'll be able to get away. Dad hates to travel and especially hates big cities, so even though it's technically a good time for him, I would be seriously surprised if he came. Tiffany is a counselor at a summer camp this year and Heather is doing an internship in Houston. I doubt she'll be able to take the time off to come. And we were never really that close, so she'll probably want to save whatever time she does get off for other things."

"Really? Isn't that a little... odd?" Will asked as he was mentally trying to place Tiffany and Heather.

"Maybe. If it was my real wedding, I'm sure they'd all come, but since it's just a reception, I don't think they'd bother. I'll ask, of course, I'm just saying we shouldn't count on it. But Jenny will be there."

"And Heather and Tiffany are your other sisters?" he asked.

"Yeah, Heather's twenty and studying engineering and Tiffany will be a junior in high school."

He smiled and looked thoughtful.

"What?" she asked.

"What, what?"

"You're smiling," she said with a nod toward his mouth. "Oh, it's the names isn't it? We get that a lot."

He grinned ruefully. "Jennifer, Heather, and Tiffany. Katherine seems a bit out of place there."

"In more ways than one," she laughed. "There's actually a funny story about that."

"Oh?" he said as he swirled his garlic bread in the sauce on his plate.

"It's like this. My parents couldn't agree on what to name Jennifer when Mom was pregnant. Dad loves books and classical names and Mom prefers more, well, Barbie names." He laughed. "She had a rough labor and by the end of it, Dad agreed to let her name the baby whatever she wanted. So that's how Jennifer got named. When she got pregnant with me, she was sure I was a boy. So the whole name thing started again. For a boy, dad liked Michael and mom wanted Corey."

He made a face.

"I know," she said. "Mom was so sure I was a boy that she agreed that Dad could name me if I turned out to be a girl, thinking he'd never get the chance. Well, obviously, Dad won the bet and named me Katherine."

Will chuckled and added more tomatoes to his plate.

"But mom got back at him."

"Oh?"

"Yeah, shortly after I was born, she asked dad if she could pick the middle name. She wanted to name me after her aunt. Of course he agreed."

"So what's your middle name?"

"Mae."

He looked confused. "What's so bad about that?"

"Nothing, on its own. But mom likes to shorten Katherine to Kitty, and often calls me Kitty Mae."

His brow furrowed. "It's a little…"

"Redneck," she interrupted.

"I was going to say rural." He smiled.

She laughed and sipped her wine. "Yes, that's an excellent word for it."

He ate a few more bites quietly and eventually said, "Okay, so probably just Jennifer here from your family, then."

"Probably."

"Alright. Well, Evelyn knows all the details and the company has an event planner that we use regularly if we want to utilize them."

"Sounds good. I'm sure between Evelyn and the planners, we can pull it off on short notice. Jen might want to help, too. She's involved with all of her charity's events and really enjoys it."

"Great."

"Do you want dessert?"

"There's dessert?"

"Tiramisu. I bought it at that little Italian bakery around the corner. I've never made it myself."

Will smiled. "I can't wait to try it," he said.

She went to the kitchen and came back a minute later with 2 small plates and a dish of layered tiramisu.

"I think registering could be a good idea. I really want a new mixer. And we need dishes," she said looking around.

"What do you mean? We have dishes."

"I mean that there are only six of these plates and two of them are chipped. There are no salad plates and no serving platters except the flea market ones I brought with me."

"Does this mean we have to go shopping?" he asked with a groan.

"Oh, stop being such a baby! It'll be fun!" He looked at her skeptically. "I'll make you a deal. You help me pick out the dishes, and I'll take care of the rest of it on my own. Sound good?"

"Perfect. Thank you, Katie."

"Don't thank me. I get to go shopping with other people's money and get anything I want, even if it's ridiculous. I think I'm the one winning here."

He smirked and took a bite of the dessert she had just given him. "Holy mother of -"

"Good?"

"Uh-huh," he moaned.

She laughed. "I'll take that as a yes."

He smiled and continued eating. When he was done, he wiped his mouth with his napkin and leaned back in his chair, his hands on his belly.

"Thank you. I haven't had a home cooked meal in ages. I was starting to forget what it tasted like."

She smiled. "Any time."

13
GAMES & PLANS

Mid-May, Tuesday
2.5 Weeks Married

"You've done it now, cuz."

"I can only assume you are referring to my rather hasty marriage," Will replied drolly as he leaned back in his chair and twisted the phone cord around his hand.

"Of course. What were you thinking? Vegas? Please tell me you got a prenup or a postnup or something," asked Calvin. *"And why haven't you returned my calls? I've left a dozen messages."*

"It's all taken care of, don't worry. I'm not an idiot, you know."

"Well, that's what I thought until you ran off to Vegas and married some American girl no one's ever heard of before."

"Kate is great, you'll like her. Quit worrying before you go gray."

"Mother is fit to be tied. She can't believe you didn't let her plan a big society wedding. I told her that was probably why you eloped, but she never listens to me. Anyway, when are you bringing her over to meet the family?"

Will hesitated. "I'm in the middle of some big negotiations right now and Kate is starting summer classes soon; I don't think we'll be able to make it for a while."

"How long is a while?" Calvin asked in that aristocratic way that managed to sound bored and demanding at the same time.

"A few months. But we're having a reception in June.

You should come then."

"Oh, no! A party and mother's not involved? You do realize that she may never speak to you again, right?"

"We have an organizer. It's not a backyard barbecue."

"Send me the details and I'll let you know. I can't make any promises."

"I understand. Cheers, Calvin."

Will leaned back in his chair and squeezed the bridge of his nose just as there was a light tapping on his door.

"Come in, Evelyn."

"It's me," Kate said as she popped her head in. "You look stressed. Everything okay?"

"Yeah, I just spoke to my cousin in London."

"And?"

"He wants us to come over there so everyone can meet you. I told him no, of course. They'll probably descend en masse on the reception."

"Is that a bad thing?"

"Not really, but one or two can be a handful. I should probably apologize for them in advance."

She smiled and sat in one of the chairs facing his desk. "What about your sister? Do you think she'll come?"

"She is coming. She invited us to visit after I told her we were married, but of course I can't leave the country right now, so I declined. She and her husband will come a few days before the reception. She wants to help you decorate the apartment."

Kate looked surprised.

"I said she'd have to talk to you then pretended to get disconnected before I could give her your number."

"William! You hung up on your own sister?"

"She knows she shouldn't be nosing around my place. I told you I never let her stay there for exactly this reason. She came over once when I first bought it and was shopping an hour later. She has to be kept under control or the whole place will look like a Mediterranean palazzo."

"Okay," she said slowly, "Well, it would be weird if we didn't have her over at all. I mean, she is your only sibling. How about I get the place done as much as possible before they get here so there's nothing for her to do? Then maybe I can ask her to go shopping with me for something else."

"Yeah, tell her you're looking for some investment property, something you can fix up. That'll keep her busy for days."

Kate cut him a look. "I was thinking shoe shopping."

"Oh." He looked around, clearly at a loss. "That could be fun, too. But wouldn't that only take a few hours? Jacqueline is a bottomless pit of energy. If we don't want to become her next project, we need to distract her."

"I guess we could go looking for property. I don't have to actually buy anything," she said thoughtfully.

"Why not? If you see something you like for the right price, you should build up your investment portfolio."

Kate raised her brows and shook her head. "I'll try to think of something. So Evelyn and I have been talking about the reception and she wants to know if we want to do all the traditional stuff like cutting the cake and the first dance and all that. I wasn't sure what all you wanted to do, so I told her we'd talk about it."

"Shouldn't we do everything? It might look odd if we didn't."

"I agree. Any ideas for our song?"

"Not a one. You?"

"No clue. We can come up with something later." She stood and smoothed her skirt. "I'll get back to planning with Evelyn."

"Kate?" he called after her.

"Yes?"

"Do you have lunch plans?"

"Not really, I thought I might order a sandwich in an hour or so."

"Would you like to eat with me? I'll be free at one."

"Sure, that would be nice." She smiled and left the room, leaving a surprisingly pleased man behind her.

An hour and a half alter, Kate poked at the chicken on her plate at the table in Will's office.

"So tell me more about your family," she said.

"What do you want to know?"

"Well, the basics about who's coming. Who's related to whom and how, that sort of thing, and maybe what they do for a living, what not to talk about in front of them, just general stuff."

"Alright. As far as taboo topics, just stay away from politics and you should be fine. Oh, and don't mention anyone's plastic surgery, no matter how obvious it is.

"There will be the Covingtons, my mother's family. I've told you a bit about them before." She nodded. "My mother's brother, Alistair, and his wife Julia will probably come. We aren't particularly close, but he and I do business together sometimes and he's a decent chap. We're working on the merger together. I don't talk to Aunt Julia much, she's a society matron and spends all her time throwing parties and shopping. They have three children, Teddy, Calvin, and Cecelia – Cece. Teddy is five years older than me and we talk about business matters and used to play polo together, but we aren't close. He's married to a woman called Caroline and expecting his first child. I don't know if they'll make it. Not sure about Cece, either. She just got married to some textiles manufacturer, Hayes. She's a good enough girl but I don't really know her well, we just see each other at family gatherings, that sort of thing. She's Jacqueline's age, so they were closer. You might like her, she seems nice enough."

"What about Calvin?"

"Calvin is only one year older than me and the only cousin I'd actually call a friend. He should be here. He's single, no children. Good chap, always good for a laugh. My mother had an older sister, Claudia, who may come, though she doesn't really travel anymore. She calls on holidays and my mother's birthday to catch up. She never had children of her own and her husband passed on a few years ago."

"Sounds like a pretty small family."

He held up a finger. "That's just my mother's immediate family. Her father had four siblings so there are plenty of cousins running around. My father had two sisters, one of whom has three daughters, the other has five children, three girls and two boys. Aunt Rebecca, the one with three daughters, married a Scottish banker and lives in Edinburgh, as do all my cousins and their husbands and children, and Aunt Helen married an American oil tycoon and she splits her time between London and Texas. Her husband retired and their eldest son runs the company now. Three of those cousins are married and the youngest is expecting her first baby."

"Wow. I should have been writing all this down. Are there more? What about great aunts and uncles and second cousins once removed?"

"Oh, there are plenty of those. My father had several cousins who live throughout Europe and America. One of his distant cousins is married to a congressman, and a few more hold seats in British Parliament. My mother's brother is an earl, so he has his seat, of course -"

Kate interrupted him, "Whoa, wait, what? An earl? As in he has an earldom?"

He smiled. "Yes, technically, though no one ever calls it that. Would it be too much to tell you now that my great uncle is a duke?"

Her mouth dropped open slightly. He was clearly enjoying her shock. "Does that make you royal or something?"

"No, not at all. My grandmother was the youngest of four children, the older three boys, so she never had much chance to inherit the title. She married my grandfather, the Earl of Maeburn, and he's not in line for the throne at all."

"And to think that I thought it was cool that my second cousin's brother-in-law was a state congressman in West Virginia."

He smiled. "You get used to it. They're just people."

"Yeah, titled people," she grumbled.

He laughed and leaned back in his chair and wisely changed the subject.

***

"What do you think about this one?" Kate held up a plate with a blue floral pattern on it.

"It has flowers on it," Will said with distaste.

Kate sighed in exasperation. "You've said no to the last twenty china patterns I've shown you. Why don't you show me what *you* like?"

Realizing he'd been a big ass but not wanting to admit it, he said, "Alright. I will."

He walked around two different aisles, then asked, "Is there another department with more selection? All of this is so..." he picked up a tiny tea cup, "dainty."

Kate cut him a look. "This is everything they have in fine china. Maybe we should look at the everyday ware."

He replaced the cup and followed her around the corner, using his gun to scan a sculptural bowl that he thought looked like a rugby ball.

"What do you think of these?" she asked.

He looked at the display before him and saw several sets of dishes that were more colorful and sturdy than what they had been looking at. "I hate it a lot less than the other stuff."

She laughed and started to walk away. "You look here, I'm going to look at the glasses over there."

Will studied the china patterns in front of him, attempting to take this exercise seriously. *This is so stupid. I can't believe I'm shopping for dishes on a Saturday afternoon.*

He finally chose three patterns he liked well enough to show Kate when she came back a few minutes later. She opted for two of his selections, saying they could mix and match.

He followed her to the next aisle over and thankfully, he liked Kate's first selection of glasses. They repeated the process with stemware, flatware, and linens. Kate finally sent Will off to electronics to pick out a new Blu-ray player while she went to the kitchen department and chose knives, a series of pots and pans, cutting boards, and anything else that struck her fancy. Will had told her that the people coming would expect to buy an expensive gift, so she should choose enough items for everyone to be able to send them something.

"That won't be a problem," she said quietly to herself.

**

"So was it fun?"

"Of course it was fun. I got to scan whatever I wanted and not worry about having enough gifts under twenty dollars to go around."

"Did William get into it?" Jen asked as she sipped a glass of wine.

"Sort of. At first he was whiny and annoying, typical guy behavior while shopping," Jen nodded understandingly, "but then he seemed to kind of get into it. It was like it clicked that this was going to be his stuff that he would be using in his home. I eventually sent him off on his own and did the kitchen stuff by myself."

"That must have been nice."

"You have no idea," Kate said dreamily. "I didn't even get halfway through before we had to leave. You should come with me next time. I have to go back Monday afternoon."

"I think I can make it. When is the reception going to be?"

"The eighth of June."

"Wow. That's only three weeks away."

"I know."

"When does summer school start up?"

"The twenty- fourth."

"Cutting it kind of close, aren't you?"

"Maybe. It's only two classes, and the first week shouldn't be too hard. It will make the fall semester a little lighter this way. And what else would I have done this summer anyway? Normally, I would just work my ass off to save money for the school year. Now that I don't have to do that, I can get a little ahead with my classes."

"Better you than me." Jen smiled at her sister and clinked her wine glass against hers, then went back to slicing okra.

*

"This looks great! What do we have here?" Andrew asked jovially as he popped into the kitchen to help carry dishes to the table.

Kate handed him a bowl. "That's Jenny's amazing fried okra," she handed him another bowl that's contents were wrapped in a towel, "and these are the best biscuits you've ever tasted."

Jen shooed him out the door and followed him with another large covered dish. "This is Katie's fried chicken. She makes the best fried chicken in the world. You're going to love it."

Kate came through behind them and placed a pitcher of iced tea on the table. "Andrew, would you mind grabbing the mashed potatoes?"

"Sure, Kate."

"I'll get the beans," Jen added.

"I'll go get Will." Kate walked down the hall to the study where Will and Andrew had been talking while she and her sister cooked. "Will?" she called as she popped her head around the corner. "It's time to eat."

"Okay, I'm coming." He got up and followed her back to the dining room. "This smells lovely."

"We made southern tonight. We call this comfort food back home."

The four of them sat around the table and began scooping food onto their plates. The men complimented the sisters several times on their fine cooking skills and everyone ate more than they should have.

"Ugh, I'm going to have to run an extra mile tomorrow," Jenny complained as she leaned back and stretched.

"It was worth it, baby," Andrew replied, patting her stomach lightly.

Kate got up and began to clear the table.

"No, don't worry about that. You two cooked, we can clean up. Right, Will?" Andrew said.

"Yeah, sure." He stood and began stacking up plates and carrying them into the kitchen.

"Let's go while the gettin's good," Jenny said as she stood and walked into the living room. "What are we playing tonight?"

"I don't know. What do you think about Pictionary?"

"Split by couples or by genders?" asked Jen.

"You'll win no matter how we do it. You'll either be with your sister or your boyfriend. This is definitely not a fair fight."

"Then why don't you partner with Andy and I'll play with Will?"

Kate's eyes lit up. "Now there's an interesting idea. But is that going to make you and Andy fight later on?"

"No, of course not. It's just a game."

Kate shrugged. "Alright, if you're sure."

45 minutes later...

"That does not look like a horse! Who could guess that?" Kate cried.

"Of course it does. Here's the tail, and here's his mane," Andrew defended.

Kate groaned and dropped her head into her hands. "You're killing me, Andy!"

Jenny and Will surreptitiously bumped fists as Kate wailed on about Andrew's deplorable drawing skills until Jenny got up to take her turn.

Jenny picked up the marker and began drawing.

"Bow and arrow." Will called. Jenny nodded. "Men. Smiley face." Jenny nodded vigorously. "Happy men? Happy men with bow and arrows? Robin Hood and His Merry Men!"

"Yes! That's it!" Jenny yelled. She gave Will a big hug as Kate shook her head. Forty-two seconds. This was so unfair.

Andrew looked at her guiltily. "I'm never playing on your team again," she said darkly.

"Sorry, Katie." He tried to appear contrite, but she could tell he was laughing behind his eyes.

"Aw, come on, sis. Don't be a poor sport," Jenny chided.

"Easy for you to say. You creamed us," Kate replied.

"I know. Wasn't it awesome?" Jenny gloated.

Kate just glared at her, then turned to begin putting away the game.

"Okay, guys' turn to pick the game. What are you up for, Will?" asked Andrew.

"Cranium?" he suggested with a sideways look at Kate, watching for her reaction.

"Ooh, I love that one!" said Jenny.

"Same teams or are we changing it up?" Andrew asked.

"New teams," answered Will. "This time, Kate is with me." He grabbed her hand and pulled her down next to him on the couch. "A man's got to stick with his wife." She looked at him in surprise and smiled slightly.

"Deal. Come on, Jenny, let's kick some ass!" Andrew added.

Harper smirked as he watched Andrew. "You two obviously didn't know before tonight what a deplorable player Andrew is," he whispered to Kate.

"Yeah, thanks for the warning," she whispered back, but her smile belied her sarcastic words.

He chuckled softly and leaned back into the cushions, placing the hand that still held Kate's on his knee as he softly stroked the skin on the back of her hand with his thumb.

An hour later, Will and Kate had left Andrew and Jenny in the dust and Kate had even developed a victory dance for every time they won a song question, which Will unabashedly enjoyed. Finally, Andrew called it a night and he and Jen left.

"That was quite a game you played tonight, Mr. Harper," Kate said as she was picking up the living room.

"You were pretty good yourself, Mrs. Harper," he responded with a smirk.

She turned off the lamp and headed for the door. "Come on, cocky, let's go to bed."

He followed her down the hall and paused to give her a quick kiss on the top of her head as he passed by. "Night, Katie."

"Night, Will."

14
LORDS & LADIES

Early June, Thursday
Married 1 Month

"What do you think of this one?" Kate stepped into Will's office and held out her arms so he could see her long blue maxi dress clearly.

He looked up from his computer screen. "It looks nice."

"Do you like it better than the other one?"

"They both look good."

"Do you even remember the first one?"

He rubbed the back of his neck. "It was a dress." She rolled her eyes. "It was very pretty," he added.

She huffed.

"I really like this one. This is definitely the winner," he said.

"Don't decide yet. I have one more I want to show you."

She scampered away and was back two minutes later in a yellow cotton dress with a full skirt and thin straps at the shoulders. She turned around and looked at him.

"Well? What do you think?"

"It's lovely."

"Yes, but is it meet-your-sister lovely?"

"Uh-"

"Does it say, sure-I-married-your-brother-in-Vegas-but-I'm-really-a-wholesome-girl?"

"Can a dress say all that?"

"And I'm-sure-we-can-be-friends-please-don't-hate-me?" she asked with a hint of desperation.

He just looked at her for a moment. "Why are you so worried about this? It's just my sister. She lives an ocean away. You'll probably hardly ever see her. Hell, I hardly ever see her. Why the freak out?"

"I'm not freaking out. I just want her to like me. She's your *sister*. Don't you want us to get along?"

"Of course. I just don't see what the fuss is about. She's a nice girl, you're a nice girl, you only have to get along for three days and she's staying at a hotel. How hard could it be?"

She rolled her eyes. "I think the first dress is out. So this one or the blue?"

"This one," he said as he rose and walked to the door. "You look happy – like sunshine."

He continued down the hall toward the kitchen as Kate stared after him, a small smile on her face.

**

Kate looked nervously around the lobby of the hotel. She wasn't sure why, but she was anxious about meeting William's sister. She'd done well with previous boyfriends' families and everyone had always liked her right away, but something about this set her off. She thought there might be something between Will and his sister that he wasn't telling her. He didn't talk about her much, and being the only two siblings, she would have thought they'd be closer. He clearly loved her, and there was a picture of the two of them on vacation somewhere a few years ago on his desk, the only picture in the apartment besides one of his father (an older version of William but with warm brown eyes and laugh lines), but otherwise, he never mentioned her.

She could be imagining things, of course. Kate definitely had an active imagination. But she still couldn't shake the nervous feeling in her belly. It didn't help that almost every woman she'd met in Will's circle so far had been rude and unwelcoming. She didn't look forward to spending prolonged time with someone who looked down on her. But that wasn't very many people, she reminded herself, and there was no guarantee that Will's sister would be like that. After all, the women who'd been rude to her were chasing after a husband, and Jacqueline Harper certainly wasn't in that category. The older and married women had been quite nice, as had most of the men.

"There she is," Will said, startling her from her thoughts.

She followed his eyes and saw a tall blonde woman walking toward them, oblivious to the heads turning as she passed. Jacqueline Harper was slender, with long limbs shown to perfection in the linen skirt and pale silk blouse she was wearing. She was very graceful, Katherine thought, like a princess. She knew how to enter a room and carried herself like she had a book balanced on top of her head. Her hair was long with gentle waves, skin tan from spending long hours in the sun, but not rough. Her face was pretty, but not beautiful. Memorable, that was the word Katherine would later use to describe her.

"Jacqueline." Will reached forward and hugged her lightly, kissing her on both cheeks as she returned the gesture.

"William. It's good to see you." She smiled at her brother for a moment before turning to Kate. "You must be Katherine."

Katherine couldn't explain it, but she suddenly had the urge to curtsey.

"It's nice to meet you, Jacqueline." She waited for her new sister-in-law to initiate a handshake or a kiss or something, but nothing happened.

Jacqueline observed her silently for a moment, and then looked back to her brother. "Where are we headed? And when can I see your flat? I've found the most wonderful chandelier for your dining room."

"I thought we'd get something to eat first, if you're

hungry?"

"My, William, you sound positively American now!" She laughed delicately while her brother looked down; Katherine was unsure of what he was thinking. "You know I never eat between meals. And Albert would never forgive me if we ate without him."

"Where is Albert?" William asked.

"He's sleeping in our room. He's never been a good flyer."

"Right. I'd forgotten," he said as he gestured for the ladies to walk out in front of him.

Katherine looked up at the sudden change in Will's voice. His whole demeanor seemed to have become more formal. His back was straighter, his head a little higher, and even his accent had taken on a more distant quality. She'd thought he was hoity-toity before, but this was a whole new level.

"About that chandelier I mentioned, a buyer at a little shop on Camden found it for me. I do think it would be perfect for your space. Shall we go fetch it?"

"Actually, Kate has nearly finished with the decorating. But she has been thinking of putting in an offer on a little brownstone on the Upper East Side. Would you care to see it?"

"Really?" Jacqueline looked at Kate with new interest. "Is it your first property? Tell me about it."

William handed Jacqueline a packet of papers with details of the property while mouthing an apology to a surprised Katherine. "I'll explain later," he whispered as he settled next to her in the back of the car.

William described what little he knew of the property to Jacqueline while Katherine looked out the window, wondering how she was going to survive the next three days.

The brownstone had once been beautiful but now it needed a lot of work. There were three bedrooms and a decent-sized bath upstairs and a kitchen, dining room, living room and study/den on the main floor. There was a pokey basement and an attic with a full set of stairs but it was unfinished and boiling hot.

"There's no central air, you'll have to install duct work throughout. This staircase is gorgeous." Jacqueline moved through the house in her own world, talking to whoever was near enough to hear her, even if it was just herself.

"What is this place?" Kate asked Will as soon as she could get him on his own in a corner of the dining room.

"I got Evelyn to look up a few listings to keep Jackie busy. Trust me, it's much better for her to spend her energy here than at our flat."

"You'd buy a brownstone just to keep your sister out of your hair for a few days?! Just tell her no!"

"So what do we think?" the realtor interrupted before William could respond.

"We'd like to see a few more this afternoon. Maybe an apartment or even a small building." Harper answered.

Kate looked at him wide-eyed but he kept his gaze trained to the over-zealous realtor.

"My wife is available tomorrow if you want to look further, maybe something in Brooklyn."

The realtor quickly agreed and began making calls and checking listings on his tablet.

"Will!" Kate hissed. "What on earth are you doing?"

"What? I told you this will keep Jacqueline busy, and more importantly, out of our flat. If you don't find anything, you spent a few hours looking at property," he reasoned.

"And if I do find something?"

"Buy it." He shrugged. "I told you you should start building your investment portfolio. Property is great for retirement planning – especially at your age. By the time you retire it should have gone up significantly in value and the rents will bring in a nice monthly allowance."

"You're serious, aren't you?"

"What? Why wouldn't I be?"

She raised a brow. "I could think of a few reasons. And one glaring one."

"We'll work out the details later, Kate. It'll be alright."

She shook her head and went to look at the house more closely. She knew absolutely nothing about renovation but if she was going to be pretending to be into it for the next few days, she should get started.

The brownstone really did have a lot of potential, she decided. There was a large bay window in the kitchen that she could imagine putting a window seat in and another in the living room overlooking the street. There was a terrace in the back, though no real yard. The basement ceiling was low and would probably never be anything other than storage, but that was at a premium in New York, so she considered it an asset. The attic could possibly be turned into something. *I can't believe I'm actually considering this.*

"What do you think, Katherine?" Jacqueline asked.

"I haven't made up my mind yet."

"It certainly has plenty of potential, and the neighborhood is good. Would you want to sell it or let it out?"

"We haven't decided that yet, Jackie," William interjected. "There's a flat a few blocks over. Shall we?"

Jacqueline nodded and led the way out the door, clearly satisfied and in her element.

"Isn't she tired or jetlagged or something?" Kate whispered to Will.

"Bottomless. Pit," he whispered back dramatically.

Kate stifled a laugh and got into the car, determined to enjoy this for what it was: A grown man running scared from his baby sister.

**

Friday was spent much as Thursday had been, but instead of looking at property all afternoon, they looked all day. Katherine learned to handle Jacqueline relatively quickly, but she still found herself being steamrolled when she let her guard down. Jacqueline wasn't bad, not really. She was polite and even kind sometimes, like when suggesting a wall be removed and a header put in to support the ceiling, then patiently explaining what a header was. Katherine was thoroughly impressed with her knowledge of building structure and wondered if she'd gone to school for architecture. But she wasn't very warm, and she was still a Harper who clearly enjoyed getting her own way. By three o'clock, Katherine was exhausted from standing her ground and suggested they head back to prepare for the family dinner that evening.

The remainder of Harper's family had flown in from England and Texas earlier that day or the night before. They were resting at their hotels and apartments and would all meet up for dinner at eight. Katherine was beyond nervous. She had agonized over what to wear and in a fit of desperation, hired a personal shopper at Saks. The end result was classy and refined but still modern. Her navy dress was modest enough with a boat neck and full knee-length skirt, but still youthful with a belted waist and sleeveless bodice. She wore simple make-up, but the navy made her green eyes stand out and her skin look creamy.

"You look great. You ready?" Harper asked as he stepped into the hall and shrugged on his suit coat.

"Yeah, I think so. Do you think I'll need a sweater?"

"No, my aunt usually keeps the house warm."

She nodded and followed him silently out the door, down the elevator, and into the car that was driving them to his family's home on the Upper East Side. She silently reviewed the names he'd given her. Jacqueline and Albert she'd met the day before, and she'd spent the entire day property shopping with Jacqueline. While they weren't great friends, she at least felt some level of comfort around her husband's sister. Albert was alright and just like Will had described him: intelligent but lazy, a dreamer who lacked vision, a trust fund baby who liked a comfortable life and couldn't be bothered with talking to those of lesser intelligence or income. He was quiet but occasionally made extremely witty observations, and Kate thought she could come to like him well enough and enjoy his conversation, but respecting him would be a little harder.

Now they were headed to Alistair and Julia's townhouse. Several extended family members would be there and her head was spinning as she tried to remember everyone's names. Will didn't have any pictures of anyone; he'd told her all the albums were at the family apartment and it was locked up and under sheets. Kate decided digging through it all just so she could put a name with an old photo seemed like too much trouble and an unnecessary invasion of William and Jacqueline's privacy.

"Here we are," Will said. She looked out the window at the opulent building and took a deep breath. "Ready?"

"Ready as I'll ever be."

"You'll be fine. It's just one dinner. And Calvin's always a safe port in a storm if you need one."

"Thanks."

The door was opened by a butler in a dark suit and Kate's anxiety immediately went up a few notches.

"Is that Harper?" boomed a man's deep voice.

"Yes, Uncle, we're here."

They stepped into a living room decorated to the hilt in creams and pale peaches, where soft classical musical played in the background, accented by the tinkle of crystal. Katherine quickly took in the room full of people. The men were in light dress pants and sport coats, no ties, while the women were in soft pastel dresses in flowy fabrics, daintily perched on the edges of pale sofas and chairs like aristocratic birds on high wires. Kate looked down at her navy dress and sighed internally. *Strike one, Katie. At least it's chiffon*, she thought.

Alistair Covington was a few inches shorter than William, though most men were, with thinning grey hair cropped close to his head. He looked to be in his early sixties and was deeply tanned with bright blue eyes, similar to William's in color but without her husband's long lashes. Kate thought he was still a handsome man and he seemed pleasant enough. So far.

Julia Covington had obviously been a beautiful woman in her younger years. At sixty-one, she still turned heads, albeit with the help of a skilled surgeon. She had a long, lean frame with a slender waist shown off by a narrow pink belt. Her dress was cream-colored sleeveless chiffon, showing off her toned arms. Two-inch heels displayed the thinnest ankles Katherine had ever seen. This woman was clearly no stranger to the gym. Kate surreptitiously felt her own upper arms and squeezed

Will's hand a little tighter.

"Aunt Julia, Uncle Alistair, this is my wife, Katherine. Katherine, my aunt and uncle." Harper performed the introductions with confidence and restraint, his accent more pronounced than it usually was, his back straight but not stiff.

Katherine said hello and thanked them for hosting this evening and for coming such a long way for their reception.

"Nice to meet you, Katherine," Alistair said. His voice was medium pitch and didn't sound hostile, but neither was it welcoming.

"Yes, it's nice to finally meet you," added Julia. "Come meet the family."

She took Katherine's arm and began to lead her away. Katherine smiled and followed, Will giving her hand an encouraging squeeze just before she let go. Julia began the introductions.

"Jacqueline you know, and her husband Albert DeWitt." The couple nodded and Julia continued around the room. "This is my eldest son Theodore and his wife Caroline." Theodore shook her hand, smiled politely and said it was nice to meet her. Caroline attempted to get up from the chair she was perched on, but struggled in her heavily pregnant state.

"Oh, please, don't get up!" Katherine gestured to Caroline and smiled. "When are you due?"

"Seven more weeks, or so they tell me!" Caroline smiled warmly and rubbed her belly. She had warm caramel eyes and honey colored hair, with cheeks flushed from the heat only she was feeling. "It's so nice to meet you, Katherine. If the reception had been any later in the summer, I don't think I could have made it."

"We appreciate you making the effort to come," Katherine said. "It can't be easy to travel this late in your pregnancy."

Caroline smiled and looked like she'd say more, but Julia took Katherine by the arm and led her to the next guest.

"This is my daughter Cecelia and her husband Robert Hayes."

Cecelia was bubbly and sweet with wide blue eyes and a

creamy complexion, her hair a golden halo of soft curls. Altogether, she reminded Katherine of a glass of champagne. She immediately insisted Katherine call her Cece because Cecelia was such a mouthful. Her husband only nodded and said it was nice to meet her. After the introduction, Cece settled next to Caroline and Katherine thought she might be able to be friends with the two of them eventually.

Julia continued with her parade around the room. Katherine met three cousins of Harper's mother and their husbands. The three sisters, Amelia (called Amy by close relations), Eloise, and Edith, ranged in age from fifty-five to sixty-five and each had the same sky-blue eyes half the room seemed to possess. They congratulated Katherine and welcomed her to the family while speaking over each other constantly and introduced their husbands before Julia had a chance to, though they weren't clear about which man went with which sister, and Katherine left them not knowing whether Eloise was married to Edward, George, or Anthony.

Next was a small cluster of brunettes, a clear minority in this room, obviously discussing business. Julia authoritatively interrupted and introduced Katherine, who was surprised to hear an American accent speaking back to her.

"It's a pleasure to meet you, Katherine. We need more Americans in the family!" laughed one of the young men.

"You're only half American, Benjamin," Julia said exasperatedly.

The easy-going young man smiled at Katherine and winked, then added, "I have to apologize for my sister Annabelle. She wanted to be here, but she's due any day now and we were all too nervous to let her travel."

"Of course. William told me she was expecting her first child. Please tell her we understand completely and wish her a safe delivery."

"I will. Have you met my brother Jake?" He gestured to a man of about thirty-five on his right. They were both roughly six feet tall with dark Harper hair and big Texas smiles. Jake smiled and shook her hand, then introduced her to his wife Joanna who suddenly appeared at his side, a lovely woman with dark red hair styled in large rolling curls and an even bigger smile. Her drawl, while not very Virginian, was comforting to Katherine who, after living in New York for five years, welcomed any kind of accent that originated south of the Mason-Dixon line.

Jake in turn introduced her to his younger sisters Margaret, whom everyone called Maggie, and Dorothy, whom everyone called Molly for some unfathomable reason. Maggie was there with her husband Michael (also red-haired and a cousin to Joanna), and Molly was single without any desire to change that any time soon. Katherine liked them, though they were a bit eccentric and clearly had more money than they knew what to do with.

Katherine tried to hold in her laughter at Julia's clear disapproval of these particular members of the family who weren't *actually* related to her. Rich they may have been, stylish they most certainly were, but Julia Montrose Covington, daughter of the Earl of Camden and wife of the Earl of Maeburn, found them a bit too *American* for her taste.

Julia nodded in what was a clear dismissal and led Katherine to the group their husbands were in. Harper quickly stepped next to Katherine and took over the introductions.

"This is Jonathon Greaves, my second cousin on my mother's side," Katherine smiled and the light-haired man returned it politely. "And this is my cousin I was telling you about: Calvin Covington."

Katherine shook Calvin's hand who then surprised her by leaning in and kissing her cheek, clearly enjoying the surprise his gesture had on everyone in their circle.

"Katherine, it's lovely to finally meet you. William has told me all about you."

Harper was about to interject when Katherine responded, "Don't worry, it can't possibly all be true."

Alistair laughed as did Calvin, and Julia smiled as much as her recent procedures would allow her.

"William, are any more of your Harper relatives coming for the reception?" asked Julia.

"Uncle John and Aunt Helen are coming up from

Houston in the morning, just for the weekend, and Aunt Rebecca and Sophie are coming from Edinburgh; they arrive late tonight. Everyone else is stuck in Scotland for the moment, I believe."

"Ah," responded Julia, who made it sound like an entire sentence. "Shall we eat?"

Dinner was unremarkable in the sense that nothing too embarrassing, interesting, or fantastic happened. However, it was terribly entertaining to Katherine who had to hide her smile more than once behind her napkin. Julia insisted on calling everyone by their full names, regardless of what they preferred. Thus Jake became Jacob, Maggie became Margaret, and Molly became Dorothy. After correcting her twice to no avail, Molly simply quit responding to Julia.

By the end of the night, Katherine learned that Jake was the typical eldest child of a large family: responsible, leader-like, and well-respected. Benjamin, or Ben as he preferred to be called, was carefree and charming, always on the lookout for the next pretty face and willing to flirt with anything in a skirt, a fact made clear when he slipped into conversation that "everything is bigger in Texas" with a suggestive look and a wink. She choked slightly on her chardonnay but recovered admirably.

Calvin was not too terribly different from Ben in essentials, but where Ben was charming in an open, relaxed, cowboy-esque sort of way, Calvin was blue-blooded through and through. Charming, but more distant, eloquent, but less familiar, easy, but less obvious. The two got along famously and were overheard making plans to go out after dinner, something Katherine was sure would be memorable for the ladies of New York. After all, how often did one meet an English aristocrat and a charming cowboy in the same night?

Maggie was mild and sweet and Molly was clearly the black sheep of the family. Joanna was nice but a little bit loud, like her hair, and Michael hardly spoke at all. The three sisters (as Katherine had come to think of Eloise, Amelia, and Edith) talked over each the entire night, never allowing another to get a word in, and Jonathon, William, and Alistair spent the entire evening discussing stocks and world economies. Cece was bubbly and endearing and listened patiently to Jacqueline's stories of renovation on her hotel while Albert occasionally chimed in a satirical word or two. Caroline looked like she was ready to go to sleep any moment, or pass out from the heat. Her husband Theodore was alternately solicitous and oblivious. Katherine came to the conclusion that he cared for his wife's comfort, but didn't really know what he ought to do.

While the Texas family seemed to like her – though Kate couldn't really be sure because she had a feeling they were like that with everyone – she got a decidedly cold vibe from several of the Covingtons. They were all polite and perfectly civil, but not overly kind or welcoming.

Theodore was in that category until the end of the evening. Katherine won him over when he left the main gathering and went into a small, out-of-the-way living room, looking for his wife, and found Katherine helping Caroline prop her rapidly swelling feet on a stool. She then carefully undid the straps of Caroline's shoes and placed them on the floor next to the chair. He watched as Katherine patiently poured her a glass of water, brought her a pillow for her aching back, and finally sat on the stool next to Caroline's poor water-logged ankles and began to stroke from her feet up towards her calves, helping to drain the water.

"Oh, Katherine, I know I shouldn't let you do this since we've only just met, but it feels so lovely I can't make myself ask you to stop!"

Katherine only laughed as Caroline leaned her head back and closed her eyes, clearly exhausted.

"Think nothing of it. My cousin Mary's feet used to get absolutely huge, especially in the summer. I'd do this for her and it always helped bring down the swelling."

"Thank your cousin Mary for me for teaching you such a wonderful technique. I think this is the first time I've felt truly relaxed since we arrived this morning."

Katherine smiled and Caroline practically purred, which only endeared her to Katherine more. She had been the most real and warm person the entire evening, and Katherine was grateful for her company and Caroline's obvious efforts to make her feel welcome in this new family.

"Would you like to have lunch tomorrow? There's a little café downtown I'd like to show you if you're available," Katherine asked impulsively.

"Won't you be preparing for the reception?" Caroline asked sleepily.

"It's not until eight and I've done all I can at this point."

"Well then, yes, I'd love to! Thank you for the invitation." Caroline smiled happily, clearly delighted with being asked. Katherine couldn't help but reciprocate.

"I'll pick you up here at noon. That should give us plenty of time to get back and dressed for the party. Now, we just need to teach that husband of yours how to do this and you'll be set!"

Caroline laughed with her and the next thing Katherine knew, there was a pair of large masculine hands on Caroline's other leg, mimicking Katherine's motions.

"Like this?" Theodore asked.

"Yes. Keep the pressure steady, but not too heavy." Katherine answered quietly. She felt a little self-conscious at her forward actions with someone who was a virtual stranger, but Theodore only looked at Caroline's lovely, tired face until his wife whispered, "Thank you, Teddy."

Katherine said goodnight and kissed Caroline's forehead, telling her she would see her the next day and left to find William and go home.

Harper was suitably impressed with Katherine's comportment that night. He hadn't been sure how she would do with his family. Katherine had said that her mother made them all take cotillion when they were younger, but he didn't really understand what it was beyond a manners class and besides, American and English manners were two entirely different things. But she had done well and in a strange way he was proud of her. This surprised him.

He was happy to see certain members of his family and less happy to see others. He didn't particularly like parties but could tolerate them when the company wasn't too tedious or the cause was worthy. In this case, it had been a necessity. Knowing himself as he did, William had decided to not openly display affection for Kate that night. Firstly, because his family didn't require it (and would likely look down on it), and secondly, because he knew it would exhaust him, as only large family gatherings combined with artificial behavior could, and he needed to be at his best the following night when people who weren't related to him would come sniffing for a juicy bit of gossip.

He hadn't thought too much about how Katherine would handle the evening, which he was slightly surprised by as he thought about it on their way home. He had told her who was who, but not much beyond that. In all honesty, he'd thought he couldn't lose. If she did well, the family would be happy for him – possibly – and understand why he did what he did and that would be the end of it. If she did badly, everyone would understand why they were divorcing two years down the line. He even went so far as to imagine how he would explain it. '*Our differences surfaced over the first year, we stuck it out a second because we had committed and wanted to try to make it work, but in the end, some rivers are just too broad to cross.*'

Now that it was over and Kate had been polite, charming, and completely un-embarrassing the entire evening, he found he was surprisingly glad of the outcome and wondered at his own feelings. Of course, what kind of man wants to see a woman he has brought into a situation, a woman whom he was growing to respect and like, fail and flounder? Not that he thought she would fail *spectacularly*. She'd held her own admirably so far and he wasn't afraid of anything glaring. But his family could be difficult, as he well knew, and they weren't all fond of Americans. Many of them were downright snobbish and he wouldn't have been surprised if they had been covertly rude. But they had behaved themselves, though they hadn't exactly been warm, but then they weren't always even warm to *him*, so he couldn't really complain there, and Katherine had been the picture of courtesy.

As they walked into the apartment, Kate put her handbag on the table and looked at Will.

"Well, what do you think? How'd I do?" she asked as she twisted her hands.

"You were amazing." He kissed the top of her head. "You won over the Harpers, that's for sure. And Calvin liked you."

"Really? How do you know? Did he say something?"

Will wasn't about to tell her that Calvin thought she had great legs and a bedroom smile and that his Texas cousins had heartily agreed. "He said you were charming. And Cece said you were very sweet."

"Oh! That's great! I liked her, too. Do you think I should have invited her to lunch tomorrow with me and Caroline?" she asked, suddenly worried.

"You're going to lunch with Caroline?"

"Yes, I told you in the car. Didn't you hear me?"

He hadn't. "Um, no, I don't think you have to invite her. I think she's spending the day with Jacqueline anyway. They haven't seen each other since Christmas."

"Okay, I won't worry about it, then." She smiled, clearly relieved. "Goodnight, Will." She reached up on her toes and kissed his cheek.

He kissed her forehead and went down the hall to his room, letting it click softly shut behind him as he released a deep breath, incredibly glad the evening of familial torture was over.

15
RECEPTION

June 8
Married 5 Weeks

Katherine had a lovely lunch with Caroline at The Southern Cross, eating her favorite foods and talking to her new friend. She found Caroline extremely likeable; kind, warm, and very funny. She laughed easily and could make Katherine laugh in turn, especially when she spoke of her misadventures through pregnancy.

"Who knew you lost all dignity! If I wet myself while sneezing one more time, I swear I will never have another baby!"

Katherine laughed until her sides hurt and Caroline invited her to her baby shower in London in July. Kate didn't think she would make it but told her she would try, and if she couldn't make it then, perhaps she could when the baby was born if it made an appearance after summer classes ended.

They took a short stroll around the neighborhood and popped into a boutique with adorable baby clothes where Caroline bought a white gown and a sweet pair or booties with yellow ribbons.

"Do you know the sex of the baby?" Katherine asked.

"No, we want it to be a surprise. Julia wanted us to find out, of course – she's anxious to know if there's a new heir – but I prefer not to know."

"Have you thought of any names?"

"I like Thomas, after my father, and Teddy likes Joseph for a boy. Of course Julia hates them both. She thinks we should call him Alistair after his grandfather or Theodore after his father, but Teddy isn't particularly fond of his name and doesn't even like me to call him that. I mostly call him darling or dear at home. Oh! Forgive me, I shouldn't speak of such things, we hardly know each other and here I am, airing my family business on a New York sidewalk! But pregnancy has made me more direct. It's as if I have no filter for my thoughts. And of course I feel like I've known you for ages! Perhaps we were boarding school chums in a past life!" She laughed lightly and Katherine smiled with her.

"What about girl names?"

"Those we have several of. Penelope, Isabelle, Charlotte, Rebecca, Diana. I think I want to see the baby first before I decide. It seems strange to name a person before you meet them, don't you think? What if she has blonde hair and we name her Isabelle? That would be ridiculous! Everyone knows Isabelle's should be brunettes!"

Katherine laughed and looped her arm with Caroline's. "You're a riot, you know that, Caroline?"

"Yes, so I've been told. An exhausted, enormous, hormonal riot!"

Kate squeezed her arm. "You must be getting tired. Shall we head back uptown?"

"Yes, let's. I can't wait to see the reception tonight! I haven't been to a party that Julia wasn't involved in for ages!" She giggled.

"You poor thing! Well, I hope you'll have a good time. What are you going to wear?"

"A tent! What else?"

Kate laughed out loud. "I'm so glad we got to spend time together today." *This is just what I needed.*

**

Kate and Will got ready separately and barely said a

word to each other as they prepared for the reception. Harper was nervous, planning what he would say, how he would act, what sort of touches would be appropriate and expected, what not to do, how to most effectively appear besotted. After nearly strangling himself with his tie, he decided to stop worrying about it and just continue as they'd been doing. Who cared what three-hundred influential people thought about him and his elopement? *Oh, God. Why did I agree to this?*

Katherine had her hair and makeup professionally done by a stylist trying to make a name for herself in New York. Kate sat on a stool in the kitchen and let her work her magic. They'd done a dry run the previous week, so Kate knew everything would work out. By the time she was ready to put her dress on, Harper was putting on his cuff links and the stylist was leaving. She slipped into her white Versace cocktail dress and carefully put on her earrings from her father and the necklace Harper had given her.

He'd suggested she wear something from the Harper vault, but it would have been a lot of trouble to retrieve them from England and have them cleaned and the settings checked. And what if she hadn't liked anything? In the end, she told him it was too short notice and when they visited after his green card came through, she'd look at the jewels then.

She dabbed perfume on her wrists and neck, slipped on her heels, and double checked her appearance in the mirror. *Here we go, Katie. It's all or nothing now.* She practiced her adoring smile in the mirror and stepped out to meet Will. He complimented her dress and she admired his suit. They were formal and awkward and walked stiffly to the car, neither saying anything until they arrived at the hotel.

They had opted out of black tie, wanting to give the event a less formal feel, but still, Kate knew the pressure would be on. She and Will had been calling each other pet names for weeks, trying various ones on and seeing what worked. They eventually settled on 'babe' for both of them. It was easy to remember and felt more natural than sweetheart – or worse, sweetie – and less forced than honey.

Andrew had briefed her in detail about who she should

be most careful of, and Will had told her everything he could remember about Alicia Winters, the woman causing them so much trouble with immigration. Steeling herself for a difficult evening, she walked into the ballroom on Will's arm with her head held high. The planner and Will's assistant quickly pulled her aside to go over a few last minute details, and within a half hour, guests were arriving.

The two of them stood at the door greeting the well-wishers, smiling broadly and acting the part of the lovesick newlyweds. All of William's family from the previous evening was there, plus four more who'd arrived that day. They were all perfectly coiffed and expensively dressed, wished her well and kissed her cheek while Will did the same for the ladies of the family. It was clear that whether or not they liked her or were skeptical about her, in public, especially in front of New York's most influential people, they would present a united front. Harpers and Covingtons did not air their private matters outside the home.

Theodore enthusiastically congratulated William and told him how lucky he was and that his wife was a gem, which clearly surprised William, especially when his non-demonstrative cousin kissed Kate on the cheek and pressed her hand affectionately. Caroline warmly hugged Katherine and kissed both her cheeks, telling her how great it had been getting to know her and repeated how much she'd enjoyed their lunch date earlier that day. Will was clearly confused by Katherine's success with this particular couple, whom he'd always found a little cold, and wondered if perhaps pregnancy had changed them.

Calvin and Benjamin swaggered through and asked Kate for suggestions on the women, which she playfully slapped their arms for and then directed them to her friend Angie across the room. Ben didn't seem interested, but she thought she saw a spark in the more buttoned-up Calvin. He looked like the type who would like a slightly wild girl. *Angie's going to looooove me!* Angie's longstanding preference for men with accents was well-known amongst her friends.

"Are all the women here Amazons?" Katherine

whispered aside to Will.

"What do you mean?" he asked between handshakes.

"They're all so tall! What is that?"

"They're not all tall," he replied with a glance at a petite woman just passing them.

"True, but all the ones you've dated before and most of the ones giving me the stink eye are stick figures on stilts!"

"I'm a tall man. Is it any wonder tall women are attracted to me?"

Kate paused in their conversation to say hello to Mr. Stevens – board member at Taggston and disappointingly monocle-free – and receive a kiss on her cheek and hearty well wishes. At a lull in the receiving line, she responded.

"Of course you only say they are attracted to you, neatly avoiding whom you are attracted to." She smiled at the next couple and shook the hand of one the VP's at HarperCo.

"What are you trying to say, Mrs. Harper?" He smiled as the mayor and his wife approached, shaking hands and kissing cheeks.

"Only that you seem to be a touch full of yourself, Mr. Harper." She said with a smile and a second later she was happily clasping hands with one of the female executives at Harper's company. As she passed by them, Kate added, "She's not one of them, is she?"

He looked at her incredulously. "What? Sarah? She works for me!"

Kate quirked a brow.

"You know I would never date someone from the office! Besides, I told you about everyone I was involved with who would be here. There shouldn't be any surprises."

"Famous last words," Kate said out of the side of her mouth before air kissing a socialite who'd gone a little heavy on the plastic surgery.

Forty-five minutes later, they were rubbing their jaws and stretching their necks in a small hall next to the ballroom.

"I've never smiled so much in my life. I can't feel my face!" Kate complained.

"At least you're used to smiling. My jaw is killing me,"

Will said as he rubbed the offending joint.

"That's what you get for being such a grump," she smirked and took his hand.

They entered the ballroom and a spotlight immediately shown on them as the bandleader announced their presence. Will smiled and held up their joined hands as he twirled Kate once under his arm. He quickly led her to the dance floor, and after a minute of dancing on their own, they were joined by a dozen other couples.

"Who knew you were such a smooth dancer, Mr. Harper?"

"Charm school. Teaches you everything you need to know," he said with a smile.

Kate laughed. "Is that so? What else did you learn?"

He quickly rolled her into his left arm, then dipped her back as she let out a small squeal.

"That will teach you to tease your husband, Mrs. Harper."

"Okay, okay, no more teasing. For now."

They danced the remainder of the song in peace, then Katherine was quickly asked to dance by Will's cousin Jake, followed by a member of the board at Taggston. Once the precedent was set, it seemed every man on the board, the presidents of other subsidiary companies she didn't even know about, and the executives at HarperCo wanted a piece of her, plus most of the men in Harper's family. After the tenth dance (and eight more promised), she was thankful that the band took a break and dinner was served. The bar was open and it was clearly time to get some food into everyone.

"Katie, it's absolutely gorgeous!" Jennifer gushed back at their table.

"Oh, thank you, Jenny! Are you having a good time?"

"Amazing! I love this band! How did you find them?"

"Will's assistant Evelyn recommended them. I told Will he'd better give her a hefty bonus for all the work she's done for this. This is above and beyond the call of duty."

"Will had better do what?" her husband asked, leaning away from his conversation with Andrew to interrupt Kate and

Jennifer.

"Give Evelyn a bonus," Kate answered.

"Don't worry. I've taken care of it. She'll have a lovely surprise waiting on her desk Monday morning."

"What is it?" asked Jennifer.

"A cruise." Jennifer gasped slightly and Katherine looked at him with surprise. "What? It's just a short one, five days in the Caribbean," he said with a shrug.

"Maybe I should become an assistant," Jen murmured to Kate. Kate hid her giggle behind her hand.

"That's very thoughtful, Will. I'm sure she'll love it. Her boyfriend has a birthday coming up next month, maybe they'll go then," Kate said.

"She has a boyfriend?" he asked, surprise evident in his features.

"Of course. She's young, smart, pretty, and apparently well employed. Why wouldn't she have a boyfriend?"

"I don't know, I guess I just never thought about it."

"So how's it going, Katie? Are you having a good time?" Andrew asked.

"I'm having a lovely time. I never sit out a dance and this food is delicious."

"Sorry about that," Harper said.

"You're sorry the food is good?"

"No, that you never sit out any dances. All the men will want to get to me through you. Be prepared for a lot of sucking up," he said as he took a sip of his wine.

Kate rolled her eyes slightly. "Are you saying that if I was just a guest, and not married to you, that no one would want to dance with me?"

Andrew made a face and leaned back, his hands across his stomach, and prepared to watch the show.

"Of course not, you're a very attractive woman. I'm just saying that it might be a little relentless and by the end of the night, your feet will be killing you."

"Attractive?"

"Yes, of course." He looked around at Andrew's amused face, Jen hiding a smile behind her napkin, and Kate looking like she could catch him on fire with her eyes. "What?"

"Nothing, dear. Nothing at all," Kate answered with a false smile, then turned to talk to her sister. *Jerk.*

Kate danced with several more men before excusing herself to escape to the ladies room. Walking into the plush lounge, she saw a familiar looking woman in a short silver dress at the mirror adding an unneeded coat of lipstick. She silently checked her hair and applied a fresh coat of color to her own lips.

"So, you're William's wife?" asked the blonde Amazon next to her. Suddenly Katherine remembered where she'd seen her. She was the one in the sparkly black mini dress from their first date at the theatre.

"Yes, Katherine Harper." She held out her hand but the woman looked at it like it was diseased. After a moment, Kate withdrew her hand and stepped into the stall, intent on ignoring the rude woman. As she was washing her hands, the woman appeared again.

"It'll never last, you know. Harper can't settle down. It's not in him."

"Well then, I'd better enjoy it while it lasts, shouldn't I? Excuse me." Katherine breezed past her and through the door, making a bee line for the ballroom.

She wasn't inside a minute before she was pulled onto the dance floor by one of Harper's college friends who insisted on telling her stories of their youthful drunken exploits. By the end of the dance, she was laughing so hard her sides were hurting and Harry Cavendish was one of her new favorite people. When he led her back to her table, he sat down in Will's chair and Kate immediately scanned the room for her husband.

"Looking for your errant lover? He's over there, dancing with the mantis, poor sod," he said.

"Who's the mantis?" Her eyes followed Harry's until she saw Will dancing with the shrewish woman from the restroom, an unhappy look on his face.

"Nicole Jamison, The Praying Mantis, or The Mantis as we like to call her. Eats men's heads when she's done with them, no doubt about it."

Kate laughed. “I know she's a bit...” She hesitated and Harry jumped in.

“Awful? Evil incarnate? Bride of Satan?”

Kate smacked his arm playfully. “I was going to say rude.”

“Of course you were.” He smirked. “Every man hates her, but we always have to dance with her because she's Andy's cousin, and everyone loves Andy. Besides, she probably has a chest filled with dolls she sticks with pins if you refuse her request.”

“I'll remember that if I have any unexplained pains.”

“You do that.”

“What are you two talking about?” asked Will as he placed his hands on Kate's shoulders and leaned over to kiss her cheek.

“Harry here has been telling me all about your wild college days.”

“Did he tell you about the time I had to bail him out of jail for urinating in a public fountain?”

She laughed. “No, he didn't.”

Harry turned red and took a sip of his drink. “Now Harper, that's not very gentlemanly of you.”

“That's not what you said when I hushed the whole thing up and snuck you back home before the papers found out.”

“Oh, are you like Will? One of England's most eligible bachelors?”

“Ha! He wishes. He's one of England's most eligible viscounts,” Will answered for him.

“Really?” Kate said eagerly.

“Thanks a lot, Harper,” Harry quipped. “You really know how to ruin a man's good time.”

“Aw, don't worry, Harry. I won't tell anyone you're nobility,” said Kate with a pat to his knee and a playful smile.

“And forty-fifth in line to the throne,” added Will. Harry glared at him.

“Oh, well aren't you important,” Kate teased.

“Haha, very funny, you two. I'm going to go dance.

There's a breathtaking blonde over there who is just dying to meet me." Harry stalked away with his nose in the air, leaving a laughing Will and Kate behind him.

"Do you think we should tell him that Jenny's my sister? Or that she's with Andy?"

"Nah, he'll find out soon enough," answered Will as he watched Harry strutting toward Jennifer where she stood next to the bar.

A slow song began and Will held out his hand to Kate. "Care to dance?"

"I'd love to."

They swayed along silently for a while, Kate's head resting on Will's shoulder, their bodies pressed closely together, Will's hand rubbing small circles on Kate's back. After smiling at a few guests who commented on how cute they were, Kate pulled her head back to look at her husband.

"I didn't know Harry was going to be here. Did he come over just for this, or was he already here?"

"Here, actually. He's in town for business and called me a few days ago to see if I wanted to grab a drink and I invited him tonight. I thought we could all go to dinner tomorrow night if you want."

"Sounds nice. Or we can have him over and I can cook. You two would have more privacy to tell your sordid stories that way."

"Thank you, Katie, that's kind of you. I'll ask him tonight if he's free."

"Are there any other surprises here tonight?"

"Not that I know of. I recognize most everyone except for your school friends, of course." Will leaned his head in the direction of three large tables that were filled with Kate's classmates from Columbia and NYU. "One of them is glaring at me."

Kate looked to the tables again. "I don't see anyone glaring. They're not even looking this way."

"Over there," Will gestured to the other side of the dance floor as the song was ending. "Did you two used to date or something?"

"No one I ever dated was invited, I can't imagine who – " Kate stopped mid-sentence as the crowd parted and she saw who Harper was looking at.

"Jeremy!" she breathed.

"Who's Jeremy?" Realization dawned. "Ex-boyfriend Jeremy?"

Kate nodded silently.

"He doesn't look too happy. Shall we say hello? Do you want me to ask him to leave?"

After another few moments of silence, Kate found her voice. "No, no that won't be necessary. Let's go say hello."

Will took her hand and led her across the floor until they were standing in front of the no longer glaring but still unhappy face of Jeremy. He looked at them calculatingly, his eyes resting on Kate long enough to make her uncomfortable.

"Hello, I'm William Harper. You must be a friend of Kate's," Will said as he extended his hand. The younger man shook it firmly.

"Jeremy Taylor. Yes, Kate and I are good friends. How are you, Katie?" he asked as he released Will's hand and turned his intent gaze to his ex-girlfriend.

"I'm great," she answered with a smile she didn't feel. "How are you, Jeremy? How's Phoenix?"

"It's great. No more rainy springs." He smiled and Will had to admit he was a handsome man. He was of medium build, tall, nearly as tall as Will himself, and he had a thick head of jet black hair that hung low over dark brown eyes. Will subconsciously stood a little straighter and pressed his shoulders back, glad that he had an inch or two over the other man.

Kate smiled in response, but before she could say anything, Jeremy asked her to dance. "That is if your husband here doesn't mind?" He tilted his head toward Harper while he kept his eyes on Kate.

"Of course not, I'd love to." Kate gave Will's hand a squeeze and followed Jeremy to the dance floor.

"Oh, you've done it now."

Will looked over his shoulder to see Harry sipping a

drink and watching Kate being pulled into Jeremy's arms.

"Done what?"

"Really, Harper, at your age, you ought to know how to hold on to your girl."

"What? They're just dancing! He's an old friend."

"Tell yourself that if it makes you feel better. He's clearly in love with her and hates you, and I've never seen Kate looking so uncomfortable."

"You just met her tonight!"

"Still... I'm just saying a little slow dancing of your own might not go amiss, that's all." Harry raised his glass, took one last drink, and left Will to observe his wife in private.

"What are you doing here, Jeremy?" a confused Kate asked.

"Aren't you glad to see me?" he teased.

She looked down. "Jeremy –"

"I know, that wasn't fair. Alright." He sighed. "I was in town for my sister's birthday and I met up with the old gang last night." He gestured to a table of Kate's friends from university. "They told me about tonight and I came with them."

She nodded, her head still slightly down, then she looked up and asked, "That explains how you knew about tonight, but not why you are here."

He smiled reluctantly, then nodded in agreement. "Well, I wanted to see you. Is that so shocking? I wanted to see how you were, if you were happy. I wanted to meet the guy who swept you off your feet so thoroughly that you married him just two months after we broke up." He tried to disguise the bitterness in his voice, but was not successful.

"Almost three months," Kate muttered under her breath. Louder she said, "You moved away to Phoenix. What was I supposed to do? Sit around pining for you? Do you expect me to believe you haven't moved on?" She struggled to keep her voice steady and at a normal volume to not draw attention.

His temper surged at her defensiveness. "No, I haven't! I haven't moved on, Katie! Okay! Is that what you wanted to hear?" he hissed.

Her gaze softened and she unconsciously squeezed her hand on his shoulder. He visibly relaxed at her touch and whispered, "I still miss you. I miss our talks. I miss reading the morning paper to you because you're too groggy to see straight. I miss the way you snuggle up to me in your sleep when it's cold. I miss the smell of your hair. God, Katie! How could I move on?"

Just then, the music stopped and everyone applauded the band. Kate clapped belatedly, then woodenly marched out a small side door into the narrow hall where she and Will had taken a breather after the receiving line. Had that only been a few hours ago?

She leaned on the wall for a minute, then looked up to see that Jeremy had followed her.

"Katie, I'm sorry. I shouldn't have said that. This is not the right time, and absolutely the wrong place."

"This is my reception, Jeremy."

"I know that."

"To celebrate my *marriage*!"

"I know," he said as he dropped his head to stare at the carpet.

"You can't just show up here and act like nothing's changed! EVERYTHING's changed!"

"I know."

Kate paced back and forth, her agitation evident.

"Is everything alright out here?"

Kate stopped and spun around when she heard Will's voice. She quickly strode to his side and ducked under his arm, wrapping her arms around his waist and leaning into his side. He reflexively pulled her closer and gave Jeremy a serious look.

"And you, Mr. Taylor? Everything all right?"

"Fine, thank you," Jeremy bit out.

"Jeremy just came to say goodbye. Isn't that right, Jeremy?"

He looked at Kate for a moment, his expression slightly tortured, then answered, "Yeah, that's right. Goodbye, Katie. Best wishes for a happy life. Harper," he said as he walked past.

The two men nodded at each other, and then he was gone.

"You okay?" Will asked gently.

"Yeah, yeah, I'm fine." She took a shaky breath. "Just surprised to see him, that's all."

She smiled weakly and Will began to lead her back to the ballroom. "Just another half hour and we can politely leave," he whispered in her ear. She looked relieved and pushed her discomfort aside until she was alone to unpack it at leisure.

**

They walked into the apartment without saying a word. Kate hung up her wrap and Harper put his keys in the dish by the door. She got a glass of water from the kitchen and made her way to her room, calling goodnight to Will on her way. He was so exhausted he barely mumbled a reply, then fell into bed and was fast asleep before he even took his socks off.

Kate took off her shoes and dress, unpinned her hair, and stepped into a hot shower. As she lathered up the shampoo, Jeremy's words ran through her mind. Did he really remember the smell of her hair? He had always been a little romantic, and she had always liked that about him. Now in the safety of her own room, she let the hot tears fall and the feelings of loss, guilt, and sadness come to the surface. After half an hour of cry therapy and strolling down memory lane, she toweled off, slipped into soft pajamas, and crawled into bed.

Her hair was cold where it lay wet across her pillow and memories of snuggling under the covers on winter nights came unbidden to her mind. She remembered the first time she had spent the night with Jeremy. A friend's father had a big cabin in the Berkshires and a group of friends from NYU went for the weekend right after midterms. There were four people present who weren't paired up: Kate, Jeremy, and their friends Carrie and Melissa. The latter took the room with two single beds, and rather than one of them sleeping on the couch in the drafty living room, she and Jeremy decided to share the queen size bed in the last guest room.

They stayed up late talking and discovered that each of

them had been secretly crushing on the other for a few weeks. Talking led to kissing and kissing led to cuddling and by the morning, they were officially a couple. Two weeks later he slept over for the first time and they started spending every spare moment together. And so it had gone for the next year, four months and two days – not that she was counting – until he accepted a job offer in Phoenix and she refused to drop out to move with him.

She remembered it like it was yesterday. It was Valentine's Day. He made her dinner, steak with roasted potatoes, the only thing he knew how to make. There were roses on the table and chocolates on the counter. He'd changed his sheets and vacuumed the rug in his tiny studio apartment. He was going to tell her that night. Tell her that the trip he'd taken at the end of January wasn't just to visit family. It was to interview for a job. A very good job. He'd had two phone interviews and then they'd wanted to meet him in person. So he'd packed his only suit and gone to Phoenix. Ten days later, they'd called. They wanted him. The job started next week and he'd given his landlord notice. He was moving to Phoenix and he wanted Kate to go with him. The ring was burning a hole in his pocket and his hands were sweating.

Kate arrived at his apartment looking gorgeous in a red dress and heels. She'd made him a frame out of candy hearts filled with little messages like "Be mine" and "True Love". Inside was a photo of the two of them at a New Year's Eve party, her in a sparkly dress with a crown, him in a leather jacket and a smile so big you could see his molars. It was his favorite picture of them, he'd said. Joy in a frame, she'd called it.

After supper, Jeremy nervously explained to her about the job interview and how he hadn't wanted to tell anyone and jinx it. She understood like he knew she would, and when he finally got around to the offer they'd made him, she congratulated him and asked him what he thought about it. He looked at her in confusion and asked what she meant, and she explained that she was asking him if he wanted to take it. What were the pros and cons of moving? What about his family in

Queens? Did he think he could handle the climate? It was with shock and disappointment that she found out he'd already accepted the job, without discussing it with her, without involving her in the decision in any way.

She sat there, staring at the wall, finally noticing the stack of broken down boxes in the corner.

"When do you leave?" she asked.

"Saturday."

Saturday. Six days away. Six days and the man she thought she'd love forever, the one she thought would father her children, was leaving her and moving across the country. And he hadn't even discussed it with her.

"Kate? Katie, say something. You're scaring me," Jeremy said.

She just looked at him, eyes wide, mouth dry, and said, "Six days."

Jeremy knelt before her and held her hand, disturbed by how cold it felt. "Katie. Katie baby, you'll come with me, won't you? We'll make Phoenix home. You and me. We'll find a little house and get a dog and you can finally have a real kitchen, one with a stove and lots of cabinets, just like you've always wanted. We'll be happy there, I know it."

"You want me to come with you?" She was filled with hope for a moment, until she realized that expecting her to go with him without even talking to her about it seemed just as bad as leaving her behind.

"Of course. You didn't think I'd go all the way to Arizona without my girl, did you?" He smiled that charming smile of his and stroked her cheek softly, his eyes looking into hers. "Kate, you're the love of my life. I need you. Come with me. Please."

He pulled out the ring box and opened it in front of her, a half carat diamond sparkling in the candlelight.

"Marry me, Katie."

She gasped and covered her mouth. "What?" she asked shakily. It was too much. The high of Valentine's with the man she loved, the fear of being left, the realization that she was basically luggage to him, and now this.

Suddenly her mind was spinning. Jeremy was saying something, but she didn't know what. He actually expected her to quit Columbia, to give up everything she'd worked for and blindly follow him into an actual desert. Who was he? How could he possibly think she would agree to that? How could he make that decision for her? For them?

She stood and grabbed her coat and bag, shakily telling him that she would have to think about it and that she would call him tomorrow. No, she didn't want him to call her a cab or walk her home. She was fine to walk, it wasn't far. She kissed his pale lips, distractedly told him she loved him, and ran out the door.

The next day, she asked him if he had just asked her to marry him because he was moving or if he really wanted to marry her. He said of course he wanted to marry her, he loved her and they were perfect together.

She said she wasn't ready. She was too young to get married. He apologized for rushing her and said they could just move in together if she preferred. He just wanted her with him.

She told him she couldn't just quit her education in the middle and that she wished he'd talked to her before he'd made such a big decision, especially if he wanted her in his life long term. He got angry and asked what that was supposed to mean and she said that it wasn't 1955 and he couldn't just expect her to pick up and follow him wherever he went. She liked her school, she had friends and a life in New York, and she wasn't ready to leave. They agreed to take a break to cool down and talk in the morning.

The next conversation went as expected. She wasn't ready to move or get married, she didn't want to drop out of her masters program, and she *really* didn't like how he'd made such a big decision without her and was afraid of what it boded for the future. He said she must not love him enough and it was best they found out now that they weren't right for each other before it was too late. She could tell he was hurt, angry, and more than a little bitter, but she stood her ground. Two days after Valentine's Day, her fairytale romance was over.

Katherine Taylor! How ridiculous would that have been? Kate forcefully pushed the memories away before she could cry again and hugged her pillow tight. Jeremy was in her past. It was time to look to the future.

16
GINGERBREAD MEN

June 9
Married 6 Weeks

The next morning, Will stood at the counter in the kitchen watching the coffee pot gurgle. He was groggy and still half asleep, but he had annoyingly woken up at his usual time and he was too hungry to go back to sleep but too tired to make himself any breakfast. So he stared at the pot as the brown liquid trickled into it, drop by precious drop.

Finally, he poured himself a cup and added a touch of cream and then sat at the counter to drink it. Halfway through his cup, he was able to think enough to grab a yogurt out of the fridge and put a slice of bread in the shiny new toaster. He ate slowly, looking through to the dining room piled high with gifts that had been arriving steadily for the last week. Seeing the elegantly wrapped presents made him think of the reception which made him think of Kate, which of course led him to the uncomfortable encounter with Jeremy.

He couldn't believe the nerve of the guy to show up at his ex's wedding reception. Who did that? At least he hadn't made a scene. Will hated scenes.

He hoped Kate was alright. She looked a bit shaken after her encounter with the lout and she had been visibly subdued the rest of the evening. To everyone else, she probably just looked tired. It was well after midnight, after all. It was nearly two by the time they got home. He'd thought about asking her if she wanted to talk, but they had never really had a personal conversation – at least one that didn't pertain to business, anyway – and he didn't really know what to say to her.

About an hour after he'd fallen asleep, he woke up to answer nature's call, then went to the kitchen for a glass of water. As he passed her door, he heard what sounded like muffled sobs, but he didn't want to intrude. He stood silently in the hall, feeling like a right idiot and hating his sense of helplessness before he went back to his own bed. The only other girl he'd ever consoled was his college girlfriend after her twelve-year-old dog had died. Besides that, his experience with comforting women in distress was pretty limited. So he left her alone and decided not to say anything unless she did. If she wanted to talk, he would be open to listen. It was too early in the morning to come up with a more elaborate plan than that.

He wasn't surprised when Kate emerged an hour later looking bleary and a little red around the eyes. He offered her a piece of toast and she nodded acceptance while she turned on the kettle to make her usual cup of tea. She sat on the stool and ate in silence while Will read the paper two stools down. After about fifteen minutes, she put her plate in the dishwasher and said she was going for a run.

An hour later, Will emerged from his room freshly showered and shaved and found Kate in the kitchen, still in her running clothes and half covered in flour, rolling out dough on the countertop, Alanis Morissette blaring angrily from the iPod dock beside the stove.

"Cooking?" he asked carefully.

"Baking." She looked up when she heard his voice and saw the understanding in his eyes. She knew she didn't have to pretend to not be bothered by last night's run-in with Jeremy. "It's cathartic."

Will nodded and looked around, his hands in his pockets. "Need any help?"

She looked at him in surprise, then said, "Sure, if you're up for it."

"I don't know much, but I know how to follow directions."

She half-smiled. "A valuable quality in a kitchen assistant. Grab an apron over there," she gestured to the hook on the wall, "and then get the oatmeal out of the pantry."

Will nodded and did as he was told, just a little pleased with himself that he'd been able to make her smile.

He slipped the red apron over his head and tied the strings around his waist. "What do you want me to do?"

"Well, these are sugar cookies," she gestured to the rolled-out dough on the counter. "All that's left to do here is cut them out and start baking. I also wanted to make oatmeal chocolate chip cookies. You can go ahead and start on those. You'll need two mixing bowls. They're in that cabinet over there."

As he reached for the bowls, he asked, "Why are you making two kinds of cookies?"

"Because oatmeal chocolate chip are my favorite and I like to decorate sugar cookies, but I don't really like to eat them."

"Ah, another Kate-ism."

"A what?"

He smiled self-consciously. "A Kate-ism. It's what I call all the strange little details about you."

"You think I'm strange?"

"No!" he said quickly. "Just that you have a few, I don't know… quirks."

"So I'm quirky?"

"Is that a bad thing?" he asked carefully.

She smiled. "You're adorable when you're flustered." He grinned slightly and rubbed the back of his neck, obviously still uncomfortable. "Don't worry, Will, I'm not offended. I don't mind that you think I'm quirky."

"You don't?"

"No. Unless you mean it a bad way…" she qualified.

"No, I don't. Not at all. It's… cute," he said after searching for the word.

She smiled and changed the subject. "Go ahead and put one and a half cups of flour in that bowl."

He began adding ingredients as she dictated them while she finished cutting out the first batch of sugar cookies, all shaped like stars, and put them in the oven. When he had thoroughly mixed all the dry ingredients, she turned to him with two metal cookie cutters in her hands.

"Hearts or gingerbread men?" she asked.

He looked at the cutters, then at her awkward expression as she glanced at the heart, clearly regretting offering that one.

"Gingerbread men. Do we have to decorate them like Christmas, though? It's June."

"Jenny and I like to decorate them like our friends." He raised an eyebrow in question. "Like Laura wears black suits, so her cookie always looks very serious. Andrew wears brightly colored ties, so we could do one like him."

"I see. Jennifer likes light colored dresses…" he suggested.

"I call hers pastel Barbie." He laughed outright. "Why don't you cut these out while I mix the wet ingredients over here?"

Will nodded and set to work. In a few minutes, he had cut out six gingerbread men and put them on the pan. He then balled up the remaining dough as he had seen Kate do a few minutes before. He picked up the rolling pin and moved it from hand to hand, feeling the weight of it and trying to think of the best way to use this new contraption. Kate saw him out of the corner of her eye but didn't say anything. When he barely caught the rolling pin before it fell to the floor, she bit her cheek to keep from laughing.

After a few minutes, Will had managed to roll out the last of the dough and eek out two more gingerbread men. As he put the last one on the pan, he was ridiculously proud of himself.

"These are ready to go."

"Great. Go ahead and slide them into the oven. It's still hot."

He did as he was told, then watched as she dumped in a large cup of chocolate chips and stirred them into her bowl.

Then she began scooping up the dough and putting it onto a large stone cookie pan.

"Do you want to do some?" she asked.

"Sure."

"Try to make each one the same size. They cook more evenly that way."

He nodded and continued scooping until the tray was full and Kate put it into the oven where the freshly removed sugar cookies had been.

"These guys look great!" she exclaimed as she placed the tray on the marble top of the island. She looked up at Will with shining eyes, then almost burst out laughing.

"What? What's so funny?"

"You have flour on your face."

"I do?"

"Right there." She pointed at his face, which of course told him nothing.

He wiped over his cheeks and she laughed more.

"Here, let me help you." She walked toward him with a towel and reached up to swipe it across his nose. "There. All better."

He grabbed her wrist where it was hovering in between them. "You have flour on you, too."

He took the towel from her hand and gently wiped along her hairline.

"I always get it there. My hair falls in my eyes and then I try to brush it away…" she stammered quietly, unnerved by his sudden closeness.

"There. All better," he said softly, his voice suddenly deeper and his eyes a little darker.

"Thank you." She swallowed. "We should put these on the cooling rack."

He looked at her without comprehending for a moment, then answered, "Right. How do we do that?"

He really was so adorably clueless. "We use that spatula right there." She pointed. "And just slide them onto this wire rack." She stepped away from him and set the rack next to the hot pan. "Once they're cool, we can decorate them. We should go ahead and make the frosting."

He carefully removed the cookies with the spatula and placed them on the rack, then turned to where Katie was using an electric mixer on fluffy white icing. She doled it out evenly into several smaller bowls. "Now we just add coloring to these bowls and everything will be ready."

Will was stirring a bowl of blue icing when Katie asked, "Do you like dough?"

"What do you mean?"

"Cookie dough. Do you like it?"

"Um, I guess. That's how you get cookies."

"No, silly. I mean to eat by itself." He looked at her strangely. "Here, try some." She gave him a spoon filled with chocolate oatmeal dough. He took a tiny bite and chewed it slowly. "Good?"

"Wow. That is good." He finished off his spoonful and dipped it back into the bowl for more.

"Just don't eat too much or you'll be sick," Kate cautioned.

The timer went off and she removed the first batch of chocolate chip cookies from the oven.

"Those smell great!" Will said with hungry eyes as he looked over her shoulder.

"Want to have hot cookies with milk?"

"Love to. Care to eat them while opening a few gifts?" he asked with a nod to the dining room and its brightly wrapped contents.

"Sounds good. You pour the milk and I'll get the next batch going," she suggested as she quickly scooped the cookies up and put them on a cooling rack. She began spooning out dough for the next batch while Will poured two frothy glasses of milk and carried them to the dining room. Just as Kate was sliding the tray into the oven, he plopped a half dozen warm cookies onto a small plate and led the way to the table.

"What should we open first?" she asked as she took a bite. "Mmm. Nothing beats homemade cookies."

"Let's open the biggest ones first. That's what I always did when I was a kid." He popped an entire cookie into his mouth at once and reached for a big box wrapped in shiny silver paper.

They tore into the paper and Kate let out a squeal of delight. "What is it?" asked Will.

"It's a dehydrator. We can dry our own fruit!"

Will wrinkled his nose in distaste and reached for the next box. An hour later, they'd made four batches of cookies, eaten ten between them, and opened nearly thirty gifts.

"It looks like we haven't even opened any," Kate said as she stared at the piles around the room and the gift-covered table.

"Want to have a little race?" Will asked as he tossed Kate's egg timer from hand to hand.

"What kind of race?" she asked suspiciously.

"We set the timer and see who can open the most presents."

"What does the winner get?"

"Loser has to clean the cookie dishes."

With a quick glance at the kitchen counters covered in flour and the sink filled with mixing bowls, she agreed. "We have to clean the whole kitchen, though. Not just the dishes."

"Deal."

Will set the timer and said 'go', and they were off. Wrapping paper was flying and bows sailed through the air. Kate cursed over a paper cut and Harper mumbled about not being able to find the seam in the paper. After the timer went off, the dining room was in shambles and they were each sitting next to a pile of opened gifts.

"How many did you get?" Will asked as he counted his presents.

"Twelve. You?"

"Damn. Eleven."

Kate laughed softly as Will trudged dramatically to the kitchen and turned on the sink, sighing loudly. He gave her a small grin as he began soaping up a bowl. She decided to clean up the dining room and got up to grab a trash bag. She picked up all the wrapping paper and stuffed it in, then looked around to make sure she hadn't missed any. Will's pile of gifts looked interesting and she began looking through them to see what they had gotten.

"This looks like more than eleven," she mumbled to herself. She counted and gasped. "Fifteen!"

She looked into the kitchen where Will was wiping flour into a trash can and humming a song she didn't know.

"He let me win," she whispered. A small smile worked its way onto her lips and she felt the urge to cry just a teeny bit. *That was so sweet. He knew I was sad and he let me win.*

She walked behind Will and put her arms around his waist, burying her face in his back and hugging him tightly.

He put a hand over hers on his belly. "Hey, you okay?" he asked gently.

"Yeah, I'm good. Thanks for cheering me up, Will."

"You're welcome."

He turned around and she smiled at him. She reached up on her tiptoes and gave him a peck on his cheek. "I'm going to go take a shower." And she walked out of the room with a new lightness in her step.

Will smiled broadly, though he didn't realize it, and finished cleaning up.

**

Harry picked up a cookie off the plate in front of him and looked at it strangely.

"That one's Andy," Kate said as she sat next to him.

"Andy?"

"Yeah. We decorated them like the people we know. This one in the white dress is me, and the blue suit is Will." She pointed to the cookies as she talked. "See?"

Harry laughed. "Don't tell me anymore, I want to guess. This one," he pointed to one with a soft pink dress with little yellow flowers on it, "is your sister Jennifer, who goes with Andrew, the lucky sod."

Katherine laughed as he bit off the head to cookie Andrew. "Yes, that's Jenny."

"This sparkly little dress must be the mantis," he said, holding up a cookie wearing a glittery black tube dress.

"Yes. Very good."

"And this dapper fellow with the excellent sense of style – who could he be?" He pointed to a cookie in a three piece suit with a full head of hair.

"That was Will's idea. He thought you'd appreciate it."

Harry chuckled. "Sounds like him. I can't believe you actually got Harper to decorate cookies with you." He raised a brow skeptically.

"Oh, he did. In fact, he did Nicole's all by himself."

"Darling, you must be amazing in bed if you got the stern William Harper to play kitchen with you."

Kate blushed and looked down for a minute to hide her smile. "Now Harry, quit blowing smoke and eat your cookie." She rumpled his hair and got up to get Will while Harry finished off eating poor Andrew with a little too much gusto.

17
FEEL THE BURN

Early July
2 Months Married

Harper opened the door to the apartment and set his bag on the floor. He loosened his tie and headed to the kitchen to grab a beer. On his way, he heard music coming out of the living room. This wasn't unusual in and of itself. However, what was unusual was the grunting he also heard. He stopped for a moment, then his eyebrows shot up to his hairline when he heard, in what was clearly Kate's voice, a loud groan that morphed into a sort of yelling whine.

A dark look on his face, he quickly stalked toward the living room. If there was another man in his house, he'd throw him out on his backside. Then he'd have a thing or two to say to Kate about contracts and abiding by an agreement.

In one loud move, he threw the door open and stormed into the room.

"Oh, hey, Will. You're home early. Would you do me a favor and turn on the fan?"

He just stood there, looking at Kate where she was on the floor on all fours, one leg extended behind her that she was moving in a semi-circle. Over to her right, touch the ground, back up as high as it could go and all the way to her left, touch the ground, then back up to center and to her right again. He watched her dumbly as her leg arced gracefully, her back sweaty and her thighs trembling slightly from her exertion. She was wearing a black pair of calf-length leggings and a pink sports bra, and that was it. He couldn't keep his eyes away from her bum, which was flexing tightly with the movement. Had it always been that round?

"Will?"

"Yeah?"

"The fan?"

"Oh, sorry."

He flipped the switch and she called out a quiet thank you. Several more minutes passed with him just standing there as she watched the movement of the people on the television screen, the TV muted while her iPod blared from the speaker on the console.

"Are you enjoying the show?"

Will started. "Huh? What did you say?"

Kate laughed. "It's okay, you can make fun if you want to."

"Make fun?"

"Of my video. It's the *Brazil Butt Lift*. I know it's weird, but it really works."

"Why are you doing a butt video?"

"Because *someone* has been taking me out for high-calorie, fattening dinners! All those carbs go straight to my butt. My jeans were feeling a little tight so I borrowed this from Laura." She walked over to stand in front of him. "See," she turned her back to him and looked over her shoulder, "it's already working and it's only been two weeks! This part right here," she ran her hand along the top of her bum, "is already higher and when you touch it, it's much firmer. It's not scary hard or anything, but you can feel the muscle under there. Feel." She grabbed his hand and placed it at the top of the swell of her bottom.

After a moment's hesitation, he pressed his hand a little more firmly into her flesh, then moved it lightly side to side.

"You're right. It's firm, but still soft. Very nice." He nodded and removed his hand. "Why do you have the volume off?"

"I don't really like the music and the guy kind of gets on my nerves after a while. I've got the moves almost memorized by now. I just use the video as a guide."

"Why haven't I seen you doing this before?"

"I usually do it when you're gone. You're home early today."

He walked over to the TV and turned the volume up, mostly to distract himself from her glistening skin and tight leggings.

"Is this guy for real?" Harper gestured to the man leading the exercises on the screen. "Why does he talk like that?"

"He's Brazilian, genius, he has an accent. You know, kind of like you do, only from another country."

"Why are you getting snarky with me? You just said he gets on your nerves!"

"Just because he can be annoying doesn't mean he's not good at his job. Besides, this is a really hard workout. Don't knock it till you try it."

He looked at the women in tiny little shorts, lifting their legs and smiling broadly.

"I don't think it would do much for me. It looks girly."

"Girly?"

Her tone should have alerted him, but it didn't. "Yeah. Men like to work out with weights, not shiny yellow bands," he said as he gestured toward the resistance band the women on the screen were using.

"Care to test that theory, big boy?"

Now he heard the tone, but he was never one to back down from a challenge.

"What do you have in mind?"

"Throw on some gym clothes and try this with me. We'll see who's the last man standing."

He raised his brows and looked at her like she was crazy. "Are you serious?"

"Dead serious." Her arms were crossed over her chest and her face was set. He was beginning to recognize that look. She was not about to back down.

"Alright, I'll be back," he said airily as he left the room.

Ten minutes later, Will was panting on the floor, an ankle weight wrapped around his leg and his thigh muscles screaming. His ass was on fire and he had given up trying to ease the pain about three minutes ago. Kate looked up at him from her place beside him.

"No, you have to keep your hips level." She stood and moved behind him, her feet on either side of his resting leg, her hands on his hips. "See, your left hip is higher than the right. They should be level. You'll get a better workout this way." He groaned as she twisted him into place and Kate stifled a snigger. "As Leandro says, 'it's all about the angles'."

Will was in so much pain, he couldn't even enjoy Kate's lycra-clad hips almost pressing into his. He watched the timer in the corner of the screen, desperately willing time to move faster so this torture would be over. With a final growl, he collapsed on the floor.

"Over your knees, Will. You're supposed to be in child's pose. It stretches out your glutes."

He mumbled some unintelligible profanity and rolled to lie across his knees.

"Are you ready to concede?"

"Concede what?" he asked arrogantly, holding onto his last shred of manly pride.

"That my 'girly workout' is actually difficult? Even for a big, tough man like you?"

He refused to take the bait. He could hear the tease in her voice and decided that if he was going to lose, he would do so with dignity and not give her the satisfaction of seeing him humiliated. He decided he would do ten more minutes, then call a truce. Okay, maybe five more minutes.

Roughly sixty reps later, Will decided he'd had enough. With muscles screaming, he sat down and looked at Kate.

"Alright, I admit it, your girly workout has merit. Now what do you want?"

"Hmmm. Let me think." She tapped her finger on her chin in an exaggerated thinking gesture while Will rolled his eyes. "Next week's date, we get to do what I want to do. I pick the restaurant, the activities, everything. And you have to go along, no complaining."

"I thought you liked my restaurants," he said, slightly offended.

"I like them fine, but they're very... you. I'd like to go somewhere more me sometimes."

He pursed his lips in thought, then said, "Okay, you pick. But not one of those weird places where you sit on the floor and eat with your hands."

She rolled her eyes and popped out the DVD. "Deal." She put the case away and turned to leave the room, leaving Will still sprawled out on the floor. *God, he's enormous. He takes up nearly half the floor!* "You might want to take some ibuprofen for that ass. It'll burn like hell in the morning."

He gave her a dirty look as she left the room, a smirk on her lips.

**

"Why did I agree to this?"

"Because my ass is stronger than yours and you couldn't admit it." She answered him with a triumphant smile and what he would have sworn was a smug expression.

"Remind me not to accept any more bets from you," he said sourly.

"Now, honey, that's no way to start the evening," she teased. She smiled and added, "Just relax – you might start to like it."

He glared at her, but turned his attention back to the front of the restaurant.

After listening to the master of ceremonies speak, he turned to Kate. "How did you hear about this?"

"Laura told me. We usually come together. It's more fun to come in a group, but I thought it might be better for you to experience your first time without an audience."

"Thank you for that," he answered dryly.

His attitude was beginning to get on her nerves, but she was trying not to show it. "Is it really so bad?" she asked quietly.

He looked around at the eclectic environment and the people in their cheap clothes who seemed to be paying zero attention to him. He sighed.

"Sorry, I'm being a bad sport. It's not so bad, just unusual for me, that's all."

She smiled and squeezed his hand. "It really can be fun if you just let yourself get into it. I promise not to make fun of you."

He responded with something incoherent and went back to scanning the menu. When the waiter finally arrived, he ordered a bottle of wine and two appetizers. Kate looked at him with a raised brow.

"What? You're the one who said it was for a good cause. Doesn't the money go to charity or something?"

"The money from the tickets goes to charity, and I believe a portion of the restaurant's revenues, but certainly not all of it."

"Well, the wine selection wasn't bad, and I could use a drink."

Seeing his tired expression, she relaxed her stance and asked gently, "Long day?"

"Yeah." He groaned and ran his hands through his hair. "There was a problem with a prototype that now basically has to go back to design, which will set launch dates back and be a very expensive mistake, and to top it off, one of our best designers resigned today. It's going to be bloody hard to replace her – especially with us being in the middle of this project. I was hoping to finalize it by the end of the year, but without Thompson, we'll probably be set back."

"Why did she resign out of the blue? Is everything okay?"

"Yes, for her anyway. She's pregnant and her husband's been transferred to LA. She apologized and I think she genuinely feels badly for leaving us in the lurch, but with the move and the baby happening at the same time, she didn't want to do the long-distance relationship thing and she thought it was a good time to move on."

Kate sat back, suddenly feeling bad for her judgmental thoughts earlier. He'd had a hard day and his attitude was understandable. "Can she not stay just for the redesign?"

"She's staying for six weeks, as required in her contract, but it would be miraculous if it was done by then."

"Could she not be persuaded to do just a few more months? When is she due?"

"I don't know, I didn't ask. I'm not even sure if I'm allowed to."

"You two are friends, right? Was she the one in the green dress at the Partners in Technology gala?"

"God, Kate, I don't know what she wore, but yes, she was there." His hands went to his hair again. "I wouldn't call us friends, but she's certainly a respected colleague."

She squeezed his forearm where it lay on the table. "I'm sorry, Will. I know this is stressful for you. Do you want to go somewhere else? We can just go home if you'd rather." She wanted to stay, but she could tell he was in a bad mood and was trying to be considerate.

"No, it's alright, Katie, we can stay. I could use a distraction. I have to start interviewing tomorrow for Thompson's replacement and it's got me in a foul mood, that's all. Let's enjoy the evening." She smiled at him. "Now, would you like to tell me what the hell is going on?"

Kate couldn't help but laugh at the expression of complete bewilderment on his face. "Well, the outside picture is that this restaurant hosts this event once a month for charity. All the ticket sales go to an orphanage in Central America. It's almost completely supported by this one event."

He raised his brows.

"See, now you can relax knowing you've done a good deed. The guy who was talking earlier will walk us through the process. It's sort of a mystery theatre, but it's interactive."

"What do you mean?"

"Well, there are actors who play parts and have a set script, but the audience participates to a certain extent. Some people are actually assigned parts to play, but I didn't sign us up for that. You take these," she held up a few small pieces of paper that were standing up in the center of the table, "and you can write down conjectures of what you think will happen, who you think did it, or what you would like to see happen, things like that, and the servers collect them. Sometimes, if a person is really close or even completely right, they kill off that person in the audience."

"What? How do they do that?"

"Well, I've never seen the killing off, but once Laura got too close to the right information and when the lights went down, they snatched her. They were really quiet and sneaky about it. When the lights came back up, she was just gone. Then we saw her locked up in a room onstage. Of course, it was a stage, so two of the walls were missing and it was all figurative, but you got the idea. She stayed put like a good little prisoner and they added her to the script. That's part of what makes it so fun – you never know what's going to happen and they don't really know either."

"I don't want to go on stage."

"I know. I don't like the idea of being kidnapped, either. Just don't be too clever and you'll be fine." She patted his knee and he sat back, taking it all in. He and Kate had a small square table set catty-cornered against the back wall and they sat on adjacent sides so both of them could see the main stage area. The atmosphere was energetic and lively and everyone seemed prepared to have a good time.

Kate seemed content to sip her wine in silence, and he did the same. After two months of marriage, they had learned how to be quiet together. There were no more awkward silences and heavy pauses. He was glad they had come to a sort of companionship. It made everything they had to go through together that much easier.

"Oh, it's starting!" she said excitedly, and he turned his attention to the front where several men in pinstripe suits were arguing over what to do about some sort of problem. He let the stress of the day go and tried to just enjoy the evening. He wasn't as successful as Kate in having a good time, but he made a valiant effort and was surprised that he actually enjoyed himself.

"Well, what did you think?" Kate asked as they walked back into their building.

"It was fun – surprisingly. Though it was way too easy."

"Well not everyone is as brilliant as you, Mr. Youngest CEO Ever," she retorted as they stepped off the elevator.

"Oh, come on! It was so obvious that Angelo did it! He was mad at Eric for stealing his girl and he had plenty of opportunity."

"But what about Sylvia? She had motive, too! She'd been in love with Eric for all those years and then he went and chose Carla instead. That kind of anger can make a girl crazy."

"It wasn't a feminine crime!" he urged as he opened the door and let her in ahead of him. "Everyone knows women prefer poison unless it's in the heat of the moment, and then they usually go for a gun. Eric's murder was clearly planned out in advance, which disqualifies Sylvia because he wasn't poisoned." He said the last with smug finality.

"So if you were so sure of your theory, why did you say you thought Eric killed himself on your answer sheet?"

"You weren't supposed to be looking at mine!" he exclaimed. She shrugged sheepishly. "And I put that, miss-know-it-all, because I didn't want to be dragged on stage in front of two hundred people for guessing the right answer!"

She laughed as she put her purse on the table and kicked off her shoes. "Well, next time, I think you should write down your real theory and see what happens. Then we'll know if you actually figured it out ahead of time or if you just said you knew all along when it was over."

He gave her a disapproving look. "You're on, missy."

She smirked, reached up to kiss him on the cheek and turned to walk down the hall. "Night, Will," she called over her shoulder.

He said goodnight in return and it was a full five minutes before he realized he'd just made another bet with her in the same night he'd sworn never to do it again.

Clever little minx.

***

"So what all do you think they'll ask us?" Kate asked Will as they rode to the interview for immigration. It had been two and a half months of studying and PDA and fake-romancing and she felt ready, but also incredibly nervous.

"I have no idea. Jamison said that in a case where there's no suspicion, it's all pretty straight forward. They look over your files and if everything's in order, you're approved and move on to the next step, which is just a doctor's appointment for me and then we get the card."

"But we might get more intense scrutiny," she said. She'd talked to Andrew and Laura and looked up a lot of information on her own, but she just wanted to talk it out again, make sure she hadn't missed anything.

"Exactly."

"We'd be alright, though, wouldn't we? I mean, we're living together, we know all sorts of things about each other. We'll be fine!" She tried to sound breezy but it came across as slightly hysterical.

"Of course." He wasn't convincing.

"I'm sorry. I shouldn't make you nervous. I talk when I'm anxious – bad habit, I know. Alright, I'll stop talking now."

"That would be helpful," he said quietly. She looked out the window then back at him, noticing the white knuckle grip he had on the steering wheel and how the muscle beside his mouth twitched every few seconds.

"Hey," she reached over and squeezed his forearm, "it's going to be okay, really. I have a good feeling," she said more calmly than she'd sounded all morning.

"Thanks," he replied. He relaxed a bit and took a deep breath, then stopped the car and announced they'd arrived.

They sat in a plain grey waiting room with several other families, the air filled with more languages than either of them could decipher. Finally, after waiting half an hour during which Will never stopped bouncing his knee, the name Harper was called and told to go to window three.

They looked at each other and rose together, Kate falling in behind Harper as he stepped up to the glass. A short man with red hair asked their names and then laid out their file in front of them. Kate recognized everything she'd put together with Andrew; her birth certificate and tax returns and school enrollment forms and copies of her driver's license.

"Alright," began the man, "there's no problem with your military or police reports, and your background check is clean. Your job checked out, as well as your personal affidavits. Your wife's financials are all in order and your residency requirements are met. In short, you're approved pending a successful medical examination." He slid the thick packet under the glass. "Here's where you go to have that done." He gave Harper a sheet of paper. "And this says that you understand what to do now, which is to set up a medical appointment and give the doctor that form. If the exam is satisfactory, you'll be granted a permanent resident visa and should receive it within fourteen days. If it is not satisfactory, your visa will be denied. Sign here, please."

Harper signed his name and slid the paper back under the glass. "Is there anything else I need to do?"

"No, you're all set. Have a nice day."

Harper thanked him, grabbed his papers and walked away.

"Well, that was anticlimactic," Kate said quietly as they retreated down the hall. "I don't know what I was expecting, but that sure wasn't it."

"Yeah, me neither. It was so, so…"

"Simple? Quick? Undramatic?"

"Yeah, and so not something we should have been stressing over."

"Don't relax yet. You still have to pass your medical exam."

"I'll pass. They're mostly checking for incurable infectious diseases and tuberculosis. I'll be fine."

"That's a relief."

When they got back in the car, Kate flipped through the folder in her lap while Harper immediately called the doctor's office to set up an appointment. She skipped over the files with their basic information and opened the Proof of Relationship file. In it were the pictures they'd taken at her little apartment on the lower east side. She felt a rush of nostalgia looking at them, not so much for the images themselves but for that time and place in her life. It had been a great place to live for the three years she'd been there and she missed it sometimes – though not terribly often.

She couldn't help but laugh at the completely made up items in the file. The pictures with Jen and Andrew, the "events" they'd orchestrated where they were both wearing party clothes and holding champagne flutes filled with ginger ale (that looked just like champagne in pictures). When she got to the emails they'd written each other, she snorted out loud.

"What's so funny?" Harper asked.

"These emails we sent each other for our proof of relationship file. I can't believe I wrote these with a straight face!"

"Which ones?"

"Listen to this: *Hey babe, I'm free after eight. Want to break in the new sofa?"*

"Did you really write that? And give it to someone?" he cried.

"You saw it before! I sent them all to you so you could change the time stamp, remember?"

"Yes, but I didn't read them *all*."

Kate rolled her eyes. "There are two more where I say my roommate is working late and suggest you come keep me company. G-d, where's my creativity!"

"You were studying for finals," he said politely. "I'm hungry. Want to get a late breakfast to celebrate?"

"Yes! Being nervous always makes me hungry."

Thankfully, the press had moved on to more interesting people, so eating out was now more about eating and less about putting on a show. Their newfound privacy improved both their appetites and their mealtime conversations.

At the table, Kate sipped her mimosa and looked through half the stack of printed emails while Will read through the rest. He sniggered as he read one of the earliest emails that was meant to come toward the beginning of their relationship.

Dear William,

I had a really great time last night. I probably shouldn't tell you this and should play hard to get and everything, buuut… emails don't count, so I'll go back to playing hard to get when I see you in person. Which is soon I hope, because you're a really good kisser and I'd like to kiss you again. I mean, really good. Did you take a class or something? You seem so serious and straight-laced and then BOOM! You should really give a girl some warning!

He held the paper up. "Do you really send this sort of thing to guys?" he asked with an amused smile.

She looked at it quickly and answered, "No! I'd been watching a bunch of mindless vlogs, don't judge me!" He laughed and shook his head. "Besides, I was trying to sound like the kind of girl that gets swept up into a whirlwind romance and says yes to a man she barely knows and follows that up with marrying him in Vegas. This was not a time for restraint."

He raised his hands in defeat. "Fair enough."

"And who are you to talk, Mr. Let-me-read-you-a-sonnet." His eyes got wide and Kate took perverse pleasure in watching him squirm. "Let me see, where was I?" She skimmed through the page she was reading.

"You weren't the only one trying to sound besotted," he said defensively.

"True, but I was the only one who didn't get to see all these emails the first time through, so I'll just take a good look now." She smiled and leaned back in her seat, a stack of papers in her lap.

Will chose not to argue with her and went back to his own stack, laughing and blushing in turn as Kate's emails became increasingly complimentary and suggestive.

Dear Will,

That thing you do with your tongue should be illegal! Who knew I was dating such a bad boy.

He was interrupted by Kate's sigh as she read his. She just waved him off when he raised a brow inquisitively and continued reading silently.

Dear Katherine,

I'm not very good with words, I never seem to know what to say and more often than not I put my foot in my mouth, so allow me to borrow from someone more talented.

How do I love thee? Let me count the ways.
I love thee to the depth and breadth and height
My soul can reach, when feeling out of sight
For the ends of being and ideal grace.
I love thee to the level of every day's
Most quiet need, by sun and candle-light.
I love thee freely, as men strive for right.
I love thee purely, as they turn from praise.
I love thee with the passion put to use
In my old griefs, and with my childhood's faith.
I love thee with a love I seemed to lose
With my lost saints. I love thee with the breath,
Smiles, tears, of all my life; and, if God choose,
I shall but love thee better after death."

— Elizabeth Barrett Browning

It's simple to say, but I love you.
William

She flipped to another for the day after the proposal.

My Darling Katherine,

Words cannot describe how happy you've made me. If I was a poet, I would write you a verse. But as it stands, "I love you the way a drowning man loves air. And it would destroy me to have you just a little."

That is how I feel – I know this has all been sudden, but I cannot imagine living without you, or having you only for a moment or an evening. I need you always. Please tell me we can marry soon. A long engagement would be torture.

Yours

Kate leaned back and sighed.

"What? Is it bad?" Will asked.

"No, it's – it's good. I like it." She smiled coyly. "If I didn't know better, I'd think you had a thing for me."

"Well, I did consult a website titled, 'How to write a great love letter.' They had a bank of quotes to choose from."

She nudged his leg under the table with her foot. "Good call."

He smiled and put the papers away to make room for the French toast that had just arrived.

"So what now?" Kate asked between bites.

"What do you mean? We're in the clear – mostly anyway," he replied.

"I know. I mean, are you off for the rest of the day or do you need to go to the office?"

"Oh, right. Technically, I don't have to go in, I wasn't sure how long all of this would take so I cleared my schedule."

"It is Friday. We could escape to the beach if you wanted. If we could pack quickly, we'd beat the weekend traffic."

"Sounds good. Let's do it."

18
HOSTILE TAKEOVER

Late July
2.5 Months Married

"Ugh," Kate growled as her textbook slid off the counter and fell to the floor. She climbed down and picked it up, then slammed it noisily onto the counter, stretching her back out after sitting so long on the hard wooden stool.

Annoyed with studying, and a little mad at herself for picking up yet another accelerated summer class, she walked down the hall and looked longingly into Will's office. The enormous desk could easily hold all her books, and the chair looked so comfortable. But she knew it would be crossing a line to use his office. It was his private space, his cave, the only part of the apartment Kate wasn't constantly mentally redecorating. Even his bedroom sported a fluffy purple pillow and pictures of them together – all to keep up the ruse, of course. This was his last bastion of masculinity, the meagre remains of his life as a bachelor. There were no throw pillows or cashmere anything, not a single picture of Kate in sight.

And yet, she was tempted.

No. She would not take over Will's space. He had a right to privacy. Of course, he had an enormous office at work to use and she just had a tiny little bedroom. Okay, it wasn't tiny, but there wasn't really space for a desk and she didn't want to spend all her time in one little room. She sighed and backed out of Will's office, or the study as he called it. *British snob.*

Walking past the spare room that housed the bed she'd banned from her room, she got an idea. Five minutes later she was changed and walking out the door.

"Feel like doing a little shopping?" Kate spoke on her phone as she walked down the hall toward the elevator.

"*Always. But I can't leave for another hour,*" Jenny answered.

"That's alright. Meet me at the Crate & Barrel on Madison when you're free."

"*See you then.*"

Kate enjoyed the thirty minute walk to one of her favorite stores and happily stepped inside.

"Can I help you with anything?" asked a young saleswoman with a perky smile and wavy brown hair.

"Yes. I'm turning a guest room into an office. I'll need a desk, some bookcases, a chair and possibly a murphy bed. Do you carry those?"

"Yes, we have three models to choose from. Follow me."

As much as she hated to admit it, her favorite part about being married to Will was probably the shopping. She'd been counting her pennies for so long, walking into a store and being able to just buy what she needed was such a relief. She'd even stopped taking a calculator to the grocery store, something she'd been doing since she left home at eighteen. She was still frugal and hadn't even gotten close to her spending limit, so she thought it was alright to spend a little on furniture.

Jen arrived a little after five just as Kate was listening to the merits of various murphy beds, and they quickly picked out two tall bookshelves, a vintage-looking swivel chair, and an oversized desk. Jen led the way to a small boutique nearby where Kate found a perfect worn leather chair and a hand-woven rug second-hand.

"Do you want to grab a drink?" Jen asked as they walked down the darkening sidewalk.

"Sure. Your turn to pick."

"You okay?" Kate asked as they sat at the bar sipping cocktails. Jenny was being unusually quiet.

"He said it."

"Said what? Who, Andy?" She looked at her sister's preoccupied expression. "The L-word?"

Jen nodded.

"That's great." Kate smiled and touched her sister's arm. "That is great, isn't it?"

"Yeah, I think so. I mean it is, I just…"

"What? I thought you loved him, too."

"I do, I just don't know if it's all moving too fast."

"It's been seven months, and you see each other all the time…" Kate trailed off at her sister's worried expression. "What is it, Jenny?"

"I think he's going to ask me to move in with him."

"And that's what you think is too soon?"

"Yes!" she said almost desperately. "You've seen his place; it's enormous! He doesn't even pay rent, his parents bought it for him as a graduation gift."

Suddenly Kate was feeling a lot better about the six grand worth of furniture she'd just bought. "Wow. I thought dad went all out with earrings."

Jen smiled wearily. "It's just, he comes from this whole other world, you know? He has a trust fund!" she cried disbelievingly.

"What's the real problem here, Jen? You never cared about Andy's money before."

"I just don't want to get sucked up, you know what I mean? I work for a non-profit. I live in a studio apartment over a drag bar. But at least it's mine. I pay for it, I earn it, nobody but me. If I move in with Andrew, and don't even pay rent because who would I pay it to, what will become of me? Of Jennifer Bishop? Will I just be Andy's girl? Just an extension of him? Will I eventually quit my low-paying job and become a corporate wife? Don't say it won't happen because we see it all the time."

Kate rubbed her back soothingly while Jen signaled the bartender for another. "I know, Jenny. Has he actually asked you to move in?"

"No, but I can tell he's going to. He commented at least five times on how small my place is last weekend. He was nice about it, but I think he's trying to convince me slowly. You know how he is – great at strategy. He plants the idea in my head that I should live somewhere bigger, nicer, with a twenty-four hour doorman. Then his place is magically offered as the answer to my better-living dreams."

Kate stifled a laugh. "Are you sure you're not taking this a little too far? Maybe he was just being honest and letting his guard down when he said your place was small. You've said it yourself plenty of times. Maybe he was taking cues from you."

Jen gave her a cynical look. "When we were getting dressed this morning, he said it would be so convenient if all my stuff was already at his place."

Kate pulled a face. "Yeah, that's pretty clear. So what will you say if he asks you?"

She held her head in her hands, blonde waves spilling over her fingers. "I don't know." She shook her head and looked balefully at her sister. "You know what the worst part of it is?"

"What?"

"I *want* to move in with him. I want to be part of his life. I don't want to lose my own identity, but I like the idea of sharing a closet and waking up with him every day. I want to cook together in that crazy modern kitchen and read the paper on the terrace every Sunday. What does that make me? What kind of feminist am I?"

"Oh, Jen! You can be a feminist and want a little romance, too! The two aren't mutually exclusive!" She tried to believe what she was saying, but she had the same fears herself and she didn't think she was very convincing.

Jen let out a deep breath and set her drained glass heavily on the wooden bar. "I know that in theory, but how do we do that in real life? I want romance, I do! I can't watch a sappy movie without crying."

"I know. You even thought Vegas was romantic," said Kate.

"But I'm an independent woman! I like my freedom, I like calling my own shots. What am I going to do? If he asks and I say no, he'll be so hurt, I might never see him again. I can't let that happen! I love him so much, I don't want to hurt him, but I can't be a crappy side salad to his steak! I don't want to be like mom, giving up everything for a man, planning my whole life around him, only to wind up disappointed. "

"Hey! You are not mom!"

Jen scoffed.

"Seriously, listen to me, Jenny. You may look like her and share her penchant for pastels, but you are nothing like her! You're smart, you're educated, you're tough. You ran a marathon last year!"

Jenny laughed shakily, but Kate could see the pride in her eyes. She'd trained for months for that marathon.

"Talk to Andy. Tell him you don't want to quit your job or lose your identity. Maybe you can put the money you'd normally spend on rent into a sort of fund for a vacation home or another apartment or something. That way if you two break up, you'll have something to fall back on."

"I would be able to pay off my student loans," Jen said thoughtfully. "But that's a terrible reason to move in with someone."

"Quit kidding yourself. You're dying to move in with him, you just need a way to justify it to your feminist sensibilities."

Jenny laughed and nudged Kate's shoulder. "You know me way too well."

"We're sisters. I'm supposed to know you well." Her phone blinked and she looked down. "The car's here. Let's get you home."

Kate led Jenny outside to the car she'd requested twenty minutes ago when she realized Jen was drinking more heavily than usual. Regular car service would have to be her second favorite thing about being married to Will.

After she dropped Jenny off, Kate couldn't stop thinking about what her sister had said. It was so easy to get sucked up into a man's life. His name, his apartment, his everything. Had that happened to her? Had the formality of their business arrangement blinded her to what was happening? Had she run away from it with Jeremy only to walk right into it with Will? And if she had, it was much worse because she didn't even love him. She'd have no excuse for her stupidity.

They'd been together such a short time and none of it was really real. She and Will were friends. But when she thought about it, was her life already blending into his? Was she the side salad to his main dish? The idea was scary and shocking and unfortunately, all too common.

**

The next evening, Kate flipped a grilled cheese sandwich while reading a textbook, her thoughts distracted. She couldn't stop thinking about what Jen had told her and wondering if she had become something she really didn't want to be.

She kept track of the calendar, Will never knew what was happening when. She went to all of his social functions, but he had yet to join her on a single group outing or dinner with any of her friends. She'd gone to Sheila's dinner party alone because Will had had to work late. She would never be allowed to skip a dinner like that; she would never consider doing it. And yes, she had redecorated almost the entire apartment, but in the end it all belonged to him. She might be able to take some furniture with her, but it was his place and ultimately, she was just a visitor. Long term, but a visitor still.

This made her sad and irritable and confused. She nibbled on her grilled cheese and began one of her regular pastimes, arguing with herself.

Sure, she kept the calendar, but Will had never asked her to. His assistant Evelyn maintained his schedule and told him every morning what he was doing that day. He had times blocked for personal scheduling, but otherwise, he was very well managed. Kate was simply copied on his personal calendar and had exercised a wife's prerogative and asked Evelyn to send her a copy of all accepted invitations. She couldn't really blame him for that. Slightly mollified, she moved on to her next point.

It was in her contract that she had to show up with Will, and he was in the public eye while she was not. Sheila and Peter were not going to care if her husband worked late and missed dinner, but her not being on her husband's arm for public functions would not go unnoticed. But still, it chafed that he felt she and her friends could be so easily moved aside. *We should have put that in the contract.*

Finishing her sandwich, she took her plate to the sink.

"Ugh!" she groaned.

There was a bowl and spoon in the sink, now covered in dried yogurt and granola, a coffee cup, again with dried black gook in the bottom, and a bread plate with a half-eaten piece of toast on it. *At least it's in the sink*, she thought dryly.

At that moment, she heard the front door opening and the sound of Will's keys plonking into the dish by the door. He was in the kitchen a minute later, looking hungry and expectant.

"Hi, Kate," he said. "Have a good day?" He grabbed a beer from the fridge and quickly popped off the top, leaving the opener on the counter next to the discarded lid. "Ooh, making grilled cheese? Is this the one with apples? I'd love one."

Kate turned toward him and met his smiling expression with fiery eyes.

"Do you have thumbs, William?"

"Pardon me?"

"Thumbs!" she exclaimed, holding up her hands and wiggling hers in front of him. "Opposable thumbs, these amazing things that allow humans to hold things and move things and wash things."

He looked at her dumbfounded. "Uh, I -"

"I just can't understand how a man with thumbs, a grown man who's lived on his own for over a decade, who is supposedly intelligent enough to run an entire COMPANY, can't manage to put a few dishes in a dishwasher!"

"Dishwasher?"

"Yes! It's this miraculous machine that spurts water and soap and cleans dishes, hence the name dish-washer!" she said emphatically while her hands gestured wildly.

"What-"

"And why on earth would you think I want to do it? Does something about me just scream 'give me your dirty dishes'? Do I seem bored? Do you really think I don't have anything better to do? I'm a very busy woman! An intelligent woman who has better things to do than scrub the crusted up granola off *your* dirty dishes!" She was nearly yelling now, her face bright pink and her heart pounding.

Will was completely lost and had no idea what was happening, but he had the distinct impression he was losing this argument. "I never said you weren't intelligent," he retorted.

"Really? You didn't? You didn't think that leaving your mess on the counter was sending a message? You didn't think that I would notice how you freely leave things lying around in the kitchen, knowing full well I spend most of my time in here, with no regard for how it might affect my day or make me feel? Really?" She gripped the edge of the counter and deliberately lowered her voice. "I graduated summa cum laude from NYU and have a 4.0 at one of the most respected universities in this country. I am not your maid. Cleaning is not in the contract."

With that, she grabbed her books and went to her room, Will staring after her in utter bewilderment. A few minutes later, he grabbed his keys and left.

*

Kate felt terrible for snapping at Will, but not at first. First, she stomped around her room. When she heard him leave, she quickly looked up the nearest kickboxing class, saw there was one starting in ten minutes, changed her clothes and sprinted the two blocks to make it on time.

After burning a few hundred calories, she felt better – calmer, more relaxed, and with a telling pain in her lower back. She called Laura as she walked down the steps at the studio.

"*Hey Katie, what's up?*"

"Don't ask."

"*Uh oh. What's going on?*"

"I just went all pre-menstrual on Will."

"*Oh, G-d. What happened?*" Laura asked.

"Well, I met Jenny yesterday and she was talking about how men take over our lives and suck us in until we become like our mothers, and then tonight I was brewing about it all and saw his dirty dishes in the sink and when he walked in I just lost it." She sighed.

"*Oh, Katie!*" Laura said through a strangled laugh. "*I would have loved to have seen you in all your hormonal glory ripping him a new one. Poor William! What did he do?*"

"Nothing, well, he didn't really have a chance." She paused as she stepped into the corner market. "I stomped off to my room and two minutes later he left. I went straight to kickboxing and haven't gone home yet." She quickly grabbed a few bars of chocolate, paid, and left.

"*Wow. Okay. What are you going to say when you get there?*"

"I don't know. I suppose I should just apologize, but it does actually bother me that he doesn't ever do his dishes, or wipe the counters, or put away the blankets in the living room. He's fine to just leave everything until the housekeeper comes to clean up after him. But in the meantime, I have to live with it and look at his shit everywhere." She felt herself getting riled up again and took a deep breath. "But I definitely could have said it better. Argh! Is this our first fight?"

"*Sounds like it. Except he didn't really fight back, so maybe not.*"

"Oh, G-d! I hate to think what I'm going home to. Do you think he'll yell? He must be mad. Do you think he's mad? He's got to be mad."

"*Of course he's mad. It's what he does with it you should be worried about. Good luck, kid.*"

"Thanks," Kate said ruefully.

"*Don't feel too bad. PMS can make anyone a little crazy. I'm not going to lie, I once put Nutella on a meat-lover's pizza.*"

Kate barked out a laugh. "And I thought my cravings were weird."

"*Hey, don't knock it 'til you try it.*"

"Well, I'm here. Time to face the music." She looked up

at her building with trepidation.

"Call me tomorrow and let me know how it goes. And hey," she said *"it'll be alright. Just explain it was the monster talking and that you are a reasonable person most of the month."*

"Thanks. Night, Laura." She put her phone in her pocket and went upstairs. "You can do this, Katie. Chin up," she told herself.

Kate walked into the apartment with a nervous feeling in the pit of her stomach. She flipped on the light and listened for sounds of Will. The apartment was silent. The clock on the wall said it was just after ten o'clock. She'd never known Will to stay out this late. Where had he gone? Was he already asleep in his room? That would have been equally unusual.

She crept down the hall toward Will's room, her stomach in knots. His door was cracked and there was a faint blue light shining. She listened carefully but heard nothing. She tapped twice on the door.

"Will?" she called.

"Yes?"

His voice held no warmth, not that she had expected it to, but the confirmation made her cringe. She pushed the door open slightly and looked in.

"Can I come in?"

He nodded silently. She took two small steps into the dim room and thought he looked a little like Clark Kent sitting in bed with his ruffled hair, black rimmed reading glasses, and old-fashioned pajamas. She had the sudden thought that he was one of the few men who could wear grandpa pajamas and glasses and still look sexy as hell. She blushed from her train of thought and made her hormone drenched mind focus on the issue at hand.

He was watching her steadily, his face blank and his eyes cold in the blue light reflected from his laptop. There were no other lights on in the room and she was somehow comforted by the idea that he couldn't see her very well.

"I wanted to apologize, for earlier. I shouldn't have snapped at you like that. I'm really hormonal and I had a rough week studying, and then Jen said something that got me all in a tizzy and the next thing I know I'm yelling at you. I'm really sorry – it was uncalled for."

"Thank you for the apology." He returned his gaze to the screen in front of him and began typing.

She waited.

"That's it? That's all you're going to say?"

He continued to type uninterrupted. "What else did you expect me to say?"

"Oh, I don't know. How about, I forgive you, or let's pretend it never happened, or it's understandable, PMS happens to everyone. You could laugh, or apologize for your part." She tried not to sound sarcastic, but couldn't help it.

He looked at her over the rim of his glasses. "So you apologize, then immediately expect me to say it wasn't necessary?"

She huffed. "Not exactly, but… sort of. Look, I know I was nasty and I definitely overreacted, but I didn't do it out of the clear blue nowhere."

He raised his brows in question but she had clamped down on her lips and wasn't opening them until he said something.

"Alright, I'll bite. What set you off, Ms. Bishop?" *Oh, shit, he must be really mad*, she thought. "What did I do in the sixty seconds I had been home that provoked such a display?"

She breathed deeply.

"What? No choice words for me? You don't want to enquire about the presence of any essential body parts? I can save you the trouble and assure you that I have all my fingers and toes and that everything is in fine working order," he said in clipped tones.

Kate stared at him, a growing sense of panic coming over her. They'd been married less than three months. They couldn't start fighting and being nasty now. If this went any further, how would they recover? Seized by a sudden need to stop this argument before it got any worse, she stepped farther into the room and walked over to his side of the bed, sitting next to him. He looked at her with surprise and she threw her arms around his neck.

"I'm sorry, Will. I don't want to fight," she said. "Can we try this again?"

It took him a moment to respond. He wrapped his arms around her slowly and finally nodded yes, not sure what she was asking but feeling his anger rapidly dissipate.

She leaned back and looked him in the eye, her hands holding his between them.

"What I should have said when you got home this afternoon was this: Will, it bothers me that you leave dirty dishes on the counter and in the sink instead of putting them into the dishwasher. It sends the message that you expect me to do it or just don't care, and that isn't fair. I would also appreciate it if you could wipe your crumbs off the counter, especially the island bar where I sit so much." She exhaled deeply and closed her eyes, as if this required great effort.

Will continued looking at her and finally took one hand from her grasp and touched her shoulder. It was rigid and tight. "Kate," she opened her eyes and looked at him, "this is really important to you, isn't it?"

She nodded, unshed tears in her eyes.

"I won't pretend to understand what happened before, but I can respect your request. I might not always do it, but I will try to put my dishes in the dishwasher. Okay?"

He caught a tear that escaped down her cheek with his finger. "Don't cry, Katie. Please."

She sniffled. "I'm fine, really. I'm just so bloody hormonal!" He smiled at her adoption of his word. "I'm sorry. I promise I'm normally quite rational."

"I know. So," he asked delicately, "is it like this every month?"

She laughed and impulsively laid her head on his shoulder. "No. Actually, it's hardly ever like this. Maybe two or three times a year. I was quite pleasant last month, remember?"

"No, I don't, which of course means you're correct." He awkwardly patted her back after a moment. "Better?"

She raised her head from his shoulder. "Yes, thank you."

She got up and began to walk out of his room. When she got to the door, he spoke. "Kate," he said quietly and seriously, "I'm sorry, too."

She smiled tiredly. "I forgive you."

They shared one last smile before she closed the door behind her and went to her own bedroom. With the assistance of a glass of water, a few painkillers, and a heating pad, she went to sleep.

19
INTIMACY?

Late August
4 Months Married

Kate looked around in confusion, wondering why she'd woken up in the living room. She smacked her lips in distaste and felt her face. Had she gone to bed with her make-up on? Her eyelashes felt caked together and the wire of her bra was digging into her ribs. She looked down and saw she still had on her cocktail dress from the night before.

It all came flooding back to her and she remembered sitting with Will on the sofa, having a drink after they arrived home. William's green card had arrived in the mail that day, complete with unflattering photo and the official USCIS stamp. They'd opened a bottle of champagne to celebrate, then they'd gone to an anniversary party for one of the board members and had gotten in after two in the morning. Too keyed up to sleep, they'd sat on the sofa with a night cap watching television until they were tired. Smacking her lips in distaste, she was regretting that last drink and the several that had come before it.

She looked at the clock. It was almost eleven. Wow. She never slept this late. She must have been really tired. Thankfully her summer classes were over and she didn't have anywhere to be until the fall semester started. She threw off the soft blanket she assumed Will had draped over her and stumbled to the bathroom to take a shower. She peeled out of her too-tight dress and the Spanx she had worn to make it fit and stepped under the hot stream. *What we suffer for fashion.*

She wrapped her hair in a towel and padded to the kitchen in yoga pants and a tank top. Today would be a lazy day. She made a pot of tea, put a slice of bread in the toaster, and began washing a bowl of strawberries. Her breakfast complete, she checked the calendar. Apparently August was a busy time of year for Harper and the Taggston companies. They'd had an event every night for the last three nights and had four more scheduled over the next week. Tonight was the engagement party for the son of the president of some subsidiary she couldn't remember. They had accepted because the father was an old friend of Will's father's and his son also worked for the company, though Kate had never met him. Apparently, he and Harper occasionally saw each other at the gym or something, but they were really going for the father.

She sighed and went to check her closet for something to wear. Once her outfit was laid out, she settled onto the sofa to watch mind-numbing television while the rest of her woke up. An hour later she felt something itching and tried to ignore it. Two hours later, she felt something burning and knew she was in trouble.

"Jenny, call me back as soon as you get this. Please." She left the message and tried to wait patiently for Jen to call her back.

Her sister was usually pretty quick, but she was in the middle of organizing a five-k for her charity and might not get the message for a while. She sent Laura a quick text. *Damn.* Laura was trapped in court all day and had to work after. She briefly considered Sheila or Angie, but Angie was working two jobs this summer and Sheila lived way out in Brooklyn. She'd just have to go to the drug store herself. She walked slowly towards the door, trying to ignore the burning. She was reaching for her purse when the phone rang.

"Jenny! Thank God!"

"*What's up, Katie? Are you okay?*"

"Yeah, I just need something from the drugstore and hoped you could help me out."

"Oh, sweetie, I would, but I'm stuck in the office for the rest of the day. Can you ask William?"

"Yeah, sure, don't worry about it. Talk to you soon."

"Bye."

Kate took a deep breath and continued walking slowly to the door. She made it into the hallway and was pressing the button for the elevator, bouncing from side to side, when she realized she wasn't wearing a bra and was still in her slippers.

"Crap!"

She shuffled back into the apartment and went to her room to dress. After getting a bra and socks on, she gave up and decided to call William. Maybe she'd ask Evelyn to run to the drugstore and Will could just bring the bag home ... without looking inside it. But then Evelyn would know and that would be awkward next time she saw her. They were friendly, but they weren't *that* close.

With a sigh, she picked up the phone and called Will.

"Hi, babe," he said as he answered the phone.

He must be around people. He always called her babe when others were around.

"Hey, Will, can you talk for a second?"

"Yes, I'm just walking out of a meeting."

"Listen, I need something from the drugstore. Is there any way you could pick something up for me and run it home real quick?"

"Actually, I was about to head out. This was my last meeting and I've been dragging all day."

"Yeah, we stayed out pretty late last night. So you can stop on the way home?"

"Sure, no problem. What do you need? Are you sick? You sound puny."

"Um, I'm having a bit of a... feminine problem."

"Oh?" he asked curiously.

"Yeah. Can you write this down?"

"Just a sec. Okay, got a pen. What am I getting?"

"Monistat 7. Not the three day, it has to be the seven day. It'll be in the feminine needs aisle."

"Anything else?"

"My pride, if you find it," she mumbled.

"*Huh?*"

"No, that's all I need."

"*Okay. I'll see you soon.*"

Kate thanked him and hung up. That was easier than she'd thought. Will could be mature; why would she think differently? He had a sister after all. Maybe he was familiar with this sort of thing.

Half an hour later, Will walked through the door with a white plastic bag in his hand.

"Kate? I'm back," he called.

"In here," she called from her room.

He stood in the open doorway and let the bag swing from his extended finger. Kate was lying on the bed looking pitiful. "Here's your stuff."

"Thanks." She got up carefully and walked over to him, gingerly taking the bag from his hand and shuffling to the bathroom.

"So what's the problem anyway?" he asked as she was closing the bathroom door.

"You don't know?" she called.

He looked around for a second, heard a flush, and waited until she finished washing her hands and opened the door.

"No, I don't know. I just asked the clerk for the Monistat, he handed it to me and I left. Is it your period?" he asked uneasily.

"You don't have to look so horrified. No, it isn't my period. It's much, much worse." She flopped onto the bed and he saw a green package of something in the sheets. "I have a..." she mumbled into the pillow.

"You have a what? Did you say infection? Do you need a doctor? And is that a bag of frozen peas in your bed?" he asked, confusion all over his face.

"Ugh! Yes, I have an infection! No, I don't need a doctor, and yes, this is a bag of frozen peas. It helps with the burning."

He watched in horrified fascination as she placed the

peas between her legs and sighed in obvious relief.

"Katie," he began, drawing out her name, "what happened?"

"Spanx! That's what happened!"

"Spanx?" he repeated, more confused than ever.

"Yes! Spanx!" she said exasperatedly. "I slept in a pair of Spanx and now I have a yeast infection. A horrible, itching, burning, yeast infection!" She buried her head in the pillow as she finished.

"What are spanx? And why did you sleep in them?"

"Because I'm not a size four!"

He just looked at her, arms crossed and leaning on the door jam, clearly confused. She sat up and sighed in exasperation.

"I saw this dress that I really wanted, but they didn't have a six, and the eight was too big, so I tried to squeeze into a four, but it didn't look quite right, so the sales lady brought me a pair of Spanx to smooth everything out. But you aren't supposed to sleep in them. But I did! And now I have a yeast infection!" She moaned the last part, falling back onto the pillows dramatically.

Will looked at her silently for a minute, then said, "So, do you want to cancel tonight?"

"Yes. No. I don't know! I can't go like this. My vag is on fire – and not in a good way!" She put her hand over her eyes. "Maybe you should just go without me."

"I don't really want to go anyway, I certainly don't want to go without you, plus it might look strange if I went on my own. If you're not well, that gives me a great excuse to stay home."

"Then it will look like you just ditched because I was perfectly fine last night and I should be fine in time to go to the dinner on Friday. You don't want to look like an ass who lies about his wife being sick to get out of parties."

"True. But my wife is sick and I don't want to leave her on her own while I go to a party that I won't even enjoy."

"Do you think they'll notice you're not there?"

He thought for a moment. "Probably. How about this:

I'll go to the party for a little while, just an hour, drop off the gift and leave early. I can tell them you're unwell and that I have to get home to you."

"You won't tell them what's wrong, will you?" she asked with a sharp look.

He held his hands up in front of him. "I wouldn't dare."

"Okay." She relaxed. "That sounds good. The gift is wrapped and on the table in the hall. And don't forget to sign the card. I left it out for you."

"Yes, dear. Shall I bring you something to drink?"

"Iced tea, unsweet, please."

"Yes, your highness," he said as he backed out.

"Shut up and bring me my tea," she mumbled.

Will chuckled and went to the kitchen. Two minutes later, he was back with a tall glass of tea, the ice clinking as he walked.

"Here you go, princess."

"Thanks," she said quietly and took a sip.

"So I don't have to leave for an hour. What can I do?"

"Nothing." She looked around the room, clearly in pain but also a bit bored. "Maybe you could pick up a movie and some take-out on your way back?"

"I've got a better idea. Why don't I go get it now so you don't have to wait so long?"

"I love that idea. Spice of India?" she asked hopefully, naming one of their regular take-out places a few blocks away.

"Sounds good. I'll put in the order now. What movie do you want?"

"I don't know. Surprise me. But nothing with explosions. Something girly. A comfort movie."

"Is that like comfort food?"

"Something like that."

"Alright. I'll be back soon."

She closed her eyes and tried to relax as she heard Will on the phone, then the sound of his key locking the front door. Thirty minutes later he was back and the smell of curry was wafting down the hall. She shuffled towards the kitchen and saw Will carrying a plate of steaming food and another glass of iced tea. She followed him to the living room and sat gingerly on the couch while he set the food on the table.

"All the new movies looked vapid, so I got *Roman Holiday*," he said as he walked to the television and slid the DVD into the player. "I remembered you liked it. Do you want me to start it?"

"No, I'll start it in a minute. You should get ready for the party."

In fifteen minutes, Harper was dressed in a fresh suit and ready to go.

"I shouldn't be too long, it's just down the street. Call me if you need me." He kissed her forehead and she gave him a sad smile.

"Have fun. Don't flirt with any leggy blondes. Or saucy redheads. Actually, don't flirt with anyone at all."

"I never flirt. You know that." He grinned at her and she winked back at him.

"Just reminding you."

"I've got my mobile," he called over his shoulder as he walked out the door.

Kate sank back into the cushions and took a bite of samosa. "He handled that really well. Who knew he had it in him?"

She flipped through the channels for a while before she started the movie. She was about twenty minutes in when Will walked in.

"I thought this would be over by now," Will said as he flopped onto the couch next to her.

"I started it late. How was the party?"

"Not too bad. You didn't miss anything."

"Anyone we know there?"

"A few people from work, no one special. The bride says she hopes you feel better soon."

"Do you think they believed you that I was sick?"

"Of course. I never lie."

She smiled and nudged him with her foot and then settled in to watch the rest of the movie. When it was finished, she got up and walked with her knees far apart to her room.

"Are you singing?" Will called after her.

Kate turned around, slightly red faced. "Uh, maybe."

"Did you just say 'to kill the yeast'?"

She flushed brighter and looked down. "It's this thing I do sometimes. You know *Beauty and the Beast*?"

"The Disney movie or the story?"

"The movie." He nodded. "They have this part at the end where Gaston is leading the townspeople to go hunt down the beast, and they sing this song. There's a line at the end where they all say 'to kill the beast,'" she delivered the line with great gusto, "so I just changed it up a bit." She shrugged and went back to looking down.

After a moment of silence, she turned slowly and began waddling back to her room.

Will caught up to her quickly and put his arm around her shoulders. "You're a weird girl, Katie Bishop."

She smacked his chest. "I am not. I'm quirky and cute!"

He kissed the top of her head outside her door like he always did and continued to his room.

An hour later, as Harper was lying in bed with his laptop open, he debated whether or not he wanted to look up a yeast infection on Google. He really had no idea what it was, so he decided to go to WebMD and get some information.

"Eww," he said to himself as he read a description of the symptoms. He clicked on 'images' and regretted it a moment later. With morbid fascination, he looked through five photographs of varying degrees of infection and cringed with each new slide.

"I am so glad I don't have a vagina," he mumbled as he turned off the computer and lay down to go to sleep.

20
POISON

Late September
5 Months Married

Kate walked in the door Thursday evening and unceremoniously dumped her bag on the floor.

"Katie?" Will called from the kitchen. A minute later he was walking towards her where she was slumped against the door. "Rough day?"

"Professor Wheeler hates me!" she cried.

"What happened?"

"She read part of my analysis of *Wuthering Heights* in class today. She said I had no vision and no understanding of the characters."

"Ouch. What's her problem?"

"She gets off on Bronte and I don't. And to think this *Women of the Classics* class was supposed to be fun," she mumbled as she walked into the kitchen and grabbed a beer roughly from the fridge. "Why are you home so early?"

"I'm not that early. It's almost seven. Did you forget we're going to dinner with your friends tonight?"

Her expression told him she had forgotten. "Crap. Sheila will kill me if I cancel. She got a babysitter and everything. Stupid Professor Wheeler. You know what she said to me at the end of class?"

"What?"

"That marrying up was all well and good, but that a woman shouldn't retire her brain to pick up an apron. Can you believe that? She might as well have told me that I'm a traitor to feminism and I wasn't even trying on that paper." She took two more gulps of beer before setting the bottle on the counter. "I'd kill for a grilled cheese right now."

Will nodded. Beer and grilled cheese had become one of his favorite meals. Kate gave herself a shake and took a deep breath.

"I just need an attitude adjustment. Screw Professor Wheeler. I'll just have to work extra hard in that class so it doesn't tank my GPA. What time are we supposed to leave?"

William looked at the calendar on his phone. "We're supposed to meet them at eight. It'll take twenty minutes to get there."

"Shit. I'd better hurry. Can you text Sheila for me and tell her we might be a few minutes late? My phone's in my bag."

She ran off to her room and he heard the shower running a minute later. He grabbed the phone from the zipper pocket of her messenger bag and quickly sent off a message.

We might be 5-10 minutes late –sorry.

A moment later her phone buzzed with a reply.

No problem, I'm running behind. What are you wearing? Better yet, what's the hunk wearing?

The hunk? Was that him? He stared at the phone for a few seconds, wondering how he should reply or even if he should reply. Sheila clearly thought she was talking to Kate.

Gray trousers and a black button down. Prada loafers. I don't know what Kate is wearing.

Almost a full minute went by before there was a reply.

Is this William? Or are you messing with me, Katie?

This is William. Or should I say 'The hunk'? Looking forward to meeting you tonight, Sheila.

In Brooklyn, Sheila was laughing so loud her husband popped into the bedroom to ask what was so funny.

Will didn't tell Kate about his little conversation with Sheila. She came out of her room in a pair of suede trousers and a lightweight red sweater, still putting her earrings in.

"Ready?" he asked.

"Mostly. I didn't have time to do much with my hair. Does it look too frizzy?"

"No, it looks good. What kind of place is this? It sounds ethnic."

"Knowing Sheila, it is. It's her turn to pick where we go. If you and Peter get along and we want to do this again, we get to pick next time."

"Fair enough. Shall we?" He held the door open and she walked out ahead of him and pushed the button for the elevator while he locked the door. "So tell me about Sheila and Peter. Did I meet them at the reception?"

"Well, I'm really more friends with Sheila. They were out of town for the reception. She's really funny, you can't help but like her. I met her last year when she was in all my classes but one. After she saw me in the fourth class, she asked if I was stalking her and we've been friends ever since. She's five years older than me and chews you out in Spanish when she gets mad – I think her mother is Cuban. Great salsa dancer.

"She had a baby after she graduated with her bachelors and waited until he went to kindergarten to get her masters. She plans to go on for her PhD. Her husband Peter – blonde Swedish looking guy – is a lawyer at some office in Brooklyn. I don't know that much about him other than he's a fun guy to have at dinner and seems pretty smart." She stopped talking when the elevator opened.

Will had guessed right and the restaurant was very ethnic. They met Sheila and Peter at the front where introductions were made and Sheila commented on how much she liked William's outfit, which Kate found odd but didn't comment on. The hostess, wearing a strange dress made out of beads, led them to a low table in the corner surrounded by pillows.

"I knew I'd end up sitting on the floor," Will mumbled just loud enough for Kate to hear him. She elbowed him in the ribs and sat down on a tasseled purple pillow, gesturing for Will to sit on the red one next to her.

"What kind of food is this?" Will asked.

"It's Persian. Have you ever had it before?" Sheila

asked.

"No, this is my first time."

"They have a few Indian dishes on the menu if those are more familiar to you. Persian food is all about balance – sweet and sour, hot and cold. There's a lovely pomegranate soup you should try." William looked uncertain so she added, "I can order for you if you want. It's easier if someone shows you what's good."

"Sure, why not," Will answered with a smile, determined to be a good sport.

Kate looked at him incredulously. "You don't know what a compliment that is, Sheila. *I've* never even ordered for Will."

Sheila smiled in triumph while Will turned to Kate in surprise. "Really? Never?"

"Not once. But now that I know strange places in questionable neighborhoods are what it takes to make you let go of the reins, I may get my chance."

He raised a brow in answer and turned to Peter, asking him about his job.

"Damn girl, he's even hotter in person!" Sheila whispered in Kate's ear.

"You do know your husband's sitting next to you, don't you?"

"I'm just appreciating the view. You think Peter didn't notice your ass in those pants?"

"Ew! I don't want to think about *your* husband looking at *my* ass."

Sheila laughed. "You are entirely too easy to rankle, Bishop." Sheila loved shock factor. "But seriously, so far he seems great. Handsome, funny, loaded."

"You think he's funny?" Kate was replaying the five-minute introductory conversation in her head. Will hadn't seemed particularly funny to her then, but to each her own.

"Yeah! And he has great hair."

"And he's a good kisser. Can't forget that one."

"You did good, kid." Sheila nudged her shoulder against Kate's. Kate just smiled back.

Sheila ended up ordering for the entire table and the next two hours were spent in lively conversation and three courses of strange but delicious food. Will had never had anything like it and looked at each new dish doubtfully, but he was a good sport and tried everything on the table, including a doughy lump floating in a red juice that burned his mouth so badly he drank an entire glass of water just to keep from breaking into a sweat while Sheila laughed so hard she fell off her pillow. Will glared at her but his mouth was too hot to do much more than pant. They all ended up laughing together and Will promised to get revenge when it was his turn to pick. The check came and Peter snatched it before Will had a chance.

"We picked the restaurant, we've got the bill." Harper nodded at Peter's determined expression and the women exchanged looks.

"Did we just witness male territory marking?" Sheila said to Kate.

"I think so. At least they settled it without peeing on anything." They both snickered as the men rolled their eyes at them.

After spending another ten minutes in idle chatter, Kate was about to begin saying their goodbyes when she noticed William had his hand on his stomach and his face looked a little green.

"You okay?" she asked him quietly.

"I think so. I feel a little," he grunted in place of a word and Kate started to get worried. In all the restaurants they'd gone to, she'd never seen him have indigestion. In fact, as she thought about it, she realized they never went anywhere remotely this ethnic and Will *never* ate spicy food. She quickly texted their driver to bring the car around to the front and said goodbye to Sheila while Will took deep breaths and looked sea sick.

"Is he alright? He looks a little green." Sheila asked.

"I think he'll be fine but I'd better get him home. Thanks for the invite, we had a great time. We'll pick next time." She kissed Peter on the cheek, hugged Sheila, and led an increasingly sweaty Will to the car.

"Go as fast as you can, Mario. Mr. Harper doesn't feel well," she told the driver as she guided Will into the back seat.

"Sure thing, Mrs. Harper."

By the time they got to their building, Will was holding his stomach and doubled over. Kate was beginning to get really worried and wondered if she should take him to the hospital to have his stomach pumped.

"Will? Babe? We're home. Do you think you can walk?"

He groaned something she couldn't understand but managed to climb out of the car. He walked in, hunched over, and headed for the elevator. The doorman immediately recognized them and ran ahead to push the button for them.

"Everything alright, Mrs. Harper?"

"Yes, Frank. I think Mr. Harper has food poisoning."

"Aw, man, that's bad. Let us know if we can help, ma'am."

"Thank you, I appreciate that." She smiled wanly as the doors closed and looked at Will where he was nearly doubled over next to her. "Will, are you going to throw up?"

"Uhhhhhhhnnnnnnnn," was his only reply.

"I'll take that as a yes," she said to herself.

Finally, the elevator reached their floor and she led him the ten steps to the front door. Once they were inside, she quickly flipped on the lights, bolted the door and shimmied Will out of his jacket. She led him as quickly as she could to his bathroom and left him kneeling in front of the toilet. She ran to the kitchen and filled a glass with sparkling water and grabbed the trash bags from under the sink. She nearly sprinted back to the bathroom and got there just in time to see Will emptying the contents of his stomach into the commode.

She reached over him and flushed, then grabbed a cloth from the cupboard, wet it with cool water, and wiped the sweat off his brow and around his mouth. When he felt the cool touch on his face, he opened his eyes and looked at Kate for the first time since the restaurant.

"Katie, you don't need to be here for this. It's okay. Go to bed."

"Like I could sleep through all this moaning you're

doing," she said as she wiped his neck.

It felt so good, he didn't want her to go, but he also didn't want her to watch him throw up and he could feel his stomach rolling again. "Kate, go on. I don't pay you enough for this."

She looked stung for a moment, then her expression hardened and she looked at him steadily. "Put your pride away, Mr. Harper. You're sick and you need help. Unless you want me to take you to the doctor, you're stuck with me."

He started to reply, but when he opened his mouth, he felt the unmistakable signs of sickness and leaned over the toilet again. Kate brushed his hair back over his ears and off his forehead, then laid the folded cloth along the back of his neck.

"Shh, shh," she crooned as he slumped against the marble floor.

"Floor. Cold. Feels good," he mumbled as he laid his cheek down.

Thank God Maria came and cleaned today, Kate thought. She rinsed out the cloth and grabbed another, giving it the same treatment. She put one on his neck to soothe his clammy skin and continued to wipe his face. When he seemed reasonably relaxed, she lined the small trash can with a trash bag, then got another can from his office and did the same with it. She put the office can next to his bed in case he needed it while he was sleeping and went back to the bathroom. Will was struggling to sit up and she immediately rushed to his side and helped him.

"How are you feeling?" she asked softly.

"Unnnnhhhhh," he tried to reply, but he was clearly spent.

"I know, baby. It'll be over soon. Can you have a sip of water?" Her voice was sweet and mellow, like a lullaby, and he was soothed by the sound and her comforting presence.

He nodded his head slightly and she brought the glass to his lips. He managed about three sips before turning his head away and she set the glass down.

"Do you think you're going to throw up again?"

He nodded slightly.

"Soon?"

He nodded again. A minute later, Kate was once again smoothing his hair back and wiping his mouth. As he leaned against the side of the tub, he made a smacking gesture with his lips.

"Do you want to brush your teeth?"

He nodded. She put a little toothpaste on his toothbrush and handed it to Will. She watched him brush excruciatingly slowly, then gave him a little water to rinse and held the empty cup for him to spit into. If he hadn't been feverish and so sick and weak he could hardly move, he would have been embarrassed at being taken care of like an invalid. But in his state he didn't notice and was only grateful for her presence of mind and ability to give him exactly what he needed before he asked for it.

Once his teeth were clean and she had once again rinsed his face, she asked, "Do you want to try to go to bed?"

"No," he croaked, "it's not over yet. Just a little break."

"Has this happened to you before?"

He tried to open his eyes to answer her. "Rio. Harry."

"Of course." She rolled her eyes. "I should have guessed he would be involved."

Will tried to smile but didn't quite manage it. He fumbled about for her hand until she realized what he was doing and grasped his clammy palm in hers.

"Thanks, Kate. You're… best… good… woman."

She looked confused for a moment, then said, "Thanks, and… you're welcome." He half nodded in acknowledgement. "Are you planning on spending the night in here?"

He tried to nod again and she got up and patted his shoulder. "I'll be right back."

She was back two minutes later with the throw blanket from his reading chair and an old pillow she was stuffing into a cheap pillow case.

"This is one I brought from my old place, so it's okay if you hurl on it. I think I paid three dollars for it at the Family Dollar." She laid it down next to him and he sank onto the pillow, letting Kate drape the blanket across his back.

"There's a trash can right here if you can't make it to the

toilet, and another by your bed if you decide you want to sleep there. Are you going to be okay if I go get ready for bed?"

He nodded sleepily into the pillow and closed his eyes. She brushed the hair off his brow and told him she'd be back in ten minutes.

She brushed her hair out and washed her face, then started flossing, keeping an ear out for Will. She heard her phone buzzing with a new text message from Sheila.

Sheila: How's William? Everything ok?

Kate: Hardly. He's ralphing all over the bathroom. Finally resting for a minute, but he's not done.

Sheila: Oh no! I feel terrible! Is he mad?

Kate: I think he's too sick to be mad. He might be mad tomorrow when he remembers that you ordered the food that made him sick. Are you both alright?

Sheila: We're fine, but we eat there all the time. Do you think it was the lamb? He's the only one that had that. I shouldn't have talked him into trying that spicy dish.

Kate: No, probably not, but you had no way of knowing this would happen. I guess it could be the lamb, who knows? Don't expect him to let you order for him again, though.

Sheila: Ha! As if I would try! You'll let me know if you need anything?

Kate: Yes, I will. If this is still going tomorrow, I might need you. I'll keep you posted.

Sheila: Sorry again, Kate. You can pick the next 3 restaurants!

Kate: I'll remind you of that when you're not swimming in guilt. Night!

Sheila: Night!

Kate put the phone away with a sigh and brushed her teeth. She slipped into a pair of flannel pajama pants and a blue tank top and looped her hair on top of her head. Padding softly to Will's room, she heard a flush and a groan. She tapped softly on the door.

"Will? Can I come in?"

"Just a minute." His voice sounded strained and she couldn't help but feel sorry for him. This was only the third place they'd gone that was her choice. Well, not his choice, anyway. She couldn't help but compare his classy, expensive, food-poison free restaurant choices to her more plebian tastes. She liked nice places as much as the next person, but she'd wanted to assert a little of herself into this relationship. He was branded all over her: his last name, his apartment, his money and credit cards and town cars and fancy events. He was clearly making a mark on her life, but was she making a mark on his?

Well, he'll certainly remember this.

She felt horribly guilty for asking him to hang out with her friends. He'd said yes with very little convincing and had agreed to this double date, even though he hated ethnic food and especially hated sitting on the floor. *No good deed goes unpunished.*

She stopped her musing when Will opened the door and stood before her, upright for the first time in an hour. He was holding a tied up trash bag in his hand.

"Is that?" she gestured to the bag, not saying the word but knowing he would understand her.

"Yeah. I needed the toilet for… other… I'll take this out."

"No! I'll take it. You stay here. Don't move around too much. I'll be right back."

She ran the bag out to the hall and into the garbage chute, then got back in time to see Will trying to cover himself up on the bathroom floor.

"Here, let me do that." She took the blanket from him and laid it across his back. "Better?"

"Yes. Thanks, Kate," he said. "You're lovely."

"Shh. Try to get some sleep. I'll be close by."

Kate went to her room and laid down with the door open, but after a few minutes of straining to hear sounds from his room, she realized she'd never be able to sleep this far away. She grabbed her pillow and went back to Will's room and climbed into his enormous king-sized bed. She could just make out where he slept on the marble floor through the crack in the bathroom door. He appeared to be sleeping and she tried to do the same.

An hour later, she was up with Will, wiping his brow

and stroking his hair. They went back to sleep, then repeated the whole process two more times before the sun finally began to rise. Will had fallen into what appeared to be a deeper sleep and she had gotten him to drink a little bit of water, but she was afraid he was becoming dehydrated. She remembered having food poisoning with Heather when they had both eaten some questionable crabs in South Carolina on family vacation. Kate had recovered in roughly a day and a half, but Heather had stayed sick for a full three days, eventually having to be hospitalized and given IV fluids, she was so dehydrated. Afraid that would happen to Will, she thought she should call his doctor. Just as she was getting up to make the call, she realized she didn't know how to find the doctor's number or even who his doctor was. *Andy will know.*

She went into her den and called Andrew. After four rings, his voicemail picked up and Kate left a message requesting the doctor's name and contact information. Leaning her head back in exasperation, she knew she didn't want to wait for Andy to call her back. That could take hours. It was only five thirty in the morning, after all. Scrolling through her contact lists, she made another call.

After two rings, a posh voice answered. "Is this the magical Katie, calling me at an ungodly hour on a Friday morning?"

"Harry, you know there's nothing magical about me. And it's after ten your time."

"Ha! Any woman who gets the impenetrable William Harper to marry her, IN VEGAS, after only two months of dating is magical. And no one decent goes out before eleven, everyone knows that."

She laughed in spite of her fatigue and suddenly felt the urge to hug him, though she barely knew him and he was an ocean away.

"Harry, I'm in a bit of a situation here. Will has food poisoning. He said he's had it once before, with you."

"Ah, you want the sordid story? Well, it was Carnival and we met these Brazilian girls, and they-"

"Actually," she cut him off, "I was hoping you could tell

me how long it lasted. I want to know what I'm in for here."

"I was out for a day or two, I think Harper had it longer. Let me think…. we met them on Friday night and I was back at the party on Sunday evening while Harper was still moaning in bed, poor sod. So there you have it. Nearly three days!"

"Ohhh," she moaned.

"Don't worry, love. Just nurse him a bit and he'll love you even more when it's all over. Men can't resist a nurse," he said conspiratorially.

"Leave it to you to make food poisoning sexual," she mumbled. "We'll see. Thanks, Harry. I'll talk to you later."

"Bye, love."

"Oh, G-d! Three days!" she said to the room. Her mind was whirring through all she had to do and their various social engagements that weekend. They were supposed to go to a dinner party Saturday night that would have to be cancelled, but thankfully that night and Sunday were clear. She needed to call Evelyn and tell her Harper would be out that day and to keep his Monday morning open in case he was still puny. She had to rewrite her paper on Bronte and had an essay due in another class. Thankfully, that one was already written and she just had to do a final polish. She decided to go ahead and do it now while she was up and Will was sleeping. Who knew how much time she would have over the weekend with him in this condition?

Forty-five minutes later, she stretched behind her desk and looked at her completed essay. At least that was one thing she could cross off her list. She quickly emailed it to her professor and then sent Evelyn a text message telling her Harper would not be in to work today and to keep Monday morning light. Evelyn immediately responded with sympathy and said she would cancel his day and his Saturday morning squash game as well. Kate thanked her and went to check on her husband.

He was just beginning to wake and seemed to have gotten back some color in his face until he sat up and he suddenly went pale again and had to lean over the toilet, dry heaving. Kate rubbed his back and said comforting words, like she had been doing all night.

"Kate?"

"Yeah, babe?"

"I know I shouldn't eat anything, but could you make me some toast? I'm hungry."

"Sure, I'll be right back." She knew he wouldn't hold it down, but surely feeling hungry had to be a good sign? She was back a few minutes later with dry toast for Will and buttered for herself.

"Why can't I have butter?" he asked like a child who'd been denied a treat.

"Because you're sick. Dry is better. I think."

He looked at her toast enviously, but ate his without further complaint.

The next several hours passed much as the night had done, with Will sleeping and vomiting in turn and Kate getting a nap or two between bouts. Sheila called at noon offering to bring lunch, which Kate quickly accepted.

She grabbed the books off her nightstand and put them in Will's room and spritzed her perfume in the sheets for good measure. She made sure her bedroom was locked and was ready for company two minutes before the bell rang. Sheila arrived with a deli sandwich and cup of soup for Kate and some bizarre looking drink for Harper.

"I promise, it'll make him feel better. Trust me," Sheila said.

"Isn't that what you said when you suggested that restaurant?"

"Ha ha. This time I mean it. Just get him to try it. It really does help."

The drink went into the fridge and Sheila offered to proofread her paper while Kate ate. A few minutes later, Kate's phone rang.

"That was Will's doctor. He'll stop by soon to check on him, but he said it mostly just needs to run its course and to keep him hydrated and comfortable."

"Your doctor makes house calls? How do I get his number?"

"I know, right? It's the first time I've ever had to call him. I guess it pays to be rich."

"So have you gotten used to it yet? Being rich?" Sheila asked as they walked into the kitchen.

"In some ways, yeah. It's nice to not have to take a calculator to the grocery store, but I still budget everything. Will teases me about it sometimes, but I think he appreciates that I'm not going spend-crazy."

"He's definitely a keeper. This place is great, by the way."

"Thanks! Sorry I haven't had you over yet. The summer was so hectic with the reception and meeting Will's family and settling in. Half the rooms didn't even have furniture in them! I'm finally coming up for air."

"Of course you haven't had anyone over! Getting married and moving is hectic. Plus you have to have all that newlywed sex. Doesn't leave time for much else." Kate laughed and shook her head to hide her blush.

"I thought we might have a little dinner party in October, let all the significant others meet each other."

"Sounds fun. Or you could just take us with you to the Hamptons for the weekend," Sheila joked to cover her friend's embarrassment. It was funny how Kate had never cared when they talked about sex in her past relationships.

"You know, that's a great idea! I'll ask Will about it when he's feeling better."

"You know I was just kidding, right?"

"Of course. But it's still a great idea."

Their talk was interrupted by a moan in the bathroom and the simultaneous buzzing for the door.

"Can you let the doctor up? I'll check on Will," Kate said.

When she got to the bathroom, Will was holding his stomach and curled in a ball on his side. She rushed to him, touching his shoulder to get his attention.

"Baby, are you alright? How can I help you?" She rubbed his back and waited for an answer.

"Can't help," he ground out.

She felt his forehead and noted with relief that it wasn't any hotter than it had been an hour ago, though it was still very warm. "Doctor Warren just got here. I'll bring him back in a minute."

Kate got to the door just as Sheila was opening it for the doctor. "Hi, I'm Katherine Harper, William's wife. This is my friend Sheila Johansen. She's helping me keep an eye on William." Kate smiled and held out her hand. The doctor shook it and smiled kindly.

"I'm Dr. Warren. Where is the patient?" he asked.

"Right this way."

Sheila stepped into the living room while Kate showed the doctor to Will's place on the bathroom floor.

"Well, you certainly look comfortable, young man," Dr. Warren commented as he knelt down. He took in Will's pale face and asked him to lie flat on the floor. Will did as he was told, but it was clear he wasn't completely aware of what was happening.

The doctor addressed his questions to Kate. When did the symptoms start? What exactly had he eaten? Did anyone else eat the same thing? Were they sick, too? How many times had he thrown up? Had he had any diarrhea? (She was only slightly mortified at that one.) Had he eaten or drunk anything since? When was the last time he vomited? How much sleep had he gotten?

The doctor felt his abdomen and checked his temperature with a digital thermometer. He looked in his eyes with a light and did the same with his ears.

"He's pretty dehydrated, but I think you're right about it being food poisoning. It's generally very violent and that seems to fit the bill here." Kate nodded agreement. "Did he have any symptoms before? Has he been feeling badly lately? Missing sleep?"

"No, he's been sleeping regularly and hasn't been sick a day since I met him. Until now, of course."

The doctor chuckled. "Well that's one way to get initiated in spousal care, huh?" She smiled weakly. "If we can get him to bed, I'd like to get an IV in him for a few hours, just to keep him hydrated."

"Yeah, sure." She bent to speak quietly to her husband. "Will, babe," his eyes fluttered open slowly. "Can you get up and make it to the bed? The doctor wants to put an IV in."

Will's eyes widened slightly and he looked at Kate with worried eyes. "An IV?"

"Some patients hate needles," Dr. Warren said to Kate. To Will he added, "Mr. Harper, just focus on your pretty wife here and don't think about the needle. Just keep looking at Katherine."

They led William to the bed and he lay down gingerly. Kate immediately climbed onto the bed on the other side of him and took his hand until he looked at her while Dr. Warren pulled out supplies on his other side. She told him about the paper she was rewriting and how she hoped this version pleased Professor Wheeler who, for some odd reason, had taken an immediate dislike to her. Dr. Warren smiled in approval at her method of distraction and within a few minutes, he had the IV stand unfolded and standing next to the bed with a clear bag of fluid hanging on it and was pulling a needle and other supplies from his bag. He surreptitiously slid a clipboard toward Kate which she glanced at long enough to read the words 'PERMISSION TO TREAT' in bold letters at the top. She signed it with her right hand while her left still held Will's without stopping her story for a moment.

In a matter of seconds, Dr. Warren had swabbed Will's arm and inserted the IV, taped it off and disposed of the packaging while William sat silently staring at Kate as she continued with her tale of unjust treatment at the cruel hands of her professor. When he looked like he was about to drop off again, Kate kissed his forehead and followed the doctor out of the room.

"Well done, Mrs. Harper. You'll be well prepared when you have children one day."

Kate just smiled and asked if there were any more instructions for Will. He told her to let him rest and that the IV stand had wheels if he needed to take it to the bathroom. He told her he'd be back to remove the IV in a few hours, but not to worry until then.

Will was in bed for all of Friday and the majority of Saturday, though he quit retching Friday night. He was able to hold down light fluids Saturday and slept the majority of the day, this time in his own bed. Saturday night he sat on the couch by Kate, watching a movie while she rubbed his neck and played with his hair. She was kind enough to eat out of his sight since he still couldn't hold much down, and by Monday morning, he was ready to go to work with strict orders to be nice to his stomach for several days. Kate made a pot of mild soup Sunday afternoon and because he'd done so well with it, she sent a container with him to work on Monday. She also sent a message to Evelyn telling her not to order Will's usual take out, no matter what he said.

By the time she got to class Monday, it felt like a vacation just to be out of the house and away from the constant threat of sickness. *So glad I'm not a nurse,* she thought.

21
GAME POINT

Late October
6 Months Married

"Man, Harper, you are really not on your game today," Andrew said as he scored yet another point.

"Thanks, Jamison. I hadn't noticed," Will bit back.

"What's the problem? You're usually mopping the floor with me by now." Will glared at him across the racquetball court. "Oh, I see!" Andrew drew out the words.

"See what?" Will's annoyance had not abated.

"You're not getting any!"

Will stared at him with shock and anger. "What do you mean 'not getting any'? I'm fine," he said through a clamped jaw.

"Yeah, right! You have a thin grip on control, my friend. Admit it, you're turning blue."

"I am not turning blue!" he nearly shouted.

Andrew held his hands up in a gesture of surrender. "Alright, alright, I'll back off. But you know Katie would help you out with your little problem if you asked her. She seemed pretty open to it in the beginning. That's why she had that clause about children put in."

"Children?"

"Yeah. Didn't you read the pre-nup?"

"I read the part about the financial settlements. I breezed through the rest. Chalk it up to my over-inflated trust in you."

Andrew ignored his jab. "Katie insisted we add a clause about children. She said with the two of you in such close quarters and all that." Andrew gestured with his hands as his friend studied his racket. "Actually, I'm surprised it hasn't happened already. It's been six months."

Will huffed. "It's not that simple, Andrew. I live with Kate. I can't just stop living with her if things aren't..."

"Sweaty? Hot and dirty? Incredibly satisfying?"

Will groaned. "Oh, come on, Jamison. You know things could be incredibly awkward afterward. And it's not like I can just go back to my place and forget about it. It's not five dates and it's over. I have to see her – EVERY DAY!"

"So what are you afraid of? Not up to the challenge?" Will shot him a dirty look. "Think she's no good? Even if it sucked, I bet you could work on it. Like you said, you live together – what better opportunity to improve your skills?"

Will gave him a cynical look.

"And I doubt she sucks." Will looked at him questioningly. "Trust me man, once you go Bishop, you don't go back."

"You did not just say that," Will replied.

Andrew just laughed. "Come on. Court time's up."

***

"Death by Chocolate Cake or the Molten Lava Brownie?"

"I'm having the tiramisu," Jen answered her sister as they perused their menus.

The waiter stepped up to the table to take their orders.

"Tiramisu and a cappuccino," Jen said.

"I'll have the Death by Chocolate Cake a la mode. And can you drizzle a little hot fudge over that? And a cup of cocoa with whipped cream and chocolate shavings."

Jen looked at her sister quizzically, but said nothing.

Kate looked at the man walking past and felt herself flush. "Wow. He's so tall. Did you see his arms?" Kate's eyes watched him until he turned the corner, then looked back at her sister who had an amused look on her face.

"Down girl!" Jen laughed. "You okay?"

"Yeah, I'm great. Why?"

"Oh, I don't know. You've just checked out every guy who's walked by in the last hour, including one who looked like Santa." She leaned back when she saw the waiter approach. He quietly set down their desserts and left. "And you just ordered about two pounds of chocolate."

"I'm just craving chocolate. It's no big deal." As she finished her sentence, she unknowingly turned her head to follow a man in a dark suit walking past their table in the busy restaurant.

"Uh-oh. Oh, no," Jen said, shaking her head.

"What?"

"How long has it been?"

"Has what been?"

Jen looked at her with raised brows and 'don't mess with me' eyes.

"Alright! It's been a while."

"How long is a while?"

"Jeremy."

"Jeremy!" Jen cried.

"Shhh! You don't have to announce it to the world!"

"You mean to tell me you haven't gotten laid since *Jeremy*?" Jen whispered furiously. "You broke up last February!"

"I know."

"It's October!"

"I *know*," she said lowly through clenched teeth, leaning over the table so know one else would hear her.

"Wow. I thought you and Will agreed to sleep together? Didn't you talk about it in April?"

"Yeah, we talked about it and we agreed it was okay, but it's kind of awkward now."

"What do you mean 'awkward'?"

"I mean I feel like we're friends now."

"And that's a problem because...?"

"I've never done it with a friend!"

"It's called friends with benefits. People do it all the time."

"I know that. I just thought it would happen naturally, but we haven't even gotten close. Now I'm afraid we're too firmly established in the friend zone."

"The zone isn't a death sentence. It's not like you're related or anything. You can adapt."

"I know that logically, but what if he doesn't want to? I don't want to humiliate myself."

"Why would you think he doesn't want to? You're hot!"

"He hasn't made a single move. He's been the perfect gentleman. Unfortunately," Kate mumbled.

"And you don't want a big awkward mess with someone you consider a friend."

"Exactly."

"Weren't you friends with Jeremy?"

"Before I dated him! Then we dated for like two months before we slept together." Jen looked at her doubtfully. "Okay, two weeks, but still!"

"But you're *married* to Will." She leaned further across the table and whispered to her sister. "And you guys go on dates – fake dates, but dates. Doesn't that count?"

"I don't know." Kate grumbled and shoved another piece of chocolate cake in her mouth.

"What about that guy before Jeremy? Mike? Mark? Mick? Weren't you friends?"

"Matt. I really liked him. And he was practically in love with me. He almost proposed, remember?"

"Oh, yeah. Why'd you guys break up again?"

"He had that weird collection of golf-balls."

"The ones with celebrities' faces painted on them?"

"Yup."

"Yeah, that's weird." Jen made a face and shook her head. "What about Phillip? You guys were great friends. He was always helping you with your homework."

"Yeah, we were friends. But I still had a major crush on him, even if it did only last a month. And we never *actually* slept together."

"You didn't? But what about that time I caught him coming out of your room?"

Katie grimaced and wagged her head side to side as if she were trying to find just the right words. "Heavy make-out session."

"Ah." Jen nodded in understanding. "So that just leaves us with the skinny tall boy from freshman year."

"Caleb."

"Ah, Kosher Caleb – how could I forget?"

Kate glared at her sister and said, "I was crazy about him and we went out for over a year. I met his *parents,* for pete's sake. He was my first – of course we weren't just *friends.*"

"So you're in uncharted territory. Big deal. Figure it out. It's not like you're not attracted to each other. Who knows? Maybe after you sleep together you'll start to like each other."

"Who says we're attracted to each other?"

"Oh, come on, Katie! First of all, this is William we're talking about. One of Manhattan's top ten most eligible bachelors – or at least he was. Every woman in the western hemisphere is attracted to him. Secondly, he's totally you're type."

"Is not. I don't have a type."

"Seriously?"

"Seriously."

"Okay, miss I-don't-have-a-type. Why haven't you ever dated a guy under six feet? Or is it six two?" Kate glared at her sister as she forcefully ate another bite of cake. "You have a thing for tall guys."

"Every woman likes tall guys. It's primal. They look like good hunters or something."

"Uh-huh. Keep telling yourself that if it makes you feel better. Have you ever dated a blonde? Or a red head?"

"That's not fair! Statistically there aren't very many red-heads. Most people have never dated one," Kate said defensively.

"Still, it seems like a pretty steady pattern you have of tall guys with dark hair. Jeremy's was black and weird Matt's was definitely dark brown."

"Phillip was blonde. Ha!"

"Light brown." Jen shot back.

"Dark blonde."

"Dark blonde? Really?" Jen looked at her skeptically. "Even if there was such a thing, you just said you never really slept together and you only went out for a month."

"So?"

"So! He doesn't really count! Obviously your subconscious was telling you he was the wrong type for you and refused to let it get serious."

"Oh, Jenny! You are really starting to crack me up!"

Jen left some money on the table and led her sister out the door. "Come on – I've got an idea."

"Where are you taking me?"

"La Perla." Kate looked at her with wide eyes. "Don't worry, there's construction on the building on the corner. I'll let you stop and gawk on the way."

**

Three hours later, Kate was unpacking her bags in her room while Jen watched, sprawled across her bed.

"I can't believe I let you talk me into this," Kate said.

"Of course you can. Subconsciously, this is what you want and I am merely helping you to achieve it."

"Would you quit talking about my subconscious? This is a ridiculous plan. I should just tell Will that I'm hormonal and ask him to oblige me."

"Oblige you? Seriously? You used to be fearless! Remember how you wrapped yourself in saran wrap for Jeremy's birthday?"

Kate got a far away look in her eye. "Yeah. That was…" She sighed dreamily.

"Hey! Snap out of it!" Kate blinked and looked at her sister. "It can't be any harder to wear a negligee than to wear plastic wrap. And definitely easier to get into."

"Not to mention it breathes better. Okay, Jenny. You win. Now help me pick which of these to wear first."

Jen held up a silky, gray-blue slip with a wide border of lace at the hem and tiny spaghetti straps. "Start with this one. It's more subtle. He won't be *completely* shocked to see you wandering around in it."

"If this blows up in my face, I'm blaming you."

"Trust me. And quit being such a coward. It's weird for you."

***

Will walked into the apartment late that night, exhausted and frustrated. "Katie," he called out from the entryway, "you will never believe the day I had! Saunders is a complete idiot and he totally cocked up the -" he stopped in mid sentence as he walked into the living room.

"Hey, Will. Popcorn?" Kate asked from the floor where she laid on her stomach, in her new negligee, watching television as if this was an everyday occurrence. She sat up and held the bowl out to him.

"Thanks." He fell onto the sofa and took the bowl from her hand, looking at her oddly.

"So what did Saunders do? Is it about the buyout?" she asked as if everything was the same as it had always been.

"Yeah." Will ate a few bites of popcorn and shook himself out of his silk-induced trance. "He pitched his plan on how to market HarperCo to the old workers at the Stenson Plant. It was complete rubbish. He even made a short film about what a caring company we are and how we look after our own."

"But you are a caring company and you do look after your people," she reasoned.

"He just made it sound so sappy." Katherine laughed at the look on his face. "Truly, it was almost painful to watch. It came complete with a theme song and motto. 'HarperCo, because Harper Cares'. I've never hated the sound of my own name so much."

"You're kidding! He really said that? Wow!" Kate laughed as Will let out a grumbling sigh and leaned his head back in exhaustion. "Aw, I'm sorry babe. It sounds awful. Beer and grilled cheese? It'll make you feel better."

"Yeah, I am a bit peckish." He followed Kate into the kitchen and sat at one of the bar stools while she gathered ingredients from the fridge. She seemed to struggle in her short nightgown with reaching down into the lower cabinet for a pan. She finally decided on squatting sideways with her knees pressed closely together. He watched her with a smile on his face as he began to relax from the day.

"So what else happened today? Is the merger still on track?" she asked him as he grabbed a beer and popped the top off.

"Yeah, so far everything is looking good. The Helgsen people will be in at the middle of the month. We'll have to do a lot of wining and dining, I'm afraid; he's bringing his wife. Are you up for it?"

"When exactly?" she asked as she set the sandwich in the pan.

"Looks like they'll arrive the fourteenth and stay the week. We're in meetings all day Monday. His wife wants to go shopping and she'll be here alone, so I was hoping you'd go with her – you know, keep her company."

"You mean keep her happy and off her husband's back so he can sign your papers faster?" she asked with a grin.

"Something like that," he smirked.

"Hasn't she ever been to New York before? Does she not have her own friends here?"

"According to Mr. Helgsen's assistant, she usually goes to Paris to shop. She's been to New York before, but usually with her sister or a friend. This will be her first time with just her husband."

"And that's where I come in."

"Exactly."

"Well, I *suppose* I can take one for the team and spend a day shopping. You know how I detest it, but I'll do it for the company," she said in a dramatic voice.

"You are too good, Katie." She set a plate with a grilled cheese sandwich in front of him. "What would I do without you?"

"You'd be sitting alone in England with no merger, eating beans on toast." She laughed. Will joined in and then grabbed her hand. He brought it to his mouth and kissed her knuckles.

"I am forever indebted to you, my lady," he said with mock gravity.

Kate backed up and pointed a finger at him. "And don't you forget it!"

Will watched her leave with a small smile on his face. Maybe getting… closer wouldn't be as hard as he'd thought.

Kate went to bed with a smile on her face, happy that the first step in her plan to let William know she was open to sleeping together had gone well.

22
MAD

Early November
Married 6.5 Months

"So this is my dad's house." Katherine pointed to a picture of an old farmhouse in the photo album sitting on her lap.

"This is where you grew up?" Will asked. He was sitting close to Kate on the couch, their legs touching and his arm on the sofa back behind her.

"Mostly. Originally, we all lived here." She pointed to a photo of a large pink Victorian house. "After the divorce my mom kept the big house and dad moved to a smaller farmhouse at the back of the property."

"Remind me how old were you when they divorced?" He played with her hair and touched her neck subtly, not terribly focused on the conversation and wondering how much longer this flirtation would go on before they got to the point.

She pointed to a picture of her and Jen in front of the Victorian house. "I was three, so I don't really remember living all together. Jenny was five, so she remembers a little more than me, but not much." She curled her legs up so her knees were halfway across his leg and her upper body was leaning against him, his breath tickling her forehead.

"Wow. That's young."

"Yeah. They talked about it before I was born, but decided to stay together for the kids. That clearly didn't last," she said sarcastically.

Will flipped the page himself and saw the same two girls, a little older now, posing with two smaller girls, one with brown hair a little lighter than Kate's and one blonde like Jenny. "Are these your other sisters?"

"Yes, that's Heather and Tiffany."

"They're your mom's right, because you said your dad never remarried?"

"No," she drew out the word, "mom never remarried either. They're not half-sisters. Just sisters."

"I don't understand." His hand was making circles on her neck now, making her skin tingle in the most pleasant way.

"My parents were obviously big believers in Bonus Night. After they'd been divorced a little over a year, Heather was born. Dad is listed on the birth certificate as the father and she calls him dad. I choose not to ask too many questions."

"Okay," he said skeptically, "what about the blonde one?"

"Three years after Heather was born, Tiffany came along. Again, I chose not to ask questions. I was only seven at the time, so I didn't really understand what was going on anyway. Of course now I realize how jacked up the whole thing was. Mom finally wised up and got her tubes tied after Tiffany."

Will was obviously having a hard time processing this information. He stopped playing with her hair and looked at her quizzically. Kate tried to explain it to him.

"My parents have what you could call a love/hate relationship. They hate each other enough that they can't live together, but love each other enough that they can't really stay away. So they live in separate houses on the same property. Dad runs the farm and mom runs the gift shop. They see each other for work things and kid stuff, though not as much since it's just Heather and Tiffany home now. It's been this way for years. I know it's weird, but you get used to it."

"Who lived with whom growing up?"

"At first we were together in the pink house, then after the divorce we all stayed with mom during the week and dad on weekends because it was the busy time in the gift shop. After Tiffany was born, I went to live full time at dad's because mom needed the space for the baby and I was the most willing to go. Jenny was about fifty-fifty at that point. After Jenny turned ten, she came to stay at dad's full time, too so mom could focus on the baby and not have to worry about the bigger kids and getting us to school and all our activities while Tiffany was napping. We'd often all have dinner together at mom's, then walk across the fields to dad's to sleep."

"What about Heather?"

"She's always lived with mom, even though I think she would have been happier with dad. Heather's the intellectual type and my mom is... well, she's not. Mom has never understood Heather, but she was quiet and stayed out of trouble, unlike me and Jenny, and she was useful in the shop, so mom kept her around. She's in college now studying engineering and seems to have really found her niche. I'm happy for her. You'll meet her when we visit. She'll probably be one of the only ones that won't give you a headache."

"So where will we stay when we go down for Thanksgiving?"

"Normally, I would say my dad's, because that's what I usually do. My mom can be trying on the nerves. But he's very perceptive and really knows me, so he might suspect something's up. Plus he likes to tease a lot and is very sarcastic, so it can get on some people's nerves if you're not used to it. Not like my teasing which is sweet and endearing." He looked at her with one eyebrow cocked and she grinned impishly.

"Okay, so your dad might blow the cover, but would probably be more pleasant to stay with. Your mom will wear us down, but isn't likely to catch that we're faking it?"

"That's about it. She's not stupid, she just doesn't see what she doesn't want to see. And she might kill me if I bring my new husband home and don't stay with her. We'll have to stay in the guestroom because my old room is at dad's."

"Too bad. I always had a thing for rooms in parents' houses." He pulled her closer so her head was on his shoulder and his hand rubbed her back gently.

"William Harper! How naughty of you! I never would have suspected it from Mr. Straight-laced."

"I think it came from my university girlfriend, Sandra. Winter break of our sophomore year, I stayed with her at her parents for New Year. It was mortifying at first because I had expected to sleep on the couch, given our ages and the fact that we weren't married. Her parents just assumed I would be staying with her and put my bag in her room." He chuckled quietly. "The walls were this hideous shade of pink, and the duvet was this ruffled affair and covered in stuffed animals. She actually had names for all of them."

"She told you that?"

"Oh yes, she told me. I was treated to a role call as she cleared the bed the first night. And she was wearing flannel pajamas with little ballerinas on them. My twelve-year-old sister had the same ones." He and Kate grimaced together. "She kept snuggling up to me and trying to start something, but I couldn't get the picture of Jacqueline out of my head. Anyway, nothing ended up happening and afterward I thought, 'What a wasted opportunity.' At least I thought that at the time." He shrugged. "I guess it will be a while longer before I live out that particular fantasy." Kate smacked his arm.

"Hey!"

"So what happened? To you and Sandra?" she asked softly, her fingers tracing random patterns on his abdomen.

"What usually happens to people you date in uni? We saw each other for a few more months after that and then grew apart. We only had one class together that spring and by autumn we were in completely different circles. We split amicably and she went on to date a rugby player whom she later married. They now live in Sussex with a dog and three children, I believe."

"Did you date anyone after her?"

"Not really. I hung out with small groups of friends and went out on a few dates of course, but nothing regular after that. I couldn't, really."

"Why not? Were you still hung up on Sandra?"

"No, that wasn't it. I knew it would never go anywhere with Sandra."

"What do you mean?" Kate asked.

"We were too different. It wouldn't have worked."

"Sometimes opposites attract."

"I suppose, but I had expectations to meet."

Her hand stilled and she sat up to look at him. "I see. You didn't mean different in personality, but different in social status. She was beneath you," Katherine said with brow raised and back stiff.

He pulled back his arm that had been around her. "I wouldn't say 'beneath me'. But we were from different spheres, yes. Don't look at me like that, Kate. A man in my position has a lot of responsibilities. I'm expected to marry a certain kind of woman, from a particular family. It's a lot of pressure and someone who didn't grow up in it wouldn't know how to handle it. She'd be unhappy, I'd be disappointed, and eventually we'd resent each other and get divorced. So why bother? Just skip the heartache altogether." He shrugged and tilted his head in a flicking gesture.

"Did Sandra know you were just slumming it with her?" Kate's voice was like ice and she was now sitting on the edge of the cushion.

"I never made her any promises," he said coldly.

"No, you just dated her for over a year, went home to meet her parents, and slept with her whenever you had the chance." Will flushed slightly. "Am I wrong? Did you tell her on your first date, 'Listen, I think you're cute and all and I'd like to shag you, but you should know right now that it'll never go anywhere because I'm expected to marry a high-society ice queen'?" Will's jaw clenched. "That's what I thought." She slid further away.

"You have no idea what it's like to live in my world."

"Don't I? What do you think I've been doing for the past six months, Will? Having dinner with your business partners, getting my nails done with their wives who wouldn't know what work was if it injected them with Botox, attending every black tie, overdone, ridiculous event where everyone *pretends* to be doing it all for charity but really just wants their picture in the paper!" Her eyes blazed as she leaned toward him, her voice hard. "You people are such snobs! Why didn't you get one of them to marry you? Nobody really cares about anybody else, anyway; it would have been easy enough to find some inflated Barbie to sign all your little papers. They probably would have been lining up to marry the Great William Harper! You didn't have to choose the daughter of a Christmas tree farmer from Virginia!"

"Would you stop freaking out? Why are you taking everything so personally? This is just a business deal. It's not like we're *really* married!" he shouted.

Kate went pale, then squared her shoulders and lifted her chin. "Of course. How silly of me. We're not friends, this is just business. Excuse me, Mr. Harper."

"Kate, wait!" Will called after her, but she was half way down the hall. By the time he got to his feet, her door had clicked quietly shut.

23
DOGHOUSE

Mid November
7 Months Married

"Cheers, mate. It's a little late, but happy birthday!" Jamison held his beer toward William and clinked his glass with his own.

"Thanks, Jamison," William said with a small smile.

"Is Kate still not talking to you?" Andrew asked as he poured ketchup onto his plate.

"Yup. It's like *Silence of the Lambs* in there. She hasn't said a single word to me outside of business deals. She needed to change our plans the other night and called Evelyn to leave a message. She won't even talk to me on the phone."

"But you're still going on your dates, right? I saw a picture of you at the hospital thing." He added mustard to his burger and signaled the server for more napkins.

"Yes, she is everywhere she's supposed to be, impeccably dressed, perfect manners, but the second we get in the car or go back home, she shuts me out. That picture from the hospital charity event?"

"Yeah?"

"That dress was backless. When I put my arm around her to pose for the picture, I swear I could feel her skin repelling me."

Andrew chuckled. "Aren't you being a little dramatic?"

"I'm telling you, Jamison, it's like she's a whole other person. No more beer and grilled cheese, no more talks after I get home from work. Nothing. She says nothing. She doesn't even watch telly in the living room anymore. She works late most nights with that professor of hers, and when I asked her about it, on a date of course so she would have to talk to me, she glared at me for a nanosecond, then did this scary sweet smile and said he just needed her a lot right now because they were getting so close to the end."

"But it wasn't that long ago that you were complaining about how she sings too much in the house and keeps talking to you. You don't like the peace and quiet?"

"Trust me, Jamison, there is nothing peaceful about this quiet. It's the kind of quiet you hear in a horror movie right as the skinny blonde girl who can't find her phone is walking into the woods in the middle of the night. It's creepy quiet."

Andrew couldn't help but laugh.

"What's so funny? I'm serious, Andrew - something's got to give. It's been two weeks! We're supposed to be going to see her parents for Thanksgiving – in six days! How are we going to pull that off if she isn't even speaking to me? We're going to have to share a room for Christ's sake!"

"Sounds like you miss Katie."

"I do. We were friends – at least I thought we were. Oh, G-d! I'm Jerry fucking Maguire! "

"Have you tried apologizing?"

"For what? I said nothing that wasn't true. She shouldn't have taken everything so personally. I wasn't talking about her."

"Harper, when are you going to get that women have this solidarity thing? If you piss off one of them, you may as well piss off all of them."

"What is that?"

"Pack mentality," Andrew said between mouthfuls of fries.

"I guess that explains why they're always going to the loo together."

And just like that, they put the difficult conversation behind them and spoke of lighter things.

***

"When do you leave for Farmington?" asked Jen as they sat on the couch in her apartment.

"I'm taking the train down in three days."

"Is William still going with you?"

"I don't know. The train is probably too *pedestrian* for him. He'll probably take the company plane. Don't know, don't care," Kate said petulantly.

"Really? Won't it look suspicious if you arrive by train and he flies down?"

"Probably. I don't even know if he's coming. Honestly, I'd be relieved if he didn't. One less thing to worry about. I can just enjoy my visit with my family. Dad's the only one who would notice anything, and I can just tell him we got in a fight and I wouldn't even be lying."

Jennifer squeezed her hand. "I'm sorry I won't be there with you."

"Don't be. It's your first holiday with Andy's family. You should be there, it's a big step for you two."

"Thanks. But all the same, this is going to be rough. And probably pretty entertaining. I'm sad I'm going to miss it," Jen added with a sly grin.

"Jenny!" Kate whined. "I can't believe I have to live through eighteen more months of this! And I almost had sex with him! What was I thinking?" She dropped her head dramatically onto the pillow she was holding. "You know what I did last night? I counted up all the days between now and when he gets his ten year green card and calculated what sixty percent of that time was. Then I tried to plan how I could spend forty percent of the time away from him and how to spread it out so it won't look suspicious."

"I thought it was seventy percent?"

"Ohhh!" she groaned. "What have I gotten myself into?"

"I'm so sorry, sweetie. If you need to come spend a few days with me, you know you're welcome. Andrew has a cabin in Vermont. Maybe we can go there for a couple of days to get away from it all – just us girls. We can get Laura to come and you won't have to pretend with us."

"That sounds wonderful, Jenny. Unfortunately, there's not enough time to go before I have to be back home. Maybe the three of us can go out together? After midterms and hosting Will's Dutch people and this fight, I'm wiped."

"I'll call Laura."

Three hours later, Jenny and Kate were sitting on the floor in Laura's loft apartment flipping through a collection of DVD's that could only be labeled as chick flicks. Laura made a pitcher of margaritas and Jenny ordered Thai food. One of Laura's clients had sent her a box of Godiva chocolates as a gift and she placed the three pound box on the coffee table with a flourish. Kate's eyes lit up and Jenny dived for the velvet ribbon surrounding the golden box. The next five hours were a blur of Julia Roberts, tequila, random tears, and nonsensical chatter.

"Was it really so bad?" Laura slurred, her glass swishing dangerously in her hand.

"You should have seen his face. He didn't care at all, like he was this great, benevolent lover who graced some lucky woman with his penis." Kate took a swig of tequila straight from the bottle.

Jen sniggered quietly and Laura guffawed. "Well, depending on the penis, she might not have minded."

Jen laughed out loud and tipped off the sofa. "Poor Katie, all hormoned up and no one to sleep with."

Kate threw a pillow at her sister. "Hey, don't taunt your drunk, sexually frustrated sister."

"Seriously, though," Laura added, putting her chin on the arm of the couch as she leaned forward from her seat on the floor, "what are you going to do? You can't cheat. You'll be in serious trouble."

Kate threw herself back on the couch dramatically. "I don't know! I guess I could get a vibrator? Do those even work?"

"Oh, G-d! This just gets better and better!" Jen howled.

"You're a bitch when you're drunk, you know that?" Kate said.

"They do work, sometimes. I'd offer to let you borrow mine, but that might be crossing the sharing boundary just a bit," said Laura.

"Yeah, thanks but no thanks," replied Kate.

By now, Jen was on the floor on her side, laughing silently while her entire body shook. Kate looked at her and rolled her eyes.

"She's so nice all the time, she has to get all her bitchiness out when she drinks," Laura surmised.

"Oh, Laura," Kate said pitifully. "Have I been wrong all along? Is William really a womanizing ass hole and I just thought he was a decent guy? What have I gotten myself into?"

"All men are ass holes. Hate to break it to you," Laura replied.

"Hey, Andy's great!" Jen slurred from her place on the floor.

"Yeah, yeah. He's rich and smart and good looking and practically perfect in every way. Just watch out. Golden boy's got to have a dark side somewhere," Laura prophesied.

Jen glared at her and let her head fall back on the pillow.

"You might have gotten the last good one, Jenny," Kate said with a slight smile in her sister's direction.

"This is why I don't do relationships. Too messy," Laura added.

"Oh, God!" Kate moaned. "I'm never going to have sex again!"

Laura snorted. "Not for the next two years anyway. Do you think your hymen will grow back by then?"

Kate kicked her leg. "Not funny!" she said while Laura laughed hysterically.

"You'll stop being mad soon enough. Then you just have to separate the man from the sex," Laura advised, gesturing with her hands.

"Ew. I don't know if I can do that."

"Sure you can. I do it all the time. It is possible for it to just be physical."

Jen moaned, clearly the only contribution she was capable of making at that time.

"Right now, the idea of letting that man touch me in any kind of intimate way makes me nauseous."

"Too bad, 'cause he is hooooootttt!" Laura dragged out the last word and broke down into giggles.

Kate sighed and closed her eyes. She knew the way Laura managed her dating life worked for her friend, but she didn't think it was her style. *It's going to be a long two years.*

It was too late to go home, so Kate crashed on the sofa and Jen slept with Laura. In the morning, they kept the shades drawn and drank tea slowly, each of them moving like they were afraid to go too fast.

Forty minutes later, Kate was on the subway heading to her 8:30 class in Laura's shirt. As she walked towards campus, she looked at her phone and saw four missed calls. She pressed the phone to her ear and listened to her voicemail.

Kate, it's Will. I was thinking about our plans for the holiday and wanted to know if you plan on flying to your parents. There's a small airport about twelve miles away that would be easy to fly into. I can leave Wednesday around five. Let me know what you want to do.

She hit erase with a huff and skipped to the next message.

Kitty, it's your mother. I've prepared the guest room for you and that husband of yours. Jenny said he was tall so I hope the bed is long enough for him. I'm expecting you Wednesday by six. The last train gets in at four-thirty and Heather or your father can pick you up, just be sure to let us know which one you're taking. We'll have a light supper then I'll need your help with the pies. Heather is absolutely useless in the kitchen! Sometimes I think that girl has feathers for brains! And of course Tiffany went and used my pie plates for some biology experiment. She's set her heart on some boy who's a bit of a nerd, sounds like, even though he is quite the looker. She's having him over to study every afternoon and they're doing God knows what in my kitchen-

The message ended abruptly when the allotted time ran out. She shook her head and clicked over to the next message.

Kate, it's Will. It's midnight and I just wanted to make sure you're alright. Please don't take the subway this late – it isn't safe. Call me if you want me to pick you up. See you soon.

Delete. Next message.

Kate, I'm really starting to get worried. I just woke up and you're not here. Please call and let me know if you're alright. I don't want to have to start calling hospitals.

She groaned and looked at the time stamp – seven forty A.M. With a sigh of resignation and a slight roll of the eyes, she sent a quick text.

I'm fine. On way to class – see you at dinner tonight.

***

Kate walked into the small Italian restaurant and gave her coat to the maître d. "Right this way, Mrs. Harper." She followed him to their usual table toward the back of the restaurant and pretended not to notice when the waiters followed her with their eyes.

Will was another story. He was immediately aware of her presence, as was every other red-blooded man in the vicinity. That was one thing he appreciated about her – she dressed to flatter her own figure. He studied her evenly as she came toward him, her body encased in a soft cashmere sweater dress. Even though it was up to her chin and down to her wrist, it was still incredibly sexy. Probably because the deep green color suited her skin perfectly and brought out her eyes, or maybe it was because the fabric looked so soft, like it was begging to be touched. It hung on her perfectly, outlining and hugging her curves without exactly clinging. It was mysterious and revealing all at once. The brown leather knee-high boots weren't exactly helping. He caught himself staring at the bit of skin revealed between her boots and her hem and it wasn't until she sat down in front of him that his focus shifted.

"Hello, William," she said evenly.

"Hi, Kate. How was your day?"

"Same as always. Yours?"

"Good, though I was worried about you. Where were you last night?" he asked quietly, leaning toward her and capturing her hand under his on the table.

She looked at his hand and said, "I spent the evening with Jenny and Laura. By the time we finished it was late and I was too tired to go back to the apartment, so I slept on Laura's couch."

He nodded. "You know I would've come and gotten you?"

"I didn't think of that. I just wanted to sleep. I was perfectly fine at Laura's."

He nodded silently and placed their order, veal Parmesan for himself and pumpkin ravioli for Kate. She pursed her lips and he asked, "What?"

"You ordered for me."

"So? I've ordered for you hundreds of times before. You don't have to get sour about it."

"What if I hadn't wanted ravioli? And I'm not sour!"

"I'm sorry. Did you want something else?" he asked sarcastically.

Kate looked down sheepishly – she was planning on ordering the ravioli anyway – then back at him with a look of defiance. "It's the principle of it. You should at least ask a person what they want instead of just assuming that you know what's best for them. I might have been in the mood for calamari, or mushrooms, or pizza!"

"You hate calamari. You always think you're going to like it, then you order it and you hate it. The only mushrooms you like are Portobello and they weren't on the menu tonight. And you hate the pizza here because the sauce is too sweet."

She huffed indignantly at his look of smugness. "So what is this? Prove-how-well-you-know-Kate night?"

"I'm not trying to prove anything. I simply ordered a meal for my wife that I knew she would enjoy. That's all."

She bristled at his use of the word 'wife'. She looked away and sipped her wine, refusing to respond. Will let out a ragged sigh and ran his hand through his hair.

"You should be careful with that. Don't want to go bald prematurely."

He glared at her. "That's an old wives' tale and you know it."

"Just saying."

They finished their meal in silence, though they did smile at each other when he helped her with her coat under the watchful eye of the maître d.

"Want to walk back? It's a clear night," he asked as they exited the restaurant.

Kate looked up at the sky, then around at the brightly lit street corner. "Sure, why not?"

He took her gloved hand in his and started down the street.

"Are you looking forward to the holiday with your family?"

"I guess," she answered.

"Did you want to come back Saturday or Sunday?"

"I thought I'd take the Sunday morning train back."

"You don't want to fly?"

"I don't want my family to know you have your own plane, no."

"I thought you said they knew about me?"

"Of course they know about you, they just don't know everything about you."

"How is that possible?"

"Easy. I didn't tell them."

"Didn't they ask questions?"

"Of course they did. They asked what you did and I told them you worked with computer chips. I'm pretty sure my mother quit listening after that. Dad just wanted to know if you paid your bills on time and if you had a savings account. Once I assured him you were financially viable, he dropped the questions."

Will furrowed his brow, unsure how to respond. He couldn't imagine being that lackadaisical about his own family. "Well, that sounds easy. Though I'm a little surprised."

"I'm not. My parents trust my judgment. My mom would love for me to marry a rich man, because of the security and the fancy Christmas gifts, but I think her idea of rich is more along the lines of a surgeon or a lawyer. As long as she's sure I'm well looked after and that you are handsome enough that she won't have ugly grandbabies, she won't ask too many questions. Dad just doesn't want me to marry an idiot or a loser. That's about it."

Will nodded. "So are you excited about going home?"

"Yes and no."

"Care to elaborate?"

"I'm not excited about lying to my parents and all my old friends, but it will be nice to see everyone."

He nodded and they went the rest of the way in silence.

***

Kate felt her phone buzz in her pocket and quickly looked at the text. *The train takes 6 hours. Are you sure you don't want to fly?*

She quickly answered. *How will I explain a private plane to my family? They'll notice when they pick us up and once they know, my mother will be out of control and my little sister will have a Christmas list a mile long.*

She set down the phone and went back to studying. Five minutes later she was interrupted by another buzz. *We could fly into the bigger Tri-Cities airport instead. It's not as close but it wouldn't raise as many questions. We can rent a car from there so no one has to pick us up.*

Her first instinct was to tell him to forget it and that she would go on her own by train like she always did, but she forced herself to consider his suggestion. It actually wasn't a bad plan.

How long will the plane take? Will smiled when he read her response.

Less than 2 hours. Private plane means no long security lines either.

Kate sighed. That definitely sounded a lot better than six hours on a train and another in the car. *You win. We can take the plane. But I have to be there by 6 to help with the pies.*

Deal.

24
THANKSGIVING

November, Wednesday Before Thanksgiving
7 Months Married

The small private plane landed at the Tri Cities Regional Airport at five-thirty the day before Thanksgiving. Will had spent the entire time on the phone between his assistant in New York and his cousin in London, going over details of the merger they were working on together.

Kate sat hunched over her laptop, finishing the draft of her last essay for her *Women of the Classics* class and working on her presentation for *Literary Critiques.* Professor Wheeler still wasn't impressed by her, but so far she had a low B in that class. Her final paper was weighted in such a way that she could pull her grade up to a low A if she got a good enough score on it. Convincing Professor Wheeler to give her a good score was the hard part.

They walked to the rental counter and got the keys for their car, Kate rolling her eyes imperceptibly when she realized Evelyn had reserved a luxury vehicle for them.

"Mind if I drive?" she asked as they put their bags into the trunk.

"Not at all," Will answered after a slight hesitation. "You know the area best."

"Thanks."

They drove the first forty-five minutes in silence, listening to the radio quietly in the background. As they passed yet another sign for a horse farm, Will broke the silence.

"Are we getting close?"

"We'll be there in about fifteen minutes. You feel ready?" she asked, her voice softer than it had been in weeks.

"Mostly. You?"

"Same."

They lapsed into silence again until Kate pulled off the highway and onto a narrow country road. A few miles later, she turned into a picturesque drive surrounded by a white fence and lined with poplar trees that had lost all their leaves. There was a wooden sign reading 'Bishop Farms' to the right of the drive. About a quarter mile up the gravel lane, they came upon a large pink Victorian house that Will recognized from the pictures he'd seen.

"It's quite lovely," he said quietly.

"Yes, my mother has a good eye for this sort of thing." She pointed to a small building that looked like it had once been a carriage house of some sort. "That's the gift shop over there. If you go over the hill and take the fork to the right, you'll hit the entrance to the tree park."

Will nodded and noticed the small sign pointing the way to the various farm offerings. They parked and Will took their bags out of the trunk. They were half way to the house when a blonde blur ran past Harper and jumped into Kate's arms.

"Katie!" the blur squealed.

"Tiffany!" Kate laughed and hugged her sister tightly. The two rocked back and forth for a minute before Tiffany grabbed her sister's arm and tugged her into the house, talking a mile a minute. She nodded at Will but otherwise ignored him.

Just inside the doorway stood an attractive woman in her early to mid-forties in jeans and a pink top, a floral apron tied around her waist.

"Hi, Mom!" Kate hugged her mother tightly, then stood back and looked at Will. "This is my husband, William Harper. William, this is my mother, Loretta Bishop."

"I'm pleased to meet you, madam."

Loretta's eyebrows shot up. "The pleasure is mine, William. Please, call me Loretta. Come on in and hang up your coats." She patted Kate on the back and squeezed her hand.

A dark-haired girl with eyes the same shade of green as Kate's appeared around the corner. "This is my sister Heather," Kate said.

"It's nice to meet you, Heather," said Harper. As Heather hugged her sister, he noticed that she was maybe an inch taller than Kate and had her coloring, but her figure was willowy, more like Jennifer's.

"It's nice to meet you, too."

"You two head upstairs and get changed. We're heading out to Papa's in twenty minutes," Loretta said.

"Papa's? Why? I thought we were making pies," said Kate.

"Most of them are done already. And the Powell's are doing something tonight. We can't miss it."

"The Powells? What are they doing?"

"Didn't you hear me say we only have twenty minutes? Go get changed! And wear something pretty!"

Kate rolled her eyes but turned to head upstairs.

"I'll help you," said Tiffany.

Kate looked at her in surprise but quickly agreed and walked with her sister while Tiffany continued telling Kate all about her boyfriend, Ryan, and how he was so smart and cute and funny and the best boyfriend ever.

When they reached the guest room, Kate smiled and shooed her sister out, telling her she'd see her in a few minutes.

Will placed the bags on the floor at the foot of the bed. It was spacious with a queen sized four poster bed in a dark cherry finish and covered in rows of frilly pillows and a fluffy duvet folded at the foot. There was a bench at the end of the bed, a nightstand on either side topped with a lamp, a low dresser on the adjacent wall and a chair and lamp next to the window.

"Sorry about all the frills. Mom loves lace," Kate said as she flicked the trim on a bolster pillow. "And flowers." She smiled and looked at the striped wall paper and floral curtains.

"No, it's fine. Nice really." Though the room was very feminine and definitely country, the colors flowed well and it wasn't entirely unpleasant to look at. It felt comfortable and loved. "It reminds me of Andrew's grandmother's place in Oregon."

"Oh, yeah?"

"Her farmhouse is a lot like this."

She waited for him to elaborate, but he didn't. "I guess Jen will be comfortable while she's there, then."

He nodded and unzipped his suitcase and began hanging things in the closet. "Where's the bathroom?"

"Down the hall, second door on the left."

He looked dismayed at not having an ensuite, but set his toiletries bag on the bureau without a complaint. "I guess there's not time to shower."

"No, not really. I'm just going to wear a simple dress. You can wear that if you want, just lose the jacket." She gestured to the navy suit and blue button down he was wearing.

He looked at his outfit and sighed at his wrinkled trousers and the tiny mustard stain on his cuff from the sandwich he'd had right before they boarded the plane. Kate caught him looking at it and began rolling up his sleeve so that his forearm was exposed and the stain hidden. He looked at her silently while she worked, thinking that this was the first time she'd willingly touched him since their fight. It felt very different from the obligatory touches and kisses she bestowed on him when they were out in public.

Abruptly, she let his hand drop and stepped back, her eyes on the buttons of his shirt. "That should take care of it. And it makes you look more relaxed."

He nodded but didn't say anything. They stood silently a few moments longer until Kate shook her head and continued unpacking her bag.

"Where's this place we're going to?" he asked as he turned his back on her and unpacked his own suitcase.

"It's called Papa's."

"Papa's? Papa's what?"

"Just Papa's." She smiled at his confused expression. "Come on, Harper, haven't you ever been to a honky-tonk before?"

His eyes grew alarmingly wide and she laughed at his discomfort. "I'm just kidding. It's not bad – just a big dance floor and a band and a bar. It's like a club, only country. Yeah, a country club." She smirked at him. "That should make you feel right at home."

She left the room to borrow a pair of cowboy boots from Heather and Will mentally prepared himself for a difficult evening.

They were in the foyer waiting for Tiffany when they heard loud steps coming from outside accompanied by a dog barking.

"Daddy!" Kate squealed as she ran to open the door. On the other side was an excited chocolate colored dog who happily jumped up onto Kate's belly and enthusiastically licked her face when she leaned down to hug it.

"Jake! Outta my house! Neal! Get that dog of yours out of here!" Loretta shouted.

Kate gently pushed Jake's paws off her and scratched his head, then looked up to see her father smiling slightly in the doorway.

"Katherine," he said simply before pulling her tightly into his arms. She squeezed her father tight and tried not to cry when she smelled his familiar scent of fir trees and firewood.

"You must be William," her father said.

"Yes, I'm William Harper. You must be Kate's father."

"Neal Bishop. Good to meet you." Neal held out his hand and Harper shook it firmly. The two men regarded each other silently for a minute until Loretta interrupted and told them to stop standing in the middle of the room and get out of everyone's way.

When they arrived, the parking lot was packed and they ended up parking in a field off to the side of the building. They'd all piled into Loretta's SUV while Tiffany drove them there, stating she needed the practice, while Neal rode in front next to his youngest daughter, calmly instructing her when she would go a little too fast or too close to the yellow line. Teaching the girls to drive fell on him since Loretta would scream and hang on for dear life as she shouted that they were about to be killed. Unsurprisingly, Tiffany took every opportunity she could to drive with her father.

The group walked into the unassuming metal structure, Will and Kate at the very back. She grabbed his hand and he squeezed it reflexively and looked at her, but she was staring straight ahead. As they stepped through the entry and into the main room, there was a loud roar as the entire room full of people yelled, “Surprise!”

Harper and Kate stopped and looked around in shock. There was a large banner on the opposite wall that read “Congratulations Katie and William!” and a table filled with brightly wrapped gifts. The guests were wearing sparkly hats and popping noisemakers. A few industrious teenage boys threw confetti on them until William glared at them and they ran the other direction. Kate kept hold of Harper’s hand but used her other to shake hands and hug what felt like every person in the place.

She introduced them all to Harper but he only retained a few names and by the end, he felt like he’d been barraged by Billys, Bobbys, Jimmys and women who seemed to have more than one name for a reason he could not comprehend. He was asked how married life was treating him by Sarah Grace and Anna Beth, and told he was lucky to marry a southern woman by an old lady named Betty Lou. There was also a Charlotte Kate, a Katie Charlotte, a Mary Jo and no fewer than three Virginia Anns.

Finally, Kate was asked to dance by a neighbor the age of her father. Will smiled and told her to have fun and gladly took the moment to regain his equilibrium. He looked around at the bare wood walls. There were signed pictures of famous and some not-so-famous musicians framed between various hubcaps and license plates from several states. The building was fairly large and full, so full that Will felt like he was in a nightclub in New York. Only there it would at least have been dark and he could sit in the corner anonymously. Here, the lights were almost fully lit and everyone seemed to know Katherine, and by extension wanted to know him, too. He couldn't remember the last time he'd shaken so many hands and smiled at so many strangers. Being congenial with new acquaintances was not his usual M.O., but he was playing the part of the besotted newlywed and he was determined to play it well.

Joshua Powell, the first person they'd met when they arrived and Laura Powell's younger brother, was on stage, playing guitar and singing in a white cowboy hat. Katie was running around the floor in a circle and twirling, doing something she called the two-step. He had no idea what this was, but she seemed to be having fun. She had on a huge smile and was laughing heartily at whatever her partner had just said. She'd barely looked at him since they got there, standing by his side and acting the happy-newlywed part while he knew she was still angry with him, then running off on her own to visit with old friends.

"Thanks, everybody. Glad to see you all dancing and having a good time." Powell's voice rose over the noise of the crowd. "Y'all may not have noticed, but we have an old friend in the house tonight." A cheer erupted through the building. "Katie Bishop, walk your sweet self up here and give everybody a good look at you." Applause and shouts filled the space while Katie walked up the three steps on the side of the stage. She was blushing, but otherwise seemed completely at ease.

"What do y'all say we get her to sing us a song or two?" The audience roared while Katie shook her head and smiled. "Come on now, Katie-Lou, you can't let down the crowd. They came all this way to be entertained."

"Isn't that what you're supposed to be doing?" Katie asked with both hands on her hips.

"Come on now. You know you want to. For old time's sake." He gave her a million-watt smile and then turned to the audience, raising his eyebrows as if to say, "now I've got her."

She let out a sigh and grabbed the microphone, a cheer going up on the dance floor. "What are we singing?"

"How about we go *Pickin' Wild Flowers*?" he answered as he plucked a melody on the guitar. Katie raised a brow that he matched perfectly. She shook her head and grinned, then started tapping her foot to the rhythm.

Harper's brows shot up to his hairline when he saw Kate give Josh a flirtatious grin as he sang the suggestive lyrics. The same flirtatious grin she gave *him*.

When Josh reached out to grab her by the waist and pull her closer as he sang, Harper clenched his jaw. Katie sang the chorus with him, her sweet voice lilting in an accent he'd never heard from her before. He'd heard her sing around the house, but not like this. Her hips swayed as she walked around Josh, one hand trailing across his broad shoulders. William's collar felt tight. As the lyrics became progressively more evocative, Harper had to fight the urge to yank Kate off the stage and send Mr. Powell a message he wouldn't soon forget.

Before he had a chance to act on any of his baser instincts, the song dwindled off and Powell started to speak.

"Katie here wants to sing us a little song. Y'all give her a big hand."

Applause filled the room and Harper reluctantly clapped along, smiling stiffly at the faces watching him.

"This is a little song for a friend of mine. You know who you are." She smiled at the audience, then caught Will's eye and winked. *Oh, no.*

The drummer hammered out an upbeat rhythm as the men in the band sang backup.

Oh God, thought Will. She sang about a *Cowboy Casanova*, a song detailing the tricks of a man who made women fall in love with him and then left them high and dry. He rubbed his temples for a moment and then made his way to the men's room.

Harper managed to hold it together as Kate sang one more song and left the stage. He ended up spending the rest of the evening talking to an old man who insisted on telling him all about his crop rotation and how they "used to do things" when he was young.

Finally, the night ended and Neal drove everyone back to the house. Will silently followed Kate upstairs to their room while the sisters called out sleepy goodnights to each other.

"I'm going to go clean up," Kate said tiredly as she grabbed a bag and her pajamas and left the room. He was tired and wished he could sleep, but the smell of fried food and cigarettes was too strong to ignore. He checked email again until he heard the shower turn off and Kate came in with wet hair and blue pajamas a few minutes later.

"Shower's free," she said dully. She sat down on the bed and rubbed moisturizer into her skin.

"Thanks."

Will gathered his things and went to the bathroom, wondering how long this stalemate with Kate would last. She seemed to have gone from being angry at him to simply ignoring him. Maybe she was close to getting over it? As he thought about this while he soaped up, he came to a conclusion. This couldn't go on. If she didn't want to talk to him, then fine. He'd quit talking to her, too. Two could play that game.

She was planning on spending the entire day tomorrow cooking with her mother anyway, so it wouldn't be too hard to avoid her. With his plan set, he dried off, pulled on his pajamas and slipped back into the hall and through the door to their room. Kate had left a small light on for him, *Well, at least that's something*, and he flipped it off and climbed into bed beside her. They hadn't slept in the same bed since their wedding night, and that one had been significantly larger.

He tried not to touch her and laid as close to the edge as he could. He could hear her even breathing and smell her lotion as it made its way to his side of the bed. Determined to ignore her and her sweet smell, he rolled over and tried to go to sleep. He stared at the wall for a while, then lay on his back and closed his eyes, attempting to still his mind.

This wasn't working. Being mad at Kate was exhausting. For one thing, no matter how much she ignored him, she was still there. Still perky and charming and a little bit weird and completely endearing, though he would never have put it that way. But examining his own feelings, now that he wasn't distracted with phone calls and mergers and clients to keep happy, he could admit that he was very fond of Kate and that they'd developed a relationship that he quite enjoyed. It was all the companionship of a woman without any of the pressure of serious expectations. He missed her. The talks, the food, the affection. She was a warm person and once that warmth had been turned off, he'd felt it acutely.

There had to be a way to fix this. What was she even mad about, anyway? She didn't even know Sandra. Did she think he'd raised her hopes and done a runner? Well, he hadn't. He'd been genuinely fond of Sandra. But it would never have worked. Surely she saw that? Sandra hadn't even seemed that upset when things ended. They'd drifted apart, and they'd never exchanged any promises or declarations of love. She wanted a quiet life in the country with a house full of kids and dogs and he was destined to follow in his father's footsteps. She had no desire to travel all over doing business deals with him, and would have been lonely in England on her own. He couldn't begin to imagine her in New York City. She would have hated it.

Oh, sod it! He was never going to figure out what Kate was so pissed about.

Just as he was wrestling with the blankets in an attempt to find a more comfortable position, he heard Kate sigh.

"Kate?" he asked quietly. "Are you awake?"

"No, I'm talking in my sleep," she answered.

He lifted his head and propped himself up on one elbow, the other arm going out to grab Kate's shoulder and turn her around so he could see her face.

"That's it! Enough! This is ridiculous. Either tell me what's got your knickers in a twist and let's have it out, or stop acting like a poor, put-upon baby!"

She looked at him with wide eyes, then sat up and pulled the blanket over her chest.

"Alright, fine. I think you're a snob."

"That's it?" he asked incredulously.

"That's the beginning."

"And the ending? The middle?"

She sighed and pursed her lips, looked away, and finally looked back at him after a few heavy moments.

"You use people. You used Sandra and you're using me. Granted, you're paying me and I agreed to it, but still. I don't like the feeling of indentured servitude."

She looked away again and he studied the side of her face, reeling slightly from her words.

"You think I use people?" he asked, his voice slightly higher pitch than normal.

"Don't you?"

"No one's ever complained before."

She just looked away again and sighed, her shoulders slumping.

"Kate, is this about you, or about Sandra?"

"Both, I suppose. How could you do that to her? Didn't she matter at all to you? Or were you just having fun? Did her feelings come into play at all in your thought process?"

"Actually, yes, they did, which is why we mutually agreed on a break-up and still keep in touch, albeit sparingly. She's very happy in her life. Her husband is a great bloke. It all worked out for the best, surely you see that?"

She looked at him skeptically. "Did you break up with her because you grew apart, or because she wasn't socially acceptable?"

"Honestly?"

She nodded.

"A little of both. I suppose that if we hadn't grown apart we would have continued on a little longer."

"What if you'd stayed together? What if you did exchange promises and declarations of love? What then?"

"What do you mean?"

"I mean, would you still have broken up with her if you'd loved her? Would it have been enough to overcome your differences and your doubts?"

"I like to think I'm capable of the kind of passion it would require to go against my family and everyone's expectations and marry a woman I loved for no other reason than because I loved her. But I have never felt that before, so I can't rightly say. Maybe I never will. Who knows?"

She looked at him a little sadly, and for a horrible moment he thought she was going to cry. "Sometimes love just isn't enough," she said softly.

He reached up and brushed away the strand of hair that had fallen across her cheek. "I suppose that's true. But maybe it is. I'll let you know if I ever find out."

She smiled weakly and took a sip of the water on her nightstand. "Will?"

"Yes, Katie?"

"Would you be against a little cuddling?"

"Not at all. Come here." He pulled her over and wrapped his arm around her shoulders, her head coming to rest on his chest comfortably. *God, I've missed this.*

"Night, Will."

"Night, Katie." He kissed the top of her head and in a matter of minutes, they were both sleeping peacefully.

*

The next morning, Will woke up alone. All sorts of warm pleasant smells had found their way upstairs. He sniffed appreciatively and quickly threw on jeans and a J Crew t-shirt. Kate had told him to dress casually. He brushed his teeth, splashed water on his face and ran a comb through his hair before heading downstairs to the kitchen.

Heather was mixing something white and fluffy in a large bowl while Tiffany stood next to her chopping celery. Their mother was cooking a pan of onions at the stove.

"Morning, William," said Heather softly. "Are you looking for Kate?"

"Yes. Do you know where she is?"

"She's in the dining room. She'll be back in a sec."

"Thanks," he said stiffly. He was looking around for coffee. He could smell it but he couldn't see it yet. Just as he was about to ask, Kate came in from the opposite doorway.

"Morning, honey." She quickly crossed the room towards him and reached up to kiss his cheek. He instinctively put his arm around her back and kissed the top of her head. "Coffee?" she asked.

"Please."

"Have a seat. I'll get you some." She led him to a large farm table in a nook of the kitchen and quickly brought him a steaming cup of coffee. "Did you sleep okay?" she asked.

"Fine. You?"

"Fine." She smiled and he wondered if everything was alright between them, but then he realized that it would look odd if they didn't speak to each other in front of her family. They were supposed to be newlyweds, after all.

He smiled back over his cup but said nothing. Kate went to the island and began chopping potatoes while Harper watched the women at work.

So this was Thanksgiving. He'd seen it like this in movies, but his only personal experience was with Andrew's family, and the staff seemed to do everything – the family just ate the meal. He was reserving final judgment until later, but this looked more fun.

"Can I help with anything?" he asked suddenly.

Conversations stopped, mixers were turned off, knives stilled in midair.

"You want to help?" Mrs. Bishop asked. He nodded. "In the kitchen?" He nodded again. "With the cooking?" Will nodded once more, slowly, and he saw a smile work its way across Kate's face.

"William's alright in the kitchen, Mom. He can follow directions. Just give him something to do. This is his first proper Thanksgiving, after all. He wants to be involved."

The two of them shared a look across the room and he shot Kate a grateful smile for explaining for him.

Mrs. Bishop shrugged her shoulders and drew out a cutting board. She placed it on the counter next to Katherine. "You can cut fruit. We need four bananas for the pudding and this kiwi for the fruit salad."

He began quietly peeling bananas next to Kate, and when Heather and Tiffany resumed their conversation and Mrs. Bishop was blending something in a Cuisinart, he leaned over and said in her ear, "How big should I cut these?"

"You want the bananas in slices about a quarter inch thick. The kiwi goes into cubes."

"Is fruit salad a normal Thanksgiving tradition? With kiwi?"

She chuckled and whispered in his ear, "Not really. My grandmother always used to make it and said it wasn't Thanksgiving without it. Mom keeps up the tradition. She's the only one who eats it and the leftovers always end up going in the fridge and getting all moldy."

"Ah, I see. So I am assisting in the least important part of the meal."

She smiled. "Just the kiwi part. Mom will make the rest herself. She doesn't trust anyone else with it. But the banana pudding is very important. It's Dad's favorite so you can't mess it up."

His eyes got round and she laughed. "Don't worry, I'll help you." He smiled uncertainly and she chuckled to herself as she chopped potatoes.

Ten minutes later, Kate's potatoes were in a pot covered by water and Will was stirring something called a whisk through a creamy yellow substance Kate assured him would turn into pudding once refrigerated. He wasn't so sure.

"Done! Now just put it in this bowl to cool," she flicked off the burner and gestured to the glass bowl on his right, "and put the whole bowl into the fridge." She rinsed the beaters while he found a space for his pudding, then grabbed his arm. "Come with me."

"What are we doing?"

"The fun part! Choose a bowl." She pointed to a china cabinet in the dining room she'd led him into. He looked confused. "For your pudding! You want a glass one, not ceramic, and preferably a footed one. As you can see, Mom likes footed bowls, so you have your pick."

He looked into the case at at least a dozen glass pedestal bowls, all cut or hand-blown glass ranging from clear to deep red in color.

"How about that one?" He pointed to a medium size bowl that was mostly clear, but had a slight blue cast to it. The sides were cut in a diamond pattern that was intricate but seemed masculine somehow.

"Good choice. Come on, I'll show you how to prep the bowl."

She handed him a box of vanilla wafers and showed him how to line the bottom rim of the bowl with them without letting them fall. Then he made another row of sliced bananas. He very carefully added a layer of the pudding mixture from the fridge, then covered that with some of the homemade whipped cream Heather had made. He repeated the entire process again until the bowl was full and Kate told him to hold it up and look at it from the side.

It was beautiful. He couldn't believe he had just made a layered pudding. He was beaming with pride as he placed it on the top shelf of the refrigerator.

"Now what?" he asked Kate.

"Now we make bread. It should be done with its first rise by now."

She removed a red checkered towel from a large bowl and showed him the puffy pale dough inside.

"Separate this into three pieces, then roll each piece between your hands until it looks like a long rope. Then I'll braid them and let them rise again."

He began rolling the dough like she showed him – which surprisingly made his arms burn – and asked why he couldn't braid them himself.

"Because most guys suck at braiding, even if they know how." He shot her a look. "Do you know how?"

"Of course I do." She raised her eyebrows, clearly disbelieving. "I used to braid my horse's tail all the time."

Kate couldn't help the laugh that bubbled up at his explanation. "You are just full of surprises, Harper."

After several more hours of cooking, and Harper being officially initiated by the Bishop women when Loretta tied a blue checkered apron on him and pinched his cheek, they were ready to eat. Neal arrived with fresh fir trimmings to decorate the buffet and Tiffany ran into the dining room to arrange them and set the table. She and Heather had polished the antique silver the day before and now she carefully laid it out next to her grandmother's china. Heather collected the freshly pressed cloth napkins and secured them in the tiny wreathlike napkin rings she'd made out of small twigs the day before. Tiffany had written everyone's name beautifully on small place cards and she and Heather giggled over who would sit where.

William finished stirring something Loretta called honey butter and walked over to where Kate was spreading whipped cream on a pumpkin pie and then carefully placing pecan halves in even spaces around the rim.

"Who else is coming? You said your grandmother and an uncle, right?"

"Yes, my great-grandmother from my mother's side is coming. She lives in an assisted living home but my uncle is picking her up. His wife and kids are also coming. They're great, you'll like them. He married late, so his kids are still pretty little. My Grandmother Phillips should be here any minute. She lives nearby and can be a handful, so don't say I didn't warn you."

"Is that Loretta's mother?"

"Yes. My father's grandparents passed away when I was a kid and his father died a few years back, but his mother lives in town with her sister. I think mom said she was coming today, too."

Just then there was a commotion at the door and a loud voice yelling, "Yoohoo, I'm here!" Tiffany rolled her eyes and looked at Will.

"Watch your back, William," she said as she left the kitchen.

"What does she mean?" he asked bemusedly.

"Just that my grandma can get a little handsy around strapping young men." She raised her eyebrows and wiggled her fingers for emphasis as she backed out the door, trying not to laugh at Will's disbelieving expression.

William looked at the dining table on his way to the living room and was concerned to find his name card next to Darlene Phillips. He quickly swapped it with one a few seats down and hoped no one noticed.

After greeting Kate's family for twenty minutes, William's head was spinning. Was this how she'd felt meeting his family? So far he'd met Kate's great grandmother, who was a quiet, bent old woman who kept hard candy in her pocket for her youngest grandchildren, Loretta's brother David and his wife Michelle, who seemed to be nice, normal people, and their three children that he couldn't begin to remember the names of. Neal's mother Edith was a sweet woman whom Katherine obviously loved and Will found her to be pleasant to talk to.

Darlene Phillips was a force of nature: loud, outspoken, and unfortunately, appreciative of a well-formed man. She hugged William just a little too long for his comfort and he was pretty sure most grandmothers didn't run their hands up and down strangers' backs like she'd done his. He saw Tiffany laughing and wiggling her eyebrows while gesturing with her hands and was slightly horrified before he could admit it was pretty funny.

The meal went smoothly enough. The children ate in the kitchen and the adults sat down in the dining room where the table was extended by two leaves and every inch was covered in food. Conversation was loud, the company was boisterous, and by her third glass of wine, Darlene was a mixture of flirtatious and sentimental. Loretta tried to contain her mother while Edith talked to Heather quietly and Neal talked to Kate. Great-grandmother Phillips – whom everyone called Granny and told William he should call her that, too, but he couldn't bring himself to do it – fell asleep and was led to the sofa to rest.

Overall, Harper was overwhelmed, overstimulated, and surprisingly pleased by the entire thing. No one was putting on a face for society, they were all just being themselves regardless of who was watching – or so it appeared to him. But after two hours of such familial closeness, he decided that while it was refreshing every once in a while, he preferred his calmer, more private existence for the day-to-day.

After the dinner, they convened in the living room where an American football game was playing. Only Neal and David paid close attention and everyone generally talked or napped during the game. Tiffany was planning a morning attack on the shopping mall in the neighboring town and trying to talk Heather and Kate into going with her. Kate resisted, but Heather was sucked in. After eating three slices of pie and a generous helping of his very own banana pudding, Will was ready for a nap himself. By the time he was drifting off to sleep that night – at nine-thirty no less – he believed everything he'd ever heard about turkey making people sleepy.

25
INTRODUCING MRS. BISHOP

November, Friday After Thanksgiving
7 Months Married

"How's it going with that husband of yours?" Loretta asked as she breezed into the kitchen.

Kate looked up from the book she was reading at the kitchen counter and slid her plate of cheese and crackers over so she could set it down. "I think it's going pretty well."

"Are you pregnant?"

"What? No! Of course not! Why would you think I was pregnant?" Kate asked with crimson cheeks.

"Well, you got married in such a hurry. What did you expect people to think?"

Kate sighed and shook her head. "Mom, it's been over six months. Don't you think I would have told you by now if I was? Wouldn't it be obvious?" She gestured to her flat stomach.

"Well, you could have had a miscarriage or ... something."

Kate shook her head again. "Well, rest easy, Mom. I'm not pregnant. Nor have I ever been. And before you ask, I'm not planning on it anytime soon, either."

"You don't want to wait too long. You're not getting any younger," she scolded.

"I'm twenty-three!"

"Soon to be twenty-four, missy. You don't want to wait forever. You can't be a student your entire life. At some point you'll have to start living in the real world." She sighed dramatically and looked at her daughter with concern and what looked like resigned pity. "Though I can't say I'm surprised. You always did have your head in the clouds, doing whatever suited you and not worrying about anyone else."

Kate stood. "Mama, I don't-"

"Just like your father. Always were, you know. Even as a baby, you were just like him." Her expression softened slightly. "At least you got your looks from me."

Kate tried to smile but was not very successful. Loretta reached across the counter and grabbed Kate's plate. She took out two small plastic bags and put the cheese in one and the crackers into the other.

"Your father never did change, you know. And if you're not careful, you'll end up just like him." She shook her head sadly and huffed. "Don't be leaving food out. I'm not made of money." She punctuated her statement with a shake of the bag she had just put the sliced cheese in before she gracelessly dropped it into the refrigerator. "We can't all be perpetual students, living off others. Some of us have to get real jobs and go to work every day."

"Mama, I'm not-" she was cut off.

"Just like a Bishop. I don't know why I bother – you've always done exactly what you wanted to do. Nobody could tell you differently; once you'd made up your mind, there was no talking to you," Loretta continued, ignoring Kate. She punctuated each statement with emphatic hand motions.

"Mama, really. That's not true!"

"And now look! You've gone and married a total stranger! And a foreigner! What were you thinking?"

"You said you liked Will! And he's English. It's not like we speak different languages. And even if we did, he's a perfectly nice guy and we're good together. Can't you just be happy for me?"

"Happy for you! Happy for you? How can I be happy when my daughter won't even invite her own mother to her wedding? Do you know how that looks? What am I supposed to tell people?"

"That was months ago! It was spur of the moment! You were invited to the reception. You said you were too busy to come."

"Of course I was! I have my own life! I can't just drop everything and run off to New York for a party. I have responsibilities here." She opened her arms and gestured to the house around her.

Kate took a deep breath. "Mom, I'm sorry you missed the wedding, truly, I am. But I can't change it now. Why don't we sit down and find a date for you to come visit? We'll pick a time when the shop is slow and ask Heather to watch it for a few days. What do you say?"

"I say it's just like you not to remember that Heather is in school right now. And that she spends every spare moment working at Johnson's Mill. She's not going to have the time to come over here and watch my store for a few days. And I certainly can't afford to close it!" She huffed and mumbled to herself, "Thoughtless girl."

Kate took a deep breath and slid off her bar stool. When her mother got to the grumbling stage, there was no reasoning with her. It was time to cut her losses and hope it would all blow over by dinner. She walked across the kitchen and into the small hallway, directly into Will.

"Oh! Sorry, I didn't see you."

He held her upper arms firmly to steady her and looked into her eyes searchingly. "Are you okay?"

"How much of that did you hear?"

He raised his brows, "Almost all of it, I think. Are you alright?"

"Yeah, I'm fine. It's Mom. She gets like this sometimes. It's all the stress. The holidays and the visitors and everything happening at once. It'll blow over soon."

"Hmm." He swiftly grabbed her hand and pulled her out the side door. He didn't stop walking until he reached the tire swing hanging from an old oak tree in the back yard, far away from the house.

"Does that happen a lot?"

She climbed onto the swing and he gave her a little push.

"Not too often. I seem to bring it out in her." She smiled ruefully and released an awkward laugh.

"Does the same thing happen with your sisters?"

"Sometimes with Heather. Not really with Jenny. *Never* with Tiffany; she can do no wrong in my mother's eyes," she said cynically.

He nodded. "So it's just you that brings out this special... side... in her."

Kate nodded slowly and held on to the rope.

"I used to wonder what it was about me that set her off, but now I just try to get out of the way when I see trouble coming. There's nothing I can do about it, so I just try to avoid it."

"Is this why you really moved in with your dad?"

Kate looked down sadly and eventually nodded. "Yeah, that was a big part of it."

Will reached out and stopped the swing. He lifted her chin and looked at her squarely. "Why didn't you tell me, Kate?"

There was something so incredibly earnest about his eyes when he asked her. Maybe it was the distant smell of fire mixed with dry leaves, or the slow gurgle of the creek just behind them. Maybe it was the way his sweater was so soft and warm, or the way his cologne tickled her nose and made her want to come just a little bit closer. She didn't know why, but suddenly Kate was overwhelmed by the understanding in his eyes and for the first time in a long time, she let herself break down.

She literally crumpled, nearly falling off the swing, while Will held her up and rubbed her back as she sobbed onto his shoulder. She clung to him desperately, taking deep, ragged breaths and releasing the tension she'd been holding in for so long. He made shushing sounds and said soothing words, all the while holding her to him and stroking her hair, rubbing her back, and rocking slightly. In her state of complete emotional vulnerability, Katherine realized that she had never felt so safe.

And that made her cry even more.

Eventually, Will spoke. "Do you want to go home tonight, baby?"

She sniffled. "No. We leave tomorrow as it is. I can hold out 'til then."

"Are you sure?"

"Yeah, I'm sure. And Dad would be upset if I missed the bonfire. It's a family tradition."

"Okay. Whatever you say. Dinner's not for another hour. Why don't you show me around the farm?"

She wiped her eyes on her sweater sleeve and nodded. "Okay."

He returned to the house for a moment to grab their jackets and scarves. As he was wrapping hers around her neck, she gave him a watery smile and said, "Thanks, Will."

He smiled back softly and said, "Any time."

Fifteen minutes later, they were walking through a field dotted high with stiff, brown grass. Kate looked over at Will, watching his expression and thinking about the last few days.

"You're being awfully friendly," she said carefully. "I thought we weren't supposed to be friends."

"Of course we're friends," he said. "Very good friends."

He touched her cheek where a single curl was blowing across her face, then tucked it behind her ear. "I'm sorry, Kate." She looked at him questioningly. "I'm sorry I ever made you think we weren't friends. We are. You're my best friend," he added quietly as he looked at the brown grass at his feet.

"I thought Andy was your best friend," she said softly.

"He was. He's been replaced." He gave her a gentle smile and she beamed back at him. "Really, Kate, we're more than just friends. We're partners. You know that, don't you?"

"I do now," she answered. "I'm sorry, too. For the song, for everything. I was a brat."

Will nodded and looked away. He pulled her to him and wrapped his arm around her shoulders as they continued walking.

"Come on," she said eventually. "I want to show you the old barn." She grabbed his hand and pulled him along behind her as she trudged through the field.

**

That night at the bonfire, Kate caught up with everyone that she hadn't seen or had a chance to talk to at the party.

After an hour of making the rounds, she saw her cousin Mary walking up from the driveway with a baby on her hip and a small boy holding her hand.

"Mary!" Kate ran over to greet them and hugged her cousin tightly before taking the baby out of her arms.

"Hi, Katie!"

"And how is little Lily?" she cooed to the baby in her arms. She looked down when she felt a tugging on her pants leg. "Hi, Joey. How are you?" He smiled and she hugged her four-year-old cousin. "Come sit down with me and tell me how everything is going."

Kate led Mary to a seat off to the side and asked Tiffany to take Joey over to the fire. She settled into a lawn chair across from her cousin and wrapped eighteen-month-old Lily in her blanket and leaned back with the baby cuddled close to her.

"So how are you?" Kate asked.

Mary sighed. "I'm doing alright. Sorry I couldn't make it to your party the other night. Joey had a stomach bug."

"That's alright. Did you have a nice Thanksgiving with Brad's family?"

She shrugged. "It was alright. His mother's a horrible cook, but what do you do?"

Kate laughed. "Are you still taking classes over in Waynesboro?"

She sighed again. "As I can. Classes are expensive and so are diapers. I'm only taking one right now."

"Do you not qualify for any kind of aid?"

"Not for the program I'm in. I'm not degree-seeking, so my options are limited." Kate nodded. "I just can't manage a full degree with four kids. I can barely manage the odd class right now, especially with Brad working the swing shift at the factory." She leaned her head back and Kate couldn't help but notice the lines beginning to form on her forehead and around her eyes, making her look older than her twenty-seven years.

"Where are Maddy and Ben? I haven't seen them yet."

"They went running straight to the fire when we got here. I saw Heather helping them put marshmallows on sticks a minute ago."

Kate nodded. "So everyone's doing alright? The kids are healthy and happy and life is good?"

Mary laughed cynically. "Oh, Kate! How you manage to put such a nice spin on everything I'll never know. There's food on the table, Maddy and Ben are doing pretty well in school, and Brad's managed to keep the same job for over a year, so that's a plus."

Kate tried to smile but knew it probably came out more like a grimace. "Are things any better between you two?"

"I don't know." Mary shook her head and looked toward the fire and the crowd of people laughing around it. "We're okay, I guess. The sex is decent, so I guess that's good. Sometimes I feel like it's the only thing we have in common anymore." Kate made a sympathetic face. "He still spends every Thursday night at the bowling alley getting drunk with the boys, though I doubt that will ever change."

"Do you want it to change? Do you want to be married to him?"

"I have four kids with him. I don't think I have much choice."

"There's always a choice."

"Not a good one. I have no marketable skills besides waiting tables, at least not yet. I'm really good at getting pregnant and changing diapers, but no one wants to pay me to do that." She laughed cynically. "Brad isn't all bad. He loves the kids and he loves me, in his way. He's just as bogged down as I am, he just deals with it differently."

Kate nodded. "I'm so sorry, Mary. I wish there was something I could do to help. What do the kids need? I can make it part of their Christmas present."

"You don't need to be spending your money on us. You have tuition bills to pay and a new husband. You should be saving up for your family."

"Save up in case I get knocked up?" Kate said wryly.

Mary laughed. "Exactly!"

"Well, William makes really good money, so we're alright in that regard. Really. So what would the kids like for Christmas?"

"Honestly, they love all kinds of toys. Ben is really into airplanes and cars right now. Joey loves trains. I've been looking on Craigslist for a track set for him but haven't had any luck yet."

"Oh, I want to get him that! Stop looking," Kate said excitedly.

"Katie! Those are really expensive." Mary shook her head.

"It's okay, really. I'm telling you, William pays all our bills and I'm still working so all that cash is just sitting in my bank account, waiting for something to spend it on."

Mary looked at her skeptically. "Are you sure this won't get you into trouble with your man?"

"Trust me, he won't mind at all. William's very generous."

"Alright, if you say so."

"Now, what about the girls."

"Maddy is still into dolls, but I don't how much longer that will last. She loves art and drawing and making stuff. I thought about asking Tiffany to show her a thing or two."

"You should. I'm sure she would be happy to do that. She'd love to have a cute little girl looking up to her and listening to everything she says."

Mary laughed. "I'm sure she would. Lily plays with whatever everyone else is playing with, but she does seem more drawn to Maddy's ponies. You can imagine how well that goes over."

Kate laughed. "Ah, sisters!" Mary rolled her eyes. "I can't wait to do some shopping!" Kate clapped her hands excitedly.

"Thanks, Katie. You know you don't have to."

"Nonsense. I want to."

Kate reached forward and grabbed her hand. They shared a sympathetic smile. Before any more could be said, Ben came running up to show his mom the s'more he'd made. Mary smiled at Kate and let herself be dragged to the fire by her son.

*

Will watched Kate and her father surreptitiously. Sure, there was a slight family resemblance, mostly in the coloring, and she and her sisters were a little taller than average, a trait obviously inherited from her father's side, but that was pretty much it. Loretta was blond and blue eyed like Jennifer and Tiffany while Heather and Kate were dark like their father. But Kate's bone structure, figure, features, everything else was more like her mother.

Neal Bishop clearly had a dry sense of humor and all his conversations had a healthy dose of sarcasm, but he was overall a quiet, reserved man who seemed to prefer more behind-the-scenes work. Loretta Bishop was completely opposite. She loved attention and the spotlight. *The prima donna and the stage hand.*

Watching the family interact around the fire, he saw that Heather was actually the most like her father. She seemed to help quietly, letting others carry the conversation and content to just enjoy everyone's presence in peace. Jennifer wasn't there to compare, but he knew she would never push herself to be the center of attention the way her mother did. At parties, she was more often found helping in the kitchen than entertaining the guests.

Tiffany was a miniature of her mother, in looks and personality, which explained why she was the favorite, and of course she was the baby on top of all of that. But watching Kate and her mother together, he saw more similarities than differences. Her mother was telling jokes that would have the entire group laughing, then Kate would pick up and tell the rest of the story, like they were a practiced duo. Then the two of them would fall onto each other laughing, as if that afternoon's argument had never happened.

No matter how hard he tried to see it, he couldn't understand why Loretta insisted on believing that Kate was just like her father. Other than having above average intelligence and loving books, they weren't that much alike. Then it hit him. *Of course, why didn't I see it before? It's so obvious!*

It wasn't that Kate was so much like her father, it was that she was so much like mother, and had done so much more with her life. At twenty-three, she was almost finished with an advanced degree, had graduated with her bachelor's summa cum laude, moved to the big city on her own and by all accounts had made a success of her life – or was about to, anyway. She already had one or two job prospects for when she finished in May, thanks in large part to her stunning recommendations from her professors and her 4.0 GPA.

Could it be that simple? Could Loretta be jealous? The more he thought about it, the more it seemed likely, and the more he thought she had to be jealous about. Loretta had gotten pregnant and married, in that order, when she was eighteen and only two months out of high school. Kate had had so many more opportunities than she'd had, and had taken advantage of every one of them. And of course Kate had two major points in her favor: brains and bravery. It probably also rankled that Kate managed to have a healthy, close relationship with Neal, something he and Loretta had never been able to manage for more than a few months at a time.

He found it in his heart to be a little sorry for Loretta, even though he was still angry with her for the way she treated Kate. It wasn't Kate's fault that her mother had gotten knocked up or that she hadn't been able to make her marriage work. But still, Loretta must have had dreams, at some point in her life at least. It couldn't have been easy to watch everything fall away like that.

"Hey, whatcha thinkin', city boy?" Kate plonked down on the log next to him and nudged his side.

"Just thinking about you and your family. You have some very interesting dynamics."

She quirked a brow at him. “Uh-oh. Don't go analyzing too closely. You might not like what you find.”

He smiled and asked, “Are you having fun?”

“Yeah. This has always been one of my favorite holiday traditions.”

“I believe it. You've been laughing non-stop for the last hour.”

She smiled and replied, “Scoot over. I'm freezing!” He opened the quilt he had wrapped around his shoulders and made space for Kate inside.

“Better?” he asked.

“Much.” She laid her head on his shoulder and he wrapped his arm around her waist, pulling her closer and sharing his warmth. “This is so much more fun with a boy.”

“Excuse me?”

“Snuggling by the fire. My sisters and I usually share a blanket, but it's not the same.”

“I should think not,” he said, sounding mildly insulted.

She giggled.

“Did you never snuggle by the fire with any of your previous boyfriends?”

“Not really. My freshman boyfriend spent the holiday with his family in Rhode Island, then for some reason I was always single over Thanksgiving after that. Jeremy was supposed to come home with me last year, but something came up last minute and I came alone. So nope, it's just you. Does that make you feel special?” she asked with an impish grin.

“Yes, I feel quite honored. I can be your first bonfire boyfriend.”

She giggled again. “Bonfire husband.”

He pulled her closer and they sat in companionable silence, watching the others laugh and talk. Heather passed out hot cider to everyone and Will listened in as Kate talked to the neighbors who stopped to ask her about her Christmas shopping plans and if she was going to any glamorous parties over the holiday season.

It was another hour before the fire started to dwindle and people began going home.

"Come on, Katie, let's get you into bed." Will stood and held out a hand to her and she groggily followed him up the stairs to their room.

"You smell like fire," she said as he removed the blanket from around her shoulders and unwound her scarf.

"So do you."

Kate blindly grabbed a t-shirt and pulled her sweater over her head. She tugged on the shirt and shucked off her jeans, leaving them in a heap on the floor. "Come keep me warm, Will. I'm cold," she said sleepily as she climbed into bed.

"I'll be right back. Just want to clean my teeth." He left the room and came back a few minutes later in flannel pajama pants and a white t-shirt, his teeth clean and minty.

He felt his way through the room without turning on the light and slid in next to Kate. She immediately scooted over close and pushed her bottom into his hips. "You're so warm. Hold me, Will. I'm freezing!"

He obeyed and wrapped his arms around her, pulling her into his chest and scooting his knees behind hers. She grabbed his hand where it lay across her belly and laced her fingers with his. His other arm was beneath her neck and she placed a sleepy kiss on his forearm before she drifted off.

"How much did you drink, Katie?" he asked in a whisper. He smiled to himself when he realized she was already asleep.

**

The next morning, Kate woke slowly and smacked her lips, instantly regretting not brushing her teeth the night before. She felt unusually warm and it only took a second to realize the cause was Will, plastered to her side. She was on her back and his leg was tossed over her knee, his head resting between her chest and chin. His hair was tickling her face and she could feel his warm exhalations on her chest. She smiled when she noticed his hand was holding her breast. *I guess some things are just universal.*

She started to move away and he gripped her tightly, groaning slightly while his head snuggled a little lower. She pried his hand away and slipped out from beneath him and slithered out of bed. She went straight to the shower and snuck back into their room to get her warm clothes on. Seeing Will was still asleep, she wrote him a quick note and slipped out of the room, heading downstairs and outside to the trail that led to her father's house.

Katherine walked slowly through the fields, listening to the crunch her boots made on the frost covered grass. She was wrapped up warmly in her faded navy coat and plaid scarf, a cloth covered basket in her hand. As she rounded the corner near the creek, she heard her father's dog barking at the door, and three seconds later she was being jumped and slobbered on by Jake, her father's Newfoundland. Katherine laughed and dodged the dog as she made her way up the creaky stairs and onto the wooden porch.

"Jake! Get down! Have some self respect, man," Neal said as he led his daughter inside. "Morning, Katie." Neal kissed his daughter's rosy cheek and took her coat, hanging it on a faded wooden peg behind the door as she unwound her scarf.

"Morning, Daddy," she said cheerfully, heading to the kitchen. "Have you eaten?"

"Not yet."

"Do you want an omelet? I got a few eggs from Bertie on my way out the door," she asked, referring to the chickens in the coop behind her mother's house.

"Sounds good. Coffee?"

"Yes, please."

They set to work in companionable silence, Neal getting cups out of an oak china cabinet that had belonged to his grandmother, Kate cracking eggs into a crockery bowl while an iron skillet heated on the stove.

"So what have you been eating?" she asked.

"Dag nabbit, young lady! You ask me that every time you come home. I'm eating! Let that be the end of it."

Kate smiled at his irritated expression as she flipped the omelet in the pan. "So beans and hotdogs?"

He gave her a look and she burst out laughing. Neal tried to keep a straight face but eventually joined her.

"It's good to have you back, Katie."

"It's good to be back, Daddy."

"So how's it going with that man of yours? Did you make up last night? "

"Yeah, we did," she answered, completely unsurprised that he'd realized they weren't getting along. "We had an argument back home and there was a misunderstanding, but we're good now."

"Good. I'm glad to hear it."

They ate in silence until Neal asked, "Have you picked out the tree yet?"

"No, I haven't had a chance. Want to do it together?"

She followed her father outside and they walked the half mile to the field until they reached a row of trees that were roughly seven feet tall.

"Douglas Fir or blue spruce this year?" he asked.

"I think the Douglas. They smell so nice!" She leaned in and took a big whiff of the tree on the end.

"The ones down here are best." He led her down the row and stopped in front of a grouping of beautiful firs, perfectly shaped with full, green bowers.

Kate took her time, walking around the trees in circles, carefully inspecting their branches to make sure none were broken and searching for the perfect pointed top.

"I think it's between this long elegant one and the fuller one over there."

Neal nodded. Every year with Katherine it was the same. She found two very different trees that were both beautiful in their way and then she went round and round about which one to pick.

"Well, this one is leaner, more regal and distant. This one is rosier, cheery. Both admirable in their way, just depends on what you're looking for," said Neal patiently.

"I think I want cheery this year, Daddy. Let's go with this one."

She took a red ribbon out of her pocket and tied it to the tree, marking it to be cut later. Katherine sighed and looked around.

"It'll be weird having Christmas without you this year," she said. "I'm going to miss this." She gestured to the rows and rows of trees around them and the forest beyond, covered in frost that sparkled under the clear morning sun. The sky was a pale blue, cold but still bright. She could see the mountains in the distance, the hazy mist surrounding them like smoke rising from a fire.

"So it's certain you won't be coming back?"

She sighed again and tucked her hand into the crook of his arm. "It looks like we'll be going to London to be with Will's family. I'm sorry, Daddy. I'd rather be here with you, believe me."

She laid her head on his shoulder as they walked slowly back toward the house, Jake running and jumping in front of them. Neal patted her head with a rough hand, then leaned over and kissed her crown.

"I know, darlin'. But marriage is filled with compromises, and you can't be in two places at once."

She squeezed his arm and they continued on, silent and slow.

**

When she got back to her mother's house, everyone was still in bed so Kate took the opportunity to do some online shopping for her cousin. Mary had written down the children's sizes – just in case – and Kate went to town. But first, she found toys for all of them for Christmas, including an extensive art kit for Maddy and a 250 piece train track set for Joey. She selected gift wrapping for all of them and gleefully typed in her cousin's address. Next she went to Amazon and set up a monthly shipment of diapers to her cousin, and added in a box of Mary's favorite chocolates for good measure.

When Tiffany joined her, she asked her little sister if she'd like to make some money and offered to pay her to watch Mary's kids for two days so Kate could send her to a spa as a Christmas gift.

"Yeah, I always want money! And Mary's kids are nice, not like those nasty Jenkinson brats."

Kate agreed and they worked out the details, but not before Tiffany asked if she would be getting such a fancy gift, to which Kate replied that if she had four kids by the age of twenty-five, she would gladly send her to a spa for the weekend. Tiffany wrinkled her nose and Kate laughed out loud. She hugged her little sister and promised her a nice gift when she graduated the next year, to which Tiffany squealed in delight and squeezed Kate within an inch of her life.

Together they went to a children's clothing site and chose new outfits for the kids: T-shirts and jeans for playing in, nicer clothes for school, and a pretty Christmas outfit for each of them. Tiffany saw some adorable new winter coats and matching snow boots which Kate eagerly put into her shopping basket and when she saw a beautiful knee length wool coat that would look great on Mary, she happily chose her cousin's size and added it to her growing pile of clothing.

In the end, she and Tiffany were practically giddy with joy and imagining how surprised and happy Mary would be when she opened everything. Kate felt like a fairy godmother and was a little embarrassed that she hadn't thought of this before.

"You don't think she'll be offended, do you?" Kate asked warily.

"No! Why would she? She's working twelve hour shifts at a diner and her husband does the swing shift at a rubber factory. I think she'll be relieved. Now she can put her money to better use, like paying for classes and cool Christmas gifts," Tiffany reasoned.

"When did you get so smart?"

Tiffany nudged her sister with her shoulder. "I am a straight A student, Katie. You didn't get all the brains in the family," she said.

Kate laughed. "I'm glad to see that. I'm proud of you, Tiffany." Her sister rolled her eyes. "No, really, I mean it. I know we don't spend much time together, but you're a really sweet girl and I'm proud to be your sister."

"Aww, I'm proud of you, too!" Tiffany hugged her sister and then pulled back and fanned her face. "Now don't make me cry! Ryan's coming over later and I don't want to be all puffy."

Kate just laughed and shook her head.

***

"What's that?" Kate asked. She'd just stepped onto the plane and was taking off her coat to hand to the flight attendant.

"Mr. Harper said it was a surprise for you." The attendant said before taking her things to the tiny closet near the cockpit.

"For me?" Kate looked at the large wrapped package strapped down in the corner of the plane. She turned around when she heard Will settling in behind her. "Will, what's that?"

"That?" He nodded toward the package. "Just a little surprise for my wife." He smiled and kissed her forehead.

He refused to tell Kate what it was no matter how many times she asked him. She finally gave up and decided to pretend she didn't want to know even though she was burning with curiosity the entire time. They finally landed in New York and made it to their apartment; Kate had mostly managed to stop thinking about the mysterious box.

"You hungry? I thought I might order some food in," he asked.

"Sure, sounds good," she said distractedly.

"Hey, you okay?" he asked.

"Yeah, I'm fine. Just thinking about home."

He looked at her questioningly.

"We have all these holiday traditions. Thursday is Thanksgiving, Friday is the bonfire, Saturday we put up the tree and all decorate it together. Gran makes ridiculously strong eggnog and mom makes this really great spiced cider. We eat leftover desserts and laugh and everybody gets along for one night. You know," she added thoughtfully, "I never thought about it before, but dad would always spend the night on this night. I've always woken up to find him puttering around in the kitchen in a navy robe that's hung on the back of my mother's bathroom door for as long as I can remember." She sighed. "Now Jenny is gone and I'm married, sort of, and everything's just… changing."

"Sounds like everyone's growing up," he said gently.

She huffed. "When did you get so philosophical?"

He chuckled. "I have my moments. You know what would cheer you up?"

"Chocolate cake?" she asked hopefully.

He laughed. "No. Why don't you take a look at your surprise?"

"Oh! I'd almost forgotten." Kate sprang up and ran into the living room where the enormous box was standing on end next to the window.

She quickly grabbed a pair of scissors and pulled the sides down as fast as she could. After she'd pulled back the protective white covering, she stood back and gasped.

"My tree! How did you…?"

"You're father said you had a tradition of choosing the tree for his house and that this was the one you picked out this year. We thought it might help you feel more at home."

Before he finished his sentence, Kate launched herself into his arms, her face buried in his neck. "Thank you," she breathed.

"You're welcome. Come on, let's get it in water."

Kate happily went about setting up the tree and fished out the decorations she'd chosen from her mother's gift shop that morning. Every year, Loretta had each of her girls choose an ornament which she then inscribed their names and the year on. This year, Kate chose two, a star for her and a gingerbread man for Will. Her mother also gave them a shiny silver heart that had their names and wedding date written in a lovely flowing script in the center.

"What's that?" Will asked as he saw her staring at the shiny ornaments.

"Oh, my mom gave this to us." She handed him the heart. "And I picked these out for us. It's a family tradition."

He smiled when he saw the gingerbread man with his name on it. "Very fitting," he said.

"I thought so." She smiled and hung the heart on the tree.

26
INTERNSHIP

Early December
7.5 Months Married

Kate was walking out of class one day when she got a text on her phone.

Mary: A small department store was just delivered to my house. You wouldn't know anything about that, would you?

Kate laughed.

Kate: Merry Christmas! I just saw a few things I thought the kids would enjoy. That's what family is for! It's my job to spoil them.

Mary: Seriously, Katie, you didn't have to do all this. But thank you. It's a huge blessing.

Kate: Good, I'm glad I was able to help.

Mary: The kids are having a blast opening everything and figuring out who gets what. They're not happy they have to wait to open the Christmas gifts.

Kate: Of course! What child enjoys waiting!?

Mary: OMG! Did you buy me a coat?! From Nordstrom's!?!? KATIE!!

Kate: I thought it would look good on you. If it doesn't fit, there's a gift receipt in the package. You should be able to exchange it.

Mary: You are the best cousin EVER!!!

Kate: Haha! You deserve it! Send me a pic of you wearing it.

Two minutes later, she was looking at a photo of a beaming Mary wearing her new coat and twirling happily. She'd also sent pictures of the kids wearing their new coats. Kate smiled and put her phone away, pleased with her good deed and the fact that someone she loved was benefiting from her decision to marry Will. It helped with the niggling fear she sometimes had that this whole thing was a really bad idea that was certain to land her in jail. She shook her head and skipped down the steps to the subway.

What's done is done, Katie. Now make it count.

**

Since they'd returned from Virginia, Harper felt like Kate had been her old self again, but somehow better. Sweeter, nicer to him, bolder in her words and actions. He was thrilled they weren't fighting any longer and basked in the warmth of her affection once more.

The week her final projects were due, she took to watching mindless television on the sofa in the living room and when Will got home, she'd hold open the quilt she was snuggled underneath and invite him to sit beside her. They'd munch popcorn and make fun of *America's Next Top Model*, Kate's I'm-too-stressed-to-function show of choice. He found her guilty pleasure amusing (especially when she strutted in imitation of Miss J) and her need to cuddle endearing.

The holidays had always been an odd time of year for him, and he found her innocent need to hold him and be held surprisingly comforting. The honesty of it was refreshing and the knowledge that he was meeting a need of hers, that he could watch her go from stressed and frazzled to calm and relaxed through his actions, made him happy and proud, feelings he chose not to examine too closely but enjoyed nonetheless. They were friends again, and it was wonderful.

The day she turned in her last project, Kate and William were eating at the island in the kitchen, laughing and talking about their days.

"Oh, I forgot to tell you. In October, my professor had to pick a few students to recommend for this really great internship next semester, and I was one of them," Kate said as she dried her hands after putting her plate in the dishwasher.

"Wow, that's great," said Will before he took another bite of his grilled cheese sandwich and washed it down with a swig of beer.

"That's not all. I went to the interview last month, and they are only choosing five students, and I'm one of them! I got my placement letter today. They're putting me in nonfiction, under nature and science." Kate waved a folded piece of paper around in front of her from the other side of the island.

"Congratulations! What sort of internship is it?"

"Editing assistant. Actually, I think it's like assistant to the assistant's assistant, and I'll probably spend most of my time fetching coffee, but I'll be in a real publishing house and make contacts and meet people that I might work with later. If they like me, they might offer me a job after graduation."

"That's exciting." He smiled at her enthusiasm. "Which publisher is it?"

"Carter House."

"Carter?"

"Yeah, are you familiar with them?"

"Um, yes. You could say that."

"Uh oh, I know that look. You're about to tell me something really bad. What is it? Is their president a horrible golfer? Does he shop at outlet stores?"

He gave her a look and she stifled her laugh. "Kate, you can't take that job," he said seriously.

She stepped back in surprise and her expression was incredulous. "What do you mean 'can't'?"

Will knew he was on dangerous ground, and their truce was so new he really didn't want to mess it up, but he had to say something. "Kate, you know Taggston Publishing?"

"Yes. It's a two-hundred year old publishing house with a stellar reputation. And it's under the Taggston umbrella. Which is basically you." She gave him a questioning look.

"Carter is our top competitor. Has been for decades. You can't work for the competition."

"What are you talking about? All publishers compete with each other. It's the nature of the beast."

"Not like this. Carter and Taggston have a longstanding, well, feud of sorts. It's a lot more than friendly competition."

"A feud? Like the Hatfields and the McCoys?"

"The who?"

"Never mind."

"Look, ages ago, a major editor left Taggston for Carter. Turns out he was about to be fired for sleeping with the vice president's wife, but no one knows that." She looked surprised and Harper continued, "Anyway, he took a lot of authors with him and spilled a lot of company secrets to boot. That started off a battle between the two companies that hasn't abated since. We never hire anyone who's worked for them, and they do the same."

"Isn't that a little extreme?"

"Maybe, but it's how it's always been done. Besides that, I don't like what I've heard of their business practices."

She shot him a look with one raised brow.

"You just can't, Kate. We're married. Think how it would look. 'Taggston Heir's Wife Goes to Work for the Competition.' It would be humiliating, not to mention the amount of explaining it would require."

She gritted her teeth and took a deep breath. *Funny how your mood can change so drastically in such a short period of time,* she thought. "This isn't 1950. You can't just tell me not to do something and expect me to just go along. This is my career, Will."

He gave her a pleading look. "Please try to understand, Katie."

She mentally counted to ten and when she felt a little more under control, she said, "Okay, so let's say I don't do the internship. I had been counting on doing one next semester and I have hours to fill in my schedule, plus I really want the experience and the contacts. What should I do? It's too late to apply for another one."

He thought for a moment, then brightened. “Why not work for Taggston? You might not be able to do it in an official internship capacity, but you could work there part time to gain experience, and maybe take another Lit class to fill up your hours.”

She sighed. “The problem with that, William,” she stressed his name, “is that this,” she gestured between the two of them, “isn't going to last forever. By the time I graduate, we'll have been married a year. If I'm lucky enough to get a job right away, I'll have been at it a little over a year when we split up. There's no way Taggston is going to feel loyalty to me after so little time. And even if they did feel some, they would never choose me over you. I would be expected to leave graciously. And depending on how the divorce is perceived, it could make other publishers wary of taking me on if they think you and your mega publishing house are holding a grudge against me.”

“I hear what you're saying, really, I do, but I think you might be taking this whole thing a little overboard. There's no reason you would need to quit Taggston. If you were doing a good job and liked it, I don't see why you couldn't stay. I have virtually nothing to do with the publishing house. We agreed we would split on irreconcilable differences, and make it known that we're still friends. We could make sure people see us having dinner together or going to the cinema or something afterward, just to make sure. You wouldn't be blackballed. I would never do that to you. I would never let my company do that to you,” he said earnestly.

She looked at him warily, her brow furrowed in thought. “But everyone there would know I got the job because of you, not on my own merit. And they would all act strangely around me. I'd be like a nark.”

“You wouldn't be a nark!” She gave him a look. “Okay, maybe a little bit of a nark, but we can work that out. Maybe in a specific department, or under a certain person, or something, it wouldn't be such a big issue.”

She gave him another look and he could tell she was starting to get really sad about the whole thing. He stepped closer to her and grasped her arms.

"Just think about a job at Taggston. You don't have to answer tonight. Just sleep on it for a bit and we'll talk later this week."

She nodded and finally put down her letter. "Okay. Goodnight, Will."

She walked down the hall, her shoulders sagging, and turned into her room. Will watched her and sighed, dropping his head to his hands and pulling his fingers through his hair. He reached across the counter for the letter she'd discarded.

Dear Ms. Bishop,

We are pleased to welcome you to the Carter House Internship Program. The Program has a long history of accepting only the most exemplary students and giving them opportunities in the publishing field. Our success rate is unparalleled; ninety-five percent of our interns go on to work in the publishing industry full time, and many find a home right here at Carter House. We look forward to adding you to our publishing family.

He stopped reading there and put the letter down. He felt guilty now, and Will HATED feeling guilty. Kate's marriage to him was supposed to be giving her more opportunities and opening doors for her, not slamming them in her face. It was too late now to figure anything out, but in the morning, he would find a way to fix this. He had to.

**

Harper walked into his office a few minutes early the next morning and immediately buzzed Evelyn in.

"Can you get me a meeting with Arnold Billington?" Harper asked.

"The President of Taggston Publishing?" she asked, obviously surprised. HarperCo was a technology firm and Harper rarely had anything to do with the other companies under Taggston.

"Yes."

"When would you like this meeting to take place?"

"As soon as possible."

"Of course, sir. I'll take care of it."

Half an hour later, Evelyn buzzed to tell him Mr. Billington would arrive at two o'clock that day. Harper thanked her and mentally went over what he was going to say and what he was going to leave out.

Arnold Billington was a contemporary of Harper's father and very good at his job, so bossing him around did not seem like a good idea, nor a palatable one. When he walked into Harper's office at precisely two o'clock in an impeccable gray suit, Harper stood and straightened his jacket, then led him to one of the club chairs by the window in an attempt to make this meeting informal.

"How are you, Arnold? How are Linda and the kids?" Will shook his hand before he sat down.

"I'm well, William, as is the family. Our youngest graduates from Dartmouth this month, so now they're all out of the nest." Arnold Billington settled back in his chair, a genial smile on his face, but his eyes were a bit tight.

Great, his youngest kid is Kate's age. "I'll get right to the point here, Arnold. I have a little problem I could use your help with." The older man looked intrigued. "A personal problem."

Arnold's brows shot up in surprise. "How can I help you, son?"

Will smiled at the endearment. It wasn't surprising, many of the older executives had known him since he was in diapers, but it was a little bittersweet.

"It's my wife, Kate. You met her at the reception?"

"Yes, lovely. Spunky little thing. Great dancer."

"Yes, she is. Well, Kate is getting her master's in literature and she's going into her final semester. She had always planned on doing an internship, for the experience and contacts, the usual thing, and she's received an offer, but I'm a little uncertain about her working for a rival house."

"Who was she going to intern with?"

"Carter," Will answered, then looked out the window at the falling rain.

"Whew, I'll bet that was a close call. So what do you want me to do? Recommend a different house? Or do you want her at Taggston?"

"I think Taggston would be best. Wherever she goes, she might be offered a job. It could create a conflict of interests for her down the road – as my wife."

"I see what you mean. Unless she went with a small, very specialized house, we could be competing for authors and readership; it could get messy."

"Exactly. But she's concerned that everyone at Taggston would treat her differently because she's my wife. She doesn't want to feel like she's on the outside and not learn what she needs to, and she doesn't want special treatment either. And she didn't say this, but I'm sure she just wants to enjoy a normal internship like everyone else, without people changing their behavior around her or buddying up to her because they think they can get to the top through her."

"I see. All valid reasons. Would she even accept a place at Taggston?"

"I don't know. I think she would if we could find a place where being my wife wouldn't influence her position, or at least not overly. Do you have a place like that?" Will asked hopefully.

Billington smiled. "I might. Let me check around. I don't handle the interns personally, but I do know that we already have them all lined up for the spring because I just reviewed the budget this morning. But there may be a slot that didn't get filled or an area that didn't have one allocated."

"And money's no object, of course, as I'm sure you know. I know you're in the habit of paying the interns, but as I understand it, Kate wasn't going to get paid with her other offer, so don't let this throw off your budget."

"Actually, only certain internships are paid. The others come with perks, but not much else. I'll see what I can do and get back to you tomorrow."

"Great, thank you, Arnold, I really appreciate it."

"Any time, William. I hope we can work something out. I'd hate for there to be trouble between you and the missus so early in your marriage."

Will laughed uncomfortably. "You and me both."

Arnold laughed jovially and slapped Will on the shoulder. "I'll call you tomorrow."

**

When Harper got home that night, he found a note on the fridge from Kate. *Christmas shopping with Sheila and Angie tonight in case you forgot. Leftovers are in the fridge – it's the bowl with the pink lid. – Me*

He had forgotten, but he didn't mind being on his own. Avoiding Kate until everything got straightened out was probably a good idea. That was why he was just getting home at eight o'clock. He heated up the dish in the microwave and went into the living room to watch television. By ten, he was heading to his room to get ready for bed. Just as he was turning off his lamp, he heard a door in the hall.

"Kate?"

"Yeah, it's me. Did I wake you?"

"Just getting to bed. Sleep well," he called.

"Night, Will," she answered.

In the morning, he left for work while Kate was in the shower. He was slightly annoyed by his cowardice, but he felt it was better to keep his distance until something could be decided. Hopefully he would have a plan sometime today.

**

It was ten o'clock when Evelyn buzzed to tell him Arnold Billington had requested his first available appointment. At ten thirty, Arnold was sitting across from him in the same seat he had the day before.

"Please tell me you have good news," Will said.

"As a matter of fact, I do. The nonfiction department, specifically biographies and memoirs, requested three interns this year. We only had the budget for two, so that's all they got. However, if your wife would agree to an unpaid internship, we could give them one more. She wouldn't be able to tell anyone about the arrangement – I don't want to create any hassles. I won't even tell the head of the department. He'll think she's being paid just like the others. Best of all, the intern supervisor doesn't pay much attention to the society pages. I doubt he even knows you got married."

"Sounds perfect. So what happens next?"

Arnold handed William an envelope. "Here's an acceptance letter from the intern coordinator. My assistant took the liberty of adding Mrs. Harper to the system. I assume that she's qualified if Carter was willing to take her on, but we'll need copies of her transcript and recommendation letters for the file. She should send them to my office; my assistant will enter them into the system so it looks like she applied months ago with the other interns. From there, she'll just need to stop by HR to fill out the paperwork and she'll be ready to start in January."

Will sighed heavily. "Thank you, Arnold. I can't tell you how relieved I am. I'm sure Kate will be very pleased with this."

"And you'll be out of the doghouse!" Arnold chuckled and Will rubbed the back of his neck as he stood and walked toward the door.

"I'll pass this on to Kate and she'll contact your assistant. Thank you again, Arnold. I really appreciate it."

"Think nothing of it, William. I'm happy to help." Billington clapped him on the shoulder and left.

**

Kate was in the kitchen, stirring a pot of something that smelled delicious and reading a book that was open on the counter next to her when Will walked in that evening. He approached her slowly.

"What are you making?" he asked gently.

"Chicken vegetable soup. It's comforting," she said softly and gave him a small smile. "We need it in this weather."

He glanced at the sleet-pounded window and nodded in agreement.

"Maria was here this afternoon. She made a fresh loaf of bread to go with it. I bought that fancy table butter, too. Should be a nice meal." She gave him that sad smile again and it made something in him ache to see her trying so hard to be nice and normal and happy when she was clearly devastated.

"I have good news," he said a little too loudly. "Or what I think is good news. The biography and memoirs department at Taggston Publishing requested three interns this term but only had the budget for two. If you're willing to work without pay, they'd be happy to have you as the third."

She looked at him skeptically. "Really? The biography department?"

"Yes. I spoke with the President today and he confirmed all the details." He handed her the letter. "What do you think?"

She read silently for a moment, then looked up with much brighter eyes. "Will they know who I am? I mean, that we're married?"

"Arnold Billington, the president, obviously knows. You danced with him at the reception. Tall chap, gray hair. Anyhow, he said the intern coordinator is none the wiser and if you want to use your maiden name, that's fine by them. You should be able to have a relatively normal intern experience."

Suddenly he had his arms full of Kate, her head pressed into his chest and her arms squeezing him tightly. He squeezed her back, lighter, and kissed the top of her head. He always forgot how much shorter than him she was without her shoes on. Finally, she lifted her head and looked up at him, her arms still wrapped around him and her chin on his chest.

"Thank you, Will," she said softly.

"Don't thank me. It was the right thing to do. You shouldn't be losing career opportunities because of me," he said seriously.

"Thank you for doing the right thing, then." She reached up on her toes and kissed his chin.

She released him and went back to her soup, giving it a quick stir before closing her book and grabbing two bowls from the cabinet.

"Let's eat!" she said happily. She was still a bit subdued, but clearly so much happier than she had been and Will gladly agreed and opened the drawer to fetch two spoons.

"How about we eat in the living room and watch a film?" he asked.

"That sounds nice. What are you in the mood for?"

"I don't know. Something old, maybe. You?"

"That sounds good. You pick."

She filled the bowls while Will set up the film, and they ate soup with homemade bread and Irish butter, watched a black and white movie, and did bad impressions of Cary Grant and Katherine Hepburn while snuggling under her grandmother's quilt.

When the film was finished, Will sighed and leaned his head on the back of the sofa.

"What's wrong? You look stressed," Kate asked, brushing the hair away from his temple.

"Just thinking about Christmas. And family."

"In a good way or a bad way?"

"Both, I suppose."

She snuggled closer and crossed her knee into his lap. "Care to elaborate?"

He sighed again and it came out more like a groan. "You met my family. They're not exactly warm. The holidays with them are always a little, I don't know -"

"Cold?"

"Yes. Everyone buys tastefully expensive gifts that their assistants likely chose and we sit down to a perfectly prepared meal. I wear an uncomfortable suit because I know my aunt would have a heart attack if I came to table without a jacket on. We discuss business and stock reports and pretend to like each other. It's not very…"

"Christmas-y?"

"Yes."

"If you had your druthers, how would you spend the holiday?"

"If I didn't have to spend it with my family?"

"Yeah."

"I don't know. One year when we were students, Jamison, Cavendish, and I went skiing with some friends from Uni. There was a storm and we were trapped in this cabin. No parents, no professors telling us what to do. No deadlines or clients to keep happy. No uncles to impress and convince I was ready to handle the business. It was lovely. I remember thinking that I'd like to do that again, get away like that with people close to me. I think, if I could, I'd do Christmas like that."

"It sounds wonderful. Where were you?"

"Cavendish has a place in the Swiss Alps. Or his family does. Just outside of this little village that has this fantastic fondue restaurant. There are only about a dozen tables, and the waitresses don't speak much English, it's not a really touristy spot, but you can eat your weight in cheese."

"Mmm. Sign me up!"

Will laughed. "I'll have to take you to Switzerland sometime. You'd love it there. Do you ski at all?"

"No, but I bet I'd look great in a ski suit," she teased.

"I bet you would, too," he growled playfully as he ran a hand across her thigh. They were both laughing and looked at each other for a long moment until Kate broke eye contact and laid her head on his shoulder.

"Maybe we can go there after London? For New Year maybe?"

"Yeah, maybe," he said huskily.

Kate felt him shift beneath her and carefully extracted her leg from his lap and scooted out from beneath the covers.

"I'm off to bed. I'll see you in the morning, Will," she said quickly without looking at him.

"Night, Kate," he said to the floor.

27
ABOUT TIME

Mid December
8 Months Married

"Are you going to tell me where we're going?" Will asked.

"Nope. You'll just have to wait and see."

Kate was driving them out of the city. It was the Friday afternoon before Christmas and she'd only told Will to pack plenty of warm clothing, then teasingly added that he should bring her Christmas gift.

"How far is this place?"

"About four hours altogether. And it's already been one, so just three more to go!" she answered cheerfully.

Will rolled his eyes and looked out the window. He finally fell asleep after another half hour and when he woke up, they were stopped in front of a familiar looking log cabin surrounded by evergreen trees.

"Is this Jamison's cabin? Are we in Vermont?"

"Yup!" Kate answered from the back of the car where she was pulling things out from the trunk. "He said we could borrow it for the weekend. He and Jen would have joined us, but they're packing for the trip to Farmington tomorrow. I can't believe he's willing to spend an entire week with my family, but that's love for you."

She kept up a running dialog as she pulled out two large bags, one filled with wrapped presents and the other with food she and Maria had prepared, plus some ingredients for making

Christmas goodies. William got out of the car and stretched, taking a deep breath of the crisp mountain air.

"When were you here last?" Kate asked as she came out of the house after taking in her sacks.

"It's been a few years," he answered. "It's not very good for a group, Andrew mostly comes up here on his own or with a-" he stopped when he noticed Kate looking at him expectantly. "There are only two bedrooms, so it's more of a private retreat," he said awkwardly as he turned his back to her and looked around, pretending to admire the scenery.

"Hmm."

Will went around the back to pick up the two small suitcases they'd brought as she grabbed the last bag and locked up the car, then bounded up the steps onto the porch and let the screen door make a satisfying smack behind her. She went straight to the kitchen and pulled out the roast Maria had made and began heating it up while she put the other groceries away.

"Do you know which bedroom you want?" Will popped his head into the kitchen. "There's a small loft room upstairs, it has two single beds. The bedroom down here has a king and an ensuite." She looked at him over the refrigerator door and he added, "You should take that one. You've never been here before and it has a fireplace. I'll just take my bag upstairs."

"Why don't we share the room?"

His brows jumped. "Share?"

"Yeah. Why not? Then we can both enjoy the fireplace."

"Right. Okay. Right then," he said as he left, his cheeks a very faint shade of pink.

A few hours later, Kate was in the bathroom brushing her teeth. They'd had a lovely meal and finished a bottle of wine while they shared holiday memories. Kate did most of the talking, as usual, and Will laughed at her exuberant storytelling skills, like he usually did. More than once their eyes had caught across the table and they'd shared a look, one of them always looking away and changing the subject before things became too heavy.

She'd finally excused herself and he'd offered to load the

dishwasher while she got ready for bed. She appreciated his consideration, with the dishes and for giving her time to use the room privately, but part of her wished he hadn't been quite so considerate.

As she brushed her teeth, she stepped to the suitcase and looked at the nightgowns she'd brought with her from her La Perla expedition with Jen. When she and Laura had heard about Kate and Will's weekend, they'd wasted no time giving her advice on how to seduce her husband. Jen had suggested subtle, of course, incorporating wine and candles and possibly some sort of massage. Laura had bluntly told her to just jump him. She did suggest the shower for creativity. Maybe the shower was a good idea? Should she just wait for him to get in tonight and then open the door and ask if she could join him?

She looked at the walk-in steam shower and thought it was definitely a possibility, but she didn't know if she wanted to have their first time in a shower. She didn't know his quirks yet. The kind of quirks you only know about someone you're sexually intimate with. What if he had a bum knee and couldn't hold her up? What if one of them lost their balance and they fell and she broke her tailbone? What if it was all just too slippery? She shook her head and told herself to stop being so ridiculous.

Looking at the nightgowns again, she saw there was a beautiful black gown. It was full-length and made of soft silk. The back was almost completely open, a deep V that went to the top of her bum. Maybe that was a good option? Surely if she went to bed in that, he'd get that she was open to the idea of… What exactly? Was it sex?

That sounded so cheap somehow. It wasn't just sex. They were friends and they cared about each other. Deeply. At least she cared about him deeply. And he'd said she was his best friend. So it couldn't be just sex. Making love then? But that sounded so romantic. They weren't really romantic. Not like Jenny and Andrew with their constant mooning over each other or even like she'd been with Jeremy when she couldn't stop thinking about him and just seeing him in a crowd made her stomach flop.

They were friends who cared about each other and had a

lot of affection for one another. *Affectionate friends*. Friends that loved each other. So it could be making love, couldn't it? Just a different kind of making love. *Friend love*. She wished that didn't sound so creepy. But they were more than just friends, right? Will had said that they were. They were partners. And what was more partner-y than having sex/making friend love?

She laughed at herself for all her silly justifications. "Just be honest with yourself, Katie," she said quietly to her stacks of folded clothes. "You want him. He's handsome and funny and sweet and smells reeeeaaaally good. It's okay to want someone. You're a grown woman, he's an adult, there's nothing wrong here. You don't have to be head over heels in love with someone to have sex. You know that."

She shook off her silliness and decided that she would go old school. She'd flirt, touch his arm, play with his hair. Let him know she was interested and go from there. All this planning was stressing her out.

Will was in the kitchen rinsing the dishes and mechanically loading the dishwasher, a skill he'd acquired in the last few months since Kate came into his life. *Kate*. He stopped mid-rinse and thought about how relaxed she'd looked at the table sipping her wine. She was so lively, and yet so laid back at the same time. He'd never felt so comfortable in his life. If the table between them hadn't placed her so far away, he knew he would have kissed her. He wasn't completely sure, but he thought she'd wanted him to. She'd been giving him shy glances for the last week, and she was the one to suggest they share the bed. Surely that was a sign?

He didn't want to assume, but he'd brought a box of condoms just in case. He wasn't sure which ones she preferred so he'd bought three different kinds, including some all-natural brand that was three times the cost of the others. He'd felt like an idiot in the drug store line, especially when the teenaged cashier looked at him with an approving smile and nodded. But when Kate had said she wanted to go away with him for the weekend, he'd hoped, wondered – no, definitely hoped – that this would be the time. It had now been over a year since he'd had sex and his body was definitely ready to move to the next level.

He considered how to go about it, thinking maybe the hot tub could be a good option, but he hadn't brought a swimsuit so would have to go without, and that might be coming on too strong at first. Maybe he could invite her to sit in front of the fire, open another bottle of wine and offer to rub her shoulders. She must be sore from the drive. One thing could lead to another … But he didn't know if the floor was a good option for their first time. What if she was turned off by the idea? Perhaps the shower? But that might be too slippery. He remembered Andrew coming back from a weekend here once with a decided limp and the explanation that redheads and showers didn't mix.

He put the last glass in the dishwasher and turned it on. He flipped off the lights and went to find Kate. Maybe inspiration would strike at the last moment.

He walked into the room to find her staring at her suitcase.

"Katie?" She turned to face him, her shoulders slightly tense but a smile on her face. "Everything alright?"

"Yes, of course. Just, um, getting ready, uh, I thought, um. How'd the cleanup go?" she asked, standing at an awkward angle but trying to appear normal.

"Fine. No problems." *Say something, quick.* "I'm a bit sore from the car ride." *Brilliant. Just brilliant.* "How about you?"

"Yeah, um, a little. Especially my shoulders." Jen's suggestion of a massage ran through her mind and she rolled her shoulders for emphasis.

"Maybe we could-," *Quick, pick something! Hot tub, shower, massage. Just choose!* "Um, there's a hot tub on the deck."

"Really?" She suddenly looked interested and walked to the door on the far wall and turned on the light. She stepped out and examined it, then stepped back in. "It's not on. It'll take a while to heat up. Maybe we can try it tomorrow?"

"Yeah, sure." He looked around and shuffled his feet, out of ideas and not sure what to say next.

"Well, I need to take a shower."

"I'm going to hop in the shower," they said at the same time. They both smiled and laughed a little.

"Did you want to go straight to bed or are you too awake?" she asked.

"I got a good nap in the car so I'm wide awake. You?"

"I could go either way." They looked at each other silently again. "Do you mind if I shower first? Do you need the bathroom?" she asked.

"Of course, go ahead. Just let me grab my toothbrush. I can use the one upstairs to clean my teeth," he said.

"Don't be silly. You can brush your teeth in here while I'm in the shower." He gave her a questioning look. "There's no reason to spread your stuff out all through the house. That's how things get lost. Just give me a quick second."

She dashed off to the bathroom before he could respond and he heard the water running a few seconds later. Kate called him to come on in and he stepped into the bathroom, walking straight to the sink and trying not to think about Kate, naked, wet and soapy just a few feet away. He looked in the direction of the shower as he cleaned his teeth. The glass door was shut and steaming up slowly, carrying a soft vanilla scent with it. The shower stretched to the left behind the stone tiles, so he couldn't see her, but he could hear her stepping lightly and the water splashing about as it came into contact with her skin. *Soft, silky skin.*

He rinsed his mouth in the sink and without thinking, pulled his shirt over his head and shucked off his socks. The next thing he knew, he'd crossed the room and opened the shower door. He couldn't see well through the steam, but asked in a husky voice, "Can I join you?"

He heard Kate's soft gasp and waited an agonizing moment until he heard her say softly, "Yes."

His pants were off in record time and then he was in and closing the door behind him. He moved forward in the orange-y red light of the shower where he could see Kate's dark hair and the pale skin of her forehead.

"Can I scrub your back?" he asked huskily, a soft sponge in his hand.

"Yes." She turned her back to him, looking over her shoulder for a moment then facing forward, her heart racing and her mind screaming that this was it. It was really happening. *Breathe, Katie. Breathe. Just relax. Everything will be fine.*

He rubbed the soapy sponge in circles over her shoulder blades, gradually dropping lower till he was near the base of her spine, then working his way back up. He set down the sponge and rubbed her shoulders, his strong fingers digging into her supple flesh and working away the knots and soreness.

"Is the pressure good?" he asked softly.

"Yes."

"Are you going to say anything else?"

"Yes," she said playfully.

He smiled. "Any time soon?"

"Yes."

He laughed. "I suppose there are worse words."

His hands dipped lower and skimmed over her ribs, making her squirm slightly, and moved on to her hips. He moved his fingers in a strong circular motion and she marveled that she'd never noticed how sore her hips were before. She leaned her head back on his shoulder in sheer bliss and felt his arousal graze against her bum. She smiled and sighed with satisfaction.

"Pleased, Ms. Bishop?" he asked in her ear.

"Yes," she said, dragging out the word.

He growled shortly and dived for her neck, greedily kissing and suckling her skin. Kate was remarkably responsive, moaning and grabbing his hair to pull him closer. He reached around and slid his hands up her torso, slowly, and Kate felt ready to scream by the time he finally cupped her breasts in his hands.

They both released a breath at the contact and Will fondled them joyfully, feeling like a teenage boy touching a woman for the first time.

Kate pressed back fully into him and Will squeezed a little firmer in response to her actions. She reached one arm around her side to grab his torso while she ground her ass into his hips. Apparently, Will approved because suddenly his hands were everywhere and she wasn't sure what was happening. She felt a thigh pressing between her legs, hands and forearms pressing across her torso and down over her hips and back again while his lips worked her neck and ears. All she could do was hang on and trust him. She blissfully let her mind go and followed where he led.

Will was in ecstasy. Kate felt amazing under his hands. Her skin was soft and silky and firm all at once. Her neck tasted like salted fruit and he couldn't keep his tongue off of her. Her wet hair was plastered to his chest and she was rubbing one foot up his shins. He couldn't think, he could only feel. Her ass against his hips made him unbelievably hard and he thought he might actually pass out when she ground into him and raked her fingernails against his scalp. He roughly wrapped his left arm around her shoulders and turned her head to face him so he could kiss her mouth while his right hand traveled down her torso. He delved into her mouth, lost to all thought or reason and only wanting to taste, touch, and possess.

Feeling like she was going to burst into tears any moment from the sheer joy of it all, Kate came out of the haze long enough to say, "bed" and they stumbled out of the shower, groping and kissing as they made their way across the room and he tried to walk and hold her ass and kiss her all at the same time.

Will roughly ground out, "Condom?" between kisses.

"Clean?"

"Yes."

"Don't need one," she said breathlessly.

Will didn't need to be told twice. He lifted her onto the edge of the bed and a moment later, her legs were wrapped tightly around his waist and her head thrown back. He knew he wasn't going to last long, but Kate beat him to it by arching her back and crying out. He quickly joined her in boneless oblivion and buried his face in her neck.

A few moments went by quietly and Kate registered the sound of the shower still running as her blood quit pounding in her ears. She could feel Will's breath on her neck and his hair on her cheek. She reached up and stroked his back, smiling when he made a soft purr-like sound.

"Will? You want to finish that shower?" she asked with a smile in her voice.

He chuckled and she felt the vibration across her chest. "I'll get up if you'll let me go."

She relaxed her legs that were still wrapped around him and he pushed up slowly. The room was dim with only one lamp turned on and he was suddenly very tired. Kate smiled at him understandingly and walked carefully to the bathroom, her gait a little lopsided.

"I didn't hurt you, did I?" he asked as he followed her back to the shower.

"No, these muscles are just out of practice." She smiled and he adjusted the control to make more steam.

They stood under separate streams and washed their hair, nearly ignoring each other, alternately absorbed in what they were doing and wondering how the other was feeling. Will was finished and about to get out when he noticed Kate gingerly cleaning her thighs.

"Allow me." He knelt in front of her and moved her hands, nudging her legs apart. He washed her gently, rubbing away the evidence of their actions that had smeared across pale skin.

"Thank you," she said softly. Her eyes had a gentleness to them he hadn't seen before and something in him responded. He smiled back and the next thing he knew, he was drying her off with a fluffy gray towel.

They padded softly into the bedroom and Will turned down the bed, watching Kate out of the corner of his eye as she fished through her suitcase. She walked towards the bed with a large T-shirt in her hand. She was about to put it on when Will spoke and stopped her.

"Do you mind," he gestured to the shirt in her hand, "would you be willing to sleep without it?" She blushed at his request and he quickly added, "Not if you don't want to. I just wondered…" She didn't respond right away and he quickly said, "If you'd rather be alone, I understand, too."

She could see he was getting anxious and quickly spoke up. "No, don't go. I don't want to be by myself. And I don't have to wear this." She held up the shirt. She smiled and added, "But you'll have to keep me warm if I go without."

"I think I can handle that." He smiled softly.

They turned out the light, climbed under the covers and scooted carefully to the center of the bed. Kate turned on her side and Will curled up behind her.

"Night, Katie," he said with a kiss to her neck.

"Night, Will." She kissed his forearm and closed her eyes. A minute later she whispered, "Will?"

"Hmm?" he groaned.

"That was great."

He placed a sloppy kiss on her neck and pulled her closer, his left hand holding her breast tightly and his knees pressed firmly behind hers.

*

Kate woke slowly, a tickling sensation rousing her from sleep. It was still dark and she could tell she'd only slept a few hours. She finally realized that Will was what had woken her and he was pressing soft kisses down the length of her arm. His lips and long lashes and thick hair were creating delightful sensations on her skin.

"Are you awake?" she asked softly, looking at his dazed expression and wondering if he was fully aware of what he was doing.

"So soft. How are you so soft?" he asked gently as he kissed her side and across her belly to her navel. "So pretty. Like a flower."

She looked at him incredulously, wondering who this suddenly verbose and complimentary man was. "Are you sure you're awake?" she asked quietly.

He ran a hand down her leg and circled her knee, drawing patterns over her skin and making her forget she was waiting for an answer. How did he know knees were her weak spot?

He continued his caresses, covering her entire body and complimenting each part in turn. Her calves were flawless and made his mouth water when she wore those red heels she loved so much. How many times had he wanted to run his tongue down the line of her muscle?

Her feet were perfectly arched and so tiny, he found her little toes irresistible and couldn't stop himself from kissing them in turn while she giggled and squirmed. Her thighs were heaven and taunted him mercilessly. Her hips kept his mind filled with indecent thoughts and her ass was hands down the most beautiful thing he'd ever seen in his life.

He must have spent nearly ten minutes touching, kneading, kissing and nibbling it while Kate clutched her pillow and blushed as Will continued to describe all the ways she had taunted him. In shorts, in long skirts, in flowy dresses and tight running pants, in low slung pajamas and red bathing suits. He ended with all the things he wanted to do with that particular part of her anatomy and in all the various places, shocking her by including his study at home and his desk at work, making her eyes widen and her cheeks burn more than they already were.

He moved up her back and traced delicious lines down her spine, sculpting and working her muscles beneath his large hands. He tickled her ribs and suckled her elbows where they rested by her sides, something that had never crossed her mind before but felt divine, and when he breathed on her neck, her entire body broke out in chill bumps.

He said her hair was luxurious and wrapped it around his hands, breathing it in and burying his face in it. He rolled her over and kissed her collar bone, commenting on its delicacy and drawing lines between the moles and freckles that peppered her skin. When he got to her breasts, she let everything go and just enjoyed his attention as he drove her from shyness to ecstasy.

When he nudged her knees apart, she was more than ready to receive him. He continued his words of praise as she moved against him, telling her how amazing she felt and how she made him feel so good. She came gently, gasping softly and pulling his head into her neck as she squeezed him tighter. Will was quick to follow and whispered her name as he collapsed onto her, suddenly spent. He kissed her and stroked her cheek, then rolled over and quickly fell asleep, leaving Kate to wonder if he'd actually been awake at all.

She went to the bathroom and then snuggled next to him with a smile on her face. She hadn't felt so thoroughly wanted in a very long time.

**

Kate woke first and took a moment to get her bearings. Will was wrapped behind her and breathing softly onto her neck, his arm over her ribs holding her securely. She tried to slide out of his embrace, but he gripped her tighter. She waited a moment for him to relax, then slithered out of bed.

She couldn't stop humming as she cooked breakfast, feeling both ravenously hungry and a burning need to feed her husband. *Hormones,* she reasoned.

Will woke to the smell of fresh coffee and frying bacon. He found Kate in the kitchen and wrapped his arms around her where she was standing at the stove.

"Good morning," he said in his rumbly morning voice that she'd always found a little too sexy for comfort.

"Good morning," she said with a smile. "You must be famished."

"Yes. What's on?"

"Bacon, eggs, and French toast – with real Vermont syrup. There's coffee in the pot over there."

He made his coffee and poured her a glass of juice just as Kate set two steaming plates on the table. They smiled at each other and tucked in.

"So what do you want to do today?" she asked after a few bites.

Thinking he shouldn't say what he really wanted to do all day, he asked, "Do you not have any plans? It was your idea to sneak up here, you know," he teased with a smile.

She looked down. "Well, I wasn't sure how everything

would go…"

Understanding, he reached across the table and took her hand. "We could have a lazy day, just hang out here if you want to? There's a decent collection of films and the town has a good restaurant if we want to go out for lunch or dinner. And of course we still need to try the hot tub."

Suddenly remembering what he'd said to her about the hot tub the night before and just exactly what he wanted to do to her in it, she blushed and fiddled with her fork. Will seemed to have the same recollection because he dropped his hand and vigorously ate his French toast.

"Can I ask you a question?" she said after a few minutes.

"Sure," he answered.

"Were you completely awake last night for… round two?" she asked.

"Round two?" he asked with a confused expression.

Suddenly she felt embarrassed for bringing it up and looked back down at her plate. "I'm just teasing you, Katie. Yes, I was awake, though not entirely. I think I came to fully somewhere around kissing your knees. Did much happen before that?"

He seemed so relaxed and comfortable talking about this. Was that a man thing? Kate swallowed her embarrassment and said, "No, not too much."

He smiled and they went back to eating their breakfast.

After breakfast, she again asked him what he wanted to do. Will suggested they take a little walk to stretch their legs. And to keep him from jumping her in the kitchen, but he didn't say that.

They walked hand in hand down the lane, the narrow road surrounded by snow banks on either side. Icicles twinkled in the sunlight and the bare frozen trees looked like frosted arms reaching to the sky.

"So," Kate spoke, "it's a little late, but we should probably have the talk."

"Yes, we should," he replied.

She wanted to ask him what they were to each other.

Besides the obvious business partners, legal spouses, and now sex buddies. But she didn't really know what he was to her and didn't think it was fair to demand to know his feelings when she wasn't sure of her own. And she was terrified of the answer. He'd made it clear he couldn't stay with her. His real wife, the one he would grow old with, had to come from the right family, have the right connections, know how to play all the games. So what did it matter how he felt right now? Even if he did have stronger feelings for her, he couldn't act on them. Well, long-term anyway, in which case she'd rather not know. Knowing would make everything awkward and uncomfortable and a bit desperate and pathetic. Eighteen months was a long time to live with those feelings every day.

And what if he felt nothing? Did she really want to hear him say that? Did she even feel anything for him beyond friendship? She wasn't sure. She agreed with what he had said back in Farmington. They were best friends, partners; two people in this together who respected and cared for one another. They were attracted to each other. Wasn't that enough? Why stir the pot with do-you-like-me-like-that questions?

"So, I was tested at my last physical and was clean, and I haven't been with anyone since," Will was saying as Kate tuned back in. "What about you? And I should be asking about birth control. We weren't exactly careful."

"Right. I was tested in the spring and I'm clean, always have been actually, and I have an IUD for birth control. I don't take the pill because they made my mother and Jen crazy so I decided not to risk it. And I don't think I could ever remember to take something at the same time every day." She knew she was giving too much information, but she always talked too much when she was nervous.

"What's an IUD?" he asked after a moment of hesitation.

"It stands for intrauterine device. It's a small T-shaped thing made out of plastic or copper that gets inserted in your uterus. The plastic one has hormones in it and lasts for five years, the copper is hormone free and lasts for ten. I've got the copper and I'm only three years in, so I'm good." *Stop talking, Katie! Geez, what are you, the sex ed teacher?*

"How effective is it?"

"It's pretty good. Better than condoms. Ninety-nine point something percent effective if I remember correctly. If you're concerned about pregnancy, we can double up and use condoms, too."

"No, that won't be necessary. I know condoms aren't as good as that, so it would be pretty pointless."

"And a lot less fun," quipped Kate.

He chuckled. "You seem to know a lot about the topic," he eventually added.

"Yeah, I think most women eventually learn all about contraception. My mother got pregnant if my dad sneezed around her and my favorite cousin had her fourth kid at twenty-five, so I've always wanted to be careful. I switched to something long-term when I was going out with Matt. It just seemed safer."

"Who's Matt?"

"He was my boyfriend before Jeremy. We should probably share numbers and exes, shouldn't we? And maybe names? It could be awkward if we met someone out or something," she said uneasily, thinking of Jeremy's intrusion at their wedding reception.

He looked thoughtful for a moment. "Numbers, sure, but maybe not names. I don't want to invade your privacy and I don't want to talk about women who aren't here to tell their side."

She shrugged. "Okay. I've had five boyfriends and slept with three men. Your turn."

He looked ahead for a minute, his face confused and thoughtful. "I think you're right. We need *some* details."

She smiled. "Joshua Powell was my first boyfriend – "

"Wait. Joshua Powell? Laura's brother? The guy you were singing with in Farmington?"

"Yup."

"He was your first…?" Will raised his brows to illustrate his meaning.

"First boyfriend. Not first time, no. We went out for almost two years, then broke up after I graduated high school and then I moved to New York. We never slept together."

"Did you," Will stopped himself before he could finish the question. It wasn't any of his business what they had or hadn't done together. He didn't know her then, they weren't married and he had no right to demand fidelity, especially given his own history.

"Did we what?"

"Nothing. So what happened after you moved to New York?"

"I met Caleb freshman year. He was in two of my classes and a business major. He's working for his father's firm now. Something to do with communications." She looked off into the woods. "He was my first. We went out for a little over a year. I was crazy about him."

"Why did you break up?"

"Oh, I don't know. It all just got so complicated. We were really young and neither of us really knew what we were doing. He was only a year older than me. We fought about stupid things a lot and then we had one really big fight and we never recovered. That was that."

He nodded. "Was Matt next?"

"No, next was Phillip. He was a bit of an anomaly. We were friends and hung out with the same crowd. He was studying theatre and I was a theatre minor. He wanted to be a director. He was pretty good at it – super bossy." She smiled fondly at the memory. "Anyway, we only went out for a month before we realized we made better friends than lovers. We never actually slept together. Probably why we're still friends now."

"You still see him?" Harper asked, surprised.

"No, not really. But I do occasionally run into him and we email sometimes. He was at Sheila's dinner party in July, that time you got caught in a meeting, and we sat next to each other. It wasn't awkward at all. And at Angie's birthday party that you missed. It was just like old times."

Kate continued speaking, unaware of Will's stony

expression beside her. He didn't like that when he'd been unable to escort her to events, her ex had been there. Nor did he like that she hadn't told him about it. Of course, his reasonable side insisted, she and Phillip were still friends, it was short-lived and they'd never actually slept together, and she had invited Will to both of those events, and he was the one who had cancelled or opted out both times. And she hadn't been responsible for the guest list in either case. It wasn't like she was sneaking around. But still, he didn't like it.

"Will? Did you hear what I said?"

"I'm sorry, my mind wandered. What were you saying?"

"I said that Phillip is working in an off Broadway show that opens in January that I'd like to see, if you want to come with me?"

"Yes, of course. I'd love to go with you." He smiled down at her and she returned it somewhat curiously. "You said five boyfriends. That's only three."

"Right. You know, I probably shouldn't even count Phillip since it was only a month, but I had a crush on him for ages before, so I always count him." Harper took a deep breath. "Okay, next was Matt. We met in sophomore year, but, as I said before, I was crushing on Phillip. Unbeknownst to me, Matt was crushing on me. We started dating right as junior year started. It was casual at first, but got serious over winter break. He was my second. We went out for about seven months."

"So that puts us where? To senior year?" Will asked, silently wondering why she hadn't given any more details about Matt.

"Yes. How much do you want to know?"

"What do you mean?"

"I mean, how much of my past do you want to know about? Not for immigration files or for sexual history purposes, but just to know?"

By now they had wandered back to the house and Will stepped in front of her to open the door. "I want to know whatever you want to tell me. Rest assured that I won't tell your secrets, if that's what you're worried about." He smiled and held out his arms for her coat.

"I'm not worried about that, I just don't want to bore you. Hot chocolate?" she asked as she walked towards the kitchen.

"Yes, please. And it's not boring."

She smiled. "Well, something odd happened with Matt." She poured milk into a pot on the stove while Harper sat on a stool at the counter. "Spring break of junior year, we'd been together several months and he invited me to go to his family's beach house for a week and meet his parents. They had a place on the gulf somewhere. Anyway, I said yes and as we were packing to go, I needed to get something from his bag. I was rifling around and found a ring. It was pretty, it looked like an antique and it was small, not too ostentatious, but it just wasn't very *me*. I tried to think of reasons he would have it other than proposing. Maybe he was taking it to his mother for some reason, maybe it was a family piece that he was delivering to her. I wracked my brain for about five minutes until I realized I was standing there like a dodo and put it back. I went into the other room and heard Matt on the phone with someone, telling them that I had no idea and that it would be a great surprise. He went on to talk about some party they were planning together and I freaked. I thought he was going to propose in front of a crowd of people and I was going to turn him down in front of all his friends and humiliate him."

"Why were you going to turn him down?"

"I didn't love him," she said simply. "I really liked him and in many ways we were good together, but he always struck me as a little bit weird. And I know I am too, everybody is in their own way, but I don't want to be with someone *despite* their weird quirks – I don't want to think my husband is *actually* odd. I want to love their quirks and accept them completely, even the parts I don't like, not wish they would quit being so weird. I'm not making much sense, but I didn't love him and I just knew somehow that I never would. And once I realized that, there was no reason to continue the relationship, especially with him being so much more serious about it than me."

"So you broke it off and never went to the coast," he

surmised.

"Exactly. It wasn't pretty. But it was the right thing to do, at least I knew that much."

"So then what? That's four, so I assume Jeremy is next?"

"Yes," she said, slightly distracted. She poured two cups full of cocoa and dolloped whipped cream on the tops. "I'd known him for years, or I should say known of him. He'd dated a girl in my dorm sophomore year, then we had the odd class together over the years. He was an English minor, so our paths occasionally crossed."

She settled onto the stool next to Will. "We started dating over a weekend away with a group of friends in autumn of senior year. He was in grad school by then; he's a little older than me. We were together until he got a job offer in Phoenix last February."

"You didn't want to go with him?" Somehow it hadn't occurred to him that Jeremy might not have asked her along.

"No, I didn't. He asked me to, but I wasn't ready to leave my life here. And he wasn't willing to give up the job. Talk about irreconcilable differences." She released a choked-sounding laugh.

They sipped their cocoa quietly for a few minutes until Kate said, a little too brightly, "Okay, you know my sordid past. Now it's your turn."

"Okay, well, I'm afraid it's nowhere near as interesting as yours. As you know, I've only had one proper girlfriend, Sandra, from uni. Before her, I was with one other girl. I was at an all boys school, so we never had any female classmates, but we did occasionally have mixers with the girls schools in the area. I met a girl, Carlotta, at one of them. She had, let's call it a... *reputation*," he said with a look.

"I see," she said with brows raised, amused at his sudden storytelling skills.

"She was known for divesting green boys like me of the encumbrance of their virginity. At one such party, I happily followed her behind some bushes out back and emerged a man."

Kate laughed. "Oh, Will! You lost it behind some bushes at a party? That's awful! You poor thing!" She meant her words, but they were lost in her amusement at his pride in the occasion.

"What? Behind a bush is a perfectly nice place to lose something and it was a much better location than my stuffy dorm room or my parents' house."

She caught her breath. "Okay, you've got me there. I can imagine your parents would not have been happy had they caught you with a girl in the house."

"No, and unfortunately I know from experience." She gave him a look that told him he needed to elaborate. "Before all of that, just before I turned sixteen, we had a gardener working at our house in London. He came on a Saturday once and brought his daughter along. I saw her outside reading on a bench and went to talk to her like any hormonal boy would have done. She was lovely. She had the smoothest skin and smelled of lavender. Anyway," he pulled himself out of his memories, "we got to talking and by the end of the afternoon, she'd given me her number. We arranged it so she would come with her dad as often as possible and once or twice I met her in town for a film or an ice cream. We were just kids, it was all very innocent now that I look back on it, but I really liked her and, well, anyway, one day, my father came home early and caught the two of us kissing in the library."

Kate's face fell with Will's when he got to this part of the story. She had a feeling she knew where this was going.

"He quickly sent her back to her father and gave me the tongue lashing of my life. He said I should never get involved with women in my employ or the daughters of people in my employ. He said that parents need to know their children are safe here and the women who work here need to know that they can come to work and feel safe with their bosses. I had never thought about it that way, that I could make someone feel unsafe, just because I was a man or because I had hiring power. Of course, I didn't have any then, but I would soon and my father assured me that everyone around knew it."

He sighed and Kate squeezed his arm. She new his

father had a point, and a good one, but her heart broke for two little teenaged kids who'd had no idea of the trouble they were stirring up.

"He went on to say that I had to be careful. Now that I was becoming a man, I had to behave differently. He followed this up with a lecture on safe sex and how I couldn't have illegitimate children running around all over town. A Harper has more restraint, a Harper is careful and responsible." Kate watched in fascination as his back became straighter and his shoulders opened, his chest high with familial pride.

"And the final nail in the coffin?" she asked, knowing there was more.

He looked at her sideways, then continued quietly. "Some people will only befriend you because of what you can give them or do for them. He told me to be especially wary of women, that many would act interested because of my wealth or position, that I would have to learn the difference between true interest and – "

"Gold digging?" she finished for him.

"Yes."

"So the easiest way to tell if someone wants you for your money is whether or not they have their own?"

"That's one way, yes."

"And how's that worked out for you so far?" she asked gently.

He raised a brow. "Touché, my dear." He raised his cocoa mug in mock salute. He sipped silently for a minute. "Anyhow, after Sandra there was a string of debutantes and society women, none that got serious, never more than a few dates."

"Did you sleep with all of them?" she asked evenly.

"No, but with several. Honestly, I don't know the exact number. I'd need to think about it." Seeing her trying to hide her expression of shock and mild distaste, he added, "I'd say it was more than fifteen and less than twenty-five."

She nodded. "Did any of them ever get pregnant? Did you get any infections?" Her voice was carefully neutral.

"Not that I know of and no, no infections. I always used

a condom. Until last night, that is."

Her head snapped up. "Really? You'd never done it without a condom before?"

"No. Does that really surprise you?"

She was about to reply that yes, it absolutely did, but stopped herself. They both knew why he hadn't. He hadn't been in relationships like she had been. He didn't know where those women had been before or where they were going after. There hadn't been trust like she'd had with Matt or love like she'd had with Jeremy. There had been no happy time of discovery, where every touch is the best touch and everything is exciting and new like she'd had with Caleb. Suddenly, she was very sad for William.

"You know, it's possible that I've had more sex than you," she said to lighten the sinking mood.

"Really?" he asked, amused.

"Yes. You've undoubtedly had more partners, but how many times did you sleep with each one? Three, four times? Sometimes only once?" He nodded slowly, a questioning look on his face. "So let's say there were fifteen for easy math. If you slept with each one three times," she could tell by his expression that she was being generous, "that's forty-five. Add in Sandra, who you dated for what? A year and a half?"

He nodded.

"So you probably have had sex roughly two hundred times, maybe two-fifty." She could see him calculating in his head as she was talking. "I definitely have you beat. I did it almost that many times with Caleb alone. Don't even get me started on Jeremy."

"Bragging, Ms. Bishop?"

"Just pointing out that while being single and playing the field may look more exciting, monogamy has its perks." She took a last sip of cocoa and got up to put her cup in the sink. She walked out of the kitchen and called over her shoulder, "I'll be in the bedroom, if you want to work on your number."

Two seconds later, Will was following her.

**

"So what do you want to do tonight?" Will asked.

They were lying in bed after lunch, having been so famished from morning sex that they ate two servings each of the casserole Maria had sent with them, which left them so sleepy they had to take a nap. Then Will woke up to Kate kissing his neck and one thing led to another. Now it was after four o'clock and they were lazing in bed, Kate's leg over Will's and his hand playing with hers.

"I don't know. I know it's ridiculous to say this after spending the day in bed, but I'm kind of tired. Do you want to just watch a movie or something?" she asked.

"That sounds nice. I'm tired, too. And to be fair, just because we were in bed all day doesn't mean we were sleeping."

"True," she said. "Oh! I know what we should do. We can open our Christmas presents!"

"Really?"

"Yes, that's why we brought them." She scrambled out of bed and turned to him with excited eyes. "Are you coming?"

Katherine sat next to the Christmas tree in the living room and sorted through the gifts. They were leaving for London a few days after they got back to have Christmas with Will's family, but she didn't want to take all their gifts all the way over there. When William told her about his ideal Christmas, she got the idea to come up here and celebrate on their own. So she had brought all the presents that they already had under their tree. She was currently shaking one from her mother.

"What should we open first?" she asked.

"There are several from your family. Why don't we start with those," he suggested.

He sat down across from her and she handed him a package.

"What's this?" he asked.

"My guess is a scarf. It's from my grandmother."

Will's face showed his surprise as he unwrapped the

oblong box covered in snowman printed paper. Inside was a long, deep red scarf.

"How did you know?"

"She called and asked what your favorite color was and Gran's an excellent knitter."

"I can see that." He examined the work and expressed sincere thanks as Katherine moved on to her gift from the same grandmother.

She laughed out loud. "Matching scarves!" She held up her own scarf and wrapped it around her neck.

Her mother had given her a new cookbook and her sister Heather a delicate charm bracelet with a graduate hat and a wedding cake charm already on it. Tiffany's gift – wrapped in hot pink paper and a glittery silver bow – was a homemade picture frame covered in random small mechanical pieces like nuts and bolts and gears. The note said she'd made it in art class. Inside the frame was a shot from Thanksgiving of her entire family, minus Jenny and plus Will. Even Jake was in the shot sitting faithfully by her father's side.

"Did she make that frame herself?"

"Yeah. She's got a great eye for this stuff. I hope she considers going to art school. I think she could have a career ahead of her."

Will nodded and opened the next box. Kate's sisters had gone together and gotten him a tie. It was pink with purple stripes and Kate couldn't help but laugh a tiny bit when she saw it. Loretta gave him a small tie pin with a Christmas tree on it and Neal gave him a collector's edition of *A Tale of Two Cities*. Kate also got a book from Neal. She read the inscription and got a little teary.

"What is it?"

"A collection of Robert Browning and Elizabeth Barrett Browning's poems." She didn't read him the inscription, which read, '*May your own heart always be this true, and may your Mr. Browning not disappoint.*' She closed the book and set it aside.

Looking around, she saw the only ones left were the ones they'd gotten each other. She handed Will a bright red package and sat back to watch him open it.

He smiled at her and began removing the paper. When he saw what was inside, he stopped and his mouth opened slightly.

"What?" he breathed out, obviously surprised.

"It's a camera!" Kate said excitedly. "You seemed so good at taking pictures last spring and I looked around and you don't have one besides the one on your phone and an old film camera. I thought maybe it was an old hobby, or that maybe it could be a new one."

He looked at the box, pulling open the seams and removing the camera. He turned it around gently, looking at all the sides of it while Kate spoke. He'd never suspected she'd get him something like this. He was expecting something simple, tasteful, and expensive. A watch, cuff links, maybe a new wallet. But this was so... personal. And so unexpected.

"Wow. Thank you, Kate, it's a lovely gift." He kissed her cheek and smiled. "Now it's your turn."

He handed her a small envelope with her name on it. Kate took it expectantly and ripped it open. There was a card inside that she read aloud.

Kate,

This is almost as much a gift for me as for you since I am sure I will benefit from it greatly. Have a great time.

Will

P.S. There's a less selfish gift for you, too.

Curious, she opened the silvery certificate inside the card. "Cooking classes! Six weeks of desserts!" she exclaimed.

"You said you'd been wanting to make tiramisu yourself but had never learned. I thought you could try this. If you don't want to do desserts, you can change it for something else. They had one for Thai cooking, too."

"Thank you, Will!" She threw her arms around his neck. "I'm so excited! I've always wanted to do a class but I never had the time. This will be so much fun!" She looked at the certificate again. "And it's for two people!"

"I thought you might like to take Jen. Or maybe Sheila

or someone else."

"Would you want to go with me?" she asked.

"Uh, I don't know. I don't really know anything about cooking."

"That's why there are classes, silly!" She smacked his arm playfully. "Now where's this other gift you mentioned?"

"Nah, ah! You'll have to wait for Christmas for that one." She pouted. "You have to have something to open in front of my family."

She sighed dramatically. "Okay. Does that mean you want to wait till Christmas for your other present, too?"

"Other present?" He looked under the tree and around the room until Kate began tracing a single finger up his arm and across his chest.

"Yes. It's black and silky. And backless. And very low cut," she whispered.

Will had gone completely still. "Totally backless?"

"Mhm," she purred. "With a very high slit."

In one swift motion, he stood and pulled Kate up with him. She yelped in surprise and then laughed as he practically dragged her to the bedroom.

***

"I'm almost sad to leave this place," Will said as he closed the trunk on the last of their bags Sunday afternoon.

"Me, too. Who knew Vermont was such a sexy place?" she teased.

He pulled her in for one last kiss before closing the door and looking back at the cabin with fondness. "I'm going to miss it here," he mumbled.

"What was that?"

"Nothing. You ready?"

"Yeah, let's hit the road."

28
ADDICTED

December 22
8 Months Married

"What are you doing?" Harper said as soon as Kate answered the phone.

"Last minute shopping."

"When will you be finished?" He leaned back in his chair, tapping the side of his desk with his pen.

"A few hours. I still have to find something for your cousin Teddy and I promised Caroline I would pick up some things for her at a baby boutique in the West Village."

Will frowned as she was speaking. "Any chance you want to take a lunch break? I can get takeaway from that salad place you love."

Her voice sounded coy. *"I could be talked into it."*

Will growled quietly. "Be here in an hour."

"*Bye Will,*" Kate said amusedly.

*

"Hello, Evelyn. How are you? Ready for Christmas?" Kate asked as she popped into Will's office.

"Almost. How about you?"

"A few more gifts to go, but I think I'll be ready to leave tomorrow."

Before Evelyn could respond, William popped his head

out of his office and said, "Has our lunch arrived?"

"Just now, Mr. Harper." Evelyn walked toward his office with a large white bag but he stopped her from entering.

"I'll take that, Evelyn. Go ahead and take your lunch break."

"Yes, sir."

He held the door open for Kate and she gave him a look as she entered in front of him. "You're being very-" Her words were cut off by Will's lips as he grabbed the back of her head and kissed her. "- abrupt," she finished as he released her.

"Hello, Katie," he said.

"Hello."

"Hungry?"

She nodded and he quickly laid the food on the table. "Is this the Asian chicken salad?" she asked as she opened her box.

"Yes."

"You want to know something strange?"

"Sure."

"None of my other boyfriends ever got my food preferences right. I mean, occasionally they would get the right thing and a few times I could tell they were trying, but it was always like, 'I know you like pistachios so here's pistachio ice cream'. As if those were the same thing." She shook her head and took a bite.

"So I'm doing well on the food thing?"

"Yes," she said with a smile. "You're doing very well." She leaned across the table and kissed him lightly.

William wolfed down his turkey on rye while Kate still had half her salad left. He stood and threw his trash away and quickly began undoing his tie. He walked over to the door and locked it, then began taking his shoes off.

"What are you doing?" Kate asked.

"I'm getting ready."

"For what?"

"To have sex with my wife. Right there on that sofa." He nodded toward the furniture.

"You are? And does your wife have any say in this?"

She took another bite and chewed while William put his socks inside his shoes and placed them under the front of the chair he had been sitting in.

Abruptly, he turned her chair to face him and Kate leaned back and tried to catch the lettuce that went flying off her fork as he placed his hands on the armrests and leaned over her.

"I'm sorry, wife. Would you prefer to have sex on the sofa or on the desk?"

She raised a brow. He continued looking at her unflinchingly. A minute passed.

"I think the sofa today. Maybe we can try the desk next time."

He smiled, straightened, and began unbuttoning his shirt. Kate ate another bite of salad and ignored the man stripping down two feet away from her.

"Hey, what are you doing?" Kate called. She looked down to see Will attempting to remove her boots.

"Helping you undress. The boots are alright, but the jeans would be hard to maneuver around."

She bit her cheek to keep from laughing. "Aren't you being a little bossy, Mr. CEO?"

"Just being helpful." He placed her boots next to his shoes and pulled her socks off.

Kate rolled her eyes and took her last bite. "Alright, I'm done." She put her fork on the table and stood up to pull her sweater over her head. Will began unbuttoning her jeans and pulling her shirt out from the waistband. He groaned after she took it off to reveal a tank top under that.

"Bloody hell, woman! How many shirts are you wearing?"

"It's cold outside!" She pulled the tank over her head and he pushed her into the seat so he could pull her jeans off, almost pulling Kate out of the chair in the process.

Looking at her in nothing but her pink bra and green panties, he sighed. "That's much better."

She smiled and held out a hand for him. He pulled her up and led her to the sofa.

"Are you sure no one will come in?" she asked.

"The door is locked, the phone is off, and Evelyn is gone to lunch. Nobody ever comes here without an appointment except for Jamison and he's in Virginia with your sister."

"Very thorough, Mr. Harper. I'm starting to see why they made you CEO."

He pulled her down onto the leather next to him and leaned over her. "No more talking, Katie."

She nodded. "You got it."

**

"How's it going with loverboy? Break your vag yet?" Laura asked as they shopped in the Chelsea Market.

Kate gave her a look. "Not yet. But he is pretty insatiable. He booty called me for lunch today."

"Can you booty call your own spouse?"

"I don't know." Kate cocked her head to the side. "Either way, the man is like a diet-er in a chocolate factory. Every time I see him, we do it."

"Seriously?"

"This is only our second day back and we've done it five times already. And something tells me we'll be at it again tonight."

"Whoa. So what is that like? Are you sharing a room now? Do you just do it and go back to your bed like nothing happened? And more importantly, how is he? Do the goods match the bank account?"

"Laura!" Kate smacked her arm.

"Hey, I'm one of your oldest friends and everything you say is protected by client privilege. Who better to tell your dirty little secrets to?"

Kate laughed and leaned forward to speak quietly "Okay, I'm kind of relieved because I've been dying to talk to someone about this! He's kind of amazing."

"Really? Better than...?" she trailed off but Kate knew who she meant.

"Apples and oranges," Kate said with a shake of her

head. "Will is like a locomotive. Once he's headed in a direction, there's no stopping him."

"Is that a good thing or a bad thing?" Laura asked hesitantly.

"So far, it's an incredibly hot thing, especially when the direction he has in mind is orgasm-town."

Laura sniggered. "So powerful like a locomotive, not clumsy?"

"No, not really clumsy. I mean, he's a large man and we're still getting to know each other, so he occasionally pinches too hard or moves too fast, but overall, he's pretty good."

"Hands?"

"Large, strong, smooth. Apparently he used to play the piano." Laura's brows shot up. "I know. That's what I thought, too. I feel like I should send his old teacher a fruit basket."

"Goods?"

"Let's just say that what they say about feet is entirely *under*rated."

"Really?"

Kate nodded. "And he's a turtleneck," she whispered over the rack of handmade purses they were looking at.

Laura gasped. "Really? I've never seen one up close. Is it as weird as they say? Does it look like an elephant's trunk, or more like a Shar Pei puppy?"

Kate laughed. "I'm not answering that! It's completely normal and un-animal-like, just a bit… extra."

Laura was silent for a few minutes as she thought over this new development, then asked, "So do you do it in your bed or his?"

"Gah, you don't quit, do you?"

"You said you wanted someone to talk to!"

Kate sighed and waited a moment, then said, "Well, when we first got back, he dragged me to his room and we used his bed. Afterward, he went to the bathroom to clean up and I said I wanted to use my own shower with my stuff. By the time I finished and came back to his room, he was fast asleep. I didn't really know what to do and I didn't want to get in his bed in case he didn't want me there, so I just went back to my own bed."

"Were you okay with that?"

"Yes and no. I prefer my room and I sleep better in there, but he is a great snuggler and it seems a little distant to sleep in separate beds after having sex with each other. I mean, it's not like I'm sneaking back to my apartment. I'm just going down the hall – seems a little pointless."

"What did he say in the morning?"

"He found me making toast and we did it on the kitchen floor," Kate said simply as she picked up a figurine and checked the price on the bottom.

Laura choked on her latte. "You're kidding?! Mr. buttoned-up three-piece-suit got frisky on the Italian marble?! I almost don't believe you!"

"Believe it. Lord knows I've got the ass marks to prove it. Anyway, we didn't have time to talk about it before he left for work. That was yesterday." They walked out of the tiny shop and further into the market.

"Soooo?"

"When he got home last night, I was reading in bed. He knocked on the door in his pajama pants and asked if I would mind if he shared my bed. It was all very Victorian, like it was 1850 and he was visiting me in my chambers."

Laura choked again. "Seriously, if you make me snort latte, I'll never forgive you." Kate patted her back. "So what did you say?"

"Yes, of course. Afterward, I led him to my bathroom to clean up and when he came out I invited him to sleep all night with me."

"How did that go?"

"I think okay. My bed is smaller than his and his feet were nearly dangling off, but it was warm. We ended up doing it again in the middle of the night."

"My G-d! You two are like rabbits! You know he'll definitely want to sleep all night with you all the time now. Men love double-headers."

Kate frowned. "I hadn't thought of it like that. I can't

keep this up indefinitely. I'm already starting to walk funny. Can you tell?" She walked ahead of Laura a few steps while her friend watcher her gait carefully.

"No, you just look tired."

"Thanks," she said wryly.

Laura pointed to the bakery they were passing. "Okay, would you say it was like that breadstick, or more like a churro?"

Kate laughed and playfully shoved her along. "That's enough detail for you, nosy Parker. Come on, I have to buy a few more things for London."

"Alright." Laura sighed as she shoved past a woman in a purple parka. "Could there be any more people here?"

"It's three days 'til Christmas. What did you expect?"

**

Will got home that night after ten. They were leaving for England the next evening and he was trying to get everything in order so he could be out of the office for a week. He had wanted to get home earlier to be with Kate, but there had just been too much to do.

Throwing his keys into the dish by the door, he stepped into the living room to find a pajama-clad Kate on the floor, surrounded by rolls of wrapping paper, several spools of brightly colored ribbon, and boxes of various sizes, Christmas music playing softly in the background.

"Hey, babe. How was your day?" she asked cheerily.

"Great." He leaned down to kiss her. "Very productive. Did you get all your shopping done?"

"You mean after you interrupted my plans with your savage desires?" she said with one brow lifted.

"Yes, after that," he said plainly.

"Well, I got these for Harry." She held up a pair silk boxers with the American flag printed on them.

"Perfect! He'll love them."

"And these earrings are for Caroline." She handed him a small embossed box.

"Very nice."

"I know you already got your sister a necklace, but I wanted to get her something just from me and thought she might like this." She handed him a heavy, large scale book with a picture of an old building on it. "It's an architecture book about beautiful hotels around the world. I know she loves buildings and with her fixing up the inn, I thought..." she trailed off as Will flipped through the book.

"Great idea. I'm sure she'll love it," he said.

"Really? You think so?"

"Yes, I'm sure of it. And Jacqueline likes you. I'm sure she'll just be pleased you made the gesture."

She smiled and handed him another book. "This is for your cousin Teddy. What do you think?"

He laughed when he saw the title, *How to Stay Hip After Becoming a Father*. "I think it's great. You've done very well, Kate."

"Thanks!" she beamed.

"So, how much longer do you think you'll be with all of this?"

"Probably another half an hour. Why don't you go ahead and eat and get ready for bed? I'll be done by then."

He nodded, glad that she understood he wanted them to go to bed together and that there would be no awkward requests for intimacy. "Did you cook?"

"I just made a quick quiche. I was craving it and there wasn't much time for anything else. It's on the island. Put the foil back over the top when you're through."

"Yes, ma'am," he said as he left the room.

29
CHRISTMAS IN LONDON

December 24, Christmas Eve
8 Months Married

The overnight flight to London was relatively uneventful, except of course for the time spent joining the mile high club, which to both their disappointment, was not as fun as it sounded. By the time they arrived at Harper's townhouse, Kate was sleeping in the back seat and Will could barely keep his eyes open.

William guided his groggy wife into the house and led her straight upstairs to his room.

"Kate, we forgot to work out the rooms. Kate? Are you paying attention?"

"Huh? Yeah, I hear you. No rooms. Got it."

He rolled his eyes. "Not no rooms, but the housekeeper will notice if we stay in separate rooms. Can you just stay with me?"

"Sure. Whatever. Where's the bed?"

He showed her into the room, which was large and impressive and pristine, none of which Kate noticed. She climbed onto the bed and was fast asleep two minutes later. Deciding she had the right idea, he climbed up and joined her.

*

It was difficult to breathe and Kate's ears rang

incessantly. The more she tried to ignore it, the stronger it became. Afraid she was coming down with the flu, Kate cracked an eye open and realized that the weight she felt on her chest was Will's head and his arms were wrapped around her torso tightly, hugging her as if she were a stuffed bear. The ringing was her cell phone on the nightstand. Stretching as best she could, she grabbed the phone and whispered a greeting.

"Katie? Did I wake you? Oh, I'm so sorry!"

"Caroline, no, don't worry about it, it's alright. I should probably be getting up anyway. What time is it?"

"Oh, you poor dear, you must be so jetlagged. It's nearly two o'clock."

"What? Two?" Kate called loudly. Will grumbled and huffed about going back to sleep. "What time are we supposed to be at your house?"

"Dinner is at six, the close family is arriving a little early."

Caroline and Teddy were hosting the annual family Christmas Eve dinner that evening. Julia had tried to claim it, insisting that Caroline was overwhelmed with the baby, but Caroline had stood her ground and said that having a baby was all the more reason to host the party. That way, the baby could be present for the dinner, then be taken to bed without his parents having to go home. Julia was not pleased, but Caroline was thrilled to be hosting her first Christmas dinner. The family had always taken turns, and between Julia and Aunt Claudia and all the cousins, she had yet to have a turn in her four years of marriage.

"Oh! I need to get up! I haven't showered and I'm sure my dress needs to be ironed."

By this point, Kate was no longer whispering and Will had given up on sleeping and had rolled onto his back to stare listlessly at the ceiling.

"I'm sure the housekeeper has taken care of that for you."

"You think? I still haven't gotten used to these servants everywhere."

Caroline laughed. "What are you wearing?"

"I wasn't sure what was best, so I brought three options and hoped you could give me your opinion before the dinner. And for Julia's party tomorrow night."

"I'd love to! And that actually works out because I was hoping I could talk you into coming over a little early and helping me with the table settings. Mrs. Lange has taken care of most of it, but I know you have a good eye for that sort of thing and I'd love your opinion."

"I'd love to help. How far are you from Will's house?"

"Really, Katie, you must start thinking of it as your house, too," Caroline admonished happily while Kate grumbled about still being a newlywed. "Not far at all. We're only a few streets over. William has the address."

"Perfect. Let me shower and get ready and me and my three dresses will be there."

Caroline rang off and Kate scrambled out of bed and rushed toward a door on the opposite wall. She was disappointed to find it was a closet. The next door was a linen closet and the one after that led to a dark hallway that she did not feel prepared to explore.

"Are you going to try all the doors?" William asked in an amused tone as he leaned back against the padded headboard.

She put her hands on her hips. "You could just tell me where the bathroom is. How many doors are in here, anyway?"

"I believe there are four closets, the servants' entrance," he gestured to the door with the dark hallway, "and the bathroom. Plus the entrance, that's seven."

"Geez! You guys don't bother with subtlety, do you?"

He chuckled and pointed to his left. "The bathroom's through there."

"Do you want to come with me to Caroline's early or would you rather wait and meet me there later?" Kate called from the bathroom as she turned on the tap.

"How early are you going?"

"As soon as I can get ready. Maybe forty-five minutes?"

"I'll go ahead with you."

He stepped into the bathroom and cleaned his teeth

while he watched Kate showering through the frosted glass panel.

"Hey babe?" she called loudly.

"I'm right here."

"Oh. Can you do me a favor?"

"Sure."

"Can you get my dresses out of my suitcase and hang them up in here? The steam from the shower will get the wrinkles out."

"Sure. Which dresses?"

"The short red one, the dark green one, and the champagne colored silky one."

They arrived at the Covingtons' with arms full of gifts and garment bags. Caroline greeted them warmly with kisses for Will and a tight hug for Kate.

"I'm so glad you're here! Come up this way. Let's get your dress sorted then we can look at the dining room." Caroline dragged Kate upstairs as Will called sarcastically that he would be fine on his own and that he would just put the gifts under the tree. Caroline called back over her shoulder that it was a great plan and continued on up the stairs.

"I think the red one is beautiful, but might be better for the party." Caroline looked at the dresses as they hung side by side in a guest room.

"Does Julia throw this party every year or is she just doing it because she's not hosting the family dinner?"

"I wouldn't put it past her to do something like that, but no, she hosts a Christmas night party every year. It's the perfect opportunity to show off your sparkly gifts. It's always terribly crowded and everyone is pissed by eleven o'clock."

"Okay, so it sounds red dress appropriate. So which for tonight? Green or champagne?"

In the end, it was decided that the green was most appropriate for the weather, the holiday, and the company. As they were walking down the hall, they heard a tiny cry coming from behind one of the doors.

"Oh, Thomas is up. You can meet the baby now!"

Caroline ushered Kate into a softly painted nursery.

"Wow!" Kate breathed. "Caroline, it's absolutely beautiful in here!"

"Thank you. I've always wanted a blue and white nursery, so I did it this way before he was born. I can just imagine the fuss Julia would have thrown if he'd turned out to be a girl and I'd dared to put her granddaughter in a blue room!"

Kate looked at the baby in Caroline's arms and said, "Now *that* is a beautiful baby."

"Thank you. Meet Thomas Joseph Theodore Covington. Thomas, this is your Aunt Katie."

Kate cooed and made baby talk at the adorable bundle in a white fuzzy sleeper.

"These Covingtons breed true. Nearly all of them have the same blue eyes," Kate commented.

"Oh, they're famous for it! And quite proud of it, too," Caroline said as she settled into a rocker by the fireplace and began nursing Thomas.

"Really?"

"Oh, yes. There's an old family story that some monarch or other, I can't remember which one, was horribly jealous of the beautiful Covington eyes. Apparently he had awful watery grey eyes or something. Anyway, he wanted them so badly that he took a Covington bride, who herself had the perfect blue eyes, just so his children could have them."

"Did it work?"

"Sadly, no. His wife delivered a boy first, with the same ugly eyes as his father. She died in childbirth with her second, a daughter who did have the eyes, but of course she married out of the family, to a Covington cousin actually, and the eyes left with her. The prince was terribly put out."

Kate couldn't help but laugh. "That's awful! Is that true?"

"I have no idea, but the whole family knows the story and passes it down one generation to the next, so there must be some truth to it."

"I suppose. They're definitely strong genes. Even Will, who looks completely like a Harper in every other way, has those blue eyes."

"True. I wonder what your children will look like?"

Kate looked away and asked about the artwork on the wall, and once Thomas was finished with his meal, they went downstairs. Caroline showed Kate the children's table in the kitchen that was decorated with a moving train as a centerpiece and the place holders that she had made herself in the dining room instead of using the heirloom ones. She knew Julia wouldn't like it, but she wanted to put her own stamp on her first Christmas dinner.

Soon the doorbell was ringing and blue eyed cousins of all ages appeared with arms full of gift bags. Kate was surprised by the number of children and realized with dismay that she only recognized about half the guests. Thankfully, Caroline handled introductions this time and the children created a boisterous enough environment that she wasn't required to carry on much conversation with new acquaintances.

Julia looked impeccable, as always, though horrified by the tiny running Covingtons bounding through the townhouse, and Alistair was dashing in a navy suit and cheery red tie. Cece was as bubbly as Kate remembered and her husband as quiet as he had been in New York. Jacqueline was elegant as usual and her husband as indolent as she'd previously found him.

Kate finally met Claudia, Harper's elderly aunt. She was half deaf and wore at least five pounds of pearls. She loudly asked Kate a number of impertinent questions, many regarding her suspected fertility and her family and how many children they each had. She was happy to hear Kate's mother had delivered four children without complications. She was less happy upon discovering all those children were girls. At one point Kate nearly told her that the choice of sex was up to the man's sperm, not the woman's egg, and that she should be examining her own family tree since William was the deciding factor in this particular relationship. Caroline squeezed her arm just in time.

The elderly aunts and a blonde man she had met in June were there with their respective significant others. She looked around and realized that she and Harper were the only dark-haired people in attendance. Cece's husband's hair was a light brown, but still, he practically looked blonde next to Harper. Caroline had placed them across the table from each other and Kate looked at Will, really looked at him while he was talking to his cousin Calvin on his left. He had a tiny scar on his chin, one that was only visible in certain lights. She'd seen it before, but somehow it had always slipped her mind to ask about it. His brows were a little shaggy, shaggier than his uncle's, whom she suspected had his waxed. They were entirely too perfect not to be. Even Calvin looked more groomed than Will.

Her husband wasn't sloppy by any means, but compared to his perfect family, he seemed more real somehow, like a live person in a wax museum. How had she not noticed that before? She watched him taking a bite of his food and laughing at something Calvin said. They were a study in contrasts. Calvin was handsome, but in a completely different way than Will. He was blond with straight hair, while Will's dark locks often curled at the ends and refused to behave. Calvin had light skin with the faintest tinge of pink at his cheeks and looked altogether English, while Will, though pale in the winter, could tan just thinking about the sun and there was nothing boyish about his appearance or his charm. Calvin was perfectly pressed in a dark, slim fitting suit that flattered his lean frame and his shave was so close she was sure it would feel like a baby's skin.

Will's suit was a bit looser – he hated it when his clothes restricted his movement and he wasn't vain enough to sacrifice comfort for fashion. Lately, he'd been letting his beard grow in a bit, partly because it was less hassle but mostly because Kate told him he either needed to grow it out till it was soft or shave it before he came near her because the whisker burn positively ruined kissing. So he didn't shave the day they were leaving and hadn't since; it was nearly two days' growth and he was looking very sexy, Kate thought, but Julia was suitably horrified. Caroline had complimented him on his American stubble and teased him about attempting to impersonate his Texas cousins.

Dinner was lovely and everyone complimented a surprised but relieved Caroline on the menu and the table decorations and the background music. Many of the parents thanked her for including the children, which made Kate wonder if they usually weren't present and how odd and quiet and restrained that must be.

Julia looked a bit pinched, but she congratulated her daughter-in-law on a successful evening. After dinner, they all settled into the sitting room where there was hot cider and coffee and the children were handed their gifts. Kate smiled at two little girls who were adorable in their matching Christmas dresses and patent leather shoes, their hair in ringlets and tied back with velvet bows.

"Almost makes you want one, doesn't it?" Caroline said quietly to Kate as she was looking at the girls piling up their gifts.

"What? No! Not at all! I just think they're really cute. My cousin Mary has a daughter about that age. I wonder what they're all doing right now."

Caroline accepted the change of subject and added, "I love having a little boy, but little girls are so fun to dress and primp. I hope the next one is a girl."

"Are you?" Kate pointed to Caroline's stomach, a questions in her eyes.

"No, at least I don't think so, but we're planning to try again when Thomas is a year old. We want to have more and I'm not getting any younger, so we don't want to wait too long in between."

"Maybe you'll get lucky and have twins," Kate teased.

"Maybe. Eleanor did." When Kate looked at her with a confused expression, she pointed across the room to yet another blond woman with sky blue eyes. "She's a cousin, second cousin I think, I can never keep them straight. She's the mother of Henry and Eisley over there." She pointed to a boy and girl of identical heights and coloring in coordinated outfits.

"I suppose it would be lucky in a way, but also really hard," Kate commented.

"Well, you know what Julia would say." Kate looked at her with raised brows. "'That's what the help is *for*, dear.'"

Kate laughed out loud at her perfect imitation and they

turned their attention to the children who were opening their gifts.

When Thomas started fussing, just as the children finished their gift opening, Julia said, "Don't you think it's time to call the nanny to take the baby, Caroline?"

"I gave her the holiday off to be with her family," Caroline said matter-of-factly.

Julia's mouth dropped open and Kate nearly choked on her cider.

"The day off? Whatever for?"

"It's Christmas Eve. She went home to Devon to spend the holiday with her family. She'll be back after Boxing Day," Caroline responded. She stood and excused herself, carrying a fussing Thomas upstairs.

"I can't believe it," Julia said quietly to Alistair. "Don't these young people know that's what the help is *for*?"

This time Kate did choke on her cider and Will had to clap her back for a full minute before she calmed.

"Have you opened your presents yet, William?" Teddy asked.

"No, I haven't even dug them out yet."

"I think the children have organized them over there." He pointed to where the children were placing gifts into small piles, nine-year-old Eisley directing the show. "She'd make a great CEO, wouldn't she?"

"Really, Teddy," said Julia, "the things you say. As if Eisley will need to run the business." By 'business' she meant the large plastics firm Eisley's branch of the family owned and ran.

"Some women do enjoy business, Mother. It isn't completely unheard of. Caroline ran an entire department before Thomas was born."

Julia's nose went up into the air, her chin firm and jaw clenched. "Caroline has no brothers," she said, as if that somehow both explained and excused Caroline's participation in the business world.

Teddy openly rolled his eyes at his mother and turned to continue talking to William. When Caroline came back downstairs without Thomas and holding a baby monitor, the adults set to opening their presents.

"I hope everyone likes their gifts," Kate said nervously. Will just squeezed her hand.

As it turned out, Calvin loved the little black book she'd bought him and Jacqueline looked a little shocked when she opened the architecture book Kate gave her. She flipped through it for a minute, said thank you quietly, and handed Kate her present. It was a guide to remodeling your home, complete with diagrams and color photos. Kate smiled and thanked her, then kissed her cheek lightly.

They were waiting until Christmas morning to exchange gifts with Teddy and Caroline, but they opened all the others. Julia gave Kate a book on how to be a proper hostess, which Kate thanked her kindly for while Julia nodded condescendingly. They gave Will a pair of platinum diamond studded cuff links and Calvin just handed him a wrapped rectangle that he advised him to open in private.

The random cousins, as Kate thought of them, all swapped out similar gifts: gloves, wallets, and cuff links for the men, earrings, necklaces, and brooches for the ladies, spotted with the odd book or scarf. Kate left with three pairs of differently shaped diamond ear studs, two books, and two silk scarves. Will got two pairs of cuff links, a tie pin, two scarves, and a cashmere sweater from his sister, plus Calvin's mystery gift.

"Well, that was fun," Kate said as they got ready for bed that night.

"Really?" Will asked incredulously.

"Well, maybe not fun exactly, but not too painful." He looked doubtful. "I think tomorrow with just Caroline and Teddy will be more enjoyable."

"Probably," he replied as he removed his tie and kicked off his shoes.

"Hey, what did Calvin give you?"

Will reached for the gift and opened it, pulling a book out of the gold wrapping. He began laughing loudly and Kate held out her hand for the book. It was a copy of *How to Keep*

Your Woman Happy: Sex Tips for the Committed Man. Calvin had written a note on the first page that read, "*Kate is great. Don't screw it up. – Calvin*"

Kate laughed as she flipped through the book. "Wow. This might actually have some good ideas."

"Like what?" Will asked as he looked over her shoulder.

"It says here that you should give your woman a massage at least once a month. 'It makes her feel loved and appreciated and will keep her from fantasizing about other men.'" Kate tilted her head to one side. "Hmm, because she's so busy thinking about your great massage?"

"Let me see that." Will snatched the book from her hand and flopped down onto the bed, crossing one foot over the other as he leaned against the headboard.

"Enjoy your reading. I'm going to brush my teeth," she said as she left the room.

"Don't be too long. We still have time for me to keep you happy tonight!"

Kate's laughter was barely muffled by the bathroom door.

**

The Harpers arrived at Caroline and Teddy's townhouse just after nine Christmas morning. Caroline had insisted on casual, so she was dressed in a pair of silky trousers and a loose, soft red sweater. Kate was in a cozy pair of wool trousers and a pale pink cashmere sweater that Will had told her once made her look like a flower in a rose garden. He smiled when he saw her in it and kissed her gently, which for some reason made her blush terribly, which only made Will smile bigger.

Caroline led everyone to the dining room where the sideboard was covered with delicious breakfast treats. They helped themselves and sat down to eat.

"What's Christmas like in America, Kate? You're from the southern part of the country, aren't you?" Teddy asked.

"Well, it's different all across the country, it is a really big place and we don't all do it the same way, but in my family at least, we all get up in our pajamas and open presents and stockings first, then we have a big breakfast together; sometimes family nearby will join us."

"What sorts of foods do you eat? In films it always looks so different from English breakfast," Caroline added.

"It depends on the year. Sometimes we prepare a casserole the day before then just pop it in the oven that morning, sometimes we make chocolate chip pancakes and eggs and bacon."

"So is your housekeeper not always with you, then?" Teddy asked. He jumped as Caroline kicked him under the table. "What?" he whispered to his wife.

Kate laughed. "It's alright, Caroline. We don't have a housekeeper, Teddy. Aside from occasionally having someone come in to do the big jobs when my mother has a busy week in her shop or is sick or something, we manage the house ourselves."

"Does that mean you can cook?" he asked. He pointed his fork to Caroline as he leaned forward. "This one has been thinking of taking a class but Mother sprouted feathers when she heard. After all, that's what the help is for."

Caroline gave him a look and Kate asked, "Do you want to learn to cook, Caroline?"

"Yes, I would love to, but it's never worked out before schedule-wise."

"I could teach you."

"Really?"

"Of course. We're here for a week, surely you can learn something in that time."

"Don't be so sure," Teddy threw in. Caroline kicked him again.

"I think that's a lovely idea, Katie, and a very sweet gesture. When would you like to begin?" asked Caroline.

"Are we doing anything tomorrow, babe?" Kate asked Will.

"Not that I'm aware of. We may be meeting my Harper relations for dinner, but it isn't confirmed yet."

"Why don't you two come over for brunch tomorrow?

Caroline and I can cook and then we can all eat it!"

Teddy looked alarmed and Caroline looked anxious but excited. "What do you think, Teddy? Sounds nice, doesn't it?"

Will jumped in before his cousin could reply. "Don't worry, Ted. Kate is a wonderful cook. I'm sure she can salvage whatever disaster Caroline comes up with."

"Hey!" cried Kate and Caroline at once.

"Alright, it's a plan. Boxing Day brunch at the Harpers. Has a nice ring to it, doesn't it?" said Teddy.

They finished and removed to the sitting room when Thomas woke up and needed to be nursed. Caroline sat with him in a chair in the corner, a large cloth covering her and the baby while Will hovered around the tree and refused to even glance in her direction. Kate chuckled and pulled him down to sit beside her on the floor.

She sorted the gifts into piles, which was basically two for each person, one from each spouse and one from the other couple. There was also a large pile for baby Thomas, who quickly fell asleep again in an ornate basket near the tree.

"Who's opening first?" Teddy asked.

"Will or Kate. They're the guests," Caroline answered.

Kate handed Will a little red box. "This one's from me."

He opened it slowly, not sure what to expect. Under the wrapping paper was a brown box with the name *Wessex and Timms* embossed in gold on the front. He flipped it open and saw an obviously antique watch on a new black leather strap.

He undid it from the cushion it was sitting on and turned it over in his hand. It was heavy and he could smell the leather and the faint tinge of metal.

"Is that an antique?" Teddy asked. "Have you shown her your father's collection?"

"Collection?" Kate asked.

"Yes, Harper's father collected watches. He must have had over a hundred of them. He used to let us look at them when we were boys. All the ticking sounded so loud when there were so many of them together. Remember, Will?"

Kate looked at William, his face blank and staring at the back of the watch. It was inscribed *'In this together.'* She wrapped her arms around him from the side and pressed her lips to his cheek.

"Merry Christmas, baby," she whispered.

"Thank you, Katherine. I love it," he said softly.

"You're welcome," she answered. Then she handed Caroline a small package wrapped in bright purple paper. "This is for you, Caroline!"

Caroline loved her earrings and immediately tried them on. Teddy opened his book and laughed out loud while Caroline teased him that he wasn't that hip before the baby was born. They gave Will a black turtleneck cashmere sweater. Kate opened her gift and laughed when she saw a red hoodie with a large British flag emblazoned on the front.

"I chose that," Teddy said proudly. Kate looked at him in surprise. "You're English by marriage now," he added amongst the laughter and jokes.

"There's something from me in the pocket," added Caroline.

Kate found a sweet little pendant necklace in the shape of an arrow and hugged Caroline. "I love it! Both of them. Thank you!" She kissed Teddy's cheek and bit back her laugh when he blushed scarlet.

Caroline almost cried when she opened a lovely string of pearls from Teddy, fanning her face and complaining about the hormones that made her so emotional. Teddy blushed again when he opened an expensive pair of deep blue silk pajamas from his wife.

Kate picked up her last gift from Will and shook it happily. Will looked a little self-conscious as she was opening it and kept twisting his wedding ring on his finger.

"Oh, Will!" Kate cried as she pulled a beautiful red silk robe out of the tissue paper. "It's so soft! Thank you!" She kissed him and immediately showed it to Caroline.

"I'm just glad I'm not the only one getting pajamas!" Teddy said. Will glared at his cousin who just shrugged in response.

The new parents opened all of their sleeping baby's gifts and Caroline did tear up when she opened the engraved ornament Kate had gotten from her mother's shop; it was an intricate silver baby carriage with Thomas's name and birth date on it.

By the time Will and Kate were packed up to go home, they'd all said thank you at least twenty times and were happily laughing at each other.

***

Boxing Day was a huge success. Caroline came early with baby Thomas and she and Kate made homemade biscuits and gravy with sausage, scrambled eggs, and huge fluffy cinnamon rolls covered in sweet white icing. Kate handled the difficult parts, of course, but Caroline felt like she learned a lot and had a great time.

The men came down to help with the baby and Will cut up fruit while Teddy made coffee. The two couples laughed and talked and Kate pictured future holidays and vacations just like this, the four of them making food together and sharing life. She quickly shook her head and threw off the melancholy that came with the remembrance that this would be over before she knew it. She told herself not to feel guilty about forming a friendship she knew had an expiration date. She and Caroline could still be friends after the divorce – they lived on opposite sides of the ocean. Surely they could stay in touch via email and phone and occasionally visit each other when Will wasn't around. And of course she and Will would still be friends.

As they were piling the dishes into the sink, Caroline suddenly turned to Kate and exclaimed, "Oh! You have to see my store before you go back!"

"The one you used to work at?"

"Yes. I check in a couple times a week now, just to keep in touch, but I'll go back full time in the new year. We have the most beautiful Christmas display up. I'd love for you to see it! What do you say we leave Thomas with the men and have a little time to ourselves?"

"Sounds great!"

Caroline's "store" turned out to be a six level

department store called Fleming's. She led Kate to the fifth floor and began showing her around.

"This is the casual women's floor. I've decided to add a maternity department for the first time in the history of the store. Designers are sending me samples, it's going to be divine!"

"So when Teddy said you ran an entire department, this is what he meant?"

"Yes, mostly, though I've run other departments before this one. I'll eventually run the entire store, but not before Thomas is much bigger and pregnancy is behind me for good."

"Feeling confident or are you in line for a promotion?"

"Both!" she laughed. "My sister doesn't want it, she doesn't really enjoy business. She's more of a musician and her heart is there."

"Wait." Kate turned to look at Caroline. "You own this? This entire store?" She gestured to everything around them.

"Yes, of course. I'm a Fleming. You didn't know that?"

Kate laughed thinly. "No, I didn't."

She turned and looked at a dress on display so Caroline wouldn't see her confusion. Kate couldn't really explain it herself. She just felt so comfortable with Caroline that she often forgot she was dealing with another of William's rich friends. She'd come to think of Caroline as more her friend than Will's, and this reminder that they were so incredibly different was unsettling. How could she have not known something so big? Everyone probably just assumed she knew and never thought to tell her – or it was just so common place in their world that it wasn't even mentioned, like the fact that she had a bicycle. What was the big deal? Everybody had one. Most of their conversations had centered on the baby and husbands and demanding in-laws. They'd rarely spoken of work, and when they had, it was in a casual, passing way.

She pulled her mind back in and listened to what Caroline was saying.

"...My father will leave his controlling shares to me and my sister will inherit my mother's shares. Still a stake in the company, but no major responsibilities."

Kate nodded. "So is it one location or do you have multiple stores?"

Caroline went on to tell her about locations in Edinburgh, Manchester, Glasgow, and Dublin. Kate listened attentively until they were back in the car and on their way home.

"It must be very different, where you're from. I can't imagine living in a whole other culture," Caroline said after a few minutes of silence.

"Well, it's William who lives in another culture. I'm just visiting here."

Caroline gave her a knowing look. "But you've entered his world." Silence hung heavy for a few minutes. "What's it like?"

"What? In my world?" Caroline nodded. Kate bit back the snarky comment she wanted to make about slumming it and seeing for herself. This was her friend who was asking out of genuine curiosity, not arrogant snobbery.

Kate sighed. "Everyone's more together. And I don't mean that in the organized sense. But we're less compartmentalized. Everyone eats together and does chores together and *does* chores! We don't all have private bathrooms and planes and cars and *staff*. We share space and breath and life."

"It sounds nice," Caroline said wistfully.

Kate nodded. "It is. But it can also be cramped, and intrusive, and annoying when the people you're sharing space and life with are not who you'd pick if you had a choice."

"We are very compartmentalized, I suppose, though I never thought about it that way. With our houses and nannies and cars." She looked around the private car they were riding in for emphasis.

"But it has its good points, too. You have an incredible amount of freedom, Caroline. That has immense value! Do you know how many women would love to take a few months off work to have a baby and go back to find their job waiting for them – and a good job at that? Having a nanny may feel less personal, but it's also an amazing gift. A gift that allows you to sleep and function better, to have time with your husband and maintain your marriage. That's huge! Do you know how many marriages break up when the kids are small? It's enormous pressure! My friend Sheila tells me all the time that they almost split up when their son was two and that's why she's afraid to have another. And he has a great job so she could stay home with her son, but it still wasn't enough!"

"You seem to have thought about this a lot for a woman without children." She looked at Katherine's belly suspiciously.

"I suppose I have. My cousin Mary got pregnant with her first when she was seventeen. It was really hard on the entire family, but mostly on her. My own parents divorced when I was three. My mother wanted to go to school, but with two little babies and a husband who was busy with his business all the time, it just wasn't realistic. It broke them. Who knows if they'd been able to pursue their own dreams if they would have made it?"

Caroline reached over and squeezed her arm. "So you think I should quit complaining?" she asked with a smile.

"No, I don't even think you're complaining. There are pros and cons to both situations, like everything else, but maybe there's a way to get the best of both worlds and not throw the baby out with the bath water. Money may not buy happiness, but it can buy options, and options lead to more choices and better choices can absolutely buy happiness."

"I think I like your way of doing math there, Katie Harper."

Kate just smiled and nudged her shoulder with her own.

30
TAGGSTON PUBLISHING

January
9 months Married

"You must be Katherine."

"Yes. Please, call me Kate." She held out her hand but he had already turned to gather something from his desk. She hugged her coat tighter and readjusted the bag on her shoulder.

"This is your orientation packet." He whirled to face her and thrust a thick envelope into her hands. She hugged it to her chest as he took off down the hall, talking over his shoulder as she scurried after him. "This is where you'll pick up your mail," he gestured to a block of cubbies along the wall. "Every Monday you report to me for assignments. You'll be rotating through the different editors' staffs. Four editors, one week each." He stopped so suddenly she almost ran into him and pointed to a hall lined with what she supposed were editors' offices. "You get two breaks a day, fifteen minutes each, and one hour for lunch. The break room is over there." He pointed to another room to her right. Her heels were clacking wildly to keep up with him.

"There's a cafeteria on the fifth floor. This is Linda." He pointed to a plump, middle-aged woman seated at a desk in front of them. "She's the intern coordinator. She gave the intern tour last month that you missed." He glared at her slightly over his glasses. "If you have any problems with your university or paperwork, etc., ask Linda. If you have any problems with the work itself or don't understand what you're expected to do, ask me. I'm your direct supervisor and therefore responsible for you." She waved at a smiling Linda as they walked off to the left and into a small room with a round table and chairs and some hooks on the wall. "This is the intern room. You can keep your belongings here."

He finally turned to face her. "While you are an intern at Taggston Publishing, you are expected to behave in a professional manner at all times. You have a copy of the employee handbook in your packet. Dress code and anything else you need to know should be there."

She nodded.

"Any questions?" he asked.

"Yes. What's your name?"

"Higgins. Russell Higgins. You may call me Mr. Higgins. Your first assignment is with John Shankman. He's expecting you in five minutes." Mr. Higgins then turned and left the room, leaving a thoroughly bewildered Kate behind him.

After hanging up her coat and bag and quickly checking the dress code to make sure she didn't need to change, she made her way back to Linda's desk.

"Excuse me, can you tell me where I can find John Shankman's office?"

"Of course. Go to the end of this hall and turn right. He's the second door on your left."

"Thank you."

Kate followed her instructions and stepped into the open door of Mr. Shankman's office and realized she was in the assistants' anteroom. There were two desks on either side guarding two matching doors. Neither of the studious-looking men looked up.

"Excuse me, I'm looking for Mr. Shankman's office? I'm a new intern here," she said in what she hoped was a quiet but steady voice.

The man on her left looked up. "Mr. Shankman is in a meeting. I'm his assistant, Paul. You actually need to speak with the associate editor under Mr. Shankman. Ralph Watson has the office across the hall." He went back to typing and ignoring Kate, so she thanked him quietly and left the room.

"Excuse me, I'm looking for Mr. Watson?" she asked the scruffy looking man behind the desk.

"That's me. You must be my intern." He stood and held out his hand.

"Katherine Bishop, you can call me Kate."

"Have a seat, have a seat," he said as he bustled around to her side of the desk and quickly cleared a stack of papers from one of the two chairs there. He was was chubby and a little clumsy, and his glasses continually slid down his nose. His hair was tousled on his head in what she supposed he thought was a stylish way and he wore corduroy trousers with a sweater vest. She saw a tweed jacket thrown over the back of the chair.

"Thank you." She sat and looked at him expectantly.

"Well, Kate, here's how this works. I'm an associate editor and I help with Mr. Shankman's authors and occasionally acquire authors of my own. I share an assistant with Kelly Green – try not to laugh – who is in the office next door. There are also editorial assistants in offices down the hall – that's the sort of job you're likely to get when you complete your internship. Now, today we have a meeting with a new author of mine, the scientist Ian Mellen. Are you familiar with Dr. Mellen's work?"

Kate stared at him, unsure of what she should respond to first and desperately searching her brain for any information on Ian Mellen.

"Um, no, I'm afraid I'm not."

"No problem, the appointment's not until ten. Why don't you take the time to read up on his work and you can sit in on the meeting. Meet me in conference room two at five till."

He stood and guided her out of the room and she wandered back to the intern room in a daze. It was already nine twenty. She sat down and googled Ian Mellen.

She was in the conference room at ten till ten and nervously wiped her palms on her skirt. She'd thought the pencil skirt and plain cotton boatneck top were a good idea; stylish, but not too expensive looking. She was a student after all. Now, she wasn't so sure. Ian Mellen was a big time scientist, as she'd just discovered, who was being considered for a Nobel Prize and had met with leaders and dignitaries all over the world. Surely that called for a pair of earrings at least? The only jewelry she had on was an old but classic watch. She felt terribly underdressed and completely unprepared. If she was going to fall flat on her face, she at least wanted to look good doing it. *Fake it till you make it, Bishop. Buck up.*

Ralph Watson bustled into the room, one of his shirttails hanging out and his arms full of papers that looked like they were about to fly from his grip. She rushed forward and took them from his arms.

"Thank you, Kate." He began arranging the papers into stacks on the table while Kate debated whether or not she should tell him about his shirt and the tuft of hair that was sticking straight up on his head. "Would you mind getting me a coffee?"

"Of course not. How do you take it?"

"One sugar, plenty of cream."

She smiled as she prepared his cup. At least this was something she knew how to do. "Should I offer Mr. Mellen any refreshments when he arrives?"

He didn't seem to hear her as he slurped his coffee and continued stacking his papers and some very colorful images of space phenomena. She waited another minute in silence, then asked tentatively, "Mr. Watson?"

"Yes?"

"What do you want me to do in today's meeting?"

"Oh, right. Sorry! Well, I will discuss the preliminary outline with Dr. Mellen and answer any questions and concerns he has. You will need to take notes. What he wants, what I respond, anything left unanswered, where we go from here, etc. Understand?"

"Yes, thank you."

Taking notes. She could do that. She'd been taking notes for the last six years.

Three hours later, Kate's hand was cramping and she'd filled more pages than she could count. She made a mental note to bring her laptop to future meetings. Ian Mellen was an eccentric Scottish scientist with a shock of red hair and an accent Kate found difficult to decipher. If she hadn't practiced on Harper's family over Christmas, she was sure she'd be completely lost.

Finally, the meeting came to an end and Kate was told to get lunch, then email the notes she'd taken to Watson and copy them to Shankman. Relieved, she dragged herself to the intern room to collect her purse.

"You must be the fresh meat." A skinny boy in black rimmed glasses and a cheap tie leaned back on two legs of a chair, eating what looked like a peanut butter and jelly sandwich.

She smiled wearily. "I'm Kate."

"Isaac. What department are you?"

"Biographies and memoirs. You?"

"Same."

Kate nodded and walked toward her bag, too tired and hungry to make idle conversation. Maybe Will had a granola bar in his desk?

"There's one more of us. Serious Asian girl. Watch out."

"Shut your pie hole, Isaac."

Kate turned around to face a short girl with spiky black hair and high cheekbones.

"I'm Alice, serious *Korean* girl," she said.

"I'm Kate."

"I'm going to the deli around the corner for lunch. Wanna come?"

"I wanna come!" called Isaac.

"You're not invited, d-bag."

Kate looked back and forth between the two, at Isaac's wide smile and Alice's gleaming eyes. Assured they didn't really hate each other, she agreed and followed Alice out of the building.

"Ignore Isaac. He's annoying but harmless, really," Alice said as they waited in line at the deli.

"Have you two known each other long?"

"Since fourth grade."

"Really?"

"We had an unfortunate incident on the monkey bars and were never really friends. We went to different colleges, but both ended up at NYU for grad school. Apparently, the universe has a wicked sense of humor."

Kate smiled and took her soup and bread to the table. She pulled out her employee handbook and began flipping through it.

"You missed orientation, didn't you?" Alice asked.

"Yes. I'm trying to get caught up!"

"The most important parts are under schedule and what's expected of you."

"Thanks," Kate said as she flipped through the thin book. "Whoa! We only work nine to four? And we get Fridays off?"

"Yeah, pretty great, huh? Most of the internships aren't paid so they can only keep you so long. And they probably want to watch the budget on those of us that are paid."

Kate nodded, mentally planning what to do with her new found freedom.

The afternoon was spent typing out her notes for Mr. Watson and getting a more in-depth tour from Linda. At three-forty, Watson handed her a manuscript and told her to read it by Thursday and give him her opinion on whether it was any good or not. She took the thick stack and nodded, praying it wasn't awful.

***

"How was your first day?" Will asked when he found Kate reading in the living room later that evening.

"Good. Hectic, exhausting," she said as she rubbed the bridge of her nose. "And completely bizarre."

"You know what's great for de-stressing after a long day," he said suggestively. She shot him a look and he laughed as he picked up her left foot and began rubbing her arch. She leaned back her head and closed her eyes in pleasure.

"I don't know why my feet are so sore. I spent most of

the day sitting," she said tiredly. "Who knows what I'll be doing tomorrow."

"Sounds like a good start," he said after a minute. "I remember being completely lost when I started my internships."

"Really? Where all did you intern?"

"First, for my dad's company, now my company. I was a general gofer and worked everywhere, starting with the mail room."

She laughed. "Aw! Poor baby!"

"The next summer I wised up and went to Covington Enterprises. I actually did a couple of summers with them. It's been surprisingly helpful to know so much about the company with the merger."

"I can imagine."

"I ended up back at Taggston, doing one summer in communications, then my final spot was back at HarperCo."

"Wow. I never realized you could do so many, but I suppose if you do one every summer, they add up."

"And I started early. So, what do they have you working on? Are you reading a manuscript?"

"Yes. This is about a Native American chief around the time of Jackson's presidency. I'm supposed to tell the editor if I think it's any good."

"Is it?"

"So far, yes. There are so many things I didn't know about that period of history. It's fascinating, really."

He smiled and felt a rush of relief at the gleam in her eyes. He really wanted this internship to work out for her. "What do you want to do for dinner?"

Half an hour later, they were sitting in an Asian fusion restaurant a few blocks from their apartment. They chatted and talked easily about their days until Kate mentioned that she sat in on a meeting with Ian Mellen.

"Ian Mellen? *The* Ian Mellen? The scientist?"

"Yeah, you know who he is?"

"Everyone knows who he is! He's one of the most famous physicists of our time."

Kate looked at him wide-eyed. "Well, he's writing an autobiography for your publishing house. I'm sure you could meet him if you wanted to. Maybe you could even get his autograph," she teased.

"Haha, you laugh now, but we both know that if you had a chance to meet Robert Frost, you'd pee your pants."

"Yeah, but he was an amazingly gifted poet!" He raised his brows and tilted his chin down in a 'so your point is' gesture. "Alright, I see your point. But still, it is awfully cute that you're fangirl-ing over a scientist."

He shook his head and went back to his food, seriously considering the idea of arranging a meeting.

31
VALENTINE'S

February
10 Months Married

Five weeks into her internship, Kate thought she might actually collapse from exhaustion. Thankfully, no one had any idea she was married to the owner of the whole thing and she was able to have a normal intern experience. She was talked down to by mean executives, commiserated with the other interns, and ran errands until she thought her feet were actually broken. She knew her way around the art department and had met a nice designer who showed her how a book cover was made from initial design to final production. Copy editors knew her by name and publicity was a department she hated going to, but came to understand fairly quickly.

The first acquisition meeting she sat through had been so fascinating, she couldn't take notes fast enough. She'd learned to keep a slim MP3 recorder on her at all times so that when things got interesting, she could just record what was going on around her. She'd tried using her phone once and had been mortified when it began singing *What's New Pussycat* in the middle of an intern meeting. She internally cursed Laura and her twisted sense of humor that thought that song was an appropriate ringtone and quickly turned the phone off. Mr. Higgins informed her that phones were prohibited and held the entire meeting while she put it away in her purse. She hadn't been so embarrassed since Bobby Klein pulled her skirt down in front of the entire class in the fifth grade.

She spent all day Monday through Thursday at Taggston Publishing, doing whatever needed to be done, and most evenings were spent reading manuscripts. She was able to escape upstairs a couple of times to have lunch with Will in his office, but not as often as she'd like. Thankfully, their social calendar was pretty light this time of year, but she knew that would only last a few more weeks. Once spring hit, things would ramp up again.

She had her regular weekly date nights with Will, which she sometimes thought were the only thing keeping her sane, and she had to meet with her advisor at Columbia every other week to discuss her internship, plus write the odd essay about various experiences. She was still working with her former professor as his writing assistant and his book was being launched the day before Valentine's. Kate was at his apartment or office all day Fridays and at least one night a week, working on his schedule with his editor and publicist, drafting statements and helping him prep for interviews. She told him over and over again that she wasn't really trained for that sort of thing and that he should find someone more qualified, but he insisted that he was comfortable with her and that it would take ages to break in someone new.

So she wrote guest blog spots for him and transcribed his answers to questions journalists emailed him. She even sat in on a few meetings with his editor, a rival house of Taggston's, and she had to admit that she was learning a lot from the entire process. She was sure that by the end of this semester, she would know more about the publishing business than she'd ever imagined.

She hadn't seen her friends in weeks, though she still talked to Sheila and Angie through texts and calls, and she'd managed to squeeze in coffee with Laura once. She'd become friends with Alice, who turned out to be whip-smart with a sharp sense of humor, and she was somewhat friendly with Isaac, who was annoying but endearing in a way, much like she thought a younger brother might be. She hadn't seen Jenny in nearly a month and it felt odd to be so removed from her closest sibling.

After the book launch, we'll have time to reconnect, she told herself. Right now, she needed to focus on finding something to wear for the party for the professor's book launch. She should probably go shopping, but she didn't really have the time. She had a semi-free night and a closet full of great clothes, she'd just have to find a cocktail dress amongst them and make it work. She saw something in her closet that she thought would do and quickly tried it on. She liked the look of it in the mirror but needed shoes to know for sure. She went across the hall to the closet in her den and chose a pair of blood red pumps to off set the black dress and back to her room to check the mirror.

This back and forth continued several times through six dresses, eight pairs of shoes, and three different bras. There was a pile of clothing on her bed and another on the chair by her desk. She couldn't decide if she should wear hose or not. She knew they were back in style, but for years she had hated to wear them unless they were thick and warm and it was freezing out. It was certainly cold enough – it was February in New York – but she would be inside and the ones she was considering could definitely not be called thick and warm. She threw the hose onto the growing pile and pulled out yet another dress, hoping she was finished with all this mess before Will came home.

**

William was having a long day. He'd been putting in crazy hours and dealing with problems nonstop for weeks. The redesign he'd been so worried about last summer was finally prepared to launch and everyone was scrambling to have everything ready in time. He'd taken two short business trips and gotten home after ten nearly every night for the last two weeks. To make matters worse, he and Kate had barely had any time together.

They saw each other on their weekly dates, but twice now he'd had to go back to the office after, and Kate had gone to meet with the professor after another. They hadn't had sex in two weeks and he really missed it. It made him feel connected to her in a way nothing else did and he was beginning to feel irritable at the lack of affection.

The book launch party was tomorrow night and Valentine's the day after. He'd asked Evelyn to put in a call to the florist and knew Kate could expect a very nice bouquet, and he had a little surprise planned, but he hadn't had time to do much else in the way of an actual gift. He stretched behind his desk and looked at the clock. Eight fifteen. If he left now, he could stop by La Perla on his way home. With new found energy, he put on his coat and headed out the door.

He walked into the apartment an hour later to the smell of Maria's meatball soup and the sound of feminine laughter coming from Kate's study. He made himself a bowl of soup as Kate and Laura came into the kitchen.

"Hey babe!" Kate said cheerfully. "How was your day?"

"Great. What are you two up to?"

"Laura's helping me choose an outfit for tomorrow's opening," Kate replied.

Laura smiled and said hi to Harper, then she and Kate quickly grabbed a drink and went back down the hall to her room.

Harper sighed. Any ideas he'd had of sleeping with his wife tonight were clearly not going to happen. *Make that two weeks and one day without sex*, he thought. He closed the fridge with a clank and popped open his beer, mentally preparing to spend another night alone.

**

The book launch was being held at a historic hotel, the kind with crystal chandeliers and original wainscoting and the tiniest bit of a dark Victorian vibe. The flowers were elegant and the music was sultry and classic. Overall, the entire party had a smoky, mysterious feeling. Kate was wearing a red dress with a dangerously high slit and black heels that made her calves look amazing. Her hair was pulled over one shoulder, large curls tumbling past her neckline. Will was in a sleek black suit with a red patterned tie the same shade as Kate's dress. Together, they were a striking pair.

They were so busy greeting friends and colleagues that they weren't able to meet the author before he was introduced. All Kate had told him was that he was from Spain and taught romantic literature at NYU. He was expecting a balding older man and a book of poetry. What he saw when the editor called for everyone's attention and introduced him was a very attractive man in his early forties, his full head of black hair speckled lightly with grey, his tan skin beginning to line in what could be called a distinguished way. He was broad shouldered and muscular, and Will began to realize he'd been completely wrong about the professor. Looking around, the atmosphere of the location, the style of the author, and, he realized belatedly, the blood red cover of the book all had a theme.

"What's this book about again?" Will whispered to Kate.

"It's about a young woman who gets involved with an older man and all of the changes that happen in her life as a result. A sort of coming of age story, set between New York and Barcelona."

Will nodded.

"It highlights the changing role of sex in literature and in recent history. It's very good – you should read it," she added.

Will listened to the professor thank everyone for coming and his editors for their valuable assistance. His eyes widened slightly when he thanked Katherine by name, then said something in Spanish that Will couldn't understand, but several people around him could and the women were sighing and holding their hands over their hearts. Even Kate had a soft expression on her face he wasn't too thrilled about.

"What did he say?" Will whispered to Kate. She waved him off and gestured that she was trying to listen.

The professor spoke for a few more minutes before beginning a short reading of the book. By the third paragraph, Will's eyes were bulging. What he was hearing was a mixture of cryptic metaphors and extremely suggestive prose. Lita, the heroine, was having all sorts of new and foreign thoughts and feelings and her mind was wandering to very strange places. Once her new lover entered the scene, things became very sensual very quickly.

"This is from chapter twelve," Kate whispered. Will nodded, not knowing how that was supposed to help him understand anything.

The professor only read one more page, then left the small stage to enthusiastic applause. Kate grabbed Will's hand and tugged him over to where the author was standing near a display of his book.

"Katerina, my angel!" Kate was quickly kissed on both cheeks and hugged tightly.

"Marco! I can't believe it's finally here!" Her smile was broad and genuine as he squeezed her tightly. "Let me introduce you to William."

The professor released her reluctantly and smiled politely to Harper. "Will, this is Mark Basurto. Mark, this is my husband William Harper." She smiled like a child as she introduced the men, unaware of their appraising looks toward each other.

Harper said hello and shook Mark's hand, and before too much could be said, Mark was being greeted and pulled away by editors and well wishers. Kate was talking to a fellow student so Will took the opportunity to pick up the professor's book. His eyes widened when he saw the dedication.

To my muse, my fair Katerina.

He spent the remainder of the party exchanging small talk with his few acquaintances there and reading snatches of Mark's book when he could. The whole way home, Kate was smiling and giddy. She practically floated down the hallway and she hummed as she put her coat away and made her way to her room to change.

"Do you want a nightcap?" she asked as she slipped off her heels in her doorway.

"No, I have a busy day tomorrow. I think I'll just go straight to bed."

Kate looked disappointed but quickly agreed. Will ran through his nightly routine and was in bed reading Mark's book in fifteen minutes.

Seven chapters in, he was sure that Kate was more than his muse, but was who the heroine Lita was modeled after. It was chapter eight, however, that made his cheeks flame red and his nostrils flare. Lita was dressing and Leandro, her lover, observed a small rose-colored birth mark on the back of her right hip, in the dim shape of a rose. He began calling her his little flower in tender moments, and just mentioning the pet name could make her blush regardless of the situation. What bothered Will, though, was that Kate had a small rose-colored birth mark on the back of her right hip, lower than her pants but just above her buttocks.

What kept him awake for the next two hours was wondering how the professor knew about it. And how was he going to find out?

*

The next morning, Will woke to the smell of coffee and sizzling bacon. He stumbled into the kitchen to find Kate flipping pancakes at the stove as she hummed quietly.

"Good morning, Will! Did you sleep well?"

"Yeah, fine. What are you making?"

"Valentine's breakfast! The pancakes were supposed to be shaped like hearts but they got a little goopy when I flipped them."

He looked over her shoulder at the odd shape. He made a "Hm" sound and walked to the coffee pot. He felt peeved about something but couldn't remember what until he noticed Kate's hip exposed above her pajama pants which made him think of her birthmark a few inches lower and of fictional Lita's matching one.

"I started reading Mark's book last night," he said casually as he sat at the island.

"Really?" she said excitedly. "What do you think so far?"

"It's interesting, not what I thought it would be."

"Oh? In what way?" she asked as she scooped up the

last pancake and slathered butter across it before adding it to the pile on the ceramic plate.

"Parts of it seemed a little… familiar," he said hesitantly. Kate set the pancake platter, scrambled eggs, and bacon on the island in front of him. She looked thoughtful as she poured herself a glass of milk and retrieved cutlery from the drawer.

"Familiar how? Like the situations, the characters, the plot?"

"I think the characters." He quickly shoved a bite into his mouth before he could say more.

"Okay," she said slowly, her face registering confusion. "Leandro, maybe? Or Lita's boss?"

He made a face and said, "No, I think it was Lita herself."

Kate tilted her head in thought as she sat down next to William and poured maple syrup over her pancakes. "That's interesting that you say that. I've heard several people say she was an authentic and true character, but no one has said she seemed familiar yet. But you know," she looked up thoughtfully, "I sometimes got a sense of dejavu when I was reading about her but I could never quite place it."

Harper fought the urge to roll his eyes. "Yeah, I got that sensation, too." He continued eating his breakfast, at least slightly relieved that Kate didn't realize the character was based on her.

"So how long have you known the professor?" he asked after several minutes of silence.

"I had a class with him sophomore year at NYU. I took another the following semester and then he was my major advisor when my original one retired."

Will nodded. "When did you start working for him?"

"Hmm, I think it was junior year. He was looking for an assistant and in one of our advising sessions, he mentioned it and asked if I was interested and I said of course I was and after a three week trial, I was in." She smiled, clearly proud of her perceived achievement. William was beginning to feel nauseous.

Kate continued eating her breakfast, oblivious to Will's struggle next to her. "What are your plans today?"

"The usual: work, meetings." She nodded. "We have plans tonight, though."

"We do? What plans?" she asked excitedly.

"Uh uh, you'll have to wait to find out." He tapped her nose gently when she made a pouty face.

"Fine, don't tell me, and I won't tell you about the awesome Valentine's gift I got for you," she said with her nose in the air.

He smirked. "Deal." He put his plate in the dishwasher and left the room to prepare for work.

The morning rushed by with nothing interesting happening except for Alice finding a sweet handmade Valentine in her cubby that Kate was pretty sure was from Isaac. After they both examined the unsigned card thoroughly, she asked Kate if she had any plans.

"I'm going out tonight, not sure where though. He won't tell me."

"Sounds intriguing. Give me details Monday."

Kate promised she would and waved her off to go to lunch. When Alice took the down elevator, Kate grabbed the next one going up.

"Hi, Evelyn. Is everything set?"

"Yes, you're good to go. All meetings for the next two hours have been rescheduled, the phones have been diverted," she handed Kate William's cell phone, "and the basket you ordered is right here." She gestured to a large basket she'd hidden behind her desk.

"Thank you so much, Evelyn! You're an angel!"

"You're welcome, I'm happy to help." She gathered her coat and bag and headed towards the door. "I'm off, then. I'll lock the door behind me. Have a good time." She winked as she closed the door and Kate couldn't help the slight blush that came to her cheeks.

She took a deep breath and crossed the room to Will's door. She had never done anything quite this daring before, but that was the fun of this type of relationship. There was no obsessing over what he was going to think about every little thing she did. If he didn't like something, he could just say so and they could move on, no hard feelings. It was incredibly liberating.

She held up her chin and knocked.

"Come in."

She opened the door quietly and stepped into the room, closing and locking it behind her.

"Evelyn, have you seen my phone? It was here on the desk a few minutes ago." He was staring at his desk and rifling through papers.

Kate set down the basket she was carrying and walked toward him slowly. "This phone?" she said lowly as she dangled it in front of her.

Will's head snapped up. "Kate! What are you doing here? I thought you were in meetings all day." He smiled and came around the desk to kiss her.

"Lunch break."

"Great. Do you want me to call something in and we can eat together? I've only got half an hour but you can finish here while I go to my meeting."

"Actually, I was thinking we could do something else." She walked over to the table near the window and plugged her iPod into the speaker there. Sultry jazz music filled the room.

Will was beginning to realize she was up to something but he wasn't sure what. Just then, his computer dinged with a message from Evelyn stating his next two appointments had been postponed to later in the day.

"Hey, good news, I'm free after all. If you want, we can go out to that little Italian place around the corner-"

His voice trailed off as he looked up and saw Kate walking toward his desk in nothing but some very skimpy and extremely well-fitting lingerie.

"Wha-" She placed a finger over his lips before he could say anything.

"Shh." She turned and removed the few papers on his desk and placed them in the chair, then closed his laptop and moved it as well. "You once said you had a fantasy of having your wicked way with me right here on this. Very. Desk." She punctuated her words by placing her hands on the desk behind her, then finally hopped onto the warm mahogany. She crossed one long leg over the other and leaned back on her hands so her breasts were displayed in the expensive lace bustier.

"I did say that," he replied, his throat dry and his voice slightly strangled. He swept his eyes over her, noticing the sky high heels and stocking clad legs held up by thin satin garters with the tiniest little bows on them. When had bows become sexy? Her panties were black lace and her sweet bottom was almost completely bared to him by her thong.

"Well? Here I am, Mr. Harper. Whatever are you going to do with me?" she said coquettishly. The thought crossed her mind that she *may* have been having a little too much fun with this, but quickly left when she saw the hungry look in his eyes.

Unable to decide if he wanted to attack her right there or drag this out a bit and play with her, he watched and waited, taking in every detail of the way her chest rose when she breathed, how her thighs looked pressed against his desk like that, how her wedding ring glimmered in the light from his lamp. Before he knew what was happening, he was hovering over her, her delectable skin on his tongue as he kissed her neck over and over again and Kate arched in invitation for more. He ran his hands over every part of her, noting the difference between the softness of the satin and the rough texture of the lace and the silkiness of her skin. He caught her hair in his hand and pulled back ever so slightly, making her arch her neck and exposing her chest to him even more. He couldn't resist plunging his face between her breasts, smelling her fragrant skin and nuzzling her gently until she laughed from the way his hair tickled her.

He couldn't help but smile and told her to laugh again, that he loved the sound and the feel of it. He ran his hands down her ribs slowly, tickling her gently and making her giggle. Finally, she wrapped her legs around his waist and pulled him to her, her eyes challenging and her body demanding.

Will would later remember it as the best sex of his life so far. He felt an amazing mix of being deeply connected to Kate and all that she had come to mean to him and insanely turned on. When they were both spent, Kate twice and him in a blindingly powerful release, he collapsed on the desk over her, too tired to care that his bare ass was in the air facing the door or that the hard wood was incredibly unforgiving on soft bodies.

"Will," Kate whispered gently. "Darling, I can't breathe."

He moved off her and slumped to the floor beside the desk next to his crumpled clothes and discarded shoes.

Kate walked over to the door, which he wasn't too tired to be able to appreciate, and came back with a large basket in hand. She quickly retrieved a bottle of water and drank half of it down in one go, then passed the bottle to him. She began unpacking the basket, setting things down in front of him and tasting and nibbling as she went.

"What's all this?" he asked.

"We're always hungry after sex; I was thinking ahead."

He smiled and popped an olive into his mouth. "Good thinking. So was this my present?" he asked with a rakish grin.

"What? Didn't you like it?"

"Yes, I did. Might be the best present anyone's ever given me."

She smiled. "So what did you get me?"

"You'll have to wait and see."

**

After an afternoon of hurried work where Will daydreamed about having Kate in other positions on his desk – he concluded that her being on all fours might be a little risky given the slick finish – and Kate desperately hoped no one could tell what she'd spent her lunch hour doing, the evening finally arrived. He'd told her to dress comfortably and to pack an overnight bag.

Excited, Kate plopped her bag on the floor by the door and called to Will that she was ready. He refused to tell her where they were going, but after an hour's ride in the car, she was beginning to get an idea. Returning to the cabin in Vermont would be wonderful. She was beginning to get ideas about the hot tub when William pulled onto a country road in Connecticut.

"Where are we?"

"You'll see," he answered.

They parked in front of a stately old Victorian mansion and followed the graveled pathway up to the front door. Kate saw the sign for the bed and breakfast and smiled. She'd always wanted to stay in one of these fancy places but had never been able to afford it before.

Their room was opulent but tasteful; the dinner was delicious and eaten by candlelight at a private table in the dining room next to a roaring fire. When they got back to their room, the fire was lit and the bed was turned down with pink and red rose petals littering the sheets.

"Do you like it?" he asked a little uncertainly.

"I love it! How did you find out about this place?"

"One of the board members recommended it."

"It's lovely. It's like stepping back into another time but with modern conveniences." She walked to the bureau and began taking off her jewelry.

"That's the idea, I believe," he said.

Kate turned around to say something and stopped when she saw William holding a large wrapped box. "What's that?"

"It's your present."

"I thought this getaway was my present?"

He shrugged. "This goes with your present, then."

She smiled and opened the box to reveal a soft pink silk nightgown that glowed in the candlelight.

"Oh, Will!" she gasped. "It's beautiful."

"Do you want to try it on?" His voice sounded calm, but she could tell looking up that he was a bit unsure about the whole thing. She smiled softly at him.

"I'd love to."

***

"So, how was Valentine's?" Kate asked Jenny as she finally sat across from her sister in her studio apartment.

"It was great. Andrew took me to his cabin in Vermont and we spent three glorious days just relaxing." She sighed. "How was yours?"

"Great. Will took me to this really beautiful old bed and breakfast in Connecticut. Our room had a fire and a claw foot tub and everything. We went ice skating on a frozen pond and even took a horse-drawn sleigh ride. It was magical."

"Sounds pretty romantic," Jenny said neutrally.

"Yeah, it was. I was a little surprised that he planned it, but I had a great time, so I'm not complaining."

Jenny nodded and left the subject alone.

"So what's up with you? Andrew still lying low or has he started hinting again?"

Several months ago, Andrew had hinted pretty heavily to Jen that he wanted them to move in together. She had freaked out and after calming down, hinted back that she thought it was unwise to move in with or make any serious commitment to someone you'd been with less than a year.

Their one year anniversary had come and gone more than a month ago and nothing had been mentioned and Jen was a little scared that she may have put him off for good. But deep down she felt she was right and she couldn't cave on something so important just to ease her boyfriend's discomfort.

"He started hinting again in January, more subtly this time. The holidays were really crazy and we barely had time to have a conversation, let alone one so important."

"So do you think you're ready now? What would you say if he asked you?"

"I'd say yes. I did say yes."

"What?"

"He asked me to move in with him when we were in Vermont. I told him I'd move at the end of the month."

"Oh my g-d! I can't believe it! Oh, Jenny, I'm so happy for you!" Kate embraced her sister tightly. "Wait, the end of this month?"

"Yes. I don't have long to pack. But my lease was up in

March anyway so I don't have to worry about that and it will give me a little time to get things out of here. Most of my furniture will be given away, it's mostly personal stuff that has to be moved."

"I can't believe it. You're moving in with a man. A rich, good-looking man." She nudged her sister. "You're the first Bishop woman to commit. I think a toast is in order." She hopped up to look for a bottle of wine in the cupboard where her sister usually kept it.

"Not completely. You are married and living with a man yourself, you know. And he's also rich and handsome, for the record."

"Yes, but yours is in love with you and mine is a business deal, dear sister. Let's not forget that." She tilted the glass of red she'd just poured in her sister's direction. "So, do you think Andrew will ask you to marry him or is this as far as his commitment abilities go?"

"He's already talked about it." Jen looked down as she spoke.

"Really? What did he say?"

"When he asked me, he made it this big romantic thing, said he wanted my face to be the first thing he sees when he wakes up and the last before he goes to bed. Cliché, I know, but it was sweet in the moment. Then he said that he wasn't playing games, that he was through with that phase of his life and he was a grown man now with a grown man's desires and plans and that those plans involved me," she hesitated, "and preferably three or four little blonde-haired angels."

"No! He didn't! He said he wants to be your baby daddy? This is serious!"

Jen playfully hit her sister's leg.

"So what did you say?" Kate asked.

"I told him that all sounded grand and that I liked a man who knew what he wanted and that I appreciated him being honest with me up front."

"What did you say about kids?"

"I told him that I wanted children, too, at least two, but that I wanted to wait awhile before I took that leap. He just had this goofy smile on his face the entire time." She looked down and fiddled with the tassels of the pillow on her lap, a soft smile on her face. "It was really cute."

Kate put her hands over her mouth. "Oh my G-d, Jenny! He's going to ask you to marry him! You're going to be a parent! With Andrew!" The sisters hugged and both had tears in their eyes by the time they separated.

"I can't believe this is happening. I mean, I always thought I would get married and be happy about it, and he hasn't even really asked me yet, but it just all seems so far past my wildest dreams, like I'm going to wake up one day and still be single in college and working as a receptionist."

"Hey, it is real, and you completely deserve it. Andrew is a great man and you two couldn't be more perfect for each other if you tried. It's almost nauseating how cute you guys are together."

Jenny smiled. "Thanks, Katie."

"So, when do you want me to come help you pack?"

"How about next weekend? It won't take long and I think we could get through the things I really need to take in a day."

"Perfect. I'll keep Saturday clear for you. Congratulations, sis. I couldn't be happier for you."

"Thanks, Katie."

32
HAPPY BIRTHDAY

Early April
11 Months Married

March flew by and before she knew it, it was early April and Kate was writing her final internship paper that was due on the twentieth. Jen was happily settled with Andrew in a scene of domestic bliss so sweet it gave Kate a headache. Things had calmed down work-wise once Mark's book was launched, and she'd only seen him twice since then. Socially, invitations picked up when the weather got warmer, but they were selective about what they accepted and less anxious to be seen than they had been the previous year. They were an established couple in the eyes of society and the press, and aside from the odd photo at an opening or charity event, their names never appeared in the paper, much to William's very vocal relief.

Her internship would be over in a few weeks at the end of April and while she would be glad to not fetch so many cups of coffee in one day, she would also miss it. She'd built friendships with the other interns and some of the younger employees, and she greatly respected the people she worked with. It had been hard and exhausting and definitely kept her on her toes, but she had loved every minute of it and wouldn't trade it for anything.

"All right, that's it. That's your fifth sigh tonight. What's wrong?" Will asked.

"It's nothing. I'm just a little sad it's almost over, that's all," Kate said from her place on the couch beside him.

He turned off the television and faced her. "Are you sad about school or work?"

"Both, I suppose. I'll still keep in touch with my classmates, but it won't be the same. Alice already got a job in Cincinnati. She's leaving in June. Sheila starts her PhD program in August. Jen's moved in with Andrew, he'll probably pop the question any day now and then she'll move to the suburbs and make babies. Everybody's moving on and life is changing and I just..." she made a face and burrowed deeper under her blanket.

"Come here, baby." He pulled her closer to him and rubbed her arm. "It's a big time of transition and everyone is scattering different directions. It's your time of life. It will continue to happen as your sisters go to college and get jobs and move around. It's what happens in your twenties. Everyone is figuring out what they're going to do with themselves and things have to shift accordingly."

She snuggled under his shoulder and said, "I know. It's natural and normal and all of that, but I don't have to like it."

He chuckled. "No, you don't." They sat like that for several minutes and he continued to rub her shoulder and hold her close. Finally, he broke the silence. "Have you decided what you're going to do next?"

"Have I decided whether I'll accept the job at Taggston? No," she pouted.

"Have you thought about going on and getting your PhD?"

Her head perked up slightly and Will continued.

"We talked about it once a while ago and you were interested. Are you still? You have the perfect opportunity to go now, if you want to."

"You would be okay with that?"

"Of course I would, why wouldn't I be?"

"It wasn't part of our original deal."

"Kate," he lifter her chin to face him. "I want what's best for you. I want you to be happy, whether that's working or continuing your education or opening a shelter for homeless cats."

"Really?"

"Of course."

"I suppose I could," she said thoughtfully.

"Just think about it. You still have a few weeks to decide."

***

"So what do you plan to do after graduation?" Laura asked when Kate met her for lunch in her office two days later.

"Why does everyone keep asking me that?" said Kate.

"Because that's what you ask someone who has spent the last six years of her life getting educated and is now about to be finished."

Kate huffed. "I don't know."

"I thought you wanted to work in publishing. What happened to that? Weren't you expecting an offer from Taggston?" Laura asked as she took another bite of her salad.

"I did get offered a job at Taggston, but I haven't decided whether I'll take it or not. I do like publishing and the idea of working in the industry, but there are so many facets of it that I don't really know which one I want, but I do know a few that I don't want."

"And where does editing assistant fall?"

"I like it okay. It's a stepping stone to associate editor and eventually editor, and I enjoy certain aspects of it, but I'm not sure I want to be an editor every day. I've spent so many years doing multiple things, doing just one thing every day feels boring somehow." Kate fiddled with the straw in her tea.

"It's hard choosing a career and a specialty within that. I remember when I was trying to choose between property and contract law. I agonized over it for weeks. Then I assisted on a divorce and custody case and bam, I knew."

"I've been waiting for my 'bam' moment, but it hasn't happened yet. I thought it would by now, especially with my internship."

"Let's think about this logically. Tell me what you're thinking so far," Laura encouraged.

"Well, I've worked with marketing and I really didn't enjoy that. I did like writing the blurbs for the jackets and talking ideas with the art department, which is something an editor could do." She looked thoughtful for a moment. "I liked talking to the authors, working with them when they were trying to figure out when something didn't mesh in the story, discussing characters. Or listening in while others discussed, I should say. They can be trying, though. Especially the 'artistic' ones."

"Of course."

"I liked putting it all together, seeing how everything came together to make this beautiful book, it was very rewarding. But it was also really frustrating when a great manuscript came in and I loved it and the editor loved it and the agent who sent it loved it, but then marketing shot it down. What do they know about books?" She waved her hand in frustration. "That feeling, that idea that something is only worth what it can be stamped as and sold for is nauseating. It didn't really matter if it was well-written or complete tripe, if it was something they could market, they wanted it. If it was challenging, or out of the box, or God forbid over their heads, they passed on it."

"So would you be able to get past those annoyances and enjoy everything else about being an editor?"

"I don't know. Probably. I also really liked what I did with Mark."

"Yeah? Like what specifically?"

"Well, I did a little bit of everything. There was some editing involved, but there were also creative aspects, like discussing the characters and the plot direction. I liked being more involved in the story, not coming in so late to the game like an editor does, but being in the thick of it right from the beginning. It was fascinating to see how the creative process actually works and I just," she sighed, "I just really liked it."

"Wow. You seem more excited about that than the other. So why don't you be a writing assistant if that's what you love?"

"Two reasons: It doesn't pay much, and there isn't

much of a market for it. Who would I even work for?"

"Maybe Mark knows someone who needs an assistant? He could at least give you a good reference and tell his editor you're looking for a client."

"Is that what I'd call the writers I'd work with? Clients?" Kate said with a smile.

"Fine, authors. Anyway, you work for a publishing house now, surely you could talk to someone there and they could send something your way. And maybe Mark will want you himself for his next book. Won't he write another?"

"Probably. Yeah, I suppose I could," Kate said thoughtfully. "Will suggested I get my PhD."

Laura coughed. "Whoa. Are you going to do it?"

"I don't know. I'm really late getting started if I decide to do it, but I could still squeeze everything in I think."

"Is that what you really want? I thought you were tired of school and wanted to get on with real life?"

"I am, I do, but Will made a good point when he said it was the perfect time to do it if I wanted to. He'd pay my tuition and I could live for free, well, you know what I mean, and it would be a lot easier to do it now than when I'm older, and it would enable me to teach at a university."

"Yeah, technically, but tenure track jobs are really hard to get and they don't really pay much either, *and* they're rife with politics."

"True."

"What about writing something yourself?"

"I don't know, I don't think I have enough life experience right now to write something people would actually want to read and not get laughed out of the publishing business."

"Sounds like you have a few legitimate options: work as an editing assistant at Taggston and start on the road to editor, continue on as a writing assistant with new authors, or get your PhD."

"Yeah, that doesn't sound confusing at all!" Kate joked.

"Hey, they're all good options. You could be looking at cosmetology school at night or babysitting in a trailer park."

Kate grimaced, both thinking of her cousin Mary who was only a few years older than Kate but had four kids and was taking night classes so she could eventually cut hair on the weekends.

"Thanks for the reminder. I'll stop being a baby now."

Laura nudged her playfully and folded her hands on the table.

"Why don't you do this: take this time that you're living with Will and be a writing assistant. A job like that will take a while to build up clientele and contacts and experience, but if you're good at it, you'll eventually build those up. When you split from Will, you'll have a place to live and enough money to live on for a few years, and by the time you even come close to running out, you should have built up enough authors to live off your income and maybe you'll be ready to write your own book by then. You could probably just invest your settlement and the interest can supplement your income so that a high-paying job isn't as important." Kate's brows shot up. "Hey, you made a very lucrative move early on, kid. Consider yourself lucky. Now you can do what you really want to do without stressing about the money." Laura shrugged. "Obviously the decision is yours, but you don't seem to really want the PhD, it just looks smart to take it."

Kate nodded. "You know me too well."

"And you've already done both of the other jobs, the publishing house and the writing assistant. You seem more excited about the writing assistant thing, even though I know you had your fair share of drama with Mark."

"Yeah, I have to admit I do like the idea of it a bit more. It just seems a little less rat-racey, like maybe I would have more freedom over my own life. And of course we can't dismiss the elephant in the room. Taggston is Will's company. If I stay on there, people will eventually realize we're married. What will happen then? Will I be shunned, sucked up to, treated like a big cheater for using my connections to get ahead?"

"All valid points, and the fact is you just don't know."

"Exactly. And what will happen when we break up? I had this conversation with Will and he said he wouldn't let anyone blackball me, but I don't know," she said hesitantly. "If someone is mad at me for using my marriage to get ahead, or just doesn't like me for some reason, that would make an excellent excuse to push me out. I feel like post-divorce, being a writing assistant might actually be the safer bet." They rose and grabbed their purses, heading out of the office.

"Well, whatever you do, make sure it's something you really want to do. No one is as good at a job they hate as they are at a job they love. Trust me, I suck at property law."

"Ah, Laura, always with a plan," she said with a smile, though her wheels were turning on what her friend had said.

"Hey, comes with the territory. Speaking of which, I have to be in court in an hour. Take care, sweetie. I'll see you later." She kissed Kate on the cheek and rushed down the sidewalk, leaving a thoughtful Kate behind her.

**

Later that night, as they were sitting down to eat dinner, Kate asked Harper, "Do you remember a while ago I asked if you would teach me how to invest money and you said that you would?"

"Yes, I remember. Why?"

"Well, will you?"

"Of course. What did you have in mind?"

"I don't know, but I was thinking about the future and how I would like something to be growing and earning income for me without me having to chase after it, you know what I mean?"

"Yes, I understand exactly. It might be a good idea to start with some simple stocks. Why don't I set up a meeting for you with one of Taggston's finance guys? They're much better at explaining all of this than I am."

"That would be great, but would they mind? Surely they have really busy schedules?"

"They will if I ask them to," he said. She saw that flicker of arrogance that sometimes showed up in him, his *Lord of the Manor* face.

"Why don't we make it something informal? Like

maybe we could all go out to dinner or you could invite him over here and I can make something for everyone?"

"Sounds good. I'll set it up."

**

Tom Donahue was an affable man in his early forties with a habit of talking with his hands. He sat across the table from Kate and William at their favorite Italian place and gave Kate a crash course in high finance. She had trouble keeping her attention on his face when her eyes were constantly drawn to the glass he was holding, the wine swishing around wildly but never actually spilling out as he punctuated words like starting capital, amortization, and economic stability.

When he stopped to take a sip, Kate asked him about smart investments for long-term growth, specifically real estate versus stocks. She knew she sounded horribly ignorant, but that's why she was there after all. In the end, Donahue recommended she invest in simple mutual funds for long term retirement goals, to begin with. Once she was comfortable with that, he thought she should look into more involved investments. He thought real estate was a good idea, given certain parameters, and answered all of her random questions graciously.

He was a little curious that she was interested in investing outside of her husband, but Harper quickly explained that Kate was an independent woman and didn't want to rely on Harper for everything she needed. She jokingly whispered "pre-nup" behind her hand and he laughed, especially when Harper elbowed her in the ribs and mock glared at her.

"How do I know you won't trade me in for a newer model when I'm forty, hmm?" she teased him.

He looked at her seriously and said, "Because you never trade in a classic."

She blushed and looked across the table to Mr. Donahue, who was smiling at their antics.

"Thank you so much for the help, Mr. Donahue. I really appreciate it." Kate smiled and Donahue nodded and assured her that it had been his pleasure.

"Any time you have any questions at all, Mrs. Harper, don't hesitate to call. I'd be happy to help."

As they were walking home from the restaurant, Harper said, "Well, what did you think?"

"I learned a lot. He really knows a lot about money. And it's even clearer that I really don't. I didn't understand half of what he was saying for a while there."

"You'll get the hang of it eventually."

"Yeah, probably."

"So what do you think you'll start with?"

"I'll probably do like he recommended and do the mutual funds." Harper nodded. "I've been thinking about property, too. It just seems more tangible, you know? I actually know people with rental houses. It doesn't seem quite so intimidating, somehow."

"Yes, I see what you mean. It can be a good long term investment if it's the right property."

"Is your sister still planning on coming over in the summer? Maybe she could help me choose something."

"Really? You do realize that if you tell Jacqueline you're interested in property, she'll call you every day and send you tile samples and lighting catalogues?"

"Yeah, but maybe that wouldn't be so bad," she said distractedly. "She knows a lot more about it than I do and it would probably be stupid to pass up the help."

"Your call, but don't say I didn't warn you."

***

"So what do you want to do for your birthday?" Jen asked.

"What do you mean? My birthday was two weeks ago," said Kate.

"I know. I wanted us all to go out and celebrate but you were busy with work and some paper with a deadline and Will was out of town, so you said we'd do something in April after you'd finished your final intern paper." Kate shot her a look.

"Well, it's April. And you said earlier that you just finished your final paper."

"Wow, you forget nothing, do you?"

"Nope. Now quit stalling and tell me where you want to go and what you want for a present," Jenny said determinedly.

"I don't know. I suppose I'd like to just have a fun dinner with friends. You and Andrew, Laura, Angie, Sheila and Peter, and of course Will."

"I know! Why don't I throw a dinner party at our place? It will be my first one there and we can have it catered or at least served so it isn't so stressful. But I want to make your cake."

"Just tell me when and I'll show up."

Jenny was a phenomenal party thrower – she was phenomenal at most things – and Kate's birthday dinner a week later was a tremendous success. She had it catered by Kate's favorite southern restaurant and made a triple chocolate cake herself. She hung homemade streamers all around the dining room – Sheila teased that she'd bought them on Etsy and was pleased when Jen blushed – and she even made a 'Who knows Kate Best' quiz for everyone to take after dinner. Laura gloated mercilessly when she won.

"Happy birthday, Kitty Cat," slurred Laura as she wrapped an arm around her friend. "Who knew when I started babysitting you all those years ago that we'd still be friends today?"

Kate laughed. "How much have you had to drink?"

"Just a few." She tried to sound authoritative but failed miserably. Kate left her sitting on the couch and found her sister.

"Well, little sister, are you having a good time?" Jen asked.

"Of course. All my favorite people in one place, how could I not?" Jen smiled and Kate added, "Though I could be slightly happier if we cut the cake."

Jen laughed. "Alright. Everyone, it's time for cake!" she called to the room.

Her friends sang off key and Kate blew out her candles,

wishing for the perfect job situation to work itself out without giving her an ulcer, and everyone cheered when she blew out all twenty-four with one breath.

"This cake is divine," Will said as he took a second piece.

"It's our mother's recipe," Jen replied. "It's always been Katie's favorite."

"She talked about opening a restaurant on the farm, and maybe a B&B, but it never worked out," Kate added.

Will nodded silently, another piece of the puzzle that was Loretta Bishop slipping into place.

"Time for presents!" Andrew called.

Kate sat in front of the small pile and rubbed her hands together like a greedy cartoon character. "Hmm, which should I open first?"

She plowed her way through the brightly wrapped boxes and shiny gift bags. Angie gave her a pair of earrings, Sheila and Peter got her a beaded scarf from a local handmade market, and Laura gave her a subscription to a wine club.

"Now that you're not a student anymore – almost – you need to start drinking like an adult," Laura said.

Jen and Andrew gave her a full spa day for the sisters to enjoy together – which Laura considered a very selfish gift for Jen to give until Jen told her she knew Laura would probably drink most of Kate's wine. Laura blushed while everyone laughed. At the end of all the other gifts, Kate looked to her husband and reached out her hands playfully.

"Alright, Richie Rich, what did you get me?" She wiggled her fingers and giggled until he slowly slid a small square box across the table toward her.

A hush seemed to settle over the small crowd and Kate stared at the box suspiciously. She opened it slowly, looking slightly confused when there was nothing but a silver keychain inside.

"Um, thanks, Will. It's cute." She smiled and held up the arrow-shaped fob for everyone to see. Sheila and Angie looked confused and disappointed, Andrew and Jen looked expectant, and Laura was starting to look green.

"Is it the arrow that pierced his heart?" Angie asked uncertainly, her voice hesitant and stilted.

Andrew was the first to laugh, and slowly they were all laughing together until William spoke over the noise.

"I thought it would make it easier to find this in those enormous bags you insist on carrying around."

He held a key between his fingers and the room got quiet. "What's it for?" Angie blurted.

Shelia elbowed her while Peter mumbled under his breath, "Not his heart."

Will heard him and laughed, then took Kate's hand and led her to the door. "It's downstairs. Come on, let's go see it."

They all piled into the elevator and chattered excitedly about what the mysterious gift could be. Ideas ranged from a Vespa to a condo to an exotic pet kept in some sort of cage in the lobby.

As they walked out the front door, Kate became increasingly nervous. Will pulled her over to the side of the building and there, parked by the sidewalk, was a bright red BMW with a huge bow on the hood.

Kate's mouth dropped open and she stared at the car, unable to hear Angie's shrieks or Jen and Sheila's squeals of glee or Peter and Andrew exclaiming over the car's various features.

"Are you alright?" Harper whispered in her ear. "You look pale."

"It's a car," she said.

"Yes, it is." He looked confused and pulled her away slightly. "If you don't like it, or want a different color or something, we can change it."

"Will! You bought me a car!" Her voice was shaky. "You can't buy me a car! That's an enormous gift! William!" She was almost pleading.

"I don't understand what the problem is. I've given you gifts before and you've never freaked out."

"Your other gifts were reasonable. Nice, expensive maybe, but not worth an entire year's salary!"

"Katie," he kept his voice low, looking to the side to see

Andrew looking their way with a questioning expression. His friend seemed to understand their need for privacy at the moment and distracted everyone else. "You're my wife. It's expected that I give you gifts, and it really wasn't that expensive. I know we have different ideas of what expensive is, but it's not like I bought you an island! It's just a car."

"A Toyota is just a car, this is a BMW," she argued.

He sighed and pinched the bridge of his nose. "Do you want me to return it?"

She felt guilty for being such a bad sport as she saw his expression: resigned, disappointed, and maybe a touch angry. She reached out and touched his arm.

"Hey, I'm sorry. I don't want you to return it, really. I'm just shocked, that's all. No one's ever bought me a forty thousand dollar gift before." She squeezed his forearm where it was crossed over his chest. "I *do* like it."

"Really?" he asked skeptically. He wisely chose not to correct her assumption of the price.

"Really. I've always wanted a little red car, actually."

"I know. That's why I got it."

"How did you know?"

"You told me. When we went away for Valentine's you said you'd always wanted a little red convertible like your doll had when you were seven."

Her brows raised. "You remembered that?"

"Yes." He looked to the side for a moment, then back at her. "You also wanted a blue house with a white porch, also like your doll had."

Her expression melted into tenderness and she held his face in her hands. "You dear, sweet, wonderful man! I – William!" This time his name sounded less like a reprimand and more like an endearment.

He finally smiled back at her. He knew she was being sincere by the twinkle in her eyes and he let some of his earlier excitement return. Kate rose up on her toes and kissed him softly, and he wrapped his arms around her waist and held her tightly to him.

They separated when they heard cheering behind them

and they both blushed as they faced their friends.

"Who wants to ride with me first?" Kate asked cheerfully. Every hand shot up and Will laughed behind her as she did eeny meeny miney mo to decide her passengers.

She squeezed his hand before she climbed into the driver's seat. "Thank you, Will. This was incredibly thoughtful of you."

He smiled. "Wait until I get you home. I'll show you thoughtful." He wagged his brows suggestively and she gave him a saucy smile.

"I can't wait."

33
CAP & GOWN

Early May
1 Year Married

Kate popped her head into the door. "Mr. Watson, do you have a minute?"

"Of course, Kate, come in, come in. Have a seat."

She moved a stack of papers off the chair in front of his desk and sat down. "I wanted to talk to you about my future here at Taggston."

"Of course, of course. Have you made a decision?" He smiled kindly and his eyes crinkled behind his smudged spectacles. Kate was filled with sudden nostalgia; she would miss this funny, unkempt, endearing man.

"Yes and no. I wondered if there was any flexibility in the offer you gave me?"

"Flexibility?"

"Yes. I wondered if the job could possibly be part time."

He leaned back in his chair and looked thoughtful for a moment. "I don't know. I'd have to talk to Mr. Shankman about it. Though I imagine you wouldn't get any benefits, or not as many with part time."

"That's alright, I have health insurance through my husband."

"You're married?"

She looked at the wedding band on her left hand. "Yes, I am."

"Well, it's more than health insurance. What about paid leave and vacations, maternity leave – which may be more important now that you're married – job security? Those are all better with a full time position."

"I understand that. The thing is," she bit her lip. "Mr. Watson, may I be frank with you?"

"Of course, Katherine." He placed his elbows on the cluttered desk and leaned toward her.

"Well, I've had a bit of trouble deciding what to do in the long term, and while I love working here, choosing this job would mean giving up working as a writing assistant, which I really love doing. However, if I could do that part time and this part time, I think that would be a really good fit for me."

"You could have more freedom and keep a toe in the publishing world," he said thoughtfully as he leaned his chair back. Kate waited anxiously. "You've been a writing assistant before?"

"Yes. I worked with Mark Basurto for three years on his first book."

"Hmm." Watson was looking at the wall, deep in thought.

"I might have just the thing, but I'll need to do some checking."

"Okay," she said hesitantly.

"Let's talk again in a few days."

The next few days were torturous for Kate. Why did she talk to Watson on a Thursday? Now she had the whole weekend to fret. She wondered if she'd screwed up her existing opportunity by asking for more and spent hours overdramatizing events that were unlikely to happen.

Finally, Tuesday morning, Mr. Watson called her in to his office.

"I've got a proposition for you."

"Yes?" she asked eagerly, completely unable to play it cool.

He smiled. "Dr. Ian Mellen, the physicist – you sat in on a meeting with him – is struggling with his book. He needs someone who can assist him, but also edit him and in some ways act as a guide. The House also needs a liaison between Dr. Mellen and us, someone keeping us informed, telling us if he's staying on track, encouraging him to do interviews. Dr. Mellen would have to approve you of course. The hours would be unpredictable at best and the pay would be hourly, as far as the assistantship goes, so I don't know if financially you could swing it – "

"I could swing it!" she jumped in.

"I thought you might say so." He smiled and handed her a piece of paper. "This is Dr. Mellen's contact information, he's expecting your call."

Kate took the paper eagerly and put it in her bag. "Thank you so much, Mr. Watson!"

Katherine wanted to rush straight up to Will's office and tell him all about her exciting news, but just as she was heading to the elevator she remembered that he was out of town until Friday and she wanted to tell him in person. She sighed and called her sister instead and then quickly contacted Ian Mellen. They set up an appointment for that evening and Katherine spent the next several hours planning what she would say and alternately celebrating and freaking out.

She had nothing to worry about. An hour into their meeting, Dr. Mellen told her she had the job and they quickly set up a schedule. He would spend a lot of the summer in Scotland, so they would have to communicate electronically, but he'd committed the next eighteen months to writing the book while his other work was in a slow phase. The two hit it off, and by the end of the week, they'd spent several hours already mapping out the manuscript.

*

"Katie! Are you home?" Will called when he walked into the apartment Friday evening. "Kate?"

"Back here!"

He found her in her study, typing away at her desk.

"How was your trip?" she asked as she kissed him hello.

"Good, uneventful. Did you meet with Watson again? What did he say?"

"As a matter of fact, I did. And he had good news."

"Really? That's great! Are they going to let you work part-time?"

"Yes and no. There is an author who needs an assistant and also a sort of guide-slash-liaison at Taggston."

"And that person is you?" She nodded. "Brilliant! Who's the author?"

"Ian Mellen." She watched him silently, wondering what his reaction would be. He just stared at her open-mouthed.

"Wow. That's, that's just, wow."

She smiled. "I know! Just think, now you'll be able to meet him!"

He was silent for a while but eventually smiled a bit. "Surely that won't be for a while yet."

"You don't want to meet him?"

"No, I do! I just meant that it wasn't likely to occur anytime soon. At least that will give me time to prepare."

"Oh, well, you better get ready quick. He's coming for dinner tomorrow night."

A loud timer went off in the kitchen. Kate jumped up and left the room, exclaiming about a casserole in the oven. Harper just stood there, frozen in place, an odd sense of excitement and nervousness running through him.

**

Saturday, Harper was a nervous wreck. He went into the office for a few hours in the morning, met Jamison for a game of squash, and was home by four in the afternoon. Kate tried not to laugh at how he changed his shirt four times or when she caught him taking his reading glasses off and on in the mirror.

"Do you want to help me with dinner?" she asked.

"Sure, what can I do?"

"See if the dough over there has risen enough to split into rolls. If it has, cut it up and put them on a greased pan and cover them, then set the timer for an hour."

"Got it."

She smiled as he got to work, remembering how a year ago he couldn't even put on an apron, let alone handle more than one direction at once. She was always the one who cooked, but he often came in and opened a bottle of wine and talked to her while she worked, pouring her a glass and helping out here and there with simple tasks.

"What kind of salad do you want?" she asked.

"What are my choices?"

"I've got the ingredients for lemon salad, but I'm not really in the mood for it, and for the goat cheese one with the candied pecans you like."

"Ooh, let's have that one. Do you have time to make the pecans?" he asked.

"Yes," she answered with a quick glance at the clock. "Can you turn the oven on to 250 please?"

She got to work whisking egg whites and mixing sugar and cinnamon together while Harper finished his rolls and placed them on the island for their second rise.

"What all are we having?"

"I made a tiramisu yesterday. It's supposed to be better the second day when all the flavors have had a chance to settle in. Cross your fingers it's good."

"It will be," he smiled. Since he'd given her the dessert classes as a Christmas gift, he'd done a lot of taste testing and loved every bite of it. She had done the class with her sister Jennifer and between the two of them, their shared meals together were always memorable.

"I made a meatloaf earlier today, it just needs to bake."

Harper made a face.

"Hey! You said you loved my meatloaf!" she cried indignantly.

"I do! It's just not the most showy thing you make and I was a little surprised, that's all," he said quickly, rubbing the back of his neck and making a sheepish face.

"Well, Mr. High Society, it just so happens that Ian specifically requested meatloaf because he's never had it and wants to try something American."

"Ah, now it makes more sense."

She swatted him with a towel. "I'm making green bean bundles right now and some sort of potatoes." She pointed to the colander filled with potatoes in the sink. "Should we have fried or mashed?"

"I love your fried potatoes. And mashed are pretty common in Scotland."

"Alright, fried it is. You want to make the honey butter now that you're done with the rolls?"

Will quickly agreed and got to work, proud of himself that he knew how to make this without any instruction now and happy to be contributing. He couldn't believe he'd missed the joy of cooking his entire life. All these years he'd been buying take away and eating at restaurants. He'd had no idea that he could very easily make delicious, wholesome food in his own home.

Kate smiled, glad Will was distracted. She'd never seen him this jumpy and nervous. She just hoped he'd be able to relax during dinner and not let his nerves get the best of him. To that end, she opened a bottle of pinot noir and poured him a glass.

Dinner was a huge success. Dr. Mellen insisted Will call him Ian and told several geeky but funny jokes that had everyone laughing and almost made Kate snort her wine. Will was tongue-tied for a little while, but halfway through the salad he loosened up and found his groove. He asked intelligent questions and gave thoughtful answers while Kate looked on proudly. She didn't know what half of the words they used even meant, and barely understood the context, but she was happy they were getting along and pleased that Will got to meet one of his heroes thanks to her.

Dr. Mellen loved the candied nuts, he thought the meatloaf was odd-looking but delicious, and declared the tiramisu to be divine. Kate thanked him and they settled in the living room with drinks and seconds of dessert and chatted until late in the evening when Will called his driver to take the doctor home. When they walked him to the elevator, Dr. Mellen declared it to be one of the best nights he'd had in this over-crowded city and kissed Kate on both cheeks, a favor she returned, and then did the same to Will while Kate nearly doubled over in laughter at the shocked look on her husband's face.

"These stodgy Englishmen," Ian leaned over and said to her as he waggled his eyebrows mischievously.

Will recovered just as the elevator opened and they parted merrily, promising to get together again soon.

"Well, you survived the night. What do you think? Does your hero live up to your expectations or are you disappointed?" she asked Will as she turned on the water to wash the dishes.

"Not disappointed. A little surprised, but pleasantly so," he said as he grabbed a towel and began drying the wine glass she passed to him.

"Just think, at work on Monday, you can tell all your nerdy friends that you were kissed by Ian Mellen," she teased.

"Don't think I won't," he said with a shake of the towel in her direction.

***

"I talked to my sister today," Will said after dinner a few nights later.

"Yeah? What did she say? Are they doing alright?" Kate asked.

"Yeah, they're great. She wants to come visit."

"Really? When? I thought she was coming in July."

"Two weeks. I told her that was when you had your hooding ceremony and party and she said she'd like to come."

"That's great!"

"It is?"

"Yeah, why wouldn't it be?"

"I thought Jacqueline exhausted you," he said.

"She can be a little… difficult, I'll grant you, but she's a perfectly nice person and more importantly, she's your sister."

"Okay," he said hesitantly.

"Plus, I'm seriously thinking about buying some property and she knows all about buildings. I'm sure she'd be willing to help me choose something."

"Oh, no doubt about that! If you're not careful, you'll wind up with more than one 'something'."

Kate smiled. "Will she stay with us or in a hotel?"

"I thought your family was staying with us?"

"We can all bunk in if we need to. Heather and Tiffany can have the Murphy bed in my den, Jacqueline can take my room and I can sleep with you."

He raised his brows.

"What? Do you not want me to sleep with you?" she asked.

"No, not at all. I love it when you sleep with me. But will your sisters want to share? And won't that be a little crowded?"

"Not at all. It'll be fun. And I don't want your sister to be the only person staying in a hotel. She'll feel left out."

"I don't know. I think she'd rather be comfortable."

"You don't think our place is comfortable?"

"Of course it is, but we don't really have proper guest quarters. And she'd be staying in your room. Aren't you afraid she'll get into your stuff?"

"Are you telling me your sister is a snoop? And what exactly are guest quarters?"

"Yes, I think she is a little bit of a snoop, thought she'd never admit it. And guest quarters are rooms designed for guests, like we have at the beach house. No personal stuff for them to go through, everything a guest could need, that sort of thing."

Kate shook her head. "Well, we can always ask her what she wants to do. Did she say why she's coming? It can't possibly be just for my ceremony."

"She said she wants to go through some things from the old apartment. And talk to me about something."

"Uh oh. That sounds ominous. Did she say what it was about?"

"No, but I have a feeling it's about the apartment. And maybe some artwork from the beach house."

"Why do you think that? And what art work?"

"I think she wants the collection of pictures of her and mother. There's a particularly nice painting done a month before she died. Jackie's always loved it and I think now that she's settled semi-permanently, she wants to have it."

"Does she have to ask you for it?"

"Technically yes, I own the house and all of its contents."

"Will you give it to her?"

"Yes, of course. I can't imagine why I wouldn't. I'd like to have a decent copy made before she drags it halfway around the world, though."

"Can I ask you a question?"

"Of course."

"Why did you get the house in the Hamptons instead of Jacqueline? From the looks of things, she was more attached to it."

"Because it was my father's and everything that belonged to him came to me," he said simply.

"Okay," she said slowly, "then why do you two share the house on the upper west side?"

"My parents bought it together. My mother had her own money; it's her half that belongs to Jacqueline now."

Kate looked confused. "Did your Harper grandparents not have a place in the city?"

"They did but my father sold it. It was smaller and in an outdated building. They spent most of their time in England and were really only here for the summers, which were of course spent at the beach house, and sporadically throughout the year for shopping and business trips."

Kate nodded. "Did your father not leave anything to your sister?"

"Of course. She has a sizeable trust fund which will keep her extremely comfortable her entire life. She has an honorary seat on the board at Taggston that she just came into when she turned twenty-five and she owns a decent percent of the Taggston stock, and even more of HarperCo which was our father's start-up. And of course she got her share of the family jewels and a townhouse in London from my mother. The house we stayed in was the Harper home."

"Wow. I'll stop thinking she got gipped, then."

He chuckled. "I do wonder what she wants to talk about in regards to the apartment in town."

"Do you think she wants to make changes or renovate it or something?"

"I don't know. She can't touch anything without my written permission. For that matter, I can't touch anything without hers."

"Then let's hope she wants to take some pictures back with her and it will all be simple."

He smiled. "I hope so, but with Jacqueline, things are rarely simple."

**

The morning of the hooding ceremony, Kate's sisters arrived.

The moment they walked in the door, Tiffany was chattering nonstop. She told them about the things they'd seen on the way to the apartment, the people they sat near on the plane, all the places she wanted to see while she was there and what she wanted to buy. Kate finally clamped a hand over her mouth and laughingly asked if her sister wanted anything to drink or eat. Tiffany laughed and followed Kate to the kitchen, Heather trailing quietly behind.

Jacqueline had opted to stay in the Covington townhouse uptown instead of staying with Kate and William. She said she didn't want to intrude on Kate's time with her sisters and that her aunt wanted her to check on the place for her, which Kate found to be a flimsy reason but didn't comment on.

Tiffany and Heather would stay with them in her room and her parents and grandmother would stay with Jen and Andrew. Kate hated to admit it, but she was relieved. She and Will were in a good place and she thought their behavior was pretty relationship-y, but if her parents stayed in her room, she was afraid one of them would find something out of place and blow the whole thing up.

She moved almost all of her clothing into Harper's closet in anticipation of her sisters' arrival, but she was still nervous that some sort of incriminating clue would be left behind. Thankfully, she kept most of her personal stuff – books, music, random mementos – in her den and only used the bedroom for sleeping and housing clothing so that if anyone stopped by unexpectedly, she could just say she used the guest room for closet space and wouldn't have to worry about being accused of having a separate bedroom from her husband. Of course since they'd begun sleeping together in December, she spent roughly half her nights in his room anyway.

The ceremony was long and drawn out, as most matriculation ceremonies are. Kate was hooded by her advisor, and by the skin of her teeth, she graduated with a 4.0, leaving her with the highest rank in her program. She was cheered on by her classmates and family and she would later declare it as the proudest moment of her life so far.

Jenny had planned a lovely party afterward at one of Kate's favorite restaurants, on Harper's tab of course, and everyone headed there following the ceremony. The private room was a raucous and cheerful place, with even Jacqueline lightening up and joining in the celebration.

Her parents and sisters had brought her gifts, ranging from the funny – a T-shirt from Tiffany reading 'I'm so much smarter than you', to the sentimental – her grandmother Bishop gave her the family pearls, the ones her grandmother had given her on her wedding day. Kate cried and laughed at herself for being so emotional. Her parents took dozens of pictures, Loretta declaring she needed plenty to show her friends and all the customers that came into the shop. Kate rolled her eyes halfheartedly and posed and smiled until her face ached.

By the time she said goodnight to her sisters and climbed into bed with Will, she was exhausted.

"Do you have the stamina for one more gift?" he asked.

"What? You got me a present?"

"Of course I did."

She smiled. "Yeah, I've got the energy for one more. Hand it over."

She playfully held out her hands and wiggled her fingers. Harper handed her a blue bag with tissue paper sticking out the top of it. She reached in happily and pulled out a snorkel mask.

She looked at it in confusion before saying, "Thanks. I don't have one of these."

He laughed and told her to look further into the bag. She pulled out an envelope with her name written on it in Will's handwriting. Inside were at least a dozen slips of paper.

She took the first one out and read, "One full body massage." She looked back up at him. "Did you make these?"

He nodded. "Keep reading," he replied with a hint of mischievousness in his voice.

"Two hours of mind blowing sex." She laughed and flipped to the next certificate. "Skinny dipping." She raised a brow. He gestured for her to continue. "Graduate's choice." She couldn't help but laugh at that one. "One make-out session on the beach and possibly more." She looked at the snorkel mask again. "Are we going to the beach?"

"Yes, we are."

Her eyes lit up. "When? Can you get away soon? Heather and Tiffany would love to see the beach house."

He stopped her before she continued. "Not the Hamptons. A different beach."

"Which beach?"

"A place I like to go sometimes to get away from it all. It's very beautiful and very secluded. And as nice as they are, we won't be taking your sisters with us."

"I can't wait! When do we go?"

"As soon as our guests leave and we work out the scheduling."

She kicked her feet and squealed on the bed, feeling like a seventeen year old girl.

"Best. Graduation. Ever!"

Will laughed and pulled her to him. "Bet I can make it better."

She giggled and kissed him, trying to be quiet so her sisters didn't hear them.

**

Kate ended up taking her entire family to the beach house Sunday evening. They had planned to make a trip of it and stay through Wednesday, so she thought it would be an ideal way to wrap things up, especially since her dad hated the city and, though her mother loved the shopping, all the energy made her feel a little frazzled.

They were all suitably impressed when they saw the outside of the house and heard the waves in the background, but they felt less out of place in the lavender, teenage-girl designed interior. For three glorious days, everyone got along and played games and laughed together. For a little while, it felt like they were all one big happy family again, especially since Jenny had managed to telecommute those days. Even though she spent a good part of the day holed up in her room on her laptop, it was great for all of them to be together, without boyfriends or husbands or anyone but the four girls, their parents and their favorite grandmother.

One morning, Kate and her grandmother were making pancakes for everyone when her grandmother asked how married life was for her now that she'd made it through the first year.

"It's good. Great, actually. We get along really well and hardly ever fight. I'm really happy. But doesn't everyone say that about their first year? Honeymoon phase and all?"

"No, not everyone! For some couples, it's the hardest time of all. Especially when one of you is older, like your William. You become set in your ways, you don't know how to adapt, or don't want to. Suddenly there's someone wanting your attention, your time, doing things their way instead of yours. It can be jarring."

"I suppose so," Kate said as she flipped a pancake. "I've always lived with someone – at home, in the dorm, then roommates – so I don't know if I really got a chance to have everything my way. I just had my room and kept to myself."

"But it's nice to run your own home now, isn't it?" Gran said with a knowing expression.

Kate laughed. "Yes, it is! I don't know if I could go back to living with roommates."

"Well, luckily you don't have to. That man of yours isn't going anywhere any time soon. He's not the leaving kind. He doesn't have it in him. Besides, it's plain to see he's head over heels for you," she said before scooping the bacon out of the pan and onto a plate covered with a paper towel.

"Yes, he's a very good man," Kate said distractedly, wondering about what her grandmother had said.

"You hold onto him. Good ones are hard to find. Especially good ones that look like that."

"Gran!" Kate turned to her with wide eyes.

Gran Bishop just laughed. "You girls are so easy to shake up. In my day, we weren't afraid to brag about our men. If he had a good job, you boasted about it; if he was smart, you told everyone; if he was good looking, you showed him off to everybody."

Kate laughed. "Gran, you are cracking me up! Somehow I can't see you running around town showing off Grandpa."

"He wasn't as handsome as your man!" she said indignantly. "But boy, was he smart, and so good to me!" She had a dreamy look on her face for a moment and looked away, blinking rapidly. "Now," she said, her voice wobbling slightly, "you take this plate to the table. I'll bring the bacon."

"Yes, ma'am," Kate said quietly as she hugged her grandmother from behind and squeezed her tightly around her shoulders. Her grandmother just patted her arm and shooed her into the dining room.

A few hours later, as they were sitting on the beach, Kate asked Tiffany about her plans for when she graduated high school next year.

"Are you going to start looking at colleges this fall?" she asked.

"I think so. Mom wants me to go to State so I'm not too far away and she can see me more, but I'm thinking about art school and their program is okay, but not the best."

"Really? That's great! You'd be amazing at art school!"

"Really? You think?"

"Of course! You don't know how many compliments I've gotten on that frame you made me for Christmas."

"Thanks," Tiffany said.

"So, have you looked into other schools?"

"Yeah. So far I'm thinking about Rhode Island School of Design, of course, and SCAD in Savannah. That would be close to the water and it's only an hour from the beach house so I could see whoever when they came down."

Kate nodded. "Have you thought about New York at all?"

"Yeah, but I'm not sure. It's a really expensive city and mom and dad could help me out a little with expenses, but not much. They've promised to pay tuition and supplies, which will probably be a lot, but I'll be on my own for living expenses."

"I could help you out a little there." Tiffany shot her a look. "I don't mean with money exactly, though I could probably slip you a little cash here and there, but you could eat with us sometimes, I could take you to lunch, that sort of thing."

Tiffany nodded. "Yeah, that would be helpful. I can't decide if I want to go someplace where I know people, like New York with you and Jenny, or go somewhere completely new and make my own mark, you know?"

"Yeah, I know exactly what you mean. I thought the same things when I was picking a school. I picked New York because it had the school and the program I wanted, and I loved the city. Jen already living here just made the choice easier for me."

"Maybe I'll come tour Pratt and NYU in a few months. Would I be able to stay with you or Jen, do you think?"

"Of course! You don't even have to ask. I could show you all my favorite places, we'd have a great time."

"Thanks, Katie," Tiffany said with a nudge to her sister's shoulder.

"Any time."

34
TAKE ME AWAY

Early June
1 year, 1 Month Married

Kate sat on the private jet, book in hand, headed to Will's mystery vacation house.

After a week of schedule rearranging and working late so they could get away, they escaped on their little graduation/anniversary trip. Their first anniversary had come and gone in a flurry of Kate's birthday, graduation, and family visits. They'd gone out to a nice dinner and Kate had worn a new lacy negligee, but otherwise, it had been pretty low key.

Now, he was whisking her off to who knows where. He had only told her to bring a bathing suit and summer clothes, though not too many since he planned to keep her naked most of the time. She'd laughed and packed happily, looking forward to spending two weeks lying on the beach with her very sexy husband.

Looking out the window of the plane, she wondered where they were.

It was dark when they landed and Harper nudged Kate's shoulder to wake her up. She groggily followed him to a car and through what she supposed was beautiful scenery but she couldn't see it because it was pitch black outside. Wherever they were, it was not near a big city.

They eventually came to a gate along a high white stone wall. The driver punched a code in and the gate swung wide, revealing a tree lined driveway, lights beneath the trees making the leaves look silvery. Kate rolled down her window and could hear waves crashing in the distance. Eventually, a large white stone house came into view, glowing in the moonlight. It was built partially into the side of a cliff with flat square roof lines and arched doorways. The path to the door was lined with small lights in blue and green, which she realized later were from the glass mosaic lanterns lining the walk.

"Oh, Will! This is magnificent!" She breathed as she stepped out of the car. "Where are we?"

"Technically, we're in Greece. This is a small island about twenty miles from Mykonos, about fifty miles from the mainland."

"Wow."

He led her around the back terrace to a low wall overlooking an infinity pool and beyond that, the Mediterranean Sea.

"Welcome to Valhalla, Katherine."

She leaned against his back and tightened her arms over his where they wrapped around her stomach. "Valhalla," she repeated. "I love it."

After three days of being in Greece, Kate was looking much browner and had lost count of how many times they had had sex. They did it in the bedroom (of course), in the kitchen after breakfast, in the pool before lunch, and between conversations of how the house got its name (a Norwegian man had named it when he bought and refurbished it years ago and Harper had left it because he liked it) and how long they could manage to stay (Kate voted for forever). They had a private stretch of beach and only shared this side of the island with five other houses, so they'd managed a few interludes in the sand and water as well.

Across the island was a village with a hotel that had a store for tourists to buy what they needed that wasn't available in the village market. Kate found bikes with baskets in the shed and they rode all over the island: to the market to get produce for the day, to the local café for dinner, and to a lovely stall where an old lady made yoghurt fresh and sold it in little glass jars. It quickly became Kate's favorite breakfast and the first week of their trip went by in a haze of lazy days and passion-filled nights.

Harper brought the camera Kate had given him for Christmas that he had heretofore only used off and on. He played with all the different settings and lenses and took hundreds of pictures. He snapped the scenery, local wildlife, a few children at the market, but mostly he took pictures of Kate. He said that since she had planted the idea in his head in the first place, she should model for him. She laughed and posed, making silly faces and teasing him about how bossy he was becoming with all his 'stand over there' and 'raise your arm higher' and 'look over your shoulder' commands.

The second week they went to Athens for a day. They spent the afternoon fighting the crowds to see all the famous statues and landmarks, then spent the night at a hotel in the city and the morning shopping for souvenirs. They went back to their island haven and went nowhere but their house and the market for the remainder of their trip. It was paradise.

Two days before they were scheduled to leave, Harper lay on the beach next to Kate and surreptitiously watched her. He never would have guessed last year when Jamison told him he had immigration trouble that it would lead to this. To her. She had quickly become his partner in life, his best friend, his lover. He realized he was glad Alicia Winters had gotten mad and turned his name in to whoever she knew at immigration. The investigation was over and he had come out on top – with a new green card, but more importantly, with Kate.

"Stop staring at me, you pervert," she said with a tiny smile.

"Who says I'm staring?"

"I can feel your eyes on me." She kept her sunglasses on and her face forward.

"How can I help myself when you're doing that?"

"Doing what? I'm just lying here."

"With your hair down and your top off," he said with a look.

She laughed. "It's a private beach! And you're the one

who suggested I go topless, not me."

"Well, I get to, it only seemed fair that you should also," he reasoned.

She snickered. "So this is all about equality then, huh?"

"Yes, of course. You should be free to enjoy everything that I do, including the sun on your bare chest."

She laughed. "I'm not sure which of us is enjoying this more."

"I am, of course. I get to feel the sun on my chest and enjoy watching it on yours as well. I'm definitely the winner here."

Kate threw a towel at him and laughed before rummaging around in her bag for her bathing suit top.

"Hey," he protested, "what are you doing?"

"Putting my top on."

"Are you cold?"

"Maybe."

"Come here," he grabbed her arm and pulled her toward him and onto his lounge chair.

"I'll hold you and then you won't need that pesky top."

"Really?" she asked with a raised brow.

"Anything for you, love. Your breasts are safe with me."

He pressed her to his chest as she giggled, then looked down at her breasts and asked if they felt warmer now. He smiled smugly at the imagined response while Kate rolled her eyes. She nestled her head onto his shoulder and relaxed, listening to the waves and the birds and feeling her husband's even breathing beneath her.

***

Eventually, it was time to pack and head back to New York.

"When can we come back?" Kate asked as she zipped up her suitcase.

"Maybe in the autumn. We can see how our schedules look. It's beautiful here in October," he answered.

"Maybe in time for your birthday," she said slyly. He

shrugged but smiled at the thought. Lying with Kate on a beach seemed like an excellent way to spend his birthday; certainly better than the stonewalled silence they'd been in for his last one.

She sighed and looked around her while Harper took the bags downstairs. She slowly followed, dragging her hand along the banister and saying a silent goodbye to the house.

"I wish we could stay longer," she said wistfully.

"Me, too. I'm glad you like it. This is one of my favorite places. It'll be nice to come here together."

She smiled gently and took his hand before turning to look at the house once more and climbing into the car.

35
HARD

Mid June
1 Year, 2 Months Married

"So what are you looking for, exactly?" Jacqueline asked at breakfast with Kate after she and Will returned from Greece.

"Well, I'm not entirely sure. Will said that property could be a good investment, and I'm looking toward long term goals. So something I could renovate and sell fairly easily, though I don't know if I know how to do that and that might make me crazy, or a decent rental property."

Jacqueline nodded slowly. "I think, with this being your first one and you not knowing as much about real estate, that it would be a good idea to start small. Maybe a small building with no more than four of five flats, for example."

"Agreed. These are the ones the realtor sent over earlier this morning." She passed the tablet to Jacqueline. "I've got a good eye for color and fabric and furniture, that sort of thing, but I don't really know anything about the structural parts of it."

"Well you're in luck. I'm not overly good at the soft part of it myself, but I know a lot about structure and hard finishes and the like. Perhaps we'll make a good team."

Kate looked a bit surprised at Jacqueline's offer of assistance but quickly covered it.

"That would be great! When do you plan on coming

back?"

"I don't really know. I'm not even sure when this visit will end," she said.

"Okay, well, would you like to go see a few of these with me?"

"I'd love to. Call the car round," Jacqueline replied.

After ten minutes of silence in the car, Kate decided to speak. "Did you study architecture in school?" she asked.

"No," she replied, her voice tight. "I studied art."

"Oh, I'm sorry, I just thought you had because you know so much about it," she trailed off, wondering what she had done to provoke her sister-in-law's ire.

"I took as many classes as I could in the subject, and I've done a lot of reading on my own, and of course my own projects have taught me a lot."

Kate nodded, unsure of what to say. Jacqueline seemed comfortable letting the topic drop.

**

"Why did your sister study art?" Kate asked that evening as they were padding around Will's bathroom getting ready for bed. She never moved her things back into her own room after her sisters left. She'd suggested it half-heartedly to Will, and he had mumbled something about it all being pointless since she spent half her time in his room anyway and leaving something for her sister's to use. She had taken it as an invitation to stay and continued to sleep in his bed, but still referred to the other as her room.

"She liked it, I suppose," he replied.

"No, I mean why didn't she study architecture? I asked her about it today and she seemed all tense."

He rinsed his mouth and gargled for a minute, then wiped his face with a towel. "I'm not entirely sure, but I do remember her talking about it and wanting to go to some school famous for its architecture program. In the end she went to Cambridge and read art, though."

"Do you think your father talked her out of the

architecture program?" she asked thoughtfully.

Will was about to retort in the negative when he remembered something from his own experience with his father. "You know, he may have. He had firm ideas about what Harpers did and didn't do, and about men and women, too. I remember mentioning that I was thinking about doubling in history or something like that, but he wouldn't hear of it. I was reading business, we both knew that, but he wanted me to study IT or robotics or something along those lines so I'd be prepared to take over HarperCo. I understood his reasons, of course, but maybe Jackie wasn't so compliant. I don't really know. He passed away in her third year – she could have changed her course if she'd wanted to."

"Doesn't that seem a little, I don't know, cold? To change as soon as he dies? Like you were waiting for him to get out of the way so you could do whatever you wanted?"

He made a face. "I see how you could think that, but I don't think it necessarily has to be that way."

"What would he have done if she'd refused to major in art and insisted on architecture? Would he have cut her off?"

"No, I don't think so, but people didn't really insist on things with my father. It just wasn't the way it worked. He was a kind man, but he was very powerful, very in command. Everyone just did what he said. Besides, he couldn't have cut her off if he'd wanted to. She had family trusts from our grandparents that he couldn't touch, plus her inheritance from our mother that she'd already come into. If she'd wanted to go for architecture, she could have. Nothing was stopping her, not really."

"Nothing but her father's approval and affection," Kate mumbled.

Will wrapped an arm around her shoulders. "Quit worrying about Jackie. She seems pretty happy with her life." He kissed her forehead and walked into the bathroom, calling over his shoulder for her to follow him. She reluctantly filed her thoughts away for another day and joined her husband in the bedroom.

***

In the end, they spent three long weeks looking and finally settled on a small building with four floors in a good neighborhood. There were seven small apartments in it already, but Jacqueline suggested making four large ones and selling them as co-ops or renting them out. Kate agreed (and had in the back of her mind that it might be a decent place for her to live when things changed in a year) and the plan was set in motion.

Harper had generously offered to finance the project for Katherine, interest free, to get her started. Jacqueline offered to handle the inspections and help with contractors, so Kate just followed along as her sister-in-law peppered the inspector with questions she never would have thought to ask. The two women had forged a tentative friendship and Kate thought that while Jacqueline was a little hard to know, it might be worth the trouble in the end.

At lunch one day after meeting with the contractors, Kate noticed that Jacqueline was a bit quiet. She wasn't a verbose woman, but she certainly spoke her fair share, especially on the topic of renovation.

"Is something on your mind?" Kate asked.

"Do you plan on spending a lot of time at the Hamptons house this summer?" Jacqueline replied.

"We usually go for weekends, but not all. Why? Would you like to spend some time there? We wouldn't mind at all."

Jacqueline took a deep breath and seemed to be trying to calm herself down a bit. "I thought I might spend some time there, yes, if you and William don't mind."

"Of course not! Go right ahead," Kate encouraged. She sat quietly for a few minutes, observing her sister-in-law and wondering if she should take the risk she was considering. "It reminds you of your mother, doesn't it?"

Jacqueline looked up at her, startled. "What?"

"The house in the Hamptons. Will told me you and your mother spent a lot of time there."

Jacqueline nodded slowly and relaxed her shoulders a bit. "Yes, the men would stay in the city working while mother and I stayed at the beach house. It was lovely."

"Sounds it."

Tentatively, Jacqueline continued, "I used to call it Misselthwaite Manor. You know, from *The Secret Garden*?" Kate nodded. "It was my favorite book. My mother read it to me when I was little and she bought me a first edition for my birthday."

"I loved that book, too."

"William and father laughed when they heard what I'd named it. They said it was nowhere near big enough to be a manor and that this wasn't England."

Kate frowned. "How old were you?"

"I must've been about nine or so. William was just a teenager, following along after father."

"Did your father spend a lot of time with you at the beach house?"

"Not at all," she said in clipped tones. "He spent very little time with me."

Just then the check arrived and Jacqueline took out her wallet to pay for it.

"No, let me get it," Kate said, reaching for the check.

Jacqueline forcefully pulled it to her. "I may not have my brother's money, but I can well afford lunch."

Kate drew her hand back, stunned, and quietly finished her drink and picked up her purse. "Shall we?" she said in a strained voice.

"Yes, let's," Jacqueline replied.

Outside, Jacqueline hailed a taxi and Kate said she would walk since she was only ten blocks from home. They said short goodbyes and a bemused Kate went home alone.

"I had a strange conversation with your sister today," she said over dinner that night.

"All my conversations with Jackie are strange," he joked. "What happened?"

She told him what was said and the weird vibe she'd gotten from Jacqueline.

"What do you think is going on?" she asked.

"I don't know. Sounds like she's mad, but if there's one

thing Harpers are good at, it's not talking about our problems."

"Do you think she wants the beach house?"

He looked thoughtful for a moment. "It's possible, I suppose. Did she say anything about it?"

"Not exactly, but she didn't seem to like the idea of having to ask permission to go to her own home."

"It wasn't home. It was a summer house."

"To you, maybe, but to her, it was home, at least here in the States. She even named it!"

"I'd forgotten about that." He smiled for a minute. "So, what are you suggesting?"

"I'm not exactly sure, but would you consider giving it to her?"

"What?"

"Why not? You could even make a trade. Her half of the upper west side apartment for your summer house. You're more attached to the apartment, she's more attached to the house. Seems fair enough. And she *is* your sister and only sibling. You're never going to get another one."

He was thoughtful for a moment. "If we did that, where would we go in the summer?"

"I have heard of this process among new money called 'buying a home'," she said with air quotes. "Scandalous, I know, but needs must." She said the last in a haughty voice, looking down her nose.

Harper laughed, "Alright, so we give the beach house to Jacqueline and buy our own. Do you like that idea?"

"Hey, it's your house and your sister. You need to make this decision."

"So you're just planting ideas in my mind?" he asked with a smile.

"Something like that."

***

"These are all awful. Can't we find something that doesn't look like it belongs in a modern art museum?" Harper complained loudly at the fifth house they looked at. He stomped across the room and flipped his hand against the vertical blinds covering an oddly shaped window.

Kate took a deep breath. "Why don't you tell the realtor what it is you're looking for exactly. Maybe he could show you something more appropriate that way," she said tensely. She'd forgotten how awful he was to shop with. Now she realized why he had a personal shopper.

"I want something with character, something without a million ridiculous angles. Is that so difficult?" he replied petulantly.

Just then the realtor came around the corner and Kate hurried over to him before Will could spout off any more.

"Mr. Harper would like to see something more classical, maybe a historic property? Do you have any listings like that?" she asked as she led him toward the kitchen and away from her disgruntled husband.

"Actually, a colleague of mine is about to list a place that might be suitable. I can call and see if it's available to view."

"That would be great," she said with a tight smile and walked stiffly back to her husband.

While the realtor talked on the phone, she marched Will onto the deck. "What is the matter with you?" she hissed.

"What do you mean?" he asked, offended.

"You're being incredibly rude!"

"I am not! It's his job to find us something we like. I told him I didn't like the first McMansion he showed us and what does he do? Show us four more!"

"What did you think he would do when you told him you wanted all the amenities and price wasn't 'really an issue'?" she asked in exasperation.

"I thought he'd bloody well do his job, that's what!" he cried. "Bloody estate agents," he murmured, pacing back and forth.

"Spoiled brat," she said under her breath.

"What?" he spun around and glared at her. She stubbornly looked over the railing and refused to face him. "What did you say?"

"Nothing," she ground out.

"Oh, no, you don't! You said something, I heard you! It sounded an awful lot like 'spoiled brat'," he enunciated perfectly.

She spun toward him. "So what if I did! You're the one acting like a huge baby, pitching a fit because no mansion is pretty enough for you!"

His mouth dropped open and his eyes widened before narrowing at her. He stalked back into the house silently.

"We won't be seeing any more houses today, Mr. Simms, thank you. We'll be in touch," he said to the realtor as he moved past him.

Kate quickly followed, making excuses to the realtor for their abrupt departure and trying to look like everything was alright when all she wanted to do was scream at her husband.

The ride back into the city was tense and silent. Neither said a word and Will kept his hands on the wheel in precisely the same position until they parked under their building.

After she'd hung up her jacket and put her purse on the table by the door, she said to Will's back as he fished a beer out of the fridge, "Would you like to tell me what that little temper tantrum was about?"

The fridge door slammed shut and for a moment, Kate wondered if she'd made the mistake of poking the proverbial bear.

Will turned around slowly and cocked his head to one side. When he spoke, his voice was deceptively calm. "Tell me, Ms. Bishop, what disgusted you so much about my behavior today?"

She paled a little and finally squared her shoulders. "You were rude to John. He's just trying to do his job and you're not making it any easier."

"But that's his job!" Harper cried. "His job is to find me what I want. For his trouble I will pay him handsomely. It's all very simple. He was doing a bad job and I was letting him know it."

"And you were so mature about it! 'These handles are too square! Why do all the doors have glass in them? Who needs an open loft?'" she imitated his deep voice and accent. "Why couldn't you just say you wanted something less modern and be done with it? Poor John didn't know what to do!"

"Why must you be best friends with everyone who works for you? Are you incapable of keeping a professional line?"

"What are you talking about?" she asked, her expression befuddled.

"You're on a first name basis with everyone you work with. I call him Mr. Simms, but you call him John. That doesn't strike you as odd?"

"No! Why should it?"

"You're too personable! I can guarantee you that if Mr. Simms, John, whatever his name is, wants to be successful in real estate, he'll have to deal with people much more spoiled than me." He laughed cynically and moved into the living room.

"So what, you're just being an ass because you can, is that what you're saying?" she asked, following him.

"I wasn't an ass!"

"Yes you were!"

"I simply didn't treat him like he was my best friend and entitled to see all my birthmarks!"

"What?" she said, suddenly confused.

"Nothing," he mumbled. "My point is that you are too close with the help. You have to maintain a professional distance. You can't keep wondering what everyone thinks of you all the time, or worrying about their feelings. You have a job to get done and you just need to do it."

"I am not too close with the help! We don't even have help!" she cried.

"Really? What about Maria?"

"The housekeeper? What about her?"

"Did you or did you not give her your recipe for butterscotch cookies?" Kate's mouth dropped open. "And you ask her about her grandchildren every time you see her. And you always sit and talk and drink iced tea together before she leaves."

"I'm being polite! I'm southern! It's what we do!" she shouted.

"And I've seen her leave here with more than one bag of hand-me-downs for her daughter," he said triumphantly.

"You may not realize this, Mr. Never-wear-the-same-thing-twice, but some people are dressed solely from hand-me-downs, and there's no shame in it! I know you can't possibly understand concepts like not having enough and depending on others to get by and actually *needing* things, but for a lot of people, it's just life! And it's hard! Something you obviously know nothing about." She was so angry she was shaking, and had risen onto her toes and was leaning toward him without realizing it.

"I know plenty about hardship!" he shouted back.

"Really? What do you know about hardship? What has ever been hard for you? Your entire life has been presented to you on a silver platter! The best schools, the nicest houses, the fanciest cars and clothes. Add to all of that you just happen to be gorgeous and have perfect hair! Your job was tailor made for you and you slid cozily into a position most people work decades to get to."

"So that's what you think? You think my life is so easy? You think everything is just handed to me? Do you have *any* idea what I've been through?" She shrank back at his vehemence. "Do you know why I'm the CEO?"

He leaned toward her and her eyes grew wide.

"Because my father isn't! Because he isn't here! Because he's dead! He's dead, Katherine! He died in my arms and there wasn't a damn thing I could do about it. Do you know what that's like? Watching the person you love most in the world struggle for breath and finally collapse? Do you have ANY IDEA!?!" he shouted.

Her mouth opened in a silent 'o', but she said nothing.

"I do. I know exactly what it's like," he said, his voice strangled. "And all the fancy educations and the nice cars didn't make up for the fact that I had a mother who never wanted me and a father I never saw. You know why I was sent to boarding school when I was eight? Because my mother finally had the little girl she wanted and she couldn't be bothered with her gangly, dirty little boy anymore. The first time I spent more than a week under the same roof as my father I was fifteen years old. He was too busy building an empire. Building all of this," he opened his arms wide and gestured around him, "and it killed him. And for what? For a loveless marriage and a bunch of toys he never had time to use. Don't tell me I don't know about hard. **I may not know about poor, but I know about hard**."

"Will," she choked, trying to hold back a sob.

He turned and walked to his room, shutting the door softly behind him. Kate sank onto the sofa and wrapped her arms around herself tightly. How had they come to this? One minute they were bickering about realtors, the next they were shouting at each other and digging up old wounds. Had his mother never wanted him? Really? But why? How had he never seen his father? She'd known Mr. Harper traveled a lot, but from the stories William had told her, he and his mother had often accompanied Mr. Harper on his trips. She'd seen pictures of the three of them in Japan together under a pagoda when William was five. There were pictures of him on the Great Wall of China in the album in his office. Surely that was something?

But still… She knew she had several pictures of her with her mother; smiling for photos, laughing together. Those did not paint an accurate portrait of their relationship. No one ever had a camera ready when Loretta once again felt the need to illuminate all of Kate's perceived faults in minute detail. In fact, she had very few pictures with her father, the parent she actually had a close relationship with. *Looks like it's true what they say. You never know what goes on behind closed doors.*

After several more minutes of thinking, she knew what she needed to do. She squared her shoulders and went to find her husband.

She opened the door and saw him lying on the bed on his side, facing the window. The room was dim and she could barely make him out, but she could tell by his breathing that he wasn't asleep. She crept over to the bed and crawled up behind him. She wrapped one arm round his waist and the other moved up to his head on the pillow where she stroked his hair. She pressed her body into his back, trying to comfort him with her warmth.

"I know how it feels not to be wanted," she said quietly into his neck. She felt him shift slightly, but he didn't respond. "I just wanted you to know, *I* want you. I don't mean in a sexual way, though that's great, but I want *you*. All of you. I want you to be my friend, I want to talk to you and spend time with you and just *be* with you. Even if we weren't married, and weren't lovers, and you didn't need a green card and never paid me a dime, I would want you in my life. *I* want you."

Will's body shuddered softly against hers and she held him tighter, pressing her face into his neck and squeezing him as hard as she could.

"Your father didn't know what he was missing. He was too focused on work, it wasn't about you, baby. He probably thought he was doing it for you, even. He must not have known what to do with a child. It wasn't you, Will."

His breath became ragged as she wracked her brain for something else to say.

"Sometimes you don't know what gift you have until it's too late. She loved you, I know she did. How could she not? You're so wonderful. Sometimes people just," she hesitated, searching for the right words, "fall short."

He shuddered and released a gut-wrenching sob. "I loved her, Katie. God, I loved her so much. She didn't, she didn't," he gasped, choking on the words.

"I know, baby, I know," she whispered.

She stroked his hair and rocked back and forth until he turned around and buried his face in her neck. The familiar scent of her soothed him and instead of quieting his sobs, it served to release even more of his pent-up pain and his shoulders shook with the force of his emotion. Had he been more mindful, he would have been embarrassed at his emotional display, but he wasn't.

Kate continued to stroke his hair and rub his back. She kissed the top of his head and whispered soothing words. Mostly she just said, "My darling. Will, my darling," as she continued her rocking motion.

Neither knew how long they stayed there, but soon, she went from kissing the top of his head to kissing his forehead, his swollen eyelids, his damp cheeks. He lay still and silent under her ministrations, only the occasional shuddering breath shattering the stillness. Eventually, he fell asleep and Kate held him while he rested, not minding the time ticking by or the buzzing of her phone down the hall. Her mind was filled with Will, and thoughts of his childhood, and wondering how on earth it had all gone so wrong.

After an hour of sleep, Will began to wake up. He squeezed her tightly, reassuring himself of her continued presence.

"G-d, Katie, I'm sorry. I didn't mean to -" she interrupted him with a swift kiss to his lips. He stopped talking and leaned his forehead against hers, closing his eyes and relaxing into her touch. Kate placed a kiss on each cheek and on his forehead, and Will sighed in relief at her acceptance.

After a few minutes of quietly rubbing his back and kissing his face and neck, she began to whisper to him. "You are so important to me. I don't know what I would do without you. My life is so much better with you in it. You bring me so much happiness, Will.

"I love the sound of your voice. It makes me happy just hearing you." She kneaded his shoulders until he began to relax under her touch. "You're the first person I want to tell my good news to, or my bad news. You're who I want to tell my stories to." She took his face in her hands and looked into his eyes. "My best friend. My lover. My partner."

He sighed and seemed to relax with her words, so she punctuated her statements with kisses and ran her hands on the skin beneath his shirt as she inched it upwards. "You're smart and funny and generous and talented." She pulled the shirt over his head as he watched her with glassy eyes and growing interest. "You are so beautiful, William." She ran her hands over his chest reverently, smoothing her palms over his shoulders and feeling his strong arms with her fingertips. "My brilliant, wonderful lover." She slid up his body and planted a slow kiss on the corner of his mouth. "Let me show you what you mean to me."

She ran her hands through his hair and scraped her nails against his scalp, making him arch his neck. "You are one of the sweetest men I've ever known. You always know just how to cheer me up." She moved on to his neck and nibbled and licked his sensitive spot there. "You're an amazing lover," she whispered into his ear before biting it gently with her teeth. "Your hands *do things* to me." She felt a slight smile where his cheek was pressed to her neck.

She kissed him softly and then pressed him back until he was lying on his back against the pillows. She reached for his pants with a naughty smile. "And you absolutely have the biggest," she undid the button, "thickest," she let down the zipper, "strongest," she gave a hard tug and pulled them down to his thighs, "heart," she smiled at him, "of any man I know." She pulled his pants past his socks and then removed those one by one.

"Even your feet are perfect. Don't you know men are supposed to have ugly feet?" She crawled back up to him, happy to see him wearing a small smile and his eyes almost cleared of sadness. "I want to make love to you, William. May I?"

He nodded slowly and almost said something, but his voice caught and she put a finger over his lips. "Shh, darling. Let me take care of you."

She trailed kisses down the length of his long muscular legs and nibbled on his stomach, something that made him squirm every time she did it. She kissed his chest and made him hold his breath when her teeth grazed across his flat, brown nipples. She suckled each finger in turn until he was moaning her name and by the time she placed a hot kiss on the inside of his wrist, he was tensing his back and obviously holding back the urge to flip her underneath him.

She straddled him and slowly pulled her sundress over her head, its light yellow fabric floating out around her. He looked at her in awe as she unclasped her bra and let down her hair, dark waves spilling about her shoulders and tumbling across her chest. Slowly, she slid over him, her silky hair and soft breasts blazing paths of fire across his skin. She started at his abdomen and slowly moved up until her breasts grazed his face, then slithered back down, this time following with her lips.

Harper bucked off the bed, his skin on fire and his heart pounding. She continued her descent slowly, torturously moving her body downward until he cried out. She retraced her movements, adding kisses in some places and nibbles in others and a few very notable licks.

When she finally slid onto him, he felt tiny bursts of energy all over his body. He couldn't describe the sensation of feeling completely accepted, of utter wholeness and joy and oneness with his wife, so he stroked her hair, and held her close, and spoke her name tenderly.

In the end, he could only say, to his surprise, that he felt loved.

36
THE TROUBLE WITH SISTERS

July
1 Year, 3 Months Married

It took a few more weekends of searching, but they eventually found a beach house that had character, charm, and plenty of modern amenities. Kate couldn't speak for a full five minutes when she saw the price tag, but Harper happily wrote an offer and called his lawyer. As luck would have it, a slightly smaller house just up the beach was for sale and Andrew put an offer on it. He had put off buying his own place because he'd always stayed at Harper's, but now that Jenny was a regular – and hopefully permanent – fixture in his life, it was decided that a little more privacy was best.

Jacqueline happily took over the Harper beach house, only a few miles from her brother's new place, and signed over her half of the old family apartment. Kate had never seen her smile as much as she did when she walked through the house, talking about how she and her mother had redone it the summer she turned thirteen and how it had been one of the best experiences the two of them had ever had together. She planned to redo the principle rooms but would leave her old room and a guest room the way they had done them all those years ago.

Several days later, Katherine met with Jacqueline to discuss progress on the building. After seeing the work and having a very confusing conversation with the plumber, they walked down the street and Kate asked how the redecorating was going at the beach house.

"So far so good. I decided to take your advice and paint the living room blue. It looks very airy and fresh."

"Good, I'm glad it worked out. Has Albert seen it yet?" Kate asked.

"No, he hasn't been over."

"Oh. Is he planning on coming over later this summer?"

"No, I don't believe he is," Jacqueline said crisply.

Kate's eyebrows rose. "Are you going back to Cyprus then?"

"Not any time soon, no." Jacqueline walked faster and Kate had to rush to keep up with her long gait.

"I don't mean to intrude, but is everything alright?"

"If by alright you mean I'm coping with the fact that I married a lying, cheating, lay about who shags the maid if I leave the house for a moment, then yes, everything is alright." She stopped briskly at the corner and turned to face Kate, her chin set and her eyes shuttered.

"Oh, no. I'm so sorry, Jacqueline."

"Don't be. It's better to find out now than years down the line. And the maid he's shagging seems very happy with her lot, so some good is coming of this," she said acerbically.

"Seriously? The maid?" The light changed and they walked briskly across the street.

"I know, it's all terribly cliché. I came home early one day and found them in bed together. He had the audacity to look me in the eye and shrug his shoulders like a boy caught stealing sweets. The little wanker actually smiled at me and said nothing had to change, he was just following his inclinations and letting his heart dictate his actions."

"And his heart told him to sleep with the maid?"

"Apparently. And in my bed, no less."

"Oh, Jacqueline," Kate said softly and squeezed her arm.

"I almost told him the supple young woman he was fondling was actually a transvestite who used to be a fisherman on a shrimping boat, but I was too angry to think clearly."

"Is that true?" Kate asked incredulously.

"No, but I would have loved to have seen his face," Jacqueline said wickedly.

Kate laughed. "Come on, I know just what you need."

Kate took Jacqueline to one of her favorite bars prior to her marriage to Will. The music was good, the cocktails were decent and the beer was cheap. More importantly, the bartenders looked like lumberjacks and all she had to do was whisper to one that her friend was a little down and he turned up the charm to eleven. Pretty soon, Jacqueline was very tipsy and feeling significantly better. Just when Kate was about to suggest she take Jacqueline home, Angie texted her asking if she wanted to join the gang for karaoke and drinks a few blocks away.

Tipsy Jackie was considerably looser than sober Jackie, and she grabbed the phone from Kate's hand before she had a chance to reply.

"Ooh, let's go! Sounds like fun!"

Kate agreed and led her sister-in-law down the street to meet Angie and three other friends she'd gone to school with.

"Wow, you're sister-in-law can really cut loose when she wants to," whispered Angie as Jacqueline cheered loudly for the stranger who'd just finished singing a popular rap song.

"I know. I'm completely shocked. Normally, she's so reserved. I can hardly get her to laugh out loud, let alone cheer and dance. Trust me, I'm just as surprised as you."

Just then, Jacqueline bounded up to them and leaned into Angie's side, one hand tentatively touching Angie's curly black hair, which she was wearing in a big natural style that day. "How does it stay up?" she asked quizzically as her open palm bounced off Angie's hair. "It's like a fern."

Katie's eyes widened like saucers and she just stared at her friend and sister-in-law, waiting for Angie to say something to Jacqueline, or worse, to smack her.

"I just put some cream on it and let it curl naturally," Angie said simply.

"Oh." Jacqueline leaned in and whispered loud enough for Kate to hear her, "I think it's beeeeea-utiful." She then smiled fondly at Angie and touched her hair once more, saying quietly, "So pretty," before moving to the other side of the table.

"Oh, G-d, I'm sorry, Angie. I didn't think she'd-"

Angie cut her off. "It's alright. Girl's completely drunk and I don't mind, really. I'm actually a little flattered. I don't think she compliments very many people." Angie sniggered.

"She's sure never complimented me," Kate mumbled, to which her friend just made an 'I told you so' gesture and turned back to face the stage.

"Come on, Katie," Jacqueline slurred as she threw one arm around Kate, "let's sing a song!"

Kate's yes widened. "Sure, Jackie. What did you have in mind?"

Before she could answer, Angie had pushed Kate up to sing and Jackie was dragging her towards the little stage in the corner.

Jacqueline was not a great singer. However, she was a decent performer. Unsurprisingly, she chose a song about a woman who found out her man was cheating and described in detail all the revenge she enacted upon him. Jacqueline belted the lines lustily, holding the microphone against her lips and bending over from the waist when she really got going. She alternately held one fist in the air and pointed the same hand at some imaginary man in the audience as she accused him of dastardly deeds. Kate sang backup with a straight face, but she nearly lost it multiple times, especially when she looked at her friends who were hysterical with laughter at her predicament.

By the time the song was up, the crowd was clapping wildly and several stood to their feet cheering and shouting encouragements like, "you tell him" and "you deserve better!"

After that, more than one attractive man stopped by their table and hit on Jacqueline, a development that didn't seem to bother her in the least, and Katie finally called the car to pick them up when she was afraid she wouldn't be able to take care of Jackie anymore. It took three of them to get her into the backseat but Katie got her into the apartment and tucked in to her old room and off to sleep without too much trouble.

Will was a slightly different matter, though.

"He did what? To my baby sister? That bastard! I'll kill him!" Will paced through the kitchen in front of Kate, his fist clenching and unclenching at his side while his other hand ran anxiously through his hair. "What was he thinking? They haven't even been married two years!"

"I know. I couldn't believe it. But when you think about what we know of Albert's character, is it really so shocking? He's lazy and indolent and expects everyone to do everything for him. He's bored with life and can't be bothered to have any ambition or actually do anything. A guy like that isn't going to make any effort to be faithful. If a chance to cheat comes up, he'll take it." Will looked at her incredulously. She shrugged. "He just follows his impulses. I doubt he'd even take the trouble to have a full-blown affair. This girl was probably just convenient and he did what he felt like without any concern for anyone else."

"Like my sister."

"Exactly. I'm sorry, honey. Can I get you a drink or something?" she offered.

"No, thanks, I'm fine. I need to call Andrew. We need to get her filed for a divorce. Thank G-d she had a prenup."

"Are you going to talk to her about this?"

He ran a hand through his hair. "Of course. Even if I wanted to, it can't be avoided. Our finances are connected through the company and even if that wasn't the case, she's my sister." He crossed his arms over his chest and leaned back against the counter. "But it's going to be damned awkward. She knows I never liked Albert."

"It's not like you're going to say I told you so." She shot him a look. "You aren't going to say that, are you?"

"No! Of course not! I would never do such a thing. But she knows that I thought he wasn't the best match for her and even if I hadn't thought that, it would still be uncomfortable."

Kate nodded as she rinsed a glass and put it in the dishwasher. "Well, if you want my advice, and I know you didn't ask for it, get her drinking. She talks a lot more when she's had a few."

"Katie! I can't get my little sister drunk just so she'll talk to me. We're perfectly capable of having a conversation without the aid of alcohol, thank you."

"She's twenty-six, not fifteen! But hey, you do what you think is best."

***

"Does Jamison have you all taken care of?" William asked as he came into Andrew's office late the next afternoon.

"Yes, I believe we're all settled here. Andrew, do you need anything else from me?" Jacqueline asked before rising gracefully from her seat in front of Jamison's desk.

"No, we're all set. I'll get the papers drawn up the way we talked about and get them sent over." He walked around the desk and shook Jacqueline's hand, pressing hers between both of his.

"Thank you, Andrew. I appreciate the assistance."

Andrew nodded and she left with her brother, casually looping her arm through his. "Where are you taking me?" she asked.

"Just out for a little bite. Kate offered to babysit for a friend tonight, so she's tied up."

"And you're avoiding the ankle biter?" she asked with a gleam in her eye as they stepped into the elevator.

He chuckled. "Only slightly. He's a perfectly decent child, but I'm not exactly proficient in answering the questions of a six-year-old."

Jacqueline laughed. "You know, sooner or later you'll have children of your own and you'll have to figure all this out."

He rubbed the back of his neck uncomfortably. "Well, not anytime soon."

The elevator opened into the lobby and Harper led his sister to the car waiting out front and on to one of his favorite restaurants. They were seated quickly and both ordered seltzer with a twist as they settled into the quiet booth.

"How are you doing?" Harper asked gently.

"I'm alright, I suppose. As well as can be expected." She gave him a weak smile and he searched his mind for something to say.

"What are your plans now?"

"I think I'll spend the summer at the beach house, then I'll think of something. I need to go back to Cyprus at some point and pack my things," she said quietly, looking down at her hands as they tore the paper napkin into smaller and smaller pieces.

He reached across the table and put his hand on top of hers. "Hey, anything you need at all, I'm here for you, alright?"

She nodded without looking up. The waiter came and took their order and the appetizer arrived without Jacqueline saying a word. William talked about his day and told what he thought was an amusing anecdote about a client lunch, but she didn't so much as crack a smile. She just nodded at intervals in the conversation and fiddled with her bracelet.

"Can we get a bottle of Malbec, please?" he asked the server. He knew Kate would gloat about it later, but he didn't know how much more of this sad silence he could take.

He took a fortifying gulp of his own wine while encouraging Jacqueline to drink hers. Every time her glass went below half way, he topped it off. At least it seemed to relax her.

"You're lucky, William," she said as she pushed asparagus around on her plate.

"How so?"

"You've always known exactly what you wanted to do, exactly how you wanted to live your life. It was all mapped out, all you had to do was follow the road signs."

He looked at her in surprise for a moment, then said, "What on earth makes you think that, Jackie?"

"Look around." She gestured with her hand. "Taggston, HarperCo, New York."

"And you think that's exactly how I wanted to live my life?"

She looked up, surprised at his vehemence. "It's not?"

"No! It absolutely isn't!"

"You always seem so sure of yourself and what you're doing. I just thought," she trailed off.

Harper tiredly dropped his forehead into his hand. "Jackie, I did what I was supposed to do, what I was told. I had a legacy to preserve, a name to uphold. It wasn't that I always knew what I wanted to do, but that I always knew what I was *supposed* to do. I just got lucky that I like it and happen to be good at it."

She opened and closed her mouth a few times. "Are you saying you wouldn't have chosen business if you'd had a choice?"

"I don't know. Maybe I would have, maybe I wouldn't. But I can tell you that I would have pursued other things, other hobbies. I would have had more of a life and other interests outside work."

"Like what?"

"Like photography." Jacqueline's eyes widened. "Kate bought me a camera for Christmas, she thought I would be good at it or something. Anyway, I've been fooling around with it, just a little here and there, but when we were on our trip I really got into it. I'm not saying I would have gone pro or anything like that, but it would have been nice to have a hobby so far removed from work all these years."

"You play golf," she said softly.

He laughed. "I hate golf! I only play it because it's useful for business. Most sports I play are actually informal business meetings except for the odd racquetball match with Jamison. The point is that I never really sat down and found out what I loved doing, what I enjoyed, because I've been too busy with work and commitments to consider my own desires beyond what I wanted for dinner."

"Are you saying I should figure out what I want?"

"No, yes, I don't know. Maybe. It couldn't hurt, right? Maybe you could go back to school for architecture. You're still young, and you used to be interested in it. Or maybe you could start a remodeling business. Lord knows you have the knowledge base."

"You think I should go back to school?" she asked.

"If you want to. I think it's a viable option. Why not?"

She exhaled loudly and turned her head to the side toward the people walking past their table. "You surprise me, William."

"Really?"

"Yes. You've changed a lot. I can only imagine it's Kate's influence that's done the trick."

"Maybe. Or perhaps you never knew me very well," he said quietly, his eyes on the table between them.

"Perhaps you're right. Maybe I just thought of you like Father and never considered you in your own right."

"Do you think dad would have been against you pursuing architecture?"

She guffawed. "Are you joking? Of course he would! He was! He made that very clear nine years ago when I was looking at universities. 'A Harper woman takes her family and position seriously.'" She said in a distant imitation of her father's voice.

"He said that to you?"

"Are you really surprised? What am I saying, of course you are. You were the golden child, you could do no wrong."

William laughed cynically. "What are you talking about?"

"Father adored you. He was always taking you with him on his trips, bragging about you to all his colleagues. I was just window dressing, you were the one he was proud of. The heir, his pride and joy," she said bitterly.

William breathed out forcibly and leaned back into the seat, then finally laughed dryly. "Wow. Katie was right," he said, shaking his head.

"What are you talking about?"

"Nothing. Listen, I'm sorry things were rough between you and dad, but I'm not him. And hey, Mother adored you. That's got to count for something, right?"

She nodded and looked down. "Sorry, William. You're right, you're not Father and I shouldn't treat you like you are."

"Just figure out what you want, Jackie. You're young, you're smart, and you have almost unlimited resources. Surely you can find contentment, hmm?"

She smiled. "You really are different, you know." He looked at her in both exasperation and curiosity. "You're warmer, more approachable. Kinder."

"Thanks, Jackie. I think."

She laughed and let the subject drop.

*

"Can you believe all this time she thought I was the favorite?" Will asked incredulously as he flossed next to Kate that night.

Kate shrugged. "Yeah, sort of." He shot her a questioning look. "Hey, I'm not trying to start anything, it's just that your family isn't exactly encouraging to its female members."

"How do you mean?"

"Seriously? Have you honestly not noticed it?"

"Aunt Julia is a bit stuck in her ways, but she hardly speaks for the entire family."

"Actually, she sort of does, but that's another topic. My point is that the women are expected to do and be certain things. Be impeccably groomed and marry the right man, stay in shape, be the perfect hostess and a force in society, and of course, produce the all important male heir. Volunteering for a charity is acceptable, but nothing that gets your hands dirty. If you must work, do it in the family firm. Of all the women in your family, Caroline is the only one I've met who actually has a job."

Will stared ahead for a moment, then opened and closed his mouth twice before responding. "So are you saying that Jacqueline has felt stifled all this time and that's why she thought I was the favorite? She perceived all this freedom?"

"Yes, basically. She obviously didn't understand that you had as little choice as she had, possibly less. She could at least pursue other things – hobbies, hotel renovations – while you have been glued to the company since you did your first internship when you were how old? Sixteen?"

"Fifteen."

She pointed her toothbrush at him. "That's my point. You never got to sit down and figure out what you want to do when you grow up. Sounds like you two had a lot in common all these years and just never talked about it."

"How did you get so smart?" he asked with a smirk and a step in her direction.

She turned to rinse her mouth in the sink. "Good genes." She flashed her freshly cleaned teeth at him and brushed past to the bedroom. "And she obviously doesn't realize that while she had a strained relationship with your father, you had the same with your mother."

"Yeah, I wonder about that." He followed her out of the bathroom. "I mean, she was old enough to remember that I wasn't around while she and Mum were doing all this stuff together. Didn't she ever ask where I was? Did it never occur to her that it was a bit odd how segregated we were?"

Kate shrugged. "It's amazing the things you don't notice when you're thirteen. Or maybe she just saw what she wanted to see. She seems to have a habit of that."

They turned down the bed together and started fluffing pillows and turning off lights.

"What was your parents' marriage like?" Kate asked after a minute.

"Distant. Hostile sometimes. They really didn't like each other. I've often wondered how they managed to have two children, though I suppose they were probably at least marginally happy when they were first married and I came along."

Kate asked the next question carefully. "Was your mother different with you before Jacqueline was born?"

He thought for a minute. "I suppose she was a bit. She was more involved. She would read to me," he said with a soft smile. "She read me *The Secret Garden* when I was five. She would sit on this little sofa in the nursery every night and we would cuddle under a quilt until I fell asleep. I'd forgotten about that." His voice faded out and he looked toward the window, blinking rapidly.

"Sounds lovely," Kate said quietly. She flipped the switch on the bedside lamp and climbed under the covers. "Come hold me, Will. My snuggle tank is low."

He smiled and climbed in beside her, spooning his knees behind hers and wrapping his arms around her, his face nuzzling her hair and neck.

"Goodnight, my Katie."

"Goodnight, my William."

**

The following week, Jacqueline and William made a tour of the old family home on the upper west side. Jacqueline needed to get her things out and Will needed to decide what he would do with it now that it was one hundred percent his. Neither had had the time recently to take a look, and of course they were both looking for reasons to avoid it. They knew it would stir up old memories, many unpleasant, and neither was eager to begin. But eventually, it couldn't be avoided, so one day Harper left work early and met his sister in the lobby of the Beresford. They gave each other identical looks of trepidation before taking the elevator up.

Most of the furnishings in the apartment were covered in sheets. After Mr. Harper Senior died, Harper spent the next year traveling to various offices all over the world, ensuring stock holders and CEOs that Taggston would continue to be a thriving conglomerate. He lived out of hotels except for when he was in London, where he spent roughly half his time. When he came back to New York to stay, he only lived in the apartment for six months before he and Jacqueline got in an enormous argument over how to handle some minor repairs. He wanted to just fix the problem, she wanted a full-scale renovation. Because they both owned it equally, neither could do anything. They agreed to disagree and she went back to England to finish college and he bought his own place. Everything in the Beresford was covered and loose items were packed until the siblings could agree on what to do with it.

Now, nearly four years later, they each had the feeling

that they were returning to the scene of a crime. Kate had suggested they do this without her, allowing the siblings some time to deal with their family issues. He was now feeling how utterly wrong that decision had been. He and Jacqueline needed some kind of buffer between them. He stepped away from his sister where she was looking under a sheet in the living room and sent Kate a text asking her to come as quickly as possible. He sent her the address and avoided his sister until his wife arrived.

"You didn't tell me you had a place in The Beresford!" Kate exclaimed when William opened the door for her fifteen minutes later. "I thought it was in just another swanky apartment building, not next door to Seinfeld."

"Seinfeld's actually three floors down," he said smoothly, guiding her into the living room. "Now, I need some help here."

"How do you mean?"

"I mean, I don't know what's happening. Are we looking through boxes? Who gets what? How do we decide? How do we not have another enormous row?"

"Okay, calm down. This is obviously a touchy situation. You said you wanted to air the whole thing out and go through things, right?"

"Yes, that was the original plan," he said, rubbing the back of his neck.

"Then why don't we start there? Let's remove all the coverings off the furniture in the living room. There aren't too many boxes in there and then you'll have a place to sit. Do you want to call a cleaning service to come in and give everything a good dusting?" She ran a hand over a side table and looked at the dust on her fingers.

"Yes, that's a good plan. I'm sorry, Kate. I thought this would be easy. We'd come in, look at a few boxes, she'd choose a few mementos to take back to England with her, we'd move on. I forgot how much stuff there was," he said looking at the boxes piled in the hall, "and I didn't count on how weird this would all be."

She rubbed his arm. "I know, babe. It's got to be bizarre

coming back after all this time. Why don't you ask Evelyn to get a cleaning service in here and I'll go find Jacqueline?"

He nodded and stepped away to make the call to his assistant while Kate went down a long hallway looking for her sister-in-law. Halfway down, a door on her right was open. She stepped inside and saw Jacqueline sitting on a pink tufted chair in the corner.

"Was this your room?" she asked softly.

Jacqueline startled and looked up. "Yes. It hasn't changed since I was a child. After Mother died, I was sent to school in England. I hardly came back here."

Jacqueline studied the bookshelf next to the chair, lost in her memories. Kate looked around quietly. Most of the furniture was covered in white sheets, but she could see that the bed had a canopy and the walls were a soft shade of pink. The floors were a light inlaid wood, a large carpet rolled up against one wall. The room was large with high ceilings and thick crown moldings, its bones very classical and almost regal-feeling.

"William is hiring a cleaning crew to come in and get the dust off everything. It will be easier to look through things that way," Kate said, feeling like she had to break the silence somehow. "I'll go see how he's getting on."

Jacqueline nodded in response and Kate backed out quietly, leaving the other woman to her memories. She found Will in the living room again, just hanging up the phone.

"That was Evelyn. A crew will be here first thing in the morning," he said. "It shouldn't take them more than a day or two to get everything cleaned and ready."

She nodded. He and Jacqueline both seemed to have slipped into awkwardness and she thought she should do something before the silence became oppressive.

"I'm starving. I haven't eaten since eleven. Do you two want to get some dinner?"

"Sure, that sounds fine," he said.

"Why don't you call Angelo's and see if we can get a table. Say twenty minutes out?"

He nodded again and she went to get Jacqueline who

was sitting in the same position she'd left her in. Shaking her head, she led both Harpers out the door and down the elevator. Being outside seemed to wake them up somewhat and dinner was subdued, but not as bad as she was afraid it would be.

Kate was not looking forward to cleaning out that apartment. If this was how they acted after only half an hour there, how would they cope with actually opening the boxes? A big part of her didn't want to know, but another was burning with curiosity.

Two days later, the apartment was clean and ready. Jacqueline had contracted a moving service that was going to ship everything she wanted to England for her. Kate suggested she start on her room since there was likely to be little argument over anything in there. William started in their father's study. Kate sent him in with two boxes, one marked 'William' for things he definitely wanted to keep, the other marked 'Optional' for things he thought Jacqueline might want or that he didn't care about either way.

Kate walked into the study looking for Will and found him sitting on a leather sofa, his elbows on his knees and his head in his hands. She walked over to him quietly and placed her hand on his shoulder.

"You alright, babe?" she asked.

He took a ragged breath and she felt his shoulders shake with the strength of it. He looked up at her with red eyes and a pale face. He just looked at her, not saying anything or even blinking.

"Baby?" she said quietly. She dropped to her knees and scooted between his legs, wrapping her arms around him and squeezing him tight. "What is it?"

"It was right there," he whispered.

"What?"

"My father. He died right there."

Kate pulled back horrified. "He died here? In this room?"

He nodded.

"Why didn't you tell me? Oh, William."

He shook his head. "We were talking about a deal with

the company, some new factory we wanted to buy out. It was late. He got a call, I don't remember who it was. They argued, he got mad and slammed the phone down, then he got this look on his face." Will opened and closed his mouth like he couldn't find the words. "The next thing I knew, he was on the floor and I was calling an ambulance. I held his hand and tried to keep his head up. I don't know why I did that." He shook his head. "But it didn't help. He was gone by the time they got here. And I was alone."

She kissed both his cheeks and embraced him tightly. After a few moments he hugged her back, squeezing her so forcefully she could hardly breathe.

"Do you want to go home?" she asked.

He nodded.

"Come on. I'll tell Jackie we're leaving."

Jacqueline didn't want to stay there alone, so the three of them left, Jackie to her family's brownstone and Kate and Will back to their apartment.

She told him she had the sudden urge to bake something and asked if he'd keep her company. So Will sat at the island in the kitchen, sipping a cup of tea and watching Kate roll out dough for a batch of cookies in the shape of gingerbread men.

Will gave her a tiny smile when she handed him several bowls of icing and a small knife and told him to get started decorating while she washed up. She watched him surreptitiously from the corner of her eye as she soaped up bowls and then made them each grilled cheese sandwiches and a small salad.

When she set a plate in front of him with a fork and napkin and a bottle of his favorite beer, she said nothing about the brown-eyed gingerbread man decorated in a dark grey suit or the one next to it that looked like Jacqueline. She looked more closely when she sat beside him and saw another in a lighter grey suit that looked like himself and a blonde woman in a blue dress with bright blue eyes; she assumed it was his mother. But nothing could prevent her surprise when she saw one with wavy brown hair and bright green eyes that looked suspiciously like herself.

**

After the fiasco in the study, Kate took over clearing out Will's family home. Luckily, she wasn't working many hours and with Ian Mellen in Scotland for the summer, she had the time to devote to it.

She sorted through his father's study and separated everything out as logically as she could given her lack of knowledge about the situation. Old business documents – the current ones had long been removed – were sent to Will's office at Taggston where he could look over them at leisure and decide what he wanted to do. Family documents – old school enrollment papers, notes about properties in other places – were sent to Will's study at home. The books she left in place, thinking Will would probably want them himself; she made a list of the titles and sent it to Evelyn. She left one family portrait of the four of them on the wall and had all the other art packed and crated and put into storage. She made a detailed list of what she put where, complete with pictures next to the description and a number for the box it was in.

The living room was easy; most of the pictures were photographs and she and Jacqueline decided the easiest thing to do was to have copies made of everything so they would each have one. While she was at it, Kate also hired an artist to copy two paintings of family members that she thought both siblings might want. Beyond the odd question or request for a photo, Jacqueline didn't seem to want much to do with the process.

The hardest room was their mother's personal sitting room. She had a desk with documents that were fairly easy to organize, but while Kate was sorting through a bookshelf, she found a few decorative boxes on the bottom shelf. She opened one and found an overstuffed white scrapbook. Opening it, she realized it was William's baby book.

There were a few photographs of his mother, young and pregnant and smiling, and a photograph of a nursery decorated in soothing colors with a red blanket in the crib. His date of birth, length and weight were all recorded. Kate smiled when she read that he'd weighed nine and a half pounds and had been twenty-two inches long. Further in, there were notes on all his achievements: rolling over, sitting up, eating solids for the first time. There was even a chart of teeth and the dates each of them came in.

One page showed a chubby smiling baby William covered in some sort of sauce and sat in a high chair, another showed him swinging in the park on a sunny day. The rest of the photos were William with his parents, a few with his cousins Teddy and Calvin, and several with older people she assumed were his grandparents. Next to the pictures, Cynthia had made short notes about the occasion or the people in them.

This continued for William's first three years of life and Kate put the book aside, planning to take it home and show it to her husband. Also in the box were two tiny keepsake boxes. One had several baby teeth in it, the other had a curling lock of baby hair tied in a blue ribbon. She set them aside to take home with her and moved on to the next box.

Three boxes of photo albums and random trinkets later, she opened the last box on the shelf and found a stack of leather books. Kate opened them to find a journal, the first date being 1980. She quickly closed the book and took the box over to the corner where she settled into the chair by the window. She knew she was snooping into things that weren't her business, but there was something she was curious about and she couldn't stop until she was satisfied.

She flipped through the first book, which only had entries every few weeks, until she got to the beginning of 1982. Kate scanned through the entries until she found what she'd been looking for. Cynthia Harper had just found out she was pregnant.

*

Kate kept the journals with her for a few days, trying to figure out what to do. She hadn't told either of the siblings about them. Partially because she thought they might come between them and damage an already fragile familial relationship, but also because she wasn't entirely sure about Jacqueline and she was afraid her sister-in-law might want them unequivocally herself and would then have ammunition on her brother, which Kate believed was unfair.

Cynthia Harper had been thrilled to find out she was expecting a child. She described her excitement for the future and her husband's happiness in the news. When Kate skipped ahead to the birth, she read of Cynthia's pride in providing the next heir to the family and her satisfaction in a job well done. Kate attempted to skip over the other woman's descriptions of her personal fears in an attempt to give her some modicum of privacy, but she read enough to know that Cynthia had felt enormous pressure to deliver a child, a male child, and that the birth of William had alleviated her fears that she would never be able to perform that particular task.

Cynthia described her baby's soft hair and dimpled cheeks and had many amusing anecdotes of what he said and did and how she liked to sneak into his room at night and sit and watch him sleep. She marveled that his first word had been been 'ball' as he pushed it to her across the carpet, and that he loved to suck on lemons and made the cutest scrunchy face when his mouth filled with sour juice. Kate thought that this was something that her husband needed to read and set it aside.

However, as the years went on, Cynthia's thoughts became more cynical. She spent more time complaining about her husband and less talking about her son. She resented her lack of influence and there was one particularly grueling argument recorded about William taking art classes. Cynthia thought he should take them – she thought he might have her gift for color and space – but James Harper was adamant. No Harper man wasted his time on such frivolous activities. Cynthia raged on about her husband's lack of understanding and culture and his small-mindedness for two pages, finally ending with a sad sense of resignation and a half-hearted wish that any future children be girls.

Eventually, Cynthia began wishing she had more children and longed for a daughter, someone she could teach everything she knew to and have more influence over. Kate rolled her eyes slightly, but it was clear the Harper marriage was crumbling and that Cynthia was a very unhappy woman.

One year, the Harpers went on a trip to Mauritius with friends to celebrate the other couples' anniversary. When they came back, Cynthia was pregnant with Jacqueline. Her happiness was once again splashed across the page. When the baby was born, her joy knew no bounds.

This was what Kate did not want William to read. While she had been happy with her first child and suitably impressed with her son, Cynthia was ecstatic about her daughter. She raved on and on about her precious little princess for pages, not mentioning her son at all for months at a time.

Years down the road, when William was a teenager, another argument with James was recorded. James wanted William to intern at the family firm that summer while Cynthia thought he should travel with her and her sister – they were taking a tour of the Greek islands on her sister's yacht and Cynthia wanted to take both of her children with her. From the looks of it, her sister Claudia doted on her children, having none of her own, and desperately wanted to spend the summer spoiling them and basking in their youthful affection.

James Harper adamantly put his foot down. It was time for William to begin learning the business. Greece wasn't going anywhere, he could go another time.

Cynthia made another plea the following year to allow William to spend the summer with her and her daughter at the beach house. She offered to compromise and do every other week or only the last half of summer, but again, James was unmoved. She made one last half-hearted plea before she gave up. She wrote one line that made Kate shiver. "*He's turning my sweet, artistic boy into a cold-hearted businessman and I can't bear to watch. I just can't.*"

William wasn't mentioned again for over a year.

The remaining journals were filled with Jacqueline and all the things she was doing – the riding show she was in, her music recitals, the shopping they did together. The two were clearly very close and Kate was afraid she was reading evidence of the parents using their children against each other. Cynthia seemed to have laid a claim on Jacqueline while James was completely in charge of William's upbringing.

Kate decided she would show Harper the journal that covered his mother's pregnancy and his early years. She thought it would do him good to see how he was happily expected and how much his mother loved him. She decided to wait on the others. Will was in a fragile emotional state when it came to his mother and she didn't think it was necessary to remind him how much Cynthia had favored his sister. If he asked her outright if there were more journals, she would tell him, but she wasn't going to offer up the information. One day, when he'd healed a little more and his relationship with his sister was a little more solid, she'd give him the rest of the journals, but today, she was sending them to storage.

The next afternoon, she placed the journal on his desk in the study with a note saying she thought he would find it interesting. Several hours later, she came home to find Will in the leather chair in the corner of the room, a blanket over his knees, reading his mother's journal.

"How's it going?" she asked tentatively.

"Hmm? Oh, it's great. I can't believe you found this," he said distractedly.

"Me neither." She watched him a minute longer, and when it was clear he wouldn't ask her anything else, she went to the bathroom to get ready for bed, trying to ignore the niggling feeling of guilt for not giving him the other volumes.

William finished the entire journal in three days. He read it in the car, between meetings, and during lunch at his desk. He couldn't believe this book had been within his grasp all these years and he'd never found it. It was edifying and confusing and terrifying all at the same time. He loved being inside his mother's head when she was pregnant, learning how she'd craved the most bizarre things including an insatiable desire for cinnamon and how she couldn't stand spicy food at all, when it had previously been a favorite. He smiled thinking about how he'd put cinnamon on everything as a child, including his jam sandwiches, and how to this day he didn't like spicy food. He wondered if her cravings had influenced him or if it had been the other way around. He liked thinking he had something in common with her, even if it was only a temporary pregnancy craving.

He thought there were probably more journals. If his mother wrote steadily for the three years covered in this one, she was unlikely to suddenly stop, but he trusted Kate and he suspected what was in the others: his parents' arguments, a narration of the steady decline of their marriage, her raptures over Jacqueline. He had no desire to read that and so he let it lie. Maybe one day, when he was feeling a little less adrift, he would read them, but for today, this was enough. It was more than enough really, and he basked in the peace he felt surrounding his relationship with his mother for the first time since his sister was born.

Four days after the first journal was laid on his desk, William found a sheet of paper in the same location. It was some sort of ledger for the storage unit. There was a box number highlighted and next to that, a small photo of several leather journals set neatly in a row. There was a post-it note on the paper written in Kate's handwriting.

Whenever you're ready, it read. He smiled and pocketed the note. He had more than enough.

***

Thanks to a very detailed pre-nuptial agreement (courtesy of her ever-careful brother), Jacqueline's divorce went fairly smoothly. Barring any unforeseen circumstances, she would be a free woman by mid-October. After a rejuvenating summer by the beach, she went back to Cyprus to take care of business there. William offered to go with her, but she said it was something she needed to do on her own. She put the hotel she'd renovated on the market and sold it quickly to another hotel in the area that was looking to expand. Albert kept their house there so he could continue to draw inspiration from the sea and the scenery. Jacqueline rolled her eyes and signed it over happily.

She went to London and stayed in her townhouse there,

the one she had inherited from her mother's family, and reconnected with her old friends in the area and spent time with her cousin Cece and various other family members that were often in the city. It didn't help that so few people expressed surprise on hearing about her divorce. It was not pleasant to realize everyone had seen coming what she'd never even considered. Her faith in men and in her own judgment had taken a beating, but she was determined that she would not let this define her life. She was entirely too stubborn for that and as Will had said, she was smart and young and had almost unlimited resources. What was stopping her from living a fulfilling life?

She researched going back to university to study architecture and eventually settled on a wonderful program right there in London. She enrolled for the January term and was happy to be moving on with her life and in a direction she was genuinely interested in, but she still felt all the humiliation of having been cheated on in such a blatant way.

She tried not to think about Albert and went through her entire collection of photographs and replaced his head with those of men in catalogs, an idea Kate had given her months ago. At first she felt silly doing it, but eventually the process became cathartic and she realized she had a beautiful life ahead of her and a pretty good one behind her, albeit a bit rocky. She would not let her cheating husband steal all her memories, hence replacing his face in the pictures. Doing this silly exercise eventually sent her into a flood of tears, only the second time she'd cried since the whole thing started in the spring, and once she'd wrung herself out, she realized she couldn't let him steal her future either.

So with great excitement and not a little trepidation, she bought her books and began studying a month before term started, just to prepare. She bought a new winter coat and a mustard colored hat – as close to cheerful as Jackie ever dressed – and even got her hair cut in a new angled bob that made her look very mod. Fresh and unencumbered, she was ready to pursue her new life, sans Albert De(fuck)Witt.

37
SUMMER FADES TO FALL

August
1 year, 4 Months Married

August eighth was a big day for Will. The merger that he had been working on for more than two years, that had kept him up nights and was so important he got married to avoid jeopardizing it, was complete. He and Kate went out with his colleagues who'd been involved and his cousin Calvin who was working the Covington side of things. They ate, drank, and made merry and didn't get home until dawn.

Without the merger hanging over his head and nothing new to launch, Harper was enjoying a pleasant lull and taking full advantage of it by spending plenty of time at the beach house and inviting his cousins to visit. Calvin only stayed a few nights, but Teddy and Caroline came with the baby and spent ten lovely days playing in the sand and soaking up the sun. Harper discovered his heretofore unknown talent for photographing children and took hundreds of pictures of young Thomas, who for some reason had taken an immediate like to Harper and smiled broadly every time the man came around.

After they'd stayed up late one night talking around the fire and laughing till their sides ached, Harper woke at his usual time. He was annoyed that he couldn't sleep in, but decided to get up and make a cup of coffee. The house was quiet and he tiptoed around the kitchen while he prepared coffee for himself and hot tea for Kate. He put the mugs on a small tray and took them to the bedroom.

Kate lay on her side, facing the opposite wall. He ran his hand slowly over her back where the sheet had drifted down, following her spine delicately and outlining her shoulder blades. She rolled onto her stomach and he saw her birthmark peeking from behind the sheet. He traced the outline of it gently. He'd wondered about it, had actually obsessed about it for a very memorable few hours, but had convinced himself that it was not his right to ask. Kate had shared her history with him and if she'd left something out, that was her right. He certainly hadn't told her the details about everyone he'd been with. Of course, that was because he couldn't actually remember their names and he was not in a working relationship with any of them. But now, they were so close, had gotten impossibly close this summer… Surely just asking wouldn't hurt?

Kate stirred.

"Good morning," she said groggily.

"Morning. Sleep well?"

"Mmhm. Is that orange tea I smell?"

"Yes. Be careful, it's hot."

She sat up and slowly brought the cup to her lips. She took a tiny sip and smiled.

"Tea in bed. What a brilliant idea."

He smiled again and looked away, slightly distracted.

"You sleep well?" Kate asked.

He nodded and made a sound she took as a yes. They drank quietly for a few minutes until Will broke the silence.

"Katie?" he said her name hesitantly.

"Yeah, babe?"

"How did Mark Basurto know about your birthmark?"

"What?"

"Your professor. In his book, the girl, she has a birthmark on her hip, just like yours." She was silent. "Did you two ever…" he trailed off, unable to voice his question.

She leaned forward and looked at him, brushing her hair behind her ear. "No, I never slept with Mark. Is that what you're trying to ask me?"

He nodded. "Did you," he hesitated, "come close?"

She touched the side of his face. "No, we never came anywhere near close." She smiled kindly. "We never kissed, I've never seen him naked, and he's definitely never seen me. Nothing remotely romantic has ever happened between us."

"Then how…?"

"He was bouncing ideas around. He wanted a distinguishing physical mark that only her lover would see. He was considering a tattoo at first, but I suggested the birthmark."

"So he's never even seen it?"

"He teased me about it and asked to see it, but I told him it would ruin the picture in his imagination."

"Hm." He felt a wave of relief wash over him. "Whose idea was it to call her his little flower? Yours or his?"

"Mine. Jeremy used to call me that."

"I'm sorry, I didn't mean to remind you," he stopped talking when she shook her head.

"It's okay. I can talk about Jeremy. I'm over it, really."

"Really? You're sure?"

"Yes, absolutely. I have been for a while now," she assured him.

"Good. I'm glad."

"How can I think about my old boyfriend when I have this hunk of a man next to me? And bringing me tea in bed, no less!" she teased, squeezing her arms around him and laying her head on his shoulder.

"Good answer." He smiled and let her pull him down next to her.

**

The next day, Caroline was feeling a bit funny and confessed to Kate that she was late for her period, but that because of the breast feeding she had been irregular and she'd taken two tests before, both negative, and didn't want to get her hopes up again. But with the recent bout of nausea, she thought this might be the real thing. Kate promised to sneak a test into the house without Teddy seeing, and so she found herself at the drug store one random Thursday morning, reading the labels of pregnancy test boxes and trying to discern which would be best. She finally settled on one that came with a simple to read plus or minus sign and four tests in the box in case one was a dud or something.

She put the bag on her dresser and joined the family for lunch, forgetting all about it. That afternoon, she went into the bedroom to change and found Will staring at something in his hand.

"Hey! Want to go for a swim? Teddy and Caroline and I are going to do some laps while the baby sleeps."

"Kate?" he said in a voice that sounded far away. "What's this?"

He held the pregnancy test box up to show her.

"Oh! You weren't supposed to see that! Caroline hasn't been feeling well and she thought she might be, but she didn't want to get Teddy's hopes up so she asked me to get the test for her. I haven't snuck it into her bathroom yet."

"So this isn't for you?"

"No! Oh, you thought I was – no, no I'm not! Everything's regular and working and – if you want me to pee on one just to be sure, I will. There are four in the box, Caroline won't mind," she rambled, scared by the strange look she saw on his face.

"You're positive you aren't?"

"Well, not one hundred percent. Anything can happen, but I did just have my period last week and I use contraceptive, so I seriously doubt it."

He nodded silently and gingerly set the box back on the bureau. He was surprised at how he felt slightly disappointed. *It's probably just being around Teddy's family, it's nothing.*

"You okay?" she asked.

"Yeah, fine. Don't worry, I won't say anything to Teddy."

"Thanks."

Caroline's test the next morning was positive. She was so nervous she made Kate read the result for her. She couldn't quite believe it, so she made Kate take one to make sure the pack wasn't bad (Kate's was negative) and just in case, she took another after breakfast that was also positive, and another after lunch with the same result. She told Teddy that afternoon while Thomas was sleeping and Kate was listening for the monitor.

That night at dinner, Teddy joyfully told Will that he would be a father of two in the spring. Harper opened a bottle of champagne and toasted his cousins eloquently. The whole party was merry and relaxed and filled with hopeful joy. Harper was only slightly discontent and told himself repeatedly that he was not jealous, rather just feeling his age and the usual urge to settle down, nothing more.

***

In September, Watson recommended Kate to an author who only needed minor help. The author was another scientist, Carol Winger, but she had some sort of weird specialty with food and was writing a 'cookbook for geeks,' as she called it. She referred to all her recipes as formulas and came at the entire thing from the point of view of a chemist. Kate loved her immediately.

As the months went on, she put in fewer and fewer hours at Taggston and took on two more authors, which was exactly how she wanted it. She thought it was smartest to maintain a good working relationship with Taggston Publishing, but the less time spent on site, the better. That way, it would be less likely for them to ask her to leave after the divorce.

Somehow, and she wasn't quite sure how this had happened, she'd become a sort of scientist-literature liaison. All her years tutoring had taught her how to teach people to write and her quick mind guaranteed that she understood the complex subjects while her lack of experience in the field helped her know when something needed to be explained more simply. By the time November rolled around, she was working with five of Taggston's non-fiction authors, four of them scientists and the other an engineer. Some required a lot of her time, like Ian Mellen, while others only needed to meet with her once a week for a couple of hours.

She had quit doing extra work for Mr. Watson, which had just been overflow for him anyway, and was putting in between thirty and forty hours a week, which was just what she wanted. The hours were flexible and erratic, sometimes working late into the night when one of her authors was feeling the muse, and other times she would have an entire day to herself. It suited her perfectly and she felt like she had really found her niche.

In October, they escaped to Valhalla to celebrate Will's birthday a little early. The actual day was November tenth, but they didn't want the beach to be too cold. They were only able to get away for five days, but it was worth the trouble. The days were a little shorter and a lot cooler, but still beautiful and absolutely idyllic. Kate felt no small amount of guilt for basically ignoring Will's birthday the year before thanks to their (what she now called) ridiculous argument.

This time, Kate made sure his birthday was memorable in all his favorite ways and Will promised to turn off his phone and electronic devices the entire time. All in all, it was a lovely holiday that ended entirely too soon, as all truly lovely holidays do.

When she left Valhalla, she had the sense that she was locking something away, like it was a secret place just for them, holding her memories tightly behind its locked doors. Here, he wasn't a business mogul and she wasn't his hired wife. They were just two people who genuinely liked each other and enjoyed one another's company, sharing a beautiful place and a few stolen moments.

***

"What do you want to do for Thanksgiving?" Will asked in early November. "Are we going to your parents' again?"

"Actually, I was thinking about doing something different. What do you think about hosting Thanksgiving here?" He looked surprised. "We've never hosted a holiday or anything together and we already promised your sister that we would go to London for Christmas. This might be our last Thanksgiving together, and I thought, I don't know, it might be a nice memory to have." She looked down uncomfortably and waited for him to answer.

"I like that idea." She looked up and smiled. "Were you thinking here or in the Hamptons?"

"Well, it probably depends on who's coming. We can fit two people in the guest bedroom," that's what they now called her old bedroom since she'd never moved out of Harper's, "two more in my den, and we could even set up an air mattress or something in your study if we needed to."

Harper pulled a face. "If your family comes, some of them could stay with Jen and Jamison. No need to put anyone of the floor." He said it so distastefully Kate had to laugh.

"They wouldn't be sleeping on the dirt! It would be a perfectly comfortable air mattress, and we would only do that for the young people like my sisters. My aunt and uncle could take the bedroom."

"If you think that many people would be coming, maybe we should do it at the beach house. It sleeps twenty and we could probably fit more if we needed to. And Jamison's place is just up the beach and has three guest rooms."

"It doesn't even have a dining table, just that little one in the kitchen."

Will sighed dramatically. "I guess you'll have to go shopping. Poor you!"

She laughed. "Very funny. Do you think it will be cold and ugly out there this time of year?"

"No uglier than it is in the city." She nodded agreement. "And there are plenty of evergreens around, so it should still have some color to it."

"Okay, so we're decided then? Thanksgiving at the beach house?"

"It's a plan."

Two hours later Harper walked into the living room to find Kate on the phone with her mother.

"I know, Mom… I know… I think so, too…. I know no place is as magical as a Christmas tree farm! – No, that's not what I'm trying to do… No one is trying to replace you! – Mom, just stop and listen for a minute, alright? Will and I bought a new beach house – Yes I did tell you about it! When we talked back in July. I said Will gave the family place to his sister and we bought a new one... Fine, whatever, that's not the point. What I'm saying now is that we have this big place and we've never hosted a holiday together and it's hard for everyone to travel for Christmas with all the activities and hauling the presents and everything, so it made sense to do Thanksgiving. Next year we'll be back at your place – I mean home, of course I still think of it as home! I just have another home here, in New York, with Will... You can go back Saturday morning, or even Friday… I know the train takes all day, maybe you can fly… I know the airports are crazy… No, I wouldn't want to get stranded for hours either… Maybe we can work something out. Just let me try for a little bit, alright? Thanks, Mom. Love you, too. Talk soon. Bye."

She sighed loudly and set the phone down.

"Rough chat?"

"Ugh! My mother! She thinks I'm trying to steal her holiday and usurp her position as hostess."

"All part of your evil plan to take over the world?" he asked.

"Exactly. Starting with Thanksgiving dinner." She rubbed her forehead. "She finally agreed, though. She is right about the trains taking all day and commercial airlines will be insane. Do you think we could send the plane down and bring everyone here at once? Would it be a huge difference in cost?"

"Probably not much, depending on how many people come. We could tell them you chartered a plane for less. People do it all the time."

"You're a brilliant and devious man, William Harper."

He just smiled.

**

In the end, they had a houseful of people. Caroline and Teddy arrived on Saturday and stayed with them in the city at first, then the women drove out to the beach house together Tuesday morning with the baby while the men spent the morning at the office, then picked up the family from the airport.

Kate and Caroline went through the house carefully, making sure that everything was ready for their guests.

"I can't believe I'm about to have my first American Thanksgiving!" Caroline enthused. "Who all is coming?"

"My mother and father, Jenny and Andrew, my little sisters Heather and Tiffany – Heather is quiet but really nice, and Tiffany is a tornado but sweet and great with kids if you need any help with Thomas. My grandmother Bishop is coming – you'll love her," she continued counting on her fingers, "my mother's brother David and his wife Michelle and their three children. My cousin Mary is coming with her four kids – her husband has to work – and I think that's it. We tried to get Calvin to come but he said he couldn't make it, especially with Teddy out of the office."

"Which is code for 'I met a hot red head'," Caroline laughed. "Wow! I don't know how I'll keep all the names straight but it sounds like it will be heaps of fun."

"It always is. I'm just glad we have the bunk room for the kids! I don't know how we'd fit everyone otherwise."

The Bishop clan arrived with a bang late Tuesday night. William had rented two vans to accommodate them. He drove one with Teddy, Mary and her four children, while David drove the other with his wife, their three children, Heather and Tiffany. Jenny and Andrew met them at the airport and brought Jen's parents and grandmother in Andrew's Land Rover.

By the time they got to the house, they all looked a little worse for the wear, but Tiffany was full of excitement about the trip and the private plane and shopping in the city on black Friday and anything else she could think of. Her father was accompanying her on two college tours on Wednesday, another thing she simply could not stop talking about. Heather thanked Kate for making the travel plans and quietly said it was exciting to ride in a private plane, then went into the kitchen to help.

Loretta took one look at the house and pinched Kate's cheek, quietly telling her she'd done well for herself. Kate flushed but knew her mother meant well and introduced her to Caroline. As soon as Loretta found out Caroline ran a store, she began talking to her about her little Christmas shop and how she'd thought about expanding and adding a tea shop onto it or even turning the house into a bed and breakfast once all her children had moved out. Caroline was kind and to Kate's surprise, got really into the conversation and gave Loretta some sound advice about inventory tracking systems. At one point, she heard Caroline taking sales advice from Loretta with rapt attention. She just shook her head in amazement and kept tending to her guests.

They all set to work on the pies Wednesday afternoon. They made chocolate and chess, pumpkin, apple, and cherry. There was also a carrot cake and the traditional layered banana pudding. Loretta made blueberry pies from berries she had grown on her farm, frozen, and brought with her. Caroline had continued learning how to cook after Kate had taught her a few things last year, and she was quickly brought into the fold. Loretta taught her how to make a blackberry pie, an experience Caroline was clearly eating up. She showed her how to make the perfect lattice top and to cut out little holly leaves made out of dough to decorate the corners.

By the time they were finished, Loretta had invited Caroline to the farm to see her store and told her she could choose whatever ornament she wished. Caroline smiled and promised to come.

The men stayed clear of the kitchen that evening, sitting in front of the television with beers while they supposedly kept their eyes on the children. Teddy was the only man there who really knew where his was, though – likely because little Thomas was sleeping in his arms.

On Thursday, Will was one of the first to arrive in the kitchen. Kate had gotten him a full sized red apron with "Good lookin' is cookin'" written on the front in big black letters. He had researched dishes he could cook this year, determined to make his own without any help from anyone else. He'd chosen an English stuffing – very appropriate, he thought – and set to work in a corner of the spacious kitchen.

Kate had bought a table that comfortably seated sixteen and could squeeze in a couple more. She figured they'd often have large groups out here and that it would come in handy. The older girls were having a great time setting it and placing tiny pumpkins and gourds down the center and special miniature white pumpkins next to each place and sticking them with nametags that looked like flags.

Looking around the kitchen at all her family making food, Teddy carefully braiding the bread Will had done last year, Caroline getting more instruction from her mother, and her sweet husband checking his stuffing in the oven, Kate felt a few moments of pure bliss before the realization that this was probably the last time they would do this slammed into her. It was so strong she lost her breath for moment and grabbed the counter to steady herself. *Don't think about it, Katie. Be here, now. Think about it tomorrow.* She took a sip of her wine and stirred the gravy.

Dinner went off without a hitch. Nothing was burnt and everyone talked and drank a little too much wine and stuffed themselves with pie. They laughed till their sides hurt and collapsed onto sofas and easy chairs then all went to bed early.

Friday afternoon, Kate's family piled back into the vans to go to the airport and head home to Virginia, Tiffany and Loretta with several bags from their shopping expedition earlier that day, and the children excitedly chattering about all the things they had seen and done. Kate waved them off and headed back inside the house where they would stay with Teddy and Caroline and baby Thomas until Sunday afternoon. Kate plopped down on the sofa next to Caroline and put her feet on the coffee table. Thomas was asleep and the men wouldn't be back from the drop-off for a couple of hours.

"Tired?" Caroline asked.

"Yup. I am really looking forward to just relaxing the rest of the weekend. How are you feeling? How's the baby?"

Caroline caressed her growing belly softly. "We're both just fine. She's been kicking a lot more lately. I think she's had a growth spurt."

"How far along are you now? Five months?" Caroline nodded. "And you think it's a girl?"

"I have a feeling. But I would be happy with a boy. Thomas would have a lifelong playmate and it would take some pressure off him down the road."

"You mean like with the business?"

"Yes. And the title and all of that. The earldom is passed through male heirs, so Teddy will inherit the title and properties, etc. when his father passes on, and on to Thomas. But there has always been Calvin to give Teddy a little leeway, you know? Like if he only had daughters, he knew his brother could inherit, or if he had no children at all."

Kate shook her head. "Now that's what you call a first world problem," she teased and Caroline shoved her arm playfully while she laughed along. "But I do see your point. Our father was the only son of his parents and I know he would have liked to have had a son to carry on the name."

"Will one of your sisters keep it and give it to her children, maybe?"

"Perhaps. Heather might. We'll just have to wait and see." She shrugged and leaned her head back on the cushion.

"When do you think you and William will have children?" Caroline asked.

Kate stared at the ceiling. "I don't know. Not any time soon. I'm just getting my career established and we're still pretty new as a couple. It's not like we dated for years before we got married, you know?"

"Yeah, I can see how that would make a difference. Teddy and I dated for nearly four years before we married, then it was three more before we got pregnant, and we're older than you two. I'd forgotten how much younger you are than me. You've got plenty of time." She squeezed Kate's knee and rose from the sofa. "I'm going to get ready for bed."

Kate said goodnight and continued sitting where she was, watching the fan go round and round and round in the vaulted ceiling. *Plenty of time.*

The thought ran through her mind and for the first time,

she thought about her life in terms of her biological clock. She was twenty-four now, she would be twenty-five in the spring, and the divorce was planned for next autumn. She would likely stay single for a while before she even started dating anyone, as much for appearances as for her own preferences. Then who knew how long it would take to find a man she liked and could love and would be a good husband and a good father and respect her and take her seriously even though she liked to cook. Not to mention someone she could actually live with without wanting to strangle.

No, she didn't think she'd be having children any time soon, likely not until she was thirty at least. She sighed and got up to head to her room. It would have been nice to have kids close in age to Caroline's and Mary's so they could play together. But who was she kidding? She would probably see very little of Caroline after the divorce, so it was a moot point anyway. Suddenly feeling very sad, Kate ran a hot bath and sank into it while she waited for Will to get home and comfort her as only he could.

38
TIT FOR TAT

January
1 Year, 9 Months Married

On a cold, mid-January afternoon, Kate sat at a table in a Ukrainian café in the west village waiting for Sheila to arrive. After waiting for ten minutes and getting through the next two chapters of the book she was reading, a harried Sheila plopped into the seat across from her, bags bustling as she tried to stuff them under her chair.

"Rough day?" Kate asked.

Sheila unwound her scarf and hung her coat on the back of her chair. "You can say that again. I hate the PTA!"

"The parent teach association? What happened?"

Sheila groaned. "There's this big fundraiser coming up next week – fancy dinner, silent auction, typical stuff." Kate nodded. "Every parent was supposed to contribute something to the auction. Well, several somethings, but they can come from anywhere. So I went around to the local businesses and asked them to donate gift certificates or items to the auction."

"Sounds good."

"Not so fast! I brought them to this morning's meeting and *Piper Sanders*," she said scathingly, "head of fundraising, said my contributions were not enough."

"What? Why not?"

"They didn't have enough 'monetary value' and weren't likely to bring in extra bids. For the first time, the auction is available online this year, too. They were hoping to get some really good stuff and advertise it around – social media, networking, etcetera – and get some bidders that aren't connected to the school. Apparently my 'little gift certificates' were thinking too small," she said bitterly.

"Ouch. What are you going to do?"

"I have no idea." She put her head in her hands on the table, corkscrew curls spilling over her fingers. "I have two days to come up with something brilliant and I don't have a clue where to start."

"Don't private schools have enough money? I mean, isn't that what they charge tuition for?"

"Apparently not." She raised her head and looked at her friend. "They want to build a new gymnasium and the fundraiser also supports the scholarship programs, which are really great, but right now I just want to scream. I don't know why I wanted to join this committee in the first place. I let all those snooty moms make me feel guilty for not being more involved in the school and now look at me! I'm a wreck!"

"You are not a wreck! You're just stressed," Kate said soothingly.

"And I'm supposed to sell ten of these stupid tickets to this stupid dinner." She waved a white rectangle in front of her. "You don't want to buy one, do you?" she asked hopefully.

"Would I actually have to go to the dinner?"

"I don't care. Give the ticket to a homeless guy or a cop or somebody who needs a nice dinner. Just buy one!"

Kate laughed at her friend's desperate expression. "Alright, I'll buy one. How much are they?"

"Ninety-five dollars."

"For dinner? Geez, no wonder you're having trouble selling them."

"And admittance to the auction," Sheila said with a smile as she pocketed Kate's cash and handed her a ticket.

"So you pay to get the chance to spend more money. Perfect."

Sheila ignored her last comment. "Now I just have to figure out something amazing to auction off."

"What sort of things are they looking for?"

"Anything, really. There have been a few historical or artistic items; a local painter donated a small piece and some prints, a parent is giving a first edition of some famous book."

"Careful, people might suspect you're a lit major."

"Ha ha." She threw her friend a look and took a bite of her varenyky. "There have been a lot of experiences. A day at a spa, a weekend at some posh cabin, that sort of thing."

"Sounds tough. Good luck." Kate smiled sympathetically.

"Thanks."

**

The next day, as Kate sat in her den going over notes from one of her authors, Sheila called.

"Hello?" she answered.

"I've got it!"

"Hello to you, too. I'm fine, a little busy with work, but otherwise doing well."

"Hi, how are you? Now listen! I know what I can sell in the auction!"

"That's great! What is it?"

"Well, I was doing a little research and I saw that in other auctions, unique experiences were the biggest sellers. Like lunch with an influential businessman or a famous actor or something. Give people a chance to pick their brain and find out something no one else knows."

"Sounds good. Who do you know? Or is Peter a fancy enough lawyer that he'll do?"

"Actually, I was thinking about William."

"William? My William?"

"Yes. Do you think he would do it?"

"Have you met William? He hates strangers! He hates business lunches! And I'm pretty sure he would hate being sold at auction."

"He wouldn't be sold! It's not a bachelor auction. Quit being dramatic! It would just be a little lunch, in public, with a time limit. He could even make it coffee in his office or an hour some random afternoon. Whatever it is, I think it'll be a huge hit."

"Do you really think so?"

"Is that a serious question? This is William Harper we're talking about here! He has controlling interest in Taggston Incorporated, one of the biggest conglomerates in THE WORLD. The WORLD, Katie. Not just the city or the state or even the country."

"Alright, alright, I get it, he's a big deal. I still don't think he'd do it, even if you told him how important he is."

"I could throw in smart and handsome."

"He hates flattery."

"I'll make him tamales. And green enchiladas. What does he want? I'll do anything!"

"It's like you said, Sheila. He's William Harper. If there's something he wants, he's probably already got it."

Sheila sighed. "So you won't give me his number?"

"No, but I know that wouldn't stop you. I'm pretty sure Peter has it, anyway. I'll ask him, but that's all I can promise."

Sheila thanked her and hung up the phone. Wanting to get her promise over with, Kate quickly called William.

"Hey babe," Harper answered his phone as he was walking out of the conference room, Evelyn walking swiftly beside him with a stack of papers.

"Hey. Do you have a minute?"

"A quick minute." He paused to listen to Evelyn tell him something about the meeting they'd just left. "What's up?"

"I just talked to Sheila and she is involved with this fundraiser dinner and silent auction at her son's school and she needs help. I already bought a ticket," he whispered instructions to Evelyn with his hand over the receiver as they reached her desk, "but she needs to contribute to the auction itself. She wants to sell a lunch or coffee meeting or something with you and let someone pick your amazing business brain."

His hand was over the speaker again. "Tell them I want to see those revised contracts on my desk by noon tomorrow, and book Wells for first thing in the morning, tell him I want to see more numbers before we decide anything," he told Evelyn. He turned his attention back to the phone. "Sure, it's a good cause. Tell Sheila we'll be there. I've really got to go, Kate. See you tonight. I'll be home late."

"Okay, bye."

Kate hung up the phone and stared at it for a minute. Had he really just agreed to be part of the auction? She quickly shot Sheila a text, who sent one back saying she was doing a victory dance and that snotty Piper Sanders was going to shit a brick.

Before she could reply, Ian Mellen called to tell her about his latest epiphany and she found herself trekking across town to his lab where she stayed charting and sketching his latest ideas with him until after ten o'clock that night. By the time she got home, Will was in bed and half asleep. Exhausted herself, she got ready for bed quietly and joined him.

**

The night of the school auction and dinner, Kate and Will had committed to a dinner party at the home of one of the Taggston board members, so they didn't attend Sheila's big event. Kate bought a second ticket and gave the pair of them to Angie who went with her latest boyfriend.

After supper, Kate checked her phone in the restroom. Sheila had sent her several texts telling her how shocked the other moms had been at her great find, how Piper Sanders didn't actually believe she'd gotten such a Big Important Person to participate in their little school auction, and how she was reveling in the glory of it all. Angie was sending texts commenting on the huge numbers she was seeing on the auction sheet in front of William's prize, and commenting on how the Facebook page was blowing up with people fighting each other to get a crack at coffee with William.

Kate laughed and rejoined the other guests. It was another twenty minutes before the party wrapped up and Kate and William said goodbye to their hosts and began the ten-block walk back to their apartment. They walked hand in hand along the dark streets, their breath making clouds in front of them as they went.

"So you're very popular," she said after two blocks of comfortable silence.

"What?"

"The auction. Sheila and Angie have been texting me about it all night. So far you're over twelve thousand dollars."

"What are you talking about?" he asked, stopping and facing her under a street light.

"Sheila's auction, at her son's school. Remember?" she said, a horrible feeling growing in the pit of her stomach. "I asked you about it last week, you said sure because it was for a good cause."

"Auction? Me? I'm sorry, Kate, I'm completely confused. What's going on?" His voice was firm and had a hard edge to it. He looked at her with his hands in his pockets, waiting for a response.

Kate squared her shoulders, resumed walking, and spoke plainly. "Sheila is on the fundraising committee for Simon's school. She was desperate for ideas for something to put in the auction. She said the most successful items were lunches or coffee or something with important people. She asked if you would do it and I told her I thought you would hate the idea, but she bugged me so much that I said I would ask, but not to count on it. When I called you, you said sure and that you thought it was for a good cause and to tell Sheila we'd be there. Of course we couldn't be there because we were already committed to this dinner, but a coffee meeting with you was still on the auction block."

"I thought she wanted us to buy tickets to the dinner, not sell me at auction!" he exclaimed.

"I didn't know that! I clearly told you what she wanted, you agreed."

"I was distracted! I didn't hear you properly."

"If you can't talk, don't answer your phone!"

"It was you! Of course I answered it! What if it had been something important?"

She smiled and tugged his hand out of his pocket,

holding it between both of hers. "I'm really sorry, baby. You can sign me up for an auction next time. I'll have lunch with whoever you want."

He looked at her skeptically. "I don't know about this, Katie. Is there any way to get out of it?"

"I don't think so. The auction ends in half an hour and Sheila will be completely humiliated if you pull out now. The only way to get out properly would be for me to buy you, and that would sort of defeat the purpose," she reasoned.

He looked hopeful and asked, "How would that defeat the purpose?"

"Well, they are trying to get more publicity for their fundraising efforts. If it's widely known that you were part of this one, and if the person who wins tells about it, and everyone sees and hears about it, it might encourage other business people or celebrities or whoever to do the same. The next auction will be more successful. Plus, the winners are published and it would look ridiculous, not to mention be super embarrassing, if it was known that I bought you."

They walked half a block in silence. "So, coffee?"

"You hate to eat with strangers, so I told her to make it simple. You have coffee with someone, you decide where, and spend one hour with them, no more." She peeked at him from the side, wondering what he was thinking.

"What do we do on this coffee date?"

"They can talk to you, ask questions, maybe get advice. Maybe they just absorb your amazingness." He shot her a doubtful look. She gave him a sweet smile and batted her lashes.

He sighed. "I guess I don't have much choice. But I won't forget this, Ms. Bishop," he said. She could see the quirk in his brow so she wasn't as worried as she usually was when he called her that. "You owe me. Big time."

"Me? Sheila is the one you're doing the favor for! Why doesn't she owe you?"

"Because she's *your* friend and *you're* the one who asked me when I was clearly distracted. And," he leaned down to whisper in her ear, "you're the one I want."

She looked at him in shock for a moment before realizing they were in front of their building. He quickly tugged her inside before she could respond.

**

In mid February, two weeks after the auction, Harper sat in his office listening to Evelyn run through his schedule and newly received invitations.

"Shall I book you at your normal hotel, then, sir?"

"Yes. Just the one night. I want to get out of there as soon as possible."

"Alright. You've also received an invitation to Mitzi Stanfield's annual fundraiser. It's the twelfth of March. Shall I forward it to Mrs. Harper?"

He leaned back in his chair and thought for a moment. "No, don't forward it and don't send anything to Mitzi. I'll take care of it myself." He extended his hand for the embossed invitation. Evelyn looked surprised for a moment, but quickly schooled her features and handed it to her boss. "That will be all for now, Evelyn. Thank you."

"Yes, sir."

After Evelyn had gone, Harper sat tapping the invitation on the edge of his desk, an idea forming in his mind. Every March, Mitzi Stanfield held an odd sort of talent-show style fundraiser to benefit the local cancer society. She invited every well-heeled, blue-blooded person in the tri-state area, and those who had any kind of talent, and some that had none, performed for the audience. Everyone voted on their favorite and the winner got some ridiculous trophy and bragging rights until the next spring when it all started again. Last year he had been out of town, so they hadn't attended. The year before that he'd gone, but Kate hadn't been in his life at the time. His mind made up, he quickly made the call.

Later that week, Kate was looking through the mail when she saw something unfamiliar addressed to her. Ripping it open, she read the letter with increasing confusion.

"Babe?" she called down the hall and stepped into

William's study. "I just got the strangest letter. Do you know someone named Mitzi Stanfield?" she asked.

"Yes. Why?" he replied, turning around in his chair to face her.

"She's sent me a dress rehearsal schedule and says I need to get my back-up music to the sound guy by March eighth. What back-up music? What is she talking about?" She handed him the letter.

"Oh, this. I signed you up for Mitzi's annual fundraiser. It's a talent show of sorts. If you win, you get a big trophy." He raised his brows and smiled, then turned back to his desk.

Kate was silent for a moment. "You did what?" she asked.

"I signed you up-"

"I heard that part!" She grabbed his shoulder and pulled him around to face her again. "Why on earth would you do that?"

"I seem to recall you saying I could auction you off to whomever I wanted," he said with a thoughtful expression, not the least bit put off by her manner.

She stepped backward, a look of horror on her face. "Oh, no. You're getting revenge!"

"I like to think of it as evening the playing field."

"What? That doesn't even make sense!" He shrugged. "You getting auctioned off was an accident. I thought you agreed to it. You deliberately did this to me without my permission!" she said angrily.

He shrugged again. Kate was beginning to find it a maddening gesture. "Don't worry, baby. I'm sure you'll be great."

She clenched her jaw and glared at his smirking face. "DON'T call me baby!"

She turned and stormed out of the room, ignoring Will's laughter behind her. She quickly grabbed her keys and went for a walk, fuming the first three blocks.

She knew his coffee date had gone badly, but revenge just seemed so… petty. There was another voice in her head telling her it was also pretty funny, not to mention a great way to deter her from volunteering him for things in the future, but still, she was not happy about this. So the guy he'd had coffee with had turned out to be an obsequious, sweaty little man who'd spent the entire hour pitching Harper on his latest 'great idea', but it was one hour. She was going to have to spend hours rehearsing for this, and then perform in front of hundreds of people she barely knew and didn't particularly like. What song would she even do?

When she got home from her walk she went straight to her old room and locked the door behind her. She was too mad to face Will without saying things she would later regret, so she kept her distance.

When Will heard her come in, he waited to hear her voice calling to him or to at least hear her stomping about in the kitchen. He didn't. He came out of his study and looked around, wondering where his wife was. He noticed her old bedroom door was shut and he saw a light shining in the crack underneath. He felt a moment of panic, wondering if he'd gone too far, and had to stop himself from turning the handle to see if it was locked.

No, she'll come out when she's cooled off, he told himself. He pushed down the gnawing fear in his gut and went to the kitchen to eat dinner. Kate had put some sort of layered dish in the crock pot. He spooned himself a generous helping and sat down, waiting for his wife to join him. When she never came out, he got ready for bed on his own. When she wasn't reflected in the mirror beside him as he brushed his teeth, he felt inexplicably alone. He climbed into bed on his side and read for a bit, hoping Kate would come in.

She never did.

He was left to wonder if perhaps he'd crossed a line. He had thought the whole thing would be a good joke. She'd performed without any preparation in Farmington their first Thanksgiving together. She had just gotten up and sung, and sung well. Of course it never occurred to him that those were musicians she'd been singing with her entire life, in front of people she'd known her entire life, in an environment she was completely familiar with and comfortable in.

He didn't think she might not enjoy putting herself on display for people who were often critical and sometimes hostile to her, nor that she might see him doing this to her as a sort of punishment suitable for an errant child. No, he did not think any of that. He simply thought that she had put him in an awkward position and he would do the same to her. His experience had had its funny side – he'd certainly relished telling the tale to Kate – and hers would, too.

But he couldn't stop himself from thinking that maybe his actions had been just a little vindictive. She hadn't meant to put him in an uncomfortable position, but he had certainly meant to do exactly that to her. An uncomfortable feeling of guilt swept through him and he told himself that if she said anything about it, he'd apologize. If it was really a problem, he'd call Mitzi and get her out of it.

Kate was not prone to long bouts of anger or anxiety, so she quickly began working out a plan. If Will thought he was so clever, she would show him that two could play that game. He might have meant to make her do something embarrassing, but she would show him that Katherine Bishop always rises to the occasion.

She spent the evening looking up songs and making a plan. She quickly drafted Sheila into singing back-up for her, since she was the one who had gotten Kate into this mess in the first place, and Jenny, being the amazingly supportive big sister that she was, agreed to take the other part. She put a call in to Mitzi Stanfield and asked her to place her husband on the front row where she could easily access him. Mitzi tittered at being in on a surprise for one of her guests and promised Kate that Harper would be at a table front and center.

The next morning, Harper walked in to the kitchen to find Kate making pancakes.

"Good morning!" she said happily. She quickly flipped a pancake and began filling a plate with bacon and eggs. "Here you go, sweetie." She set the plate on the bar on the island and went back to her pancakes.

"Thanks," he said suspiciously. "What are your plans today?" He didn't want to ask why she hadn't slept with him last night; he knew why, and he hated arguing. Best to avoid the whole thing unless she brought it up.

"I'm meeting an author at eleven and then I have to meet with an editor at Taggston at four-thirty. I'll probably be there pretty late; do you want to go to dinner from there?"

"Sure. That sounds good." He was still watching her carefully, but she seemed completely back to normal, if a little saccharine. "Where are we going?"

"It's your turn to pick."

"Is it just us?" he asked.

"We can ask Jenny and Andrew if they want to join us if you want. I haven't seen Andy in weeks."

"I'll see him later today and mention it. Let's say Le Cirque at seven. Will you be done by then?"

"Yeah, I should be done by six-thirty. I'll text Jen and come by your office when I'm finished with my meeting."

"Great."

They ate their meal in silence, Will reading the news on his tablet while Kate read the latest chapters her author had sent her. They said goodbye distractedly and parted ways for the day.

**

Kate spent the next few weeks working on her routine, as she had come to call it. Jenny and Sheila were dancing and singing back-up, and Andy, Peter and Sheila's son Simon had often played audience for them while they practiced, working hard to get it right. It ended up being a lot of fun, like memorizing dance moves to their favorite songs when they were kids, but she wasn't about to tell Will that.

Eventually, it was the big day and Kate arrived early at the venue. It was a large ballroom with a stage at one end and a wooden dance floor in the center with tables around three sides. She joined Sheila and Jen and they took their places in the green room. They were the second performers to go on, so they wouldn't be mingling beforehand. The show was divided into three parts. The first happened during appetizers, then there was a break for more mingling and congratulating and a little dancing while the band played, then the main course was served and the second, longest act came on. More mingling and dancing, then finally dessert was served accompanied by the third and shortest act. It was basically a really fancy and expensive dinner theater, or at least that was how Kate had come to think of it.

They could hear the sound of laughter and voices from their places backstage, which was really just a small conference room next to the ballroom with the hall shielded by a curtain. The first act was called and Kate held hands with Jenny and Sheila, all three saying a quick prayer and wishing each other luck. Before they knew it, the stage manager was calling them out.

The lights were dimmed and Kate took her place in the center, Jenny on her right and Sheila on her left. The three of them stood with their backs to the audience, lights dark. The music started and they bounced one hip to the rhythm, the spotlights coming on a few beats in. Jen and Sheila began snapping their fingers to the side in time with their hips, long hair streaming down their backs and swaying with their movement.

Finally, Kate turned her head over her shoulder and began singing, red lips forming the opening lines to *Hey, Big Spender*. The crowd went wild when they realized what she was singing. She turned to face the audience and sashayed around, one long perfect leg reaching out through the slit in her blood red gown. The three women moved in perfect time down the steps of the small stage and onto the dance floor, Jenny and Sheila moving to the sides while Kate walked directly toward her husband, moving her hips seductively and singing every line slowly and perfectly. Before she got to him she backed up, meeting her partners in the center. Together they kicked and turned and sang the chorus in perfect harmony.

The lyrics rang out clearly through the ballroom, followed by the whoops of a few men, likely egged on by Andy and Peter who were the designated cheerleaders of the night. The three of them continued to strut around the room, two of them meeting and sliding downwards back to back, Jenny reaching a leg out through her slit and sliding so low the audience was afraid she couldn't get up, but then bouncing back with a bang.

Kate pointed at Will and sang directly to him, winking and making come here motions with her finger when she sang. He wouldn't admit it, but he found the entire thing unbelievably sexy and had to shift more than once in his chair. Kate seemed to sense his discomfort and smiled her mischievous smile, walking up to him and placing one finger beneath his chin and tilting his face up to her while she sang and edged ever closer, stopping just an inch shy of his mouth. When she turned and danced away, he sat frozen for a minute, not moving until the people around him clapped and jostled him out of his stupor.

The girls ran back on stage as the music wound down, hiding behind the curtain until the very end when the final drum thumped and they each flicked out a long kick before giggling and running backstage.

The emcee took the stage and commented on how amazing their performance had been and how all the other performers had some serious competition. They hardly noticed. The three of them were jumping and laughing backstage, thrilled with how well it had gone and high on the rush of performing.

"Did you see his face? He was completely surprised!" Jenny said.

"What was he expecting, anyway?" asked Sheila.

"I don't know. Maybe he thought I'd just stand there and sing a little song." Kate answered.

The three of them laughed and quickly changed out of their costumes and into their cocktail dresses. They joined the party during the first break between acts.

"You were amazing!" Andrew was the first to greet them, kissing Jen soundly on the lips, then bussing Kate and Sheila each on the cheek. "Very well done, ladies!"

Peter quickly joined them and added his praises.

"Thank you! It was a lot of fun. Has anyone seen Will?"

Kate asked.

"Look behind you."

She turned in time to see her husband headed toward her with a glass in each hand. He kissed her firmly as soon as he saw her, making everyone around them snicker softly. "You were magnificent," he said quietly. He handed her a glass of champagne and tipped his in her direction, then congratulated Jen and Sheila. They all raised their glasses with a small cheer and a quick toast from Andrew.

After they'd drunk and accepted more congratulations, Harper smiled that enigmatic smile of his. "Point taken," he whispered in her ear. "I won't challenge you again."

She blushed and looked down, then smiled up at him flirtatiously. "Glad we understand each other," she said softly.

The remaining acts were a mix of funny, entertaining, and difficult to watch. But it was all in good fun and for a good cause, so Harper happily wrote a check to the local cancer society and promised his attendance for the next year.

When the time came at the end to award the prizes, Kate was shocked when her name was called as the first place winner. She was sure one of the repeat performers or someone with more influence would win. Kate, Jenny, and Sheila thanked everyone for voting for them and held the trophy up high as they smiled and posed for photographs. When Mitzi Stanfield encouraged Kate to say a few words, she took the microphone with a mischievous smile.

"I just want to say thank you to everyone who voted for us and to Mitzi for making this event possible and allowing all of us to support such an important cause in such a fun way. Maybe next year we should invite the cancer patients to view the show – I'm sure it would raise their morale." The audience laughed and a few cheered. "I will display this trophy proudly in our home. Thank you for encouraging me to do this, William Harper, I certainly wouldn't have done it without your influence. Thanks again!"

The audience cheered and she took the heavy trophy back to their table where it stood proudly for the rest of the night. The remainder of the evening, people stopped by to congratulate her on her win and William on his choice of wife.

Will watched her with pride and a feeling he couldn't quite describe. Sure, he was proud that she'd won, but it was more than that. She had taken his poorly thought-out revenge and turned it into something beautiful and worthwhile. She had risen above so elegantly – he was in awe of her and, in the end, he felt like he was the one who'd been taught a lesson.

God, she's amazing, he thought as he watched her shake hands with yet another man currying her favor. *I really love her.* His eyes widened at his own thoughts. *Oh, shit!*

39
OH, MAMA

Last week of May, Thursday
2 Years, 1 Month Married

Kate had just shut her car door and turned to look at the wildflowers blooming in the neighboring field when she heard the loud smack of the screen door followed by a shriek.

"Katie!" Tiffany came flying out of the house and jumped into Kate's arms. "Can you believe I'm graduating? Aah! Will!" She hugged her brother-in-law as he was slamming shut the trunk on the rental car. "Are you hungry? Mom's been cooking all day! Where's Jenny?" She looked behind them then continued talking. "Ryan's going to be at the barbecue tonight! Do you want to meet him?"

"Tiffany, give your sister some breathing room," Loretta called from the porch. "How was the flight down?" She hugged Kate and pulled William lower so she could kiss his cheek. She held his chin in her hand and turned his face side to side. "You look thin. What are you eating?" She gave Kate a sharp look. "Are you feeding him properly?"

Kate suppressed an eye roll. "Will actually knows how to feed himself, Mom, but yes, I do a fair amount of cooking. He's just lean naturally. Leave him alone."

Loretta released William's face and turned to lead the way back into the house. "Where's your sister?" She asked over her shoulder.

"She and Andrew got their own rental car. She wanted to show him around the area and said she might make a stop on the way. Probably something to do with the wedding." Andrew and Jennifer had gotten engaged over New Year and were planning an autumn wedding at the family farm.

Loretta nodded and ushered them into the kitchen. She quickly pulled a few glasses down from a cabinet and opened the fridge. "Do you like sweet tea, William?"

"He likes half and half, Mom," Kate answered for him.

Loretta nodded and filled his glass with half sweet tea and half unsweet.

"What time does the barbecue start?" Kate asked.

"Six, but Ryan will be here a little early. Mary's coming, too," Tiffany answered.

"Perfect. That gives us enough time to shower and change. Where do you want us, Mom?"

"You can have the guest room. Jenny and Andrew can have Heather's room and she can stay at your father's, or Jenny can stay at Neal's and Heather can keep her room, or you can all stay here and Heather can bunk in with Tiffany. I'm too busy to worry about the details. I'll let you kids work it out." Loretta swished a dish towel for emphasis and turned to stir something on the stove.

Kate quickly grabbed Will's hand and led him around the corner. "Do you want to stay at Dad's?" she whispered.

"Why? Do you want to?" he whispered back.

"You're the one with the fantasy about a girl's room," she said with a look he couldn't possibly mistake the meaning of.

"Ah, yes, I think that could be a good idea. Jamison will be more comfortable in the guest room here."

Kate smirked. "I'm sure he will."

William took their bags back out to the car and Kate quickly told Tiffany that they would stay at their father's and they'd be back by five thirty for the barbecue.

"I probably should have asked this sooner, but you do have a big enough bed at your dad's, right?"

She laughed as they drove over the hill and through a

small forest of trees. "Yes, I got a queen when I turned fifteen. It's not as big as our bed back home, but it'll do."

They parked in front of the old white farm house and Kate shook her head at the peeling paint she noticed by the front window. She wasn't halfway up the porch steps before she heard a swishing in the grass and a few seconds later, she was nearly bowled over by Jake, her father's dog.

She laughed and cooed at the dog while she scratched his ears and Will waited behind her, tapping his foot on the porch.

"Come on in," she finally said. She opened the door and called out loudly. "Daddy! It's Katie!" There was no response. "He's probably in the fields. Come on up."

She led the way up a narrow staircase into a whitewashed hall with three doors. "That's Jen's room," she pointed to the door on her left, "that's the bathroom," she pointed straight ahead, "and this is my room." She nudged open the door on her right as she hefted her bag in. Jake followed her, nudging William out of the way and lying down on the small braided rug by the bed.

"It's nice," Harper said, looking around. The walls were painted a sunny yellow, the floors were a natural wood, and the curtains were white with tiny yellow flowers on them. "So this is where you grew up," he said speculatively, turning around slowly before focusing on a bulletin board over a small green desk. "Wow. You won a spelling bee."

"I won on the word 'expeditious'," she said proudly, looking at the medal hanging from the corner of the board.

He looked at photos of her with Laura and Jennifer on horseback; standing by a row of trees next to her father; laughing with Josh, his arm around her shoulders.

"You know, we've never gone riding together," he commented.

"You're right, we haven't. Do you want to go for a ride while we're here?"

"Does your father have horses?"

"Not anymore. Jen and I shared a mare that our grandfather bought us when we were kids, but she died a few years ago. The Powells raise horses, though, and they're just the next farm over. They'd let us borrow for the afternoon. I do it every summer, Josh doesn't mind. He's great fun on a ride."

Will pursed his lips. "Does he run the family farm now?"

"Sort of. He handles all the training and the hands-on stuff now, but his dad still takes care of the paperwork and business side of things."

Will nodded.

"Hey, you okay?" she asked, touching his arm lightly.

"Yeah, fine." She raised a brow. "Honestly? I'm not too fond of spending a lot of time with Joshua Powell."

She looked surprised. "Oh. You don't have to go if you don't want to. We can ride on our own; Josh won't mind."

He frowned. "I'm even less fond of you going riding with him without me."

She wrinkled her brow in thought for a moment, then it cleared suddenly. "Are you jealous?"

"No! I just don't like the thought of my wife spending hours alone riding through the picturesque countryside with her first love, that's all."

She smiled. "What do you think about *you* spending hours riding through the picturesque countryside with your wife?"

"Without Mr. Powell?"

"Without Josh."

He smiled. "I like that idea."

She gave him a quick peck and turned around to unpack her bag. "You don't have anything to worry about with Josh, you know. It was all over ages ago." She hung a dress in the closet and walked back to the bed where her suitcase sat. "Besides, I'm not his type."

"What do you mean? You're every man's type."

She grinned. "While I appreciate the compliment, that is not true." She put her t-shirts in the drawer. "And what I meant is that Josh prefers his lovers a bit taller and broader, with shorter hair and a flatter chest."

"What? Josh is gay?"

She nodded.

"But he went out with you!"

"He was a kid. He was figuring everything out. Why do you think we're still friends now? I'm not friends with any of my other exes."

William wondered why he had never noticed that before and shook his head. "Is it common knowledge?"

"It's a bit don't ask don't tell. Most people around here aren't straight-up homophobes, but it isn't super accepted either. I imagine most people who know him at all suspect it, but no one wants to come right out and ask."

Will nodded absently, lost in thought.

"Please keep that to yourself. I don't want Josh to feel uncomfortable or anything," she added.

"Of course. I won't say a word."

***

Friday afternoon, William enjoyed a leisurely stroll around the farm while Kate visited with her sisters and helped Tiffany prepare for her graduation ceremony that evening. Neal's dog Jake faithfully, and surprisingly, followed him through the rows of trees as he explored the property.

Tired and thirsty, he headed inside the pink house to get a drink and collect his wife before heading back to Neal's to dress for the evening. He stepped into the mud room, but before he could slip off his dirty shoes and leave them next to the door, he heard the sound of Kate and Loretta's raised voices in the kitchen. Stepping into the doorway, he saw Kate standing on one side of the island, Loretta on the other, a wooden spoon in her hand as she stirred something on the stove.

Kate put her hands in the air and said loudly, "Why are you so mad about this? It's not you who's doing it!"

"Because I want you to be okay! Because I don't want you to make bad decisions!" her mother cried.

"I'm not making bad decisions! I chose very carefully! Why can't you believe that? Why does everything have to look a certain way in order for you to understand it? Why can't you see that this is what's best for *me* now, at this point in my life?" Kate was gripping the edge of the counter tightly and her body was rigid.

"How do you know that? You're just a kid! You're twenty-five! You don't know what life's going to throw at you. Security may look boring, but it's the only thing standing between you and the welfare line. Why can't you think practically sometimes?" Loretta was shouting, steam from the pot giving her face a red, waxy glow.

"Am I interrupting something?" Will said.

Both women snapped their heads toward him. "No, I was just about to go back to Dad's and change. Walk me?"

"Of course. Loretta." He nodded at his mother-in-law and followed a steaming Kate out of the house.

She stomped half the way to her father's before Will said, "What was that about?"

"I made the mistake of telling my mother that Taggston offered me a full-time position last spring that I turned down in favor of what I'm doing now, what I happen to love, and she didn't agree with my choice." She ruthlessly whacked at a branch as she passed.

"Ah."

He followed her the rest of the way in silence, then started a pot of tea when they got to Neal's. Kate stomped straight up to their room. Ten minutes later, he took two steaming cups up the stairs and nudged her door open.

Kate sat on the bed, a large teddy bear in her lap and her chin resting between its ears. He placed her tea on the side table and sat at the foot of the bed silently until he couldn't stand it anymore and spoke up.

"So what are you going to do?" he asked.

"About what?" she asked.

"You know what. About your mother."

"Nothing. What can I do? It's always been this way, it probably always will be. Talking about it will just start another argument. It will all blow over, just like it always does."

"Katie," he said gently but with a slightly reproachful tone.

She continued to look at the quilt on her bed, tracing the pattern with her eyes. "My grandmother made this quilt, you know. When I moved over here, dad took me shopping for paint colors. He wanted me to make it my own space. He thinks it's important to have a place in the world. Gran said something similar. When she found out I'd painted it yellow, she bought all this different fabric and I picked out the quilt pattern myself. She let me help cut out some of the pieces. It's pretty, isn't it?"

He looked at her, at the way her shoulders were slumped and how she wouldn't look up at him. He sat on the bed beside her and touched her arm.

"Kate, I know it's difficult, but you should talk to your mother. This happens every time you come for a visit. It's not getting any better. If you have something you want to say, or questions you want to ask, now's the time."

She huffed. "You say that like it will make everything better."

"I don't know if it will be better, but I do know that not knowing can eat you up inside. That you'll lie awake nights wondering if it all could have been better if you'd just had the courage to speak up. I don't want you to live with that."

She looked up at him with red rimmed eyes. "Is that how you felt about your mom?"

"Yes. For years. Until last summer. I don't want you to feel that way, Kate, not ever. Life is fragile. You never know how much time you have with someone. One day my mother was perfectly fine, the next she bent over to tie her shoe and she collapsed on the tennis court. She was forty-five. I'm not saying your mother has an aneurysm like mine did, but that you never know what tomorrow will bring, and if you have something to say to your mother, you should say it."

"What would you have said to your mother?" she asked quietly.

He scuffled his feet for a minute and leaned back on his hands. "I would have asked her why. Why she was so distant, why she was so silent. I could have; I was twenty when she died. I'd had plenty of time; I was an adult. I was just too afraid of the answer and I kept thinking it would get better on its own." He huffed. "Like that's ever happened."

"So you think I should ask her why she always blows up at me?" she asked uncertainly.

"If that's the big question for you, yes. But I think you might have a bigger question." He smiled at her gently. "I'll go with you if you want. Or be here when you get back, whatever you need."

"Thanks, Will. I think I'll be alright on my own, but I'll definitely find you when it's over."

"Okay."

**

After dinner that night, Kate knocked on her mother's bedroom door. Will had wished her luck and sent her up the stairs, saying he would wait in the living room with Andrew and Jennifer. She waited in the hall for a minute until her mother's voice called for her to come in.

Kate looked around the room decorated in purple flowers and lace and sat gingerly on the bench at the end of the bed. She hadn't been in there in over two years and it felt a little foreign, but also a little too intimate a place to be having this very intimate conversation.

Loretta came swishing out of the bathroom in a long cream robe over a pair of pink silky pajamas. She was patting wrinkle cream onto her face, her blonde hair pulled back.

"What is it, Kitty? Sorry, Katie," she corrected when Kate gave her a look.

"Mom, I wanted to talk to you about something. Something serious."

Loretta looked at her expectantly. "You're pregnant! I knew it!"

"No! I'm not pregnant! Why do you always think that? I want to talk to you about something else. Are you up for that right now?"

"I suppose. What do you want to talk about?"

Kate took a deep breath. *Say it quick, Katie. Like ripping off a Band-Aid.* "Why haven't you ever liked me?" she said in a rush. Her hands gripped her knees and her eyes focused on a framed needlepoint bouquet on the wall.

Loretta sunk into the chair in the corner of the room. "Not liked you? What are you talking about?"

"What do you mean what am I talking about? I'm talking about you always acting like I'm in your way, like I'm a huge disappointment, like you wish I was anyone but who I am." Her voice rose with each word until it cracked, her nerves shot and her legs bouncing rapidly.

Loretta looked confused for a moment, then leaned back in her chair and covered her eyes with her hand. After several minutes of awful silence, she very quietly said, "I'm a terrible mother."

"What?" Kate asked in disbelief, her feet finally stopping their incessant bouncing.

"I need to tell you something. Will you listen?" Kate nodded. Loretta took a deep breath and looked away. "When your father and I first got together, we were full of big ideas and fanciful dreams. He wanted to expand the farm, I wanted to open a restaurant and B&B on the property. We were going to turn it into a tourist destination. We used to sit up in the hayloft talking about all our plans, watching the stars. We'd talk until dawn and then he'd help me sneak back into my parents' house. It was a magical time."

Kate watched her mother in fascination. Loretta had a soft look on her face and her eyes had a dreamy quality. In all the years she'd spent with her mother, Kate had never heard her talk about the beginning of her relationship with Neal. Kate leaned forward and put her elbows on her knees, listening carefully.

"I wanted to go away to culinary school. I loved cooking and was always trying new recipes. Neal was very supportive. He was older than me and already working on the farm, but he said he'd drive down on weekends and that somehow we'd make it work. He was quite dashing back then.

"Anyway, one night, things in the hayloft went further than either of us planned and we weren't careful. We did better after that, but once was all it took and Jennifer was on her way. My father threatened to kick me out if I didn't get married immediately, not that I didn't want to. Neal offered to do the right thing and marry me, of course, but it wasn't a hardship. We were so in love with each other, it was only a matter of time before we decided it for ourselves.

"But getting pregnant changed all my other plans. I couldn't go near a kitchen – every smell made me nauseous. There was a school in Richmond that had an excellent cooking program. I signed up for a two week course in pastries in my sixth month after my stomach had settled. I stayed with my aunt Betty in town. Every day was spent in the kitchen, rolling out dough and learning and experimenting. I did really well; the teachers thought I showed great promise." She looked toward the window and out at the inky night sky, lost in thought for several moments.

"Jen was born shortly after that and life was consumed with taking care of an infant for a while. Then one day, one of my teachers called me. One of the scholarship students had dropped out and there was a vacancy in the year-long program. She encouraged me to apply." She sniffled and touched the corner of her eye. "I got the slot. With my triple chocolate cake, the one I always make for your birthday." She gave Kate a watery smile.

"I didn't know you went to proper cooking school," Kate said.

"That's because three months into the program, I had to run out of the kitchen to throw up in the bathroom. I was expecting you." She looked at Kate and smiled cryptically. "I tried to muscle through and ignore the nausea and the dizziness. I always found it ironic that Heather and Tiffany's pregnancies were so easy." She paused and looked heavenward, then looked back at her daughter. "Your father had rented us a little studio apartment near the school, and my aunt kept Jenny while I was in class. Everyone was doing so much to make this work for me. Neal was stocking shelves at a grocery store, for Pete's sake! But he'd said it was only for a year and that we should consider it an investment in our future."

"What happened?"

"One day I fainted. I was standing over a hot stove, had been standing over a hot stove for days on end, it felt like. Anyway, something happened and it got to me. The director sat me down and told me I'd been missing a lot of information with my frequent escapes to the ladies' room and that as a scholarship student I had to maintain a certain attendance and performance level. I was slipping. She gave me until the end of the week to master the sauces that had been giving me trouble and then she said they would revoke my scholarship. When I told her I was pregnant, that I wasn't just sickly or worse – on drugs or something – she was very kind about it and suggested that I might want to come back after the birth.

"I told her I thought I could do it and spent every extra moment that I wasn't taking care of Jenny in the kitchen. I was determined to get it right. But everything tasted off: the salt was too salty, the lemon not nearly strong enough.

"The next Friday, we did our blind tasting for the teachers like we usually did, and we were scored like always. I failed by two points." Kate gasped and put her hand over her mouth. "There was too much tarragon and not enough pepper. I'd gone heavy on the lemon. I wanted to scream at them that it wasn't my fault, that my tastes were altered because of the pregnancy, but it was over and I knew it. I packed up my bags and we came back here. I'd lost my chance."

"Because of me," Kate said quietly.

Loretta just looked at her for a long moment, then finally said, "Because of bad timing. I was a wreck. I was bitter and disappointed and I shouldn't be surprised you picked up on that. Your father and I started fighting when we got back. Nothing could please me, nothing could compensate for what I'd lost. He couldn't understand what I was so upset about, why I couldn't just be happy with what we had. Then you were born and it was really hard for a really long time. Two children under two isn't easy under the best of circumstances. Your grandparents were living here with us and I felt like I was being watched all the time. When it was just one baby, I felt like I could get away. I had options, I could have made it work with just one – school, a job, whatever. But two just felt so impossible, so overwhelming for the twenty-year-old girl I was.

"Now look at me. A forty-five-year-old woman whose daughter is asking her why she was such a bitch all her life." She laughed cynically.

"I didn't say that!" Kate protested.

"You may as well have. Don't worry, I'm not offended. Lord knows it's true enough. So to answer your question, I don't dislike you. In fact I like you very much, but you were born in a very difficult situation to two completely unprepared people. Your father doted on you, always has, but I had a hard time. It was so easy to bond with Jenny, she was so sweet and we were so naïve, but with you, I knew exactly what I was getting myself into, the sleepless nights and the earaches, and I was terrified." Kate thought that the disappointment of being another girl and not the hoped for son probably also added to the difficulty, but she said nothing. Loretta sighed and looked toward the window. "And if I'm being completely honest, I've been a bit jealous."

"Jealous? Of me? Why?"

"Do you really need to ask? You're charmed!" Kate looked at her incredulously. "You're smart and talented and beautiful." Kate started to interrupt but Loretta held up a hand to stop her. "And most importantly, you make better decisions than I ever did."

"You did the best you could with difficult circumstances," Kate said uneasily, unsure if even she believed her words.

"Let's not kid ourselves, honey. I could have done better. I had a chance and I blew it, plain and simple – with your father, with cooking school. I've had to accept that."

"Could you not go back later? Was there no way to try again?"

"Your father wouldn't have been willing to do that a second time. Remember this, Katie." She faced her daughter fully. "In the beginning, a man is desperate to please you, to make you happy, but after a while, that fades. He's less willing to put himself out when he gets little in return. The few times we talked about it were so tense and he always brought up logistical problems that I couldn't argue with. Then his father bought the farm next door and it was time to expand and Neal was needed here. My window closed."

"Oh, Mom! I'm so sorry!"

"It's not your fault, baby. You were an innocent child, and I'm so proud of you. I'm sorry I ever made you feel like you weren't wanted here or that I didn't like you. I adore you. I just don't always know what to *do* with you. You're so smart and worldly, and you and your father always have these private jokes; I feel like the two of you are laughing at me half the time. And I'm so worried you'll end up like me and so worried you'll be like your father. He's so alone now, with just his stubbornness to keep him company." She shook her head.

"Mom, I – We weren't laughing at you. I'm sorry if we made you think that."

Loretta jumped in. "Don't apologize to me, honey. You're a brilliant girl. You always have been. You get that from your father. I'm smart enough, but he's really intelligent. That's what drew me to him, you know? He wore those glasses when he read that made him look so scholarly. And he was always quoting poetry to me. He'd say the sweetest things. I'd pack us a picnic and we'd go for a ride up into the hills. We'd lie on a blanket and he'd read aloud to me; Bronte, Dickens, Henry James. I'd feed him pie and we'd while away the days. I wasn't as smart as him, we both knew it, but we were good together, for a while." Loretta laughed softly. "He once wrote a poem about my strawberry pie. He said it was like poetry in his mouth and I teased him to write it down for me. I still have it somewhere." She sighed.

They were silent for several minutes, soaking it in and looking everywhere but at each other.

"Thanks for telling me all this, Mom. It helps."

Loretta smiled softly. "I'm so sorry you've been caught in the middle of this mess, baby girl. I'll be better going forward – I promise."

She rose and sat down next to Kate, wrapping her arm

around her daughter's shoulders. She slowly rocked side to side, stroking her hand up and down Kate's arm as she hummed softly. Kate shifted and lay her head in her mother's lap, trying to stifle the tears that were threatening to overwhelm her. Loretta stopped her rocking and ran her hand through her daughter's hair and began singing softly.

"*'Hush little baby, don't say a word. Mama's gonna buy you a mockingbird.'*" Loretta continued in her soft voice while Kate cried quietly, until finally, lulled by her mother's voice, she fell into a peaceful sleep.

***

Sunday afternoon, the family all gathered around the dining table at Loretta's house to celebrate the matriarch's birthday. The birthday itself was Wednesday, but they were celebrating together before half the family returned to New York.

The food was delicious, the cake was divine, and the champagne flowed freely. After the meal, Loretta sat down on the sofa to open her gifts. Tiffany had made her a metalwork necklace that had everyone exclaiming while Heather gave her mother a cardigan she had knitted herself. Originally, Jen had gotten her a beautiful bracelet and Kate a matching pair of diamond stud earrings, but after their discussion two nights ago, Kate had another idea. She bit her lip anxiously as Loretta opened the small flat box with a simple label saying it was from all her daughters.

Loretta looked at the heavy cardstock inside, then looked at her daughters in confusion.

"What is this?"

"It was Katie's idea," Tiffany said. "Jen said you can stay with her, and Heather and I will watch the store for you. Isn't it great?" Tiffany clapped her hands together gleefully, but Loretta was still too shocked to say anything.

She looked at the card in her hands and read it for the third time. She was invited to attend a special week-long intensive for chefs in New York. There were several happening throughout the summer, each focusing on different aspects of cooking and pastry making. The card said two week-long courses were paid for; she could take them consecutively or on their own. Everything was arranged and her acceptance was guaranteed.

"How? When?" Loretta stammered.

"William knows one of the chefs leading the course. He made a call. Do you like it?" Kate asked tentatively.

Loretta fanned herself with the box lid and said, "Like it? Of course I like it! I love it! You sweet girls! Thank you so much!"

All her daughters piled around her for a group hug. When everyone broke away, Loretta held onto Kate and whispered in her ear, "Thank you, Katie. That was incredibly generous of you."

"You called me Katie," Kate replied in surprise.

"I know you prefer it." She smiled tearfully at her daughter and Kate smiled back, kissing her mother on the cheek and walking away before she got emotional.

Harper watched it all with hopeful skepticism. He wanted Kate to have a good relationship with her mother, to have the relationship he'd never had with his, but at the same time, he knew change took time and Loretta's negative habits and Kate's defensiveness were well ingrained. Still, he couldn't help the deep sense of satisfaction he felt looking at Kate hugging her mother so affectionately and being genuinely embraced in return.

Even Neal looked affected. William couldn't miss the look of understanding that passed between his wife's parents when Loretta had opened her gift. Neal knew how much this meant to Loretta, that was obvious.

After anther hour of chatting and hearing all about Tiffany's acceptance and plans for Rhode Island School of Design, Kate, William, Jenny, and Andrew said emotional goodbyes and piled into their rental cars, promising to visit again soon and congratulating Tiffany once more on graduating high school.

"How do you feel?" Will asked in the car.

"Good. Drained. How about you?" she replied.

"Fine, but I'm not the one who just had a come-to-Jesus moment with my mother. You sure you're alright?"

"Yeah, I'm great, actually. It's not perfect and we have a long way to go, but I feel like we've made a good start and cleared up some misunderstandings. That's more than I ever thought would happen."

He held her hand over the console. "Good. I'm glad."

"Thanks for encouraging me to clear the air. You were right. Questions needed to be asked."

"You're welcome. Any time."

40
STALLING

Late July
2 Years, 3 Months Married

Monday evening, Will took the mail from his box in the lobby and flipped through it in the elevator. His heart stopped for a moment when he saw a USCIS stamp on the corner of a white envelope. He stepped into the apartment and listened carefully. All was quiet. He took the letter to his study and ripped open the top, quickly scanning the letter inside.

There it was, attached to the bottom of a sheet of watermarked green paper. His ten-year permanent resident card. He'd known this was coming, but for some reason, he was shocked to see it happening so soon.

Of course, he could delay it all. He could tell Kate there was some kind of hiccup, or better yet that he'd decided to get citizenship and ask if she'd stay on longer. That would buy him a whole year more.

Get a hold of yourself, Will. You can't bribe her into staying. As he told himself that, though, he wondered if he could, just a little bit. It didn't have to be a complete bribe, just enough to get her to want to stay.

He shook off his wayward thoughts, ashamed of himself. He couldn't live with himself if he manipulated Kate like that. Besides, immigration was nothing to play around with. And she probably didn't want to stay anyway. *It's not like she's in love with me.*

Sometimes, in his more desperate moments, he thought she was, at least a little, or that she could be down the road, but he always dismissed the idea. Kate was so open, when she felt something for you, you knew it. And she had always been direct with him, even with difficult topics. Surely she would have said something if she wanted to try a real marriage?

On top of all of that, he knew her history. Every time the men in her life asked her to commit, Kate cut and ran. Maybe it was because she didn't love them, or love them enough, or maybe she just didn't feel it was right. But he had to admit that part of him wondered if she wasn't just frightened of commitment. Lord knows watching her parents' marriage could have put anyone off the idea. If she hadn't found that ring with Matt, she likely would have stayed with him longer. Maybe she would have changed her mind about him eventually.

And of course she freely acknowledged that she'd loved Jeremy. By her own admission, they were great together and deeply in love. But still, *still* she hadn't been willing to commit to him. Will had Googled Jeremy; he had a good position at a PR firm in Phoenix and was already climbing the ranks admirably. He was on track for management and possibly more. According to everything Will had found (thanks to a bottle of scotch and a late night in front of the computer), Jeremy was well liked and respected and disturbingly single. He had a niggling fear that Kate would go back to him when their relationship ended. He had no idea how she still felt about Jeremy; she said she was over it, but he knew too well how one's own heart could surprise a person.

He found himself oddly hoping that she did have a fear of commitment and that it would keep her far away from Phoenix and its eligible bachelors.

No, it was much safer to keep her in his life as a friend than to risk losing her altogether by making an uncomfortable request.

He would call Jamison in the morning and tell him it was time to prepare the papers. He shoved the letter in his briefcase and told himself not to worry until he had to.

**

One week later

"I've got the settlement ready for you to sign whenever you're ready, Harper," Andrew said during their next meeting in his office. He pulled a sheaf of papers from a drawer and plopped them down in front of his friend.

Will absentmindedly flipped through the documents on the table. "Five hundred thousand and a house? That's all she's getting?"

"Those were the terms we originally agreed to. You thought they were adequate two years ago."

"Adequate? How is she supposed to live on that? The interest won't even cover her living expenses!"

"I believe she expects to work full time, similar to what she is doing now," Jamison said carefully.

"Make it two million."

"What?"

"You heard me. Make it two million. And she can have the apartment. I don't need it, I've got the family place, I can easily move in there."

"Whoa, wait a minute, Harper," Andrew said agitatedly. "I know this is Kate and you want to do right by her and all, but the original settlement is perfectly adequate, generous even, by some standards."

"This is not a case of 'some standards', Jamison," Harper spat scathingly. "This is my wife we're talking about here. I want her taken care of. Make it two million, plus the apartment in town and whatever house she wants. No limits on that."

"No limits! Harper! You can't just give her carte blanche to buy whatever she wants. The original limit of six hundred thousand is perfectly reasonable."

"Quit making me repeat myself, Jamison. *Whatever* she wants. I trust Kate."

With a final look at his friend and lawyer, Harper left

the room.

Later that night, Harper sat in his office, looking at pictures of their last vacation on his computer. They had gone to London for Christmas, then on to Switzerland for New Year with a group of friends and family, or as Kate had referred to them, a motley crew. Teddy and six-months-pregnant Caroline had come and brought their nanny and little Thomas. Calvin Covington and Harry Cavendish each came with their most recent girlfriends, Jennifer and Andrew came after their visit with his family in Dorset, and Jacqueline came on her own.

They'd stayed in Harry's family place outside Geneva in a small French-speaking village. The chalet was beautiful, the scenery was pristine, and the company was perfect. Andrew finally popped the question and Jen accepted joyfully; they celebrated for what felt like days. They laughed and drank and ate more fondue than they could hold. Will taught Kate how to ski, something they each enjoyed immensely, and with a grin, he remembered how cute she had looked in her ski suit.

She had really been horrible when she started. She couldn't balance or keep her skis straight or maintain the correct posture. He'd been equally exasperated and amused with her. But when she smiled at him so sweetly after fumbling his instructions, his annoyance would dissolve and he'd find his patience again. After a few days, she finally got the hang of it and they spent many pleasurable hours skiing down very gentle slopes. Next year, he wanted to take her down something a bit more challenging. Maybe they could – he stopped himself.

There wouldn't be a next year. Now that he had his ten year green card, they needed to start distancing themselves. He'd have to go to society functions without her, she would spend more time with her friends without him. All strictly social functions would have to be attended without the other and their dates would cease. Andrew had orchestrated a detailed plan for the break up, just as he had the beginning of their relationship. Once they'd quit spending time together publicly, he'd move into his parents' apartment – his apartment now – and they would admit to a separation. A month after that, they'd file for divorce officially. It would all be done by

Christmas, February at the latest.

His stomach rolled just thinking about it.

Ignoring his feelings of discomfort, he opened another file of pictures on his computer. They were from Valhalla the previous spring. They'd gone for a week to celebrate their second anniversary. Kate was in nearly all of them, except for the ones she'd taken of him and a few of the local scenery. They were on the beach, lying in the sand, playing in the water, laughing at stupid jokes and drinking too much. He felt a tightening in his throat as he looked at her, running on the beach, looking over her shoulder at him, her hair flying behind her and a teasing grin on her lips. It had been a blissful holiday and for a brief moment, he wondered if Kate might want to go back, for one last hurrah as it were.

Why would she want to do that, Harper? This is a business deal, plain and simple. He shook his head to dispel his gloomy thoughts. Quit feeling sorry for yourself. She does love it there, maybe she would like to go…

Before he could talk himself out of it, he shot off a quick text to Kate. *Want to go to Valhalla one last time?*

Kate immediately responded. Is that a serious question? YES!!! Just say when.

Before he left for the night, he sent an email to Evelyn requesting she make all the arrangements.

The next morning, he met with Jamison again.

"Did you change the papers?" Harper asked as Jamison sat down.

"Yes. Harper, as your lawyer, I have to ask. Are you sure about this? Really sure? This is a lot of money," Jamison asked uneasily.

"Yes, Andrew, I'm sure. And I want you to add one more thing." Andrew raised his brows as Harper turned and walked toward the window, his hands in his pockets and his eyes on the city. "Give her Valhalla."

Andrew spluttered. "What?"

"You heard me."

"But you love it there!"

"So does she."

"How is she even going to get there? International tickets are expensive. Can she even afford the upkeep?"

"Good point. Add two trips per year on the Harper jet, whenever she needs them. And a small trust to keep the place up. It shouldn't take much, I'll check with the caregiver." He kept his back to Andrew, his face to the window and his gaze steady.

"Harper, I have to ask. Why?"

Harper's shoulders tensed. "I believe it's your job to write up contracts, Jamison, not question my personal decisions."

Jamison stiffened and stood to leave. "Point taken. I'll have the new papers on your desk by the end of the day."

"Thank you," Harper said without turning around.

Jamison left without another word, the door clicking shut behind him the only sign that he had gone.

***

"You know, I've been thinking," Will said that night over Chinese take out.

"Yeah? 'Bout what?" Kate asked.

"If we get divorced immediately after I get my ten-year green card, won't that look suspicious?"

"It could," she agreed.

"I mean, it would be pretty ridiculous to have put all this time and effort into it only to have it all fall apart at the twelfth hour."

"Yeah, no, I see what you mean. We wouldn't want that. So," she said hesitantly, "do you want to stay together a little longer?" She kept her eyes glued to her lo mein as she waited for his response.

"Well, yeah, but only if you want to. I mean, we don't have to. You've fulfilled your part of the deal and I don't want to overstep or anything."

"No, it's alright. It's not overstepping." She smiled at him. "I could be married to you a little while longer."

"Alright. So, one more Christmas?"

"One more Christmas."

***

They escaped to Valhalla a week later, though they could only stay six days. Whenever they got away, Will usually would spend a few hours each day on his own; early walks in the morning, solitary swims. This time, he never left Kate's side. He felt slightly disgusted with himself and his neediness, and he was afraid his constant presence would get on Kate's nerves and she would tell him to leave her alone, but oddly enough, she seemed to like his presence. She smiled when he joined her in the kitchen when she was making breakfast and happily chatted while she sliced fruit. When he asked if he could sit by her when she was relaxing by the pool with a book, she would set the book down and give him her attention. They talked about everything and nothing. What they were reading, his latest business transactions, their friends and family, whether Kate should run in Jenny's five K again this year and if he should do it with her.

She told him about the authors she was working with and how proud she was of the two that had recently finished their manuscripts and were now in final production stages with Taggston Publishing. He told her how well the new company with Helgsen and Covington Enterprises was going and how excited he was about the direction Taggston was headed in.

Their dinners were quiet and intimate, often eaten outside at sunset or on the patio in candlelight. They made love every night, the sound of crashing waves in their ears and seaside breezes blowing through the open curtains.

Alone in the dark with her, William felt a sort of desperation, a craving he couldn't describe. He knew his days were numbered and like a man possessed, he wanted to memorize every inch of her body and every constellation of freckles on her skin. He wanted to have every sigh, every moan, imprinted on his soul to remember, to take out and examine on lonely days after she was gone, after her light had left him. With a strength he didn't know he was capable of, he carried her to new heights and together they transcended the familiar and inhabited a world apart.

Kate seemed to understand his need and met him there, finding a well of vigor inside her rising up just when she thought she was ready to collapse. She dug her nails into his back, viciously hoping she could leave a scar and that every woman who came after her would know she had been there, she had made a mark on this man, she had left something permanent behind her. He may be the great William Harper, force of nature and unconquerable demi-god, but she, Katherine Bishop, had left her mark on him, at least for a little while, and that had to mean something. *She* had to mean something.

This meant something. She knew it did.

41
DESPERATE MEASURES

August
2 Years, 4 Months Married

A few days after they returned from Valhalla, Kate had a physical at the gynecologist. As she lay there in a paper gown with her feet in the stirrups, she told herself to relax and that it would all be over soon.

"Alright, everything looks good," said the doctor as she pulled her gloves off and stood up. "Do you have any concerns you want to talk to me about? Are you happy with your current contraceptive?"

"No, no concerns," she shook her head, her mind suddenly filling with a desperate idea. "How's my IUD?" she asked. "Still in the right place and everything?"

The doctor smiled reassuringly. "Yes, it's fine. Have you experienced any discomfort with it?"

"Not really, but my husband does say he can feel it sometimes, but I don't know if that's true."

"Some men say that, though they likely wouldn't feel anything if they didn't know it was there."

"Yeah, I'm sure," Kate said. She tried to keep her voice light, but her mind was reeling. She could have her IUD removed. There was a strong possibility that she would get pregnant relatively quickly. William would surely stay married to her if she was pregnant. Wouldn't he? She wouldn't have to tell him she'd had it removed; that was confidential. She could say the pregnancy was a fluke and that she had the device removed afterward. She was his best friend, surely he would believe her.

Stop it, Katie! You do not trick a man into marrying you! What kind of marriage would that be?! She scolded herself. An awesome one, like the one you already have, said her traitorous heart.

"Are you alright?" asked the doctor.

"Yeah, sorry, I'm fine. Just a little distracted today." Before she could think about it, she added, "You know, I think I want to have my IUD removed. It's really bothering my husband and we can just use condoms for a while." *What are you doing, Katie! Stop talking!* "Is that possible?"

The doctor looked at her earnestly. "We don't have any more time today, and it's a serious step. You need to be completely sure and have alternate contraception in place."

"Right, of course," Kate agreed, unable to look her in the eye.

"You can schedule the removal at the front desk if you're ready, but I want you to think about it carefully. Your body doesn't handle chemical contraceptives well, and the diaphragm just isn't as effective. If your IUD isn't giving *you* any trouble, it really is the best option for you. Maybe you could try different positions so your husband wouldn't mind it so much," she suggested.

Oh God, how had this become so horribly awkward? *Because you're a sneaky little liar, that's how.* "Got it, I'll think about it. Thank you," she said. She smoothed the sheet over her knees and kept her eyes on the buttons of the doctor's coat.

"Alright, you do that. Regardless, I want to see you again next year for a check up. Call me if you have any problems before then."

Kate nodded and got up to get dressed when the doctor left the room. Where had those thoughts come from? She was getting divorced in a few months. It was all planned, had been planned for ages. She had to get out of there, and fast. She dressed as quickly as she could and sped past the receptionist, not bothering to schedule another appointment.

*

"Oh, Jenny! It's awful!"

Jenny held her hysterical sister while she sobbed. "What's awful, honey?"

"Will!"

"Will's awful? What happened? You've been getting along so well."

"Exactly! That's what's so awful!" Kate sobbed again and blew her nose noisily.

"I don't understand," said Jen with a confused look on her face.

"He's perfect! Don't you see that? He laughs at my stupid jokes and he thinks I'm quirky and not weird and he hangs out in the kitchen while I cook. He gives the best presents!" she added in a high pitched voice. "Where am I ever going to find another guy like that? Huh? He actually remembers the things I tell him and he's such a good kisser." She sank back dramatically on her sister's sofa.

"Couldn't you talk to Will, suggest that you stay together, at least for a little while to give it a try?" Jen soothed.

Kate shot her sister a look. "And have him tell me no? I don't think so."

"How do you know he'll tell you no? Maybe he feels the same way. You'll never know if you don't ask."

"I already know." She sprang forward and leaned over her knees. "He's made it very clear from the beginning. He has to have a wife from the right circles," she said disgustedly. "I don't fit the bill." She slumped back into the couch cushions again.

"But surely that doesn't matter so much now? Your families' have met and accepted each other, you know almost all of his coworkers, you've met all the society players. Maybe he doesn't think that kind of wife is as important now."

"I don't think so, Jen. I mean, I suppose it's possible the way anything is possible, but I really doubt it. I don't think he'd stay, even if he wanted to. His sense of duty is too strong. But more importantly, I can't bear to see the look on his face when I beg him to stay and be *really* married to me and he makes that face, the one he makes when he feels sorry for someone that he has to give bad news to. I couldn't take it directed at me, I know I couldn't."

"Oh, sweetie. I'm so sorry." Jen patted her knee and sat beside her sister, silently supporting.

"Me, too, Jenny. Me, too."

***

"Katie, this is Laura, your lawyer. You really need to call me back. This is the fourth message I've left you. We have things to discuss. Call me."

Kate deleted the voicemail and decided to finally bite the bullet and call Laura back. She knew her lawyer wanted to talk about the divorce settlement. She just didn't want to think about it.

Deciding to be adult about this, she quickly sent a text to Laura and asked if she could come by her office the next day. Surprisingly, Laura asked if she could come to Kate's apartment instead. Kate was confused but agreed, then waited on tenterhooks for the next morning to come.

When Laura arrived, Kate was in black yoga pants and a grey tank top with a long black cardigan hanging past her wrists and slipping over one shoulder.

"Going out? Or dressed for mourning?" Laura teased.

"I made tea. Want some?" Kate asked dully.

"Sure," Laura replied. She grabbed her cup and followed Kate silently to her den and sat at her friend's desk while Kate took the comfy leather chair in the corner and curled her knees up to her chest.

"I have good news for you!" Laura said cheerily.

"How could you possibly have good news? Don't you have a briefcase full of divorce papers?"

Laura shot her a dark look. "Actually, they're settlement papers, and yes, it's very good news. You remember the agreed upon settlement?"

"Yes. How could I forget about my thirty pounds of silver?" Kate said darkly.

Laura rolled her eyes. "Quit being dramatic."

Now Kate rolled her eyes but turned her attention to her friend in her smart navy skirt suit. "What's your good news?"

"You, oh wayward friend of mine, are now a wealthy woman."

"What? What are you talking about?"

"I'm talking about your swanky new settlement, that's what!"

"New settlement? Why haven't I heard anything about this?"

"Maybe because you haven't been returning my calls." Kate looked down. "Now, according to the old settlement, you got five hundred thousand cash plus a house and the right to live here for a year while you shopped for it. Now you've got two million cash," Kate's head snapped up, "a house with *no price limit*, and you keep this apartment outright."

"What? You're kidding! How did this happen? Did you negotiate for this, Lar?"

Laura put her hands up in front of her. "No, not at all. It was all Harper. His idea to change it and he set all the new limits." Kate was staring at the wall silently. "Apparently, he wants to make sure you'll be okay," she added quietly.

Kate just nodded and a tear tracked down her cheek.

"Hey, now! What's this?" Laura grabbed a box of tissues and handed it to Kate. "Why the tears? This is good. Now you can buy a little house on the beach for summers, you could even rent it out for extra income when you're not using it. Hell, this place is big enough to make money off roommates, not that you'll need it now. Don't you see what this means, Katie? You're going to be okay! Like forever okay! Like the kind of okay our mothers always wanted us to be. You have a place to live and a steady income now, if you invest this properly, which I'm sure William will help you with. He's a very decent man."

Kate let out a ragged sob and hugged her knees. Laura knelt in front of her and rubbed her arms, asking what was wrong.

"Don't you see? Doesn't anybody see it? Oh, G-d, Laura! What have I done?" Kate cried.

"See what, sweetie? What are you talking about?" Laura asked in a soft voice.

"I love him," Kate whispered.

Laura rocked back on her heels, eyes wide. "Oh, Kate." Knowing her friend as she did, she knew Kate didn't throw around that word lightly.

"I'm in trouble, Laura," Kate said quietly. "What am I going to do now?"

Laura rubbed her arm again, and asked, "Are you sure? Totally sure? It's not just really great sex?"

Kate snorted. "I'm sure. He's so, he's just so perfect, Lar. Not overall, he's too sedate for you and too serious for Jen, but for me, he's just right. He's perfect for me." Laura looked at her with wide eyes and Kate felt compelled to continue, to give voice to the thoughts that had been torturing her endlessly lately. "You know how I know it's love? Because I've never felt anything quite like this before. I know him, so well, and I respect him. The more I know, the more I find to respect and like about him. He's generous, and kindhearted, and so sweet to me.

"Josh was friendship love and Caleb was puppy love and Matt was strong like. Jeremy was passionate love, and everything I thought love was supposed to be, but this, this…" she trailed off. "This is so much more than any of that. It's like the friendship I had with Josh, plus the passion of Jeremy and the sweetness of Caleb. It's everything I ever had before and so much more, more than I ever wanted or thought to want or believed I could have. He respects me, really respects me. He's not intimidated by my mind or my grades or my crazy ideas."

Laura made a sympathetic face and squeezed her knee, knowing that feeling all too well.

"You know what he told me?" Kate continued. "He thinks I'm smarter than him. Me! The head of HarperCo, heir to Taggston Incorporated with a degree from Cambridge, thinks I, Katie Mae Bishop from Virginia, am smarter than him. Can you believe that?! And he likes it! He LOVES it! He wants to talk with me and debate politics and throw around ideas. He actually *asks* for my opinion, and he listens, really listens." She looked earnestly at her friend and lowered her voice. "How could I not fall in love with a man like that?"

"So what are you going to do?" Laura asked.

"What can I do? Take the money graciously, like I know he'd want me to, and try to move on."

"Seriously? That's it?"

"What? What do you expect me to do?"

"To at least try, to talk to him or make an effort or *something*!"

"You know how he feels about this. And since when are you so romantic?" Kate cried, rising from the chair and pacing across the room.

"I'm not, but you are, and you're behaving completely out of character! What happened to fearless Katie, the one who followed her gut and would try anything?"

"She fell in love," Kate said sadly. "I'm sorry, Laura, I hate to let you down, but I just don't think my heart could take a rejection right now."

"What if he feels the same way?"

"I don't think he does."

"How do you know?"

"Because he knows the only thing stopping this from being a real relationship is his need to marry the right kind of woman. He's the one with stipulations, not me. If he changed his mind about that, he could easily tell me that he's realized those things aren't as important. Will is direct when he wants something. And he's been completely silent." She turned to the window and looked out at the alley, her fingers fiddling with the trim on the curtains.

"There's something else you should know," Laura added in a serious voice.

"What is it?"

Laura waited for Kate to turn around and face her before she continued. "He gave you Valhalla," she said simply, holding up the settlement papers as proof.

Kate's eyes widened and she sank into the chair. "He

what?"

"Valhalla. It's yours. Free and clear, with all its contents and the private jet will take you there twice a year at least, more if you ask."

Kate was staring off in front of her, her mind whirling. "Valhalla," she whispered.

Laura watched her, wondering what her friend was going to do next and beginning to get worried when suddenly Kate leapt up and grabbed Laura by the shoulders.

"Do you know what this means!?" Kate cried. Laura just shook her head. "He loves me! That's his favorite place in the world, in the whole world! He wouldn't give it to me if he just wanted me to be okay, I don't need a villa to be okay. He loves me! Laura! He loves me!" she cried excitedly, jumping and moving around her friend in a circle, joy beaming out of her.

"Where are you going?" Laura asked as Kate ran out of the room.

"I have to find Will!" Kate cried.

She grabbed her phone and texted Will. *Where are you?*

Will: In the car. Was headed to a meeting but it just cancelled, going back to office.

Kate: Are you close to home?

Will: Yes. Should I stop by? ;-)

Kate: Yes, stop by. I want to see you.

Will: I'll be there in 15 minutes.

"Laura, you have to leave," Kate said, shrugging out of her cardigan.

"What? Why?"

"Because Will's on his way over and I don't need an audience when I jump him in the foyer, alright?"

Laura laughed. "Alright, alright, I'm going." She packed her papers into her briefcase and waved the last packet at Kate. "I'm guessing you won't be needing these, then?"

"Leave them. I might need them as evidence," Kate said, her eyes sparkling again.

Laura nodded. "I like your style, Bishop."

Kate was now in their bedroom, ripping off her tank and

digging in her drawer for something sexy to wear.

Laura leaned in the doorway and said, "Wear the red one. It makes you look like sex on a stick."

Kate turned and quickly embraced her friend. "Thank you, Laura, for everything."

"That's what friends are for. Go get your man, Katie Bishop," she said thickly, squeezing her friend's shoulder and walking to the front door.

She was reaching for the handle when Kate called out, "That's Katie Harper!"

Laura laughed and shut the door loudly behind her, leaving Kate alone and excited and terrified out of her mind.

42
KEEP YOU

August
2 Years, 4 Months Married

Will wasn't in the door a minute before Kate jumped into his arms, furiously kissing him.

"Hello to you, too," he said happily as she released his mouth and moved on to his neck.

She tore his clothes off with no regard for silly things like buttons or belt loops. His pants were thrown behind her where they landed on a lamp and his shoes were tossed into the dining room. It took him a minute, but he finally realized she was wearing nothing but a pair of lacy red panties and a matching bra. Those, too, quickly met the floor.

Kate seemed to be in the throes of some sort of desperate passion, and thinking himself the lucky recipient of feminine hormones, he gladly went along. But after a few minutes, something began to shift. There was a light in her eyes. Actually, the first thing he noticed was that her eyes were open, nearly the entire time, an unusual action for her. But after he noticed that, what little attention he could spare he used to study her. Something was different. Her green eyes were glittering, seemingly speaking volumes to him, and once his eyes had locked on hers, he couldn't look away.

Like a man hypnotized, he touched and caressed her all the ways he knew she loved and thrilled with each approving "yes" she uttered. Somehow, in his mind, her cries of agreement were not mindless expressions of ecstasy but answers to all the questions he hadn't had the courage to ask her. Do you love me? Will you stay with me? May I keep you forever?

The look on her face was almost better than spoken acceptance. In her expression he saw devotion, love, passion, and a fierce determination that fascinated him.

Her arms were wrapped tightly around his neck and her legs around his waist. Her eyes were glued to his and as she came to him, so beautifully, she cried out his name and then, to his very great surprise, burst into tears. Unsure what was happening, he stroked her back and whispered to her.

"Katie, my Katie, don't cry darling. Everything's alright. I've got you. I've got you, darling."

She buried her head in his neck and let her tears fall unchecked before finally choking out, "I'm alright. I'm just so happy."

"You're happy?"

"William! My William!" she whispered into his neck.

She moved her hips against him and he met her motions with his own stronger thrusts. She returned her eyes to his and continued to call his name, sweet and breathless, low and passionate, whispered and intimate. It had an intoxicating effect on him and he lost control, growling her name and holding her so tightly he was sure to bruise her pale skin.

"Katie! Katie!" He was incoherent, every sense filled with the taste and scent and feel of his wife, her sweet voice in his ear urging him on to greater abandon. "I need you, baby, I need you so much. My wife, my perfect wife." He continued to call her name and whisper endearments until they cried out together and he collapsed in boneless oblivion.

After several moments of lying next to each other on the living room floor (he wasn't exactly sure how they had gotten there) he reached for a throw blanket and wrapped it around them.

He stroked her cheek and asked gently, "Are you alright?"

"I'm perfect." She smiled blissfully and he noticed again

that something was different about her. She was… luminous.

She ran a hand through his hair and traced the features of his face with a possession she had never allowed herself to feel before. "William." She smiled that radiant smile again and said simply, "You gave me Valhalla."

He looked at her with wide eyes. *She knows. She knows I love her. Oh, G-d.* He flushed in embarrassment and looked away, only to return his eyes to her a moment later. She was still smiling at him, her eyes more serene and happy than he had ever seen them. *Is she happy that I love her?*

Before he could lose his courage, he said, "Are you happy? To have Valhalla, I mean."

"Yes, of course. I love it there. But I'm even happier to have you." She smiled again and he looked away, overwhelmed with emotion.

For a dreadful moment, fear gripped Kate's heart. Had she misunderstood? Did she not have him?

"William?" She said in a small voice laced with fear.

He looked back at her and saw the look of trepidation on her face. He brushed a curl from her forehead. "Katie, I don't want just one more Christmas."

"You don't?"

"No. I want every Christmas. And Thanksgiving and Valentine's and New Year. Stay with me, my darling girl. I love you so!"

Kate's breath whooshed out of her in a long sigh of relief and she hugged him tightly. "Oh, thank G-d! For a minute there I thought I'd fallen in love with the wrong man!"

He pulled back and looked into her eyes, holding her face in his hands. "You love me?" She nodded. "Are you sure?" She nodded again, this time accompanied by a bright smile. "Say it, Katie. I want to hear you say it."

"I love you. I love you completely and wholeheartedly, with every fiber of my being. And I don't want to get divorced." She rested her forehead against his.

"I couldn't leave you if I tried, my darling," he whispered.

***

Harper had to go back to the office a few hours later for a meeting that couldn't be missed. When it was through, he walked into Andrew's office just as his friend was packing up for the day.

"Hey, are you all ready to sign the papers?" Andrew asked.

William sat in the chair in front of his lawyer's desk and leaned back, his long legs stretched in front of him and his hands folded across his middle.

"There's been a change of plans, Jamison," he said with a small satisfied smile.

"Oh? What's up?" Jamison sat on the edge of his desk, in the same room and position he'd sat in when he made Kate an offer she didn't refuse more than two years ago.

"We need a new settlement."

Andrew closed his eyes for a moment. "Will, we've discussed this. The settlement is very generous. More than generous, considering."

Will raised his brows and looked at Jamison until the other man asked, "Alright, what changes do you want made?"

Will sat up and leaned forward slightly. "In the event of divorce, she gets half of everything. All my personal holdings. Taggston is separate, of course, but my personal wealth should be split in half. She can have Valhalla and the apartment, that part stays, but add in the house in the Hamptons. And she should get alimony. Something fair, but generous. Oh, and her little loan on her building is forgiven," he looked at his watch, "starting now."

Andrew looked at his friend in confusion, then opened his mouth and tried to speak without success.

"If there are children involved, I will assume the cost of their educations as high as they care to go, and she gets regular child support and fifty percent custody. And they can all take art classes if they want – put that in there."

"Harper, what – "

Will cut him off. "Oh, and under no circumstances is

Taggston Publishing to sever their working relationship with her." He looked thoughtful for a moment. "You know, she should have a house in London so she has somewhere to stay with the kids while I'm there. Add in a townhouse near mine."

"Aren't you forgetting the infidelity clause?" Andrew asked sarcastically. He stood and walked to sit behind his desk.

"If she cheats," he thought for a moment, then waved his hand in dismissal, "lower her alimony, but still be generous. If I cheat, give her my stock in HarperCo."

Andrew spluttered. "Will! What, how – what are you even talking about?"

"Or I could give her more money, though it hardly seems a fitting punishment," he said thoughtfully.

"That isn't a settlement!" Andrew cried incredulously.

"I suppose it is more of a prenup. Or is it a postnup? I'll let you work that out," Will said casually.

"William Harper! I insist you tell me what you are talking about this moment!" Andrew stood and nearly shouted.

William leaned his head back and laughed. Then he rose smoothly from his chair and smiled at his friend. "Sorry, Jamison, no time to explain. I've got to get home to my wife." With that, William turned and walked toward the door, whistling a suspiciously cheerful song.

"You dog," Jamison said quietly. Will glanced over his shoulder and smiled, and Jamison added loudly as his friend stepped through the door, "It's about bloody time, you daft git!" He heard Harper's laughter in the hallway.

"I can't believe he finally did it." He reached for his phone to call Jenny.

**

When Will got home that evening, the lights were dim and the table was set with crystal candlesticks and elaborate place settings. Sultry music was coming from the console in the corner. He could smell something delicious wafting out of the kitchen. He popped his head in the door and saw several dishes covered with lids, but no Kate. He went to their bedroom and changed out of his wrinkled suit into comfortable chinos and a soft shirt Kate could never resist hugging him in. How could he have thought she didn't love him because she supposedly didn't show it? She showed it all the time. Through warm affection, cooking his favorite meals, laughing with him, cheering him up, holding him, listening to him, partnering with him in every way. No one was that good of an actress all the time. How could he have been so blind?

He walked slowly back to the dining room, looking for his wife. *My wife*, he thought with a satisfied smile. Kate was standing next to the table, wearing a simple pink sundress he'd always loved her in. Something about the tiny flowers on it reminded him of England in June and made her look fresh and rosy.

"Hello," she said sweetly. He smiled and she immediately blushed, which made him smile more.

"Hello, Katie." He reached for her and she came willingly, wrapping her arms around him tightly. "How was your day?"

"Good. Great, actually. How was yours?" she asked.

"Excellent." They pulled back and smiled at each other for a moment.

"I made dinner," she said.

"Yes, I saw."

She led him to the table, now covered with the dishes that had been in the kitchen and told him what was what while he poured them each a glass of wine. He listened to her in rapt attention and felt unbelievably happy, unbelievably lucky, that this is what his life would look like going forward. He could come home to this, to her, every day. He grabbed her hand as she turned to take her seat and pulled her back to him. He gave her a quick kiss before letting go, laughing quietly at her once again rosy cheeks.

Kate was quiet during dinner, but she often was when something was on her mind, and he knew his own mind was practically swimming, so he didn't worry about it overmuch. Finally, they finished and took their plates to the kitchen where Kate sliced them each a piece of strawberry cheesecake. They sat at the table again, Will eating happily while Kate fiddled with her fork.

"Are you alright?" he asked, a nervous feeling creeping up his spine.

"Yeah, fine, I just wondered, now that we're really married, what do you think about doing it again?"

"What do you mean?"

"I mean another ceremony. Where we can promise more things, real things."

"Our first wasn't too far off," he said as he reached across the table to take her hand. "Do you want to do another ceremony just the two of us, or would you like to include friends?"

"Ideally I'd like to include friends – not many, but I would like it if Laura could be there, and Caroline and Teddy and Harry, and my parents and sisters and my grandmother."

"That's quite a list."

She looked down. "I guess that isn't really feasible, is it?"

He looked at Kate with sadness. She'd never worn a wedding gown – she'd worn a little blue dress at their Vegas ceremony. She didn't walk down the aisle with her father or dress her sisters in frilly matching frocks. She hadn't had photos taken of her with her parents in all her finery or worn a veil or put a penny in her shoe. She was so young, and he'd cost her so much already. Perhaps there was a way.

"Maybe we can think of something," he said.

"Yeah, maybe."

Wanting to lighten the mood, he said, "Katie, did you just propose to me?"

She looked up, startled. "I guess I did!" She laughed and suddenly everything was right again.

43
HERE COMES THE BRIDE

Late August
10 Days in Love

Knowing her dream of having a wedding with her family and friends present wasn't a possibility (after all, who renews their vows after only two years?), Kate began thinking of other options. She thought they could have a small ceremony on a beach somewhere with just Jenny, Andrew, and Laura present and maybe Teddy and Caroline. The two couples had grown close and they could consider telling them the truth. Or maybe they would believe it was just a renewal.

She also considered telling them that they had thought she was pregnant the first time and it was why they had really married, but that it had turned out to be a false alarm or maybe they could say she'd had a miscarriage. She didn't like the idea of more lies, but she would really like Caroline especially to be there. And Wouldn't William like to have someone from his family there? Thomas was two now and could be a ring bearer. He would be adorable in a little tuxedo. The baby was too small, but she could war a pretty white dress in the pictures.

She shook her head and made herself focus on the task at hand. They could have an elaborate anniversary party in April, or do it sooner in the autumn as a celebration for Will's thirty-fifth birthday, or even have something at Christmas. If they did a super private ceremony before, with just the people who knew the truth already, maybe they could have a reception disguised as a party. She wanted a simple dress – it didn't have to be obvious it was a wedding dress.

She continued to wrack her brain for ways to make this work, and just when she'd convinced herself one way would be feasible, she realized something that would make it impossible.

With a sigh, she gave up for the time being and went for a run. She needed to clear her head.

Her run led her near Andrew and Jen's apartment and she decided to pop in and see her sister. Jenny was sitting at the dining table, surrounded by magazines and pictures of floral arrangements she'd cut out.

"Wedding planning?" Kate asked. Jen's October wedding is what had made her scratch the big October birthday idea.

"Yes. There are so many details to organize! Mom's been a big help, but I still have to tell her what I want before she can put the order in with the florist."

"This is pretty." Kate held up a picture of an elegant centerpiece.

"Thanks. I was talking to Gran the other day. After I told her what a hard time I was having finding a dress, she suggested I wear her wedding dress."

"Oh, really? Will you?"

"I'm not sure. I'm a little taller than her, and my arms are longer, so the sleeves may be too short. But we could probably have it altered."

Kate nodded. She'd always loved her grandmother's wedding dress. Jen would look beautiful in it. Both were tall and thin, with willowy figures and porcelain skin. Her sister would look very elegant walking through the trees in the gown. Jen's wedding was being held at their parents' farm, in a beautiful glade the girls had played in as children.

"Gran said she was sad she never got to see you in a wedding dress. She'd always thought we'd both get to wear her gown. I told her you could wear it in the fittings and we'd take pictures of you. What do you think about that? I'm sure Gran would love to have them. We could get your hair done and everything. It would look like a real wedding."

Kate nodded. "I like that idea. Gran would really love it,

too. She could add it to her wall of photos."

"Actually," Jen hesitated, "I had an idea I wanted to run by you. It's a little crazy but, it could be really fun."

***

October in Virginia was beautiful. The leaves were vibrant shades of red, gold, and orange and the evergreens were the perfect backdrop for a ceremony. The secluded glade at the back of the farm had been transformed into a wonderland. There were wide ribbons hanging from branches and lights strung through the trees.

Several rows of white wooden chairs faced an arbor decorated in white flowers where the actual ceremony would take place. Jen's colors were simple and clean, much like her own personal style. Most everything was some shade of white, with lots of wood accents and the occasional bit of green moss or pale pink flower. The whole effect was soft and ethereal.

The bridesmaids were all in creamy white, each in her own beautiful gown and styled to suit her personality. Jen had always wanted a snowball wedding, and this suited their plans perfectly.

Once everyone was seated, the string quartet began playing Pachelbel's *Canon* and Tiffany waltzed down the aisle, smiling brilliantly and winking at her boyfriend. Mary followed more sedately, then Heather, Laura and finally Kate as the matron of honor. Mary's two daughters skipped down the aisle, the younger throwing rose petals and the older ringing a large brass bell in time to the music. When they reached the front, the music swelled and everyone rose and faced the back, eyes searching for the bride.

Jenny was resplendent. She wore her grandmother's gown and looked positively angelic as she floated down the aisle on her father's arm. Neal was tall and proud, his eyes misty and his shoulders back. There was hardly a dry eye in the house as the couple declared their vows to each other, written on their own of course, and exchanged beautiful platinum rings.

The audience cheered and clapped as an extremely joyful Jenny and Andrew practically ran down the aisle and down a small pathway out of sight. They were followed by Kate and Will – the best man, and the other bridesmaids with the groomsmen: Harry, Calvin, Andrew's brother-in-law Samuel and his cousin David. After they had all disappeared into the trees, the preacher asked everyone to make their way to the reception site, gesturing into the distance where there was a large tent set up out of sight, and asked the close family to remain for pictures.

The guests made their way over the hill, some walking, some riding in the Land Rovers that had been rented for the occasion. Once the space was cleared, the preacher spoke to the remaining people.

"As you saw in your invitations, we'll now be moving on to the next portion of the program. Is everyone in their places?"

There was a general murmur of consent and Caroline and Jacqueline quickly stood and removed their coats, revealing elegant long, white bridesmaid dresses. Beside them, Teddy quickly pinned a boutonniere to his tuxedo lapel and went to stand next to his brother to the right of the clearing. Caroline led Thomas to the back (their six-month-old daughter Christine was with the nanny in Loretta's house) and showed him how to hold his ring bearer pillow and Laura quickly refilled the flower girls' baskets with petals.

"As you know," the preacher spoke again, "when Katherine and William married some two years ago, they did so without their families present. Her family never even got to see her in a wedding gown. The young couple would like to rectify that today."

He then stepped back and the music began, followed quickly by the entrance of William, the groom, and his groomsmen, Andrew – now in the place of best man, Calvin, Harry, Teddy, and his Harper cousins Ben and Jake, who'd flown in from Texas especially for this.

The small audience of family and close friends smiled, then turned their attention to the back as the bridesmaids began their processional down the aisle, Jenny in the final position as her sister's maid (now matron) of honor.

Kate entered on her father's arm, her smile so wide her cheeks ached, wearing a simple white cap-sleeve dress, her grandmother's veil, and the family pearls. William lit up when he saw her, his heart pounding in his ears and making it difficult to hear the music or the words of the preacher.

William's voice was strong and deep as he recited his vows. "I promise to always love you, to never lie to you, to always be there when you need me, to support and comfort you, to provide for you whatever you may need, to listen and really hear you. I will be the proudest witness of your life, your strongest encourager, and I will always be on your side. I promise to put you first, always."

Kate smiled and said her own vows, her voice quiet but steady. "I promise to love you well and with all my heart, to support you through every endeavor, to take care of you when you're sick, to hold your hand when you're scared, to walk through the ups and downs of life by your side. I will always want you, no matter what. I promise to put you first, always."

The preacher guided them through lighting the unity candle and exchanging the rings. Will wanted that portion of the ceremony to be traditionally English, so when he slid the ring on her finger, he said, "With this ring I thee wed, with my body I thee worship, with all my worldly goods I thee endow."

Kate batted her eyes to keep from crying and repeated the words as she slipped the simple band onto his finger. She almost laughed at the "worldly goods" portion, but didn't. Traditionally, only the man spoke that part, but they had wanted a more equal ceremony, so they both said it.

The preacher smiled and said, "I now pronounce you husband and wife. You may kiss the bride."

A loud whoop went up, courtesy of Will's Texas cousins, and they laughed through a light kiss, both with shining eyes.

"May I present Mr. and Mrs. Harper."

They walked back down the aisle at a brisk pace, followed quickly by smiling bridesmaids and groomsmen.

The two wedding parties laughed their way through photographs, changing out family members where necessary and switching brides and grooms as the photographer ordered. Jenny and Kate had several wonderful shots of the two of them together and the two grooms as well. The foursome together was stunning. Loretta was beside herself with happiness and continually fanned her face to keep the tears at bay. Neal was quiet, as always, but he radiated a solemn joy that his two eldest daughters recognized.

The entire party walked over the hill for the reception, joining the already boisterous crowd. This portion was for Jen and Andrew alone; Kate and Will had had a reception, after all, but they didn't mind. In fact, William thought it was the best possible way to do it. He got to have a beautiful small ceremony with his wife and all his best-loved people, and then blend nicely into the party afterward without having to stand for hours in a receiving line or be the center of everyone's attention.

"Are you having a good time?" Kate asked as they danced.

"Yes, I am. You?"

"Yes. This is a lovely party." He turned her under his arm, then brought her back into his embrace. "I heard something interesting from my mother."

"Oh?"

"Yes. She said the tearoom connected to the store is ready to open. Apparently, she somehow got the money necessary to build the addition and put in a kitchen."

"Hmm."

"Can you imagine who would do such a thing?" she asked.

"Perhaps Andrew. Or maybe she saved it."

Kate shook her head. "Her store is successful, but she has two daughters in college. She's been complaining that that's where all her money goes for years."

He shrugged. "Does it really matter where it came from? If she's running the business well, what difference does it make?"

He twirled her under his arm again. When she returned, she gave him a playful glare. "Don't think spinning me around will distract me."

He dipped her backwards. "I wouldn't dream of it," he said when she popped back up with a surprised expression.

"William Harper!"

He laughed and spun her around again, then a second time for good measure.

"Alright, alright, I give in! No more questions!" she exclaimed, dizzy and out of breath.

They danced quietly for another minute.

"Will?"

"Yes, Katie?"

"I'm really happy," she whispered. "I just wanted you to know."

He held her a little tighter. "Oh, my Katie, I'm happier than I ever remember being."

"Really?" she asked, leaning her head back to look up into his face.

"Really. The love of my life has just promised to live with me and love me forever. How can it get any better than this?"

"Oh, Will."

EPILOGUE

October
4 Years, 6 Months Married
2 Years, 2 Months in Love

"How are you feeling?" Kate asked Caroline.

They were sitting on the patio of Caroline's home in London, their feet propped up on a chaise, Caroline's pregnant belly peeking out from underneath her shirt. Caroline's children played happily in the garden.

"I'm fine. I feel old hat at this now. I am much bigger than usual, though I suppose that's to be expected with twins."

"I can't believe you're really having twins!"

"I know! For all our joking about it, I never thought it would actually happen to me. What about you? How are you feeling these days? The morning sickness still bothering you?"

"No, it's pretty much gone now, thankfully. We have our first ultrasound tomorrow."

"Are you going to find out the sex?" Caroline asked. She smiled at Christine, her two-and-a-half-year-old daughter who brought her a handful of rocks she'd collected from the garden.

"I don't think so. My mother wants to know, of course, and Jen wants me to find out so she can start planning play dates." Kate tied four-year-old Thomas's shoe that he had propped up on her chair and sent him back to play.

"How far along is she?"

"Thirty-four weeks. Just a little while longer and Baby Boy Jamison will be here."

Caroline shook her head. "I can't believe we're all

pregnant at the same time. Who would have thought it?"

"It's all the hormones flying through the air. It was bound to happen," Kate replied.

Caroline laughed and leaned her head back. "Well, I'm just glad you're here for a while. It will be so nice for the children to play together."

"Yeah. Will wants the baby to be born here and have English citizenship and everything, but I just don't know if I want to give birth in a foreign country. No offense."

"None taken. It's a scary enough process without adding in all the extra cultural stuff."

Kate nodded. "Well, William's project will be over sometime in late winter. We could probably make it back just in time for the birth if we wanted to, but I have a feeling I need to get used to the idea of giving birth here. March will be here before I know it. And hey, it has the added advantage of keeping my mother out of the delivery room."

**

"Are you nervous?" Kate asked.

"No, why would I be nervous?" Will answered as they parked at the doctor's office.

"You have your nervous face on."

"No I don't. I'm just excited. This is what excited looks like," he said.

She gave him a disbelieving look. "Uh huh. Okay. Well, we should go in. Our appointment is in five minutes."

Kate lay back on the table, her belly exposed and one hand behind her head. The nurse was measuring her stomach with a thin tape and jotting things down in the chart. She then took Kate's blood pressure and listened to her heartbeat, then told them the doctor would be in shortly and to sit tight.

"You alright?" Will asked.

"Yeah, I'm great. You?"

"Yes, just a little anxious."

She smiled. "Everything will be fine, baby. I have a good feeling."

He let out a relieved sigh. Kate didn't use the "I have a feeling" line often, but when she did, she was unerringly correct.

Just then the doctor came in and extended a manicured hand toward Kate.

"I'm Dr. Fletcher. You can call me Rachel. How have you been feeling?"

She proceeded to ask Kate questions about her sleeping patterns and nausea and digestion. Finally, they were ready to see their baby.

She slid the ultrasound wand over Kate's small belly, collecting measurements and talking as she went. She asked them about their plans for the birth and if they were going to take any classes, and mentioned the course their office offered.

She pointed out the head and spinal cord to the new parents and they oohed and aahed appropriately. When Kate heard the rapid heartbeat, she unsuccessfully tried to hide the tears that slid out.

After what felt like an hour but had probably been closer to fifteen minutes, Dr. Fletcher wiped off Kate's belly and pulled her shirt back down, then gave Kate her hand and pulled her to a sitting position.

"Mr. and Mrs. Harper," she said, looking at the two of them, "are you planning on delivering here or in the States?"

"We're not sure yet, it depends on my husband's work schedule," Kate answered, swinging her legs over the side of the table and taking Will's hand.

The doctor nodded. "Is everything alright with our baby?" Will asked, his voice strained. He had been watching her face during the ultrasound and had definitely noticed some concern.

"Yes, the baby is fine." Will relaxed his rigid posture. "In fact, they're both fine."

He sighed in relief. "Good. I'm glad she-"

Kate cut him off with a hand on his arm. "Do you mean both as in me and the baby? Or both as in two babies?"

Will suddenly looked at the doctor in alarm.

"Two babies," the doctor replied calmly.

"We're having twins?!" Kate cried.

"Are you sure?" Will asked.

Dr. Fletcher smiled. "Yes, I'm sure. See here?" She showed them the grainy print-out. "That's the first head, and that is the other baby peeking around. It's like they're hiding behind each other," she added fondly.

"Oh, God! Two mischievous Katie's!" Will cried, turning around and running his hand through his hair.

Kate studied the picture the doctor had given her and carefully listened to explanations of what was what.

"Could you see the sexes? Don't tell me, I just want to know if you could tell," Kate asked.

"It's a bit early to say for sure. I have a pretty good guess for baby one, but baby two is completely hidden. They are in separate sacks, but they can still be somewhat identical if they separated early enough. They could be completely fraternal, even different sexes. It's too early to tell."

Kate nodded. A surprise with one baby was fun, but with twins, they might want to be as prepared as possible.

Will took the strip of pictures the doctor handed him.

"Twins. I can't believe it. I knew they ran in my family, but I never thought *I…*" he trailed off, his voice soft and his eyes wide as he looked at the pictures of his children.

"The family is going to freak," Kate mumbled.

August
8 Years, 4 Months Married
6 Years in Love

"Neal! Put that down!" Andrew called.

"That's James," Will told his friend. "His eyes are blue. Though it's hard to tell when he's running!" He scooped up his giggling three-year-old and took the glass paperweight from his hand. "Have you been playing in Uncle Andy's office again?"

James shook his head vehemently, shaggy brown hair falling across his brow.

"Are you sure?" Will asked sternly.

The boy burst into giggles again.

"Apologize to Uncle Andy."

"Sowwy, Unca Andy," James said, his eyes cast down.

Andrew rumpled his nephew's hair. "All is forgiven. Just don't play in there again, alright?"

James nodded and scampered off to find his cousins.

"Paul has a room full of toys, but do they want to play in there? No!" Andrew said, referring to his oldest son.

Kate walked in with Jenny just behind her.

"Is Madeline sleeping?" Will asked his wife.

"Just went down." Kate set the monitor on the table and sat next to her husband on the couch.

Jen lowered herself carefully down next to Andrew. He automatically picked up one of her swollen feet and started massaging it.

"Next time I decide to be pregnant in summer, smack me," Jen said tiredly, leaning back with her eyes closed.

"Planning another already?" Will teased.

"Haha, William." She didn't even open her eyes to respond to him.

"Just one more week, sweetheart." Andrew soothed. "You're almost there."

Jen nodded tiredly. She was on her third pregnancy and had no patience for anyone or anything. Their oldest son, Paul, would be four at Christmas, and their son Nicholas had turned two last month. This one was a girl and Jen was very excited – when she had the energy to be.

Kate smiled. "When Madeline wakes up, we should get home. Teddy and Caroline arrive tomorrow and I want to be ready. What time does Tiffany get in?"

"Her plane lands at eleven tomorrow. I'm picking her up and bringing her here," Andrew answered. Tiffany was coming to help Jen with her last few days of pregnancy and would keep the boys for a bit after the baby was born. Of course, she felt that staying at a beach house for free was more than enough compensation, but Jen insisted on paying her since she was giving up her summer job to be with them. Tiffany was getting a masters in fine art and her final semester would begin in September.

The next day, everyone gathered at the Harpers for dinner. Will flipped meat on the grill while Kate carried sides to the table and Jen sat with her feet up, Tiffany rubbing her shoulders. Caroline and Teddy were sleeping off their jetlag and their children were running outside with their cousins, Andrew attempting to corral them into some kind of order. After several minutes of futilely chasing his son Paul and Teddy's twins, he gave up and joined the adults.

"So what will you do after you're finished with school, Tiffany?" he asked.

"Actually, I wanted to talk to you guys about that."

"Oh? Something exciting happening?"

"Sort of. I'm thinking of opening up an arts camp on the farm," Tiffany told them.

"Really?" Kate asked, taking a seat by her sisters.

"I talked to Mom and Dad about it. You remember the old creek cabin?"

The sisters nodded. There was an old cabin without running water or electricity in a picturesque setting by the creek at the back of the property.

"Well, I was thinking of modernizing it and making it the center of the camp. We could make it a classroom, or even a bunk room and build a second building nearby so we can have boys and girls."

"That sounds great, Tiffany!" Kate encouraged.

"When do you hope to get started?" William asked.

"Well, Mom's B&B is doing so well, she suggested I start with some weekend workshops for the visitors there. I already sell my own work in the gift shop, so it wouldn't be completely out of the blue."

"What does Dad think?" asked Jenny.

"He likes the idea. With Heather in Texas and you two here, someone will have to take over the farm. Why not me?" she said the last a bit uncertainly. After all, she was the youngest.

Jen squeezed her hand. "I think that's a lovely idea."

"So do I," Kate added. "Are Mom and Dad going to fund you or do you need start up money?" Tiffany had long ago

Googled her brothers-in-law and knew they were very wealthy men. Her parents knew to an extent, but they would likely be shocked if they were privy to the true numbers.

"I'm not sure yet. Dad offered some, but I'd rather he save for retirement. He's already paid for my grad school tuition, which I never expected. And eventually someone will have to be hired to manage the trees themselves. I don't know enough about that. But Josh Powell's "friend"," she said with air quotes, "has been helping out in the busy season. If he and Josh are serious, that could be a perfect solution."

"I'd like to help, Tiffany," Will said unexpectedly.

"Really?"

"Yes. Your parents should concentrate their money on building up their retirements and expanding their businesses to increase revenue. I'm sure your endeavor will be successful. We can work something out."

Kate smiled and squeezed his hand.

*

William turned out to be very helpful. The original spring house was modernized and turned into a workshop of sorts, and two bunk houses were built nearby in order to host weekly camps. Tiffany had been a camp counselor every summer since her fourteenth birthday, and she was beyond excited about the plan. William funded all the building and renovations at a low interest rate. He wanted to make it interest free, citing family as the cause for his generosity, but Tiffany insisted he get something. In the end, one percent was settled on and Tiffany was ready to open her camp the following summer. Children of varying ages came for one week at a time and learned how to paint, sculpt, work with metals, and make paper.

The Harper boys, James and Neal, along with their Covington cousins Thomas, Christine, and the twins Adele and Alistair, plus the Jamison boys Paul and Nicholas (though little Nick could only make it through a couple of hours before needing a nap) attended a day camp Tiffany's first summer.

James liked it so much that his parents promised he could come back the next year. Will found it highly ironic that the son he named for his father would be so interested in art, but he said nothing about it.

Tiffany taught weekend workshops during the year to the adult guests of her mother's B&B, and they eventually branched out and offered entire artisan weekends, where the guests would learn how to can and cook from Loretta, and how to paint, weave, and create mosaics from Tiffany.

Tiffany's venture was successful relatively quickly, between the after school classes for older children and teenagers, the nightly classes for adults, weekend workshops, and school field trips. She became known as the 'art lady', a title she wore proudly, and frequently hosted her nieces and nephews and even Caroline's children, who called her 'auntie' even though they weren't technically related. It was no secret she was everyone's favorite aunt, another title she loved.

December
10 years, 8 Months Married
8 Years, 4 Months in Love

Harper was brooding. He didn't want to admit it, he knew it was childish, but he was brooding all the same. If he'd admitted why he was brooding, which he would never do, he would be embarrassed for anyone to know it, but he never did, so he never was.

But still, he brooded.

His wife was being unreasonable. Alright, maybe he was being unreasonable, but he genuinely thought she was the unreasonable one in this instance. Surely she understood that if he could carry the baby, he would? But he couldn't. He simply didn't possess the necessary equipment. Which he had tried to tell her, but she had only gotten angry and thrown a pillow at him and shouted something about not being manipulated by her own uterus, whatever that meant.

He knew her last pregnancy had been difficult. The

twins had actually been relatively easy. They had gone almost to full term, making it thirty-seven weeks, very impressive for twins, and she'd delivered them naturally, again, very impressive. Caroline, poor thing, had had both. She'd delivered the first one naturally, then the second simply wouldn't cooperate and she'd been rushed to surgery for a caesarean.

But when William reminded Kate of her good luck, she simply glared at him again. Their daughter Madeline had been a bit of a surprise, but a happy one. They had talked about trying again soon anyhow, so when they found out they were pregnant, they were happy. But the pregnancy had been hard on Kate. She'd pulled her pelvic ligament in the fifth month, something she described to Will as excruciating and he tried, but failed, to understand. He would find her up at all hours in the night, heartburn keeping her awake. She'd lost eight pounds in the first trimester with morning sickness, which looked more like morning, noon, and night sickness, and then gained it all back with a vengeance once her movement was restricted due to the pulled ligament.

One good thing had come out of all the difficulty. Jacqueline had come to stay with them when she heard about Kate's injury and helped with the twins, which brought the two of them closer and created a new bond between William and his sister and between the twins and their aunt. But could Kate see any of that now? No! She insisted on focusing on how bad the whole experience was, how labor had come so quickly Madeline had almost been born in the car, how she had been in some kind of pain nearly every second of every day for nine horribly long months.

So here they were, at an impasse. William wanted another child, Kate did not. Actually, it would be fair to say that Kate would be happy to have another child if said child simply arrived, but she did not want to have another pregnancy or another delivery where her husband would drive as slowly as possible, telling her she was doing great and they'd be there soon, while she passed out between contractions in the back seat because he didn't think she was as close as she was and refused to go faster or drive in the shoulder past the traffic jam or do *anything* remotely helpful.

So now, Madeline was two and a half years old. The twins would be five March first. He was over forty, for pete's sake! If they were going to have another one, it should be now. But Kate was being stubborn and every time he brought it up she said she felt cold chills all over and a feeling of dread swept through her. So he'd let it go for a while, but now… Surely she was over it?

He quit pacing and shook his head. There was no forcing Kate when she didn't want to do something. Besides, this wasn't something he would want to force her into, anyway. He just wished she agreed with him that a sister for Madeline would be a good thing. Kate was so close to her own sisters, he knew she must want that for their daughter.

Maybe they should look into adopting. They could be sure to get a girl that way. But he really wanted another of their own. A daughter with Kate's bright smile and the Covington eyes. Madeline looked very much like a Harper. She had William's smile, his brow, his cheekbones, everything. Her eyes were green like Kate's, but otherwise, she was all William. Kate sometimes called her a little traitor. After all Kate had gone through with that baby, she had the nerve to look just like her father. She even spoke with his snooty accent in her tiny toddler voice.

It was a few days before Christmas and they were heading to Virginia the next day to have a big family gathering. Heather was coming and bringing a boyfriend that she'd gotten pretty serious about. The Jamisons would be there with their brood. They'd recently had their fourth – and final – baby, another little girl. She was just a few weeks old now and Will hoped being around such a small baby would make Kate reconsider her rigid stance.

*

The reunion at the Bishop family farm was as expected. There were hugs and kisses and pinched cheeks all around. The Harper family was supposed to stay at the B&B, taking up two of Loretta's paying rooms while she was in one of her busiest seasons, while the Jamisons would stay at Neal's so the newborn wouldn't keep any guests up in the night.

Kate offered to ride over to her father's with Jenny to help her get settled in and Will and Andrew offered to come along and do the heavy lifting, leaving the older children with their grandparents. At the top of the hill, where he was supposed to turn right to go to Neal's, he went straight, deep into the tree farm.

"Will, you missed the turn, babe. You can turn around in the clearing up here," Kate said when she looked out her window.

"Oh, I wanted to see the new playground Tiffany put in before it gets dark. Do you mind driving past?"

The baby was asleep so the sisters agreed. Another few minutes passed and the rows of trees changed into a wilder forest. They climbed a hill steadily until they turned a corner and Will stopped the car. The sisters were talking and didn't notice until Will told them to look outside.

"What on earth!?" Kate exclaimed. "Will, what is this?"

"Where are we?" Jenny asked.

"Merry Christmas, ladies," Andrew said exuberantly.

Before them was a large white farmhouse with a wrap around porch and an enormous red ribbon tied to the front.

"I don't understand," Jen said.

"What's going on?" Kate asked.

"Well, there are too many of us to fit comfortably in your parents' houses, and you two like to come back here so much, and the kids really love playing on the farm, so we thought we should have a place of our own. It's almost two houses, really. Come have a look," Andrew explained.

The women got out of the car in a daze, looking around at the beautiful view and the fully fenced in yard. They walked up the steps slowly, their hands gingerly resting on the white railing. To their surprise, the front door opened and a flood of yellow light came out. Standing in the doorway was Jacqueline.

"Jackie!" Kate called and ran to embrace her sister-in-law. "What are you doing here? Happy Christmas!"

Jacqueline embraced her sister-in-law and kissed Jenny's cheek. "I'm here to show you around your new house." She smiled and led them inside.

Their husbands had been very sneaky and hired Jacqueline, who was making a name for herself as a residential architect, to design a house for them to share. She had talked to each of the women to find out what they wanted, asking sly questions like, "Do you like the master on the same floor as the children or separate? I have a client who can't decide."

It had two wings, so each family had privacy and their own kitchen with an eating nook. The two sides were connected by an enormous dining room that seated twenty, suitable for large family gatherings, and an enormous great room with a large stone fireplace and a wall of windows looking out over the farm and the mountains in the distance.

Jacqueline took them on a tour, showing them the bookcases that were built in and the steps that folded right out of the lower cabinets so the children could reach higher shelves without climbing. Each side had four bedrooms: a master with its own bath, two children's rooms with shared baths, and a room suitable for guests or eventually, older children who didn't want to share. Next to each kitchen was a cozy sitting room with a fireplace, French, doors and shelves ready to be stuffed with books and family photos.

The attic was finished out into a playroom and designed to look like a pirate ship, with planked walls and the support posts decorated like ship masts. There was even a rope ladder leading up to a small lookout in the center of the room where the pitch was highest, and a pole going to the lower floor for them to slide down when a quick escape was necessary. It had the added bonus of keeping all the noise high above when the adults were trying to hear themselves think downstairs.

Not all of the decorating was done, the men knew their wives would want to do that themselves, but there were beds and kitchen tables, so they could function for this trip. Before the tour was through, Kate and Jenny were planning a raid on the furniture store.

Within three days, the two women had nearly bought

out the two local furniture stores and one in a neighboring town. They'd paid extra to get everything delivered early and the house was looking settled, if not entirely finished.

Neal had taken the older children on a Christmas tree hunt and they'd chosen a lovely eleven foot fir to put in the shared great room. The tree was already crowded with gifts – the ones the families had brought with them and those the grandparents and great grandparents had added to the pile.

Christmas Eve, after a sumptuous dinner and sprinkling magic oats in the yard for the reindeer and leaving out milk and cookies for Santa, Will and Kate finally went to bed.

As she joined her husband under the sheets, Kate said, "I have a present for you."

"Oh?" he said with a playful smile. "Can I open it now?" He reached for her and she giggled and pushed his hands away.

"No, a real present." She passed him a small box wrapped in shiny red paper.

He opened it slowly, giving his wife suspicious looks throughout.

"What is it?" He turned the purple and white rectangle over in his hands.

"It's a pregnancy test."

He looked at her with wide eyes. "Are you? Are we?" he asked breathlessly.

"No, at least not yet. The box hasn't been opened. See?" She showed him the sealed end. "I just wanted to let you know that I'm willing to try now. I went to the doctor last month and, well, I pulled the goalie, so to speak, so we're good to go whenever you want to start trying."

He immediately pulled her underneath him. Kate let out a surprised squeal and he smiled brightly.

"Let's start trying right now."

***

Mary Cynthia Harper never understood why her parents called her their little Christmas gift when she was born on

September twenty-fourth. It was one of the many things she did not understand about them. Like why were they always kissing when they thought no one was in the room with them? And why did they call Uncle Andy and thank him each year on their anniversary? Why did her father always say he would be lost without her mother? How would he get lost? And why would they never let her sleep in their bed? It was big enough for all of them and she promised not to kick, but every time she snuck in, she would wake up as she was being carried back to her own room.

There were other things, too. Her parents always talked about Vermont like it was a magical place, but she didn't understand what was so special about it. Her grandpa's Christmas tree farm was way better. And every time her mother made sugar cookies, she would save one gingerbread man for her father and wouldn't let anyone else touch it, not even guests!

Mary Cynthia decided parents were simply weird creatures and left it at that.

THE END

KATE'S GO-TO RECIPES

Lemon Salad

Salad
1 Pound Romaine lettuce or 1 large head
1/3 cup grated Swiss cheese
1/3 cup parmesan cheese
1/3 cup slivered almonds
4 strips of bacon, cooked crispy and cut into bite sized pieces
Cherry tomatoes (optional)

Combine all ingredients in a large bowl

Dressing
1 clove of garlic, pressed or diced
¼ cup lemon juice, usually 2 lemons
¾ grapeseed oil or vegetable oil (grapeseed oil is MUCH better)

Mix all together in a jar and pour over salad. Last 36 hours in the fridge

Summer Salad

Salad
1 pound spring mix
1 cup candied nuts (recipe follows)
4 oz. crumbled feta cheese
About 10 medium strawberries, sliced

Dressing
2 parts Grapeseed oil (usually ½ cup)
1 part Balsamic vinegar (usually ¼ cup)
Mix in jar; stir or shake before using

Toss spring mix in dressing, then add nuts, cheese and strawberries. Stir and serve.

Autumn version:
Substitute apple chunks for strawberries (1 small apple) and add ½ cup dried cranberries
Plain or roasted walnuts can be used in place of candied nuts for a less sweet salad

Candied Pecans

1 pound pecan halves (or mix with walnuts)
1 cup sugar
1 teaspoon cinnamon
1 teaspoon salt
1 egg white
1 tablespoon water

Preheat oven to 250 degrees F
Mix together salt, sugar, and cinnamon
Mix egg white and water in separate bowl until frothy; toss pecans in mixture
Add sugar mixture to pecans and toss until coated
Spread on baking sheet and cook for one hour, stirring every fifteen minutes
Remove from pan and cool before serving

Oatmeal Spice Cookies

1 ½ cups all purpose flour (spelt works nicely in this cookie)
1 teaspoon baking soda
½ teaspoon salt
1 teaspoon ground cinnamon
½ teaspoon nutmeg
½ teaspoon ginger
½ pound (2 sticks) butter, softened
½ cup granulated sugar
1 cup firmly packed brown sugar
2 eggs
1 teaspoon vanilla
2 cups uncooked oats (quick or old fashioned)
2 cups semi-sweet chocolate chips (may sub. butterscotch chips)

Heat oven to 350 degrees F
In medium bowl, Combine dry ingredients (first 6) and mix well
In large bowl, beat butter and sugars until creamy; add eggs and vanilla, beat well
Add flour mixture to butter mixture
Stir in oats and chocolate chips gradually
Spoon onto cookie sheet (best on stone sheet) and bake 10-12 minutes or until light golden brown
Cool 1 minute on cookie sheet, then remove to cooling rack

Comfort Soup

2 tablespoons mild oil
1 onion, diced
2 cloves of garlic, pressed or minced
4 stalks of celery, diced
6 large carrots, sliced thin
½ pound mushrooms, baby bella or white (bella adds more flavor)
1 rotisserie chicken or boiled whole chicken, meat pulled from

the bone and cut into bite-size pieces
2 quarts chicken stock
1 quart water
1 teaspoon parsley flakes
1 teaspoon dried rosemary
1 teaspoon thyme

Heat oil in large stockpot and cook onions, garlic, and celery until celery is soft and onion is translucent. Add spices and stir on medium-low heat.
In separate pan, saute carrots until softened slightly, then saute mushrooms until color darkens, about 4 min.
Add stock and water to stock pot, then add cooked carrots and mushrooms.
Add chicken to stock pot.
Simmer on low heat for two hours (quick version: simmer 30 min), then reduce heat to low. The longer the flavors blend together, the better the taste.

Quick Sausage Pepper Quiche

1 roll out pie crust, softened and placed in pie plate
1 package ground sausage, mild or spicy, depending on preference
1 red pepper, diced
½ cup milk
6 eggs
¾ cup cheddar cheese

Preheat oven to 375 degrees F; place crust in pie plate
Whisk eggs and milk together in medium bowl; set aside
Cook sausage in pan over medium heat; remove with slotted spoon when browned and add to egg mixture
Cook pepper in sausage pan, do not drain first; when soft, add to egg mixture; stir in cheese
Pour into pie plate and bake for 45 minutes or until knife inserted in center comes out clean. Let set for five minutes before serving

ABOUT THE AUTHOR

Elizabeth Adams loves sunshine and a good book, is learning Italian, and believes baking is cathartic. This is her second book.

For more information, outtakes, and a peek at what's coming next, go to ElizabethAdamsWrites.wordpress.com.

Made in the USA
San Bernardino, CA
21 May 2015